The Rabbi

The Rabbi

by Noah Gordon

McGraw-Hill Book Company

New York   Toronto   London

THE RABBI by Noah Gordon.

For my mother and father,
Rose and Robert Gordon
—and for Lorraine

CONTENTS

When I consider thy heavens, the work of thy fingers,
The moon and the stars, which thou hast ordained;
What is man, that thou art mindful of him?
And the son of man, that thou visitest him?
For thou hast made him a little lower than the angels,
And hast crowned him with glory and honor.
Thou madest him to have dominion over the works of thy
hands;
Thou hast put all things under his feet. . . .

—PSALM VIII

BOOK I:

The Beginnings
of Things

CHAPTER ONE

On the winter morning of Rabbi Michael Kind's forty-fifth birthday he lay alone in the oversized brass bed that had once belonged to his grandfather, clinging to the numbness of sleep but listening against his will to the noises made by the woman in the kitchen below.

For the first time in years he had dreamed of Isaac Rivkind. Once when Michael was a little boy the old man had told him that when the living think of the dead, in paradise the dead know that they are loved and they rejoice.

"I love you, Zaydeh," he said.

It didn't occur to Michael that he had spoken aloud until his ear caught a momentary halt in the noises below. Mrs. Moscowitz wouldn't understand that a man who had just crossed the line into middle age could find comfort in talking to a man who had been dead for almost thirty years.

Rachel was already seated at the old-fashioned dining-room table when he came downstairs. It was a family custom that birthday mornings were celebrated with cards and small gifts piled on the breakfast table. But the perpetuating force behind the custom was Leslie, the Rabbi's wife, and she had been away nearly three months. The place by his plate was empty.

Rachel was slouched forward with her chin buried in the linen tablecloth, her eyes steadily following the text of the book she had propped against the sugar bowl. She had on her blue sailor. All the buttons were buttoned and she wore clean white socks, but as usual her thick blonde hair had been too much for her eight-year-old patience. She was reading with furious concentration, her eyes darting from line to line as she tried to cram in as much as she could before the interruption she knew was inevitable. She gained a few seconds through the entrance into the dining room of Mrs. Moscowitz with the orange juice.

"Good morning, Rabbi!" the housekeeper said warmly.

"Good morning, Mrs. Moscowitz." He pretended not to notice her frown. For weeks she had been urging him to call her Lena. Mrs. Moscowitz was the fourth housekeeper they had had in the eleven weeks Leslie had been gone. She kept a dusty house, she made rubbery fried eggs, she disregarded their pleadings for *tsimmis* and *kugel,* and everything she baked came from packaged mixes, for which she expected lavish praise.

"How do you want your eggs, Rabbi?" she asked, setting before him a glass of frozen orange juice he knew would be watery and improperly diluted.

"Soft-boiled, Mrs. Moscowitz, if you please." He focused his attention on his daughter, who had gained two pages in the interval.

"Good morning. I had better brush your hair for you."

"Morning." She turned a page.

"How's the book?"

"Cool."

He lifted it up and looked at the title and she sighed, knowing that the game was over. It was a juvenile mystery. The Rabbi placed it on the floor beneath his chair. From upstairs a burst of sweet sound indicated that Max had awakened sufficiently to reach for his harmonica. When there was time, Rabbi Kind enjoyed playing Saul to his sixteen-year-old son's David, but he knew that unless he interrupted, Max would eat no breakfast.

He called and the music stopped in the middle of one of those ersatz folk songs. A couple of minutes later Max was sitting with them at the table, his face scrubbed shiny and his hair wet.

"Somehow this morning I feel like an old man," the Rabbi said.

Max grinned. "Hey, Pop, you're still a kid," he said, reaching for the underdone toast.

The Rabbi tapped his eggshell with a spoon while self-pity settled around him like Mrs. Moscowitz' perfume. The soft-boiled eggs were hard. The children ate theirs without complaint, satisfying their hunger, and he ate his own without tasting, content to watch them. Fortunately, he thought, they resembled their mother, with hair the soft color of candlelight on copper, good white teeth and complexions that demanded the freckles.

For the first time he noticed that Rachel was pale. He reached over and took her face in his hand and she nuzzled against his palm.

"Go outside this afternoon," he said. "Climb a tree. Sit on the ground. Get some cold air in your lungs." He looked at his son. "Maybe your brother will even take you skating, the big athlete?"

Max shook his head. "No chance. Scooter cuts the team this afternoon and gives permanent positions. Hey, can I get some hockey skates when my Chanukah check comes from Grandpa Abe?"

"You haven't got it yet. If it comes, then ask me."

"Poppa, can I be Mary in our Christmas pageant?"

"No."

"That's what I told Miss Emmons you'd say."

He pushed back his chair. "Run upstairs and get your brush, Rachel, so I can part your hair the right way. Hurry up, I don't want to keep them from having a *minyan* at the temple."

He drove through the town in the gray morning light of Massachusetts winter. Beth Sholom lay just two blocks north of the Woodborough business district. It was a twenty-eight-year-old building, old-fashioned and well-constructed, and so far he had managed to fend off those in the congregation who wished to build a more modern temple in the suburbs.

He parked under the maple trees and walked from the tiny parking lot up the red brick stairs and into the temple, as he had done every morning for eight years. In his study he took off his overcoat and traded his old brown fedora for a black skullcap. Then, murmuring the blessing, he touched the fringes of his *tallis* to his lips, threw the prayer shawl around his shoulders, and walked down the deep-shadowed corridor to the sanctuary, automatically counting with his eyes as he said good morning to the men seated on the white benches. Six, including the two mourners, Joel Price, who had just lost his mother, and Dan Levine, whose father had died six months before.

The Rabbi made seven.

Even as he mounted the *bema* two more men came through the front door, stamping the snow from their shoes.

"One more," said Joel, sighing.

Michael knew he was nervous about the possibility that they wouldn't assemble the ten men necessary to say *Kaddish,* the prayer pious Jews offer each morning and evening for eleven months following the death of a parent. The tenth man was the one he always sweated out himself.

He looked out over the empty temple.

Hello God, he thought.

Please Lord make this the day she improves. She is deserving of you. I love her so.

Help her, Lord. Please God. Amen.

He started the service with the morning blessings, which are not community prayers and do not require a *minyan* of ten men: "Blessed art Thou, O Lord our God, King of the Universe, who hast given to the cock intelligence to distinguish between day and night. . . ." Together they blessed God for granting them faith, freedom, masculinity, and strength. They were praising him for removing sleep from their eyes and slumber from their eyelids when the tenth man arrived—Jake Lazarus, the cantor, with sleep still in his eyes and slumber on his eyelids—and the men grinned at the Rabbi and relaxed.

When the service was over and the other nine men had dropped coins into the *pushkeh* for indigent transients and said good-by and hurried off to their businesses and jobs, Michael left the *bema* and sat on the white bench in the first row. A shaft of sunlight came through a high window and struck the spot; when he had arrived at Beth Sholom the illuminating ray had appealed to him because of its beauty and melodrama; now he liked it because sitting in its warmth on a winter morning was better than the sunlamp at the YMHA.

He sat for five minutes watching the motes of dust dance up and down the long sun-column. It was quiet in the empty temple, and he closed his eyes and thought of the slow surf in Florida and of the orange trees budding tight and green in California, then of the other places they had been, of deep snow drifting in the Ozarks and of the sound of katydids in Georgia fields and of the woods wet with rain in Pennsylvania. If nothing else, he told himself, failure in many places gives a rabbi a good geographic background.

Then, feeling guilty, he jumped up and set out to make his pastoral calls.

His first stop concerned his wife.

The grounds of Woodborough State Hospital were sometimes mistaken by strangers for a college campus, but halfway down the long, winding driveway the presence of Herman left no doubt about the hospital's identity.

Michael had a crowded morning schedule, and Herman would see to it that it took him ten minutes to negotiate the rest of the driveway and ease his car into a parking space, a process that otherwise would have taken about sixty seconds.

Herman wore bell-bottomed dungarees, an old pea coat, an Orioles baseball cap, and fluffy earmuffs that had once been white. In each hand he carried an orange ping-pong paddle, the kind covered with tiny rubber pips. He walked backward, guiding the car's progress with a fierce intentness, conscious that the Rabbi's life and the fate of an expensive government aircraft were on his shoulders. Twenty years before, Herman had been flight operations officer on a wartime aircraft carrier. He had chosen to continue the assignment. For the past four years he had been meeting cars and guiding drivers in to landings on the hospital parking lot. He was an annoyance, but an appealing one. No matter how hurried Michael was, he found himself acting out a role that made him a willing part of Herman's illness.

Michael was the hospital's Jewish chaplain, a post that occupied half a day of his weekly routine, and he had arranged to work in the chaplain's office until notified that Dan Bernstein, Leslie's psychiatrist, was free.

But Dan was waiting for him.

"I'm sorry I'm late," he said. "I always forget to leave a couple of extra minutes for Herman."

"He bothers me," the psychiatrist said. "What will you do if some day he decides to wave you off at the last minute and signals you to fly around and make a new approach?"

"I'll pull back hard on the stick and my station wagon will roar up over the administration building."

Dr. Bernstein settled himself in the one comfortable chair in the room, slipped off his brown loafers and wiggled his toes. Then he sighed and lit a cigarette.

"How's my wife?"

"The same."

He had hoped for better news. "Is she talking?"

"Very little. She's waiting."

"What for?"

"For her sadness to go away," Dr. Bernstein said, rubbing his stockinged toes with fat, blunt fingers. "Something grew too strong to face, so she withdrew. It's not uncommon. If she reaches understanding she'll come out and face it, and allow herself to forget what is causing her depression.

"We had hoped to help her to do this with psychotherapy. But she doesn't talk. I think electric shock is indicated."

Michael's stomach twisted. Dr. Bernstein looked at his face and snorted in undisguised contempt. "You call yourself a mental hospital chaplain? Why the hell should shock frighten you?"

"Sometimes they thrash around. Broken bones."

"Not for years, not since we've had muscle-paralyzing drugs. Today it's a humane treatment. You've seen it, haven't you?"

He nodded. "Will she experience aftereffects?"

"Of the treatments? Probably some slight amnesia, partial loss of memory. Nothing serious. She'll remember everything that's important in her life. Little things, things that don't matter, will be gone."

"What kinds of things?"

"Perhaps the title of a movie she's seen recently, or the name of the film's leading man. Or the address of a slight aquaintance. But these will be isolated incidents. Most of her memory will be retained."

"Can't you attempt to make progress with psychotherapy for a little while longer before you try the shock?"

Dr. Bernstein allowed himself the luxury of mild annoyance. "But she's not talking! How can therapy be conducted without communication? I have no idea what's *really* making her depressed. Have you?"

"She's a convert, as you know. But she's been completely Jewish for a long time."

"Other pressures?"

"We moved around a lot before we came here. Sometimes we lived in situations that were difficult."

Dan Bernstein lit another cigarette. "Do all rabbis move around that much?"

Michael shrugged. "Some men go to one temple and stay there for the rest of their lives. Others keep traveling. Most rabbis are on short-term contracts. If you struggle too hard, break too many lances in the congregation's tender skin, or if they break too many in yours, you move on."

"You think that's why you've moved so often?" Dr. Bernstein asked in a flat, impersonal way. Michael knew intuitively that the tone was part of his session technique. "Have you broken the lances, or received them?"

He took a cigarette from the pack Dan had left on the desk between them. He noticed with annoyance that his hand trembled slightly as he held the match. "A little of both," he said.

Dr. Bernstein's eyes were on his face, gray and direct. They made him uncomfortable. The psychiatrist pocketed his cigarettes. "I think electric shock is your wife's best bet. We could start her on a course of twelve treatments, three times a week. I've seen marvelous results."

Michael nodded in reluctant agreement. "If you think it's best. What can I do for her?"

"Be patient. You can't reach out to her. You can only wait for her to reach out to you. When she does, you'll know she's taken her first step toward recovery."

"Thank you, Dan."

He rose to his feet and Michael shook his hand. "Why don't you drop around the temple some Friday night? You might get some therapy out of my *shabbos* service. Or are you another atheistic man of science?"

"I'm not an atheist, Rabbi." He pushed first one pudgy foot into a loafer, then the other. "I'm a Unitarian," he said.

On Monday, Wednesday, and Friday mornings of the following week Michael was very irritable whenever approached. He silently cursed the fact that he had ever become a chaplain; it would have been so much easier if the details were shrouded in mystery.

But he knew that by seven the treatments would begin in Templeton Ward.

His Leslie would wait in an anteroom with other patients until her turn came. Then the nurses would lead her to a bed and she would lie down. The attendant would take off her shoes and slip them under the thin mattress. The anesthetist would slip a canula into her vein.

Each time he had watched the treatments there had been several patients whose veins were so small they could not be pierced, and the doctor had sweated and grumbled and cursed. Leslie's veins would give them no trouble, he thought thankfully. They were narrow but distinct. When you touched them with your lips you could feel the blood pumping up strong and clean from the core of her body.

The canula would drip a barbiturate into her bloodstream, and thank you, God, his wife would fall asleep. Then the anesthetist would inject a muscle relaxant, and the tensions that kept her functioning as a living machine would slacken. Her chest muscles would grow flaccid, no longer operating the lovely bellows of her chest. Instead, from time to time a black cup would be fitted over her mouth and nose and the anesthetist would force oxygen into her lungs, breathing for her. A rubber wedge would be placed between her jaws to protect her tongue from her fine white teeth. The attendant would rub her temples with electrode jelly and then the electrodes, the size of half-dollars, would be pressed into her skull.

The anesthetist would say "All right," in a bored voice, and the resident psychiatrist would press his fingertip down on a button in a little black box. The alternating current would surge silently into her head for five seconds, an electrical storm that in the tonic stage would jolt her arms rigid despite the relaxant, and then in the clonic stage would leave her limbs twitching and jerking like those of the victim of an epileptic fit.

He drew books from the library and read whatever he could find about electric-shock treatments. He realized with a slow horror that Dan Bernstein and every other psychiatrist in the world didn't know exactly what happened when they buffeted his wife's brain with electric bombardment. All they had were theories, and the knowledge that the treatments got results. One of these theories said that the electrical charge burned out abnormal circuits in the switchboard of the brain. Another said that the shock was close enough to the death experience to satisfy the patient's need for punishment and assuage the guilt feelings that had plunged him into despair.

That was enough; he stopped his reading exercises.

Each treatment day he called the hospital at 9 A.M., and a ward nurse with a flat, nasal voice told him that the treatment had been uneventful and that Mrs. Kind was resting comfortably.

He wanted to avoid people. He did paperwork, catching up with his correspondence for the first time in his life, and he even cleaned out his desk drawers. On the twelfth day after Leslie began the shock treatments, however, the rabbinate caught up with him. That afternoon he attended a *bris*, blessing a baby named Simon Maxwell Shutzer as the *mohel* slit away the fore- skin of the little bloody penis and the father trembled and the mother wept whitely and then laughed in joy. Then, covering the life span from birth to death in two short hours, he officiated at the funeral of Sarah Myerson, an old lady whose grandsons wept to see her lowered into the grave. Darkness had fallen by the time he returned home. He was bone-weary. At the cemetery the sky had begun to spit a fine sleet that stung their faces until they burned, and he felt chilled through to the marrow. He was on his way to the liquor cabinet for some whiskey when he saw the letter on the foyer table. When he picked it up and saw the handwriting he had trouble ripping it open. It was written in pencil on inexpensive blue stationery, probably borrowed.

My Michael,

Last night a woman down the hall screamed that a bird was beating its wings, beating its wings against her window, and finally they came and gave her a needle and she fell asleep. And this morning an attendant found the bird, an ice-covered sparrow, lying on the walk. Its heart was still beating, and when they fed it warm milk with a dropper it lived, and he brought it to show the woman it was all right. They left it in a box in the dispensary but this afternoon it died.

I lay in my bed and remembered the sound of the birds in the woods outside our cabin in the Ozarks, and how I would lie in your arms and listen to them after we had made love, our hearts the only thing we could hear in the cabin and the birds the only thing we could hear outside.

I want to see my children. Are they well?

Wear your thermal underwear when you make pastoral calls. Eat leafy vegetables and stay away from your spices.

Happy birthday, my poor old man.

Leslie

Mrs. Moscowitz came in to announce dinner and stared in amazement at his wet face. "Rabbi, is anything wrong?"

"I just got a letter from my wife. She's going to be all right, Lena."

The dinner was burned. Two days later Mrs. Moscowitz announced that she was needed by her widower brother-in-law whose daughter was ailing in Willimantic, Connecticut. Her place was taken by a fat, gray-haired woman named Anna Schwartz. Anna was an asthmatic with a wen on her chin, but she was very clean and she could cook anything, including a *lochshen kugel* with two kinds of raisins, light and dark, and a crust that was so good you hated to chew.

CHAPTER TWO

When the children asked what their mother had written he told them she had wished him a belated happy birthday. He wasn't hinting—or perhaps he was—but the next day resulted in a crayoned card from Rachel and a store-bought one from Max, plus a gorgeous loud tie from the two of them. The tie matched nothing he owned, but he wore it to temple that morning.

Birthdays made him optimistic. They were turning points,

he told himself hopefully. He remembered his son's sixteenth birthday, three months before.

The day Max had lost his belief in God. *

In Massachusetts, at sixteen a boy becomes eligible to apply for a driver's license.

Michael had taught Max to drive the Ford and he had an appointment to be examined for his license at the Registry of Motor Vehicles on the morning before his birthday, which fell on a Saturday. On Saturday night he had a date with Dessamae Kaplan, a child-woman with blue eyes and red hair who made Michael envy his son.

They were supposed to go to a square dance at a barn overlooking the lake. Leslie and Michael had asked a group of their son's friends to a small birthday party before the dance, and they had planned to hand him the keys to the car so he could celebrate by driving for the first time without parental escort.

But it was on the Wednesday before Max's birthday that Leslie fell into the deep emotional depression that sent her to the hospital, and by Friday morning Michael had been told that she would be there for an indeterminate stay. Max canceled his appointment for the driver's test and called off his party. When Michael heard him breaking his date with Dessamae, too, he pointed out that Max's becoming a hermit wouldn't help the state of his mother's health.

"I don't want to go," Max said evenly. "You know what's on the other side of that lake?"

Michael knew, of course, and he stopped urging Max to attend the dance. It would not be pleasure for a boy to stroll with his girl at the water's edge and gaze out across the lake at the sanitarium his mother had entered a few days before.

Most of the day Max stayed on his bed, reading. Michael could have used his son's customary ability to clown, because he was having a bad time with Rachel, who wanted her mother.

"If she can't come here, let's go and visit Momma."

"We can't do that," he told her again. "It's against the rules. There are no visiting hours now."

"We'll sneak in. I can be quiet."

"Go and get dressed for services," he said gently. "We have to be at the temple in an hour."

"Daddy, we can make it. We don't have to drive all the way around the lake. I know a place where there's a rowboat. We can float right across and see Momma and then we can go right back again. Please," she said.

He could only slap her on the behind and leave the room in order not to hear her cry. He poked his head into Max's room as he went by.

"Better get ready, son. We'll be going to the temple soon."

"Would you mind if I didn't?"

Michael stared at him. Nobody in their household ever missed services unless he was ill.

"Why?" he asked.

"I don't want to be a hypocrite."

"I don't understand."

"I've been thinking about it all day. I'm not sure there's a God."

"God's a phony?"

He looked at his father. "He may be. Who really knows? Nobody's ever had any proof. He may be a legend."

"You think I've spent more than half my life serving a puff of smoke? Perpetuating a fairy tale?"

Max said nothing.

"Because you mother has taken sick," Michael said, "and you in your wisdom have reasoned that if there were a God He would not take her away from you?"

"That's right."

His argument was hardly new and Michael had never learned to refute it, nor did he desire to do so. A man either believes in God or he doesn't.

"Stay home, then," he said. He washed Rachel's red eyes and helped her dress. As they left the house a short time later he heard Max's harmonica begin to shrill a blues. Ordinarily his son refrained from playing on Friday night out of respect for the *shabbos*. But on that night Michael understood. If, as Max suspected, there were no God, why observe any of the meaningless scribbling on the totem pole?

Michael and Rachel were the first ones at the temple and he

opened the windows wide, trying to court a small breeze. Billy
O'Connell, the organist, arrived next, and then Jake Lazarus,
the cantor. As usual Jake hurried into the men's room as soon as
he had struggled into his black robe and put on the skullcap. He
always stayed there exactly ten minutes, leaning over the wash-
bowl and staring into the mirror as he practiced scales.

By eight-thirty, when the service was scheduled to start,
only six other people had arrived. Jake looked at the Rabbi ques-
tioningly.

Michael motioned to him that they would begin: God should
not have to wait for laggards.

For the next thirty-five minutes the people drifted in, until
there were twenty-seven—it was easy to count from the *bema*.
He knew that a number of families were away on vacation. He
also knew that at least a *minyan* could be collected in a bowling
alley within driving distance, that several cocktail parties were
being held that night, and that tent theaters, supper clubs, and
several Chinese restaurants no doubt held more of his congregation than the temple did.

Years before the knowledge that only a handful of his people
had come to the synagogue to greet the *shabbos* would have been
a knife mincing his innards. But he had long since learned that to
a rabbi even one Jew is satisfying company in prayer; he was at
peace as he led the service for a tiny group that barely filled the
first two rows of benches.

Word of Leslie's illness had spread, the way such things
always do, and several of the ladies fussed over Rachel during
the *oneg shabbat*, the refreshment period following the service.
Michael was grateful. They stayed late, desiring the company of
the herd.

When they got home the light was out in Max's room and
Michael didn't disturb him.

Saturday was a replica of Friday. *Shabbos* as a rule was a
time of rest and meditation, but there was no peace in the Kind
house that day. Each of them suffered in his own way. Shortly
after dinner Michael received word that Jack Glickman's wife
had died. It meant that he would spend the evening in a condolence call. He hated the thought of leaving the children.

"Do you want to go out?" he asked Max. "If you do, I'll call in a sitter to stay with Rachel."

"I'm not going anywhere. She'll be all right."

Later Max recalled that after his father left he had put his book down and had stopped in Rachel's room for a moment on the way to the bathroom. It was hardly dusk, but she was already in her pajamas, lying with her face to the wall.

"Rache," he said softly. "You asleep?" There was no reply, so he shrugged and ambled along. He returned to his book, this time not setting it down until he felt hunger pangs half an hour later. On his way to the kitchen he passed Rachel's room again.

The bed was empty.

He wasted five minutes roaming through the house and then the yard, calling her name and not daring to think about the lake and the boat she had been wanting to float away in, into her mother's arms. He didn't even know whether it was a real boat or an imaginary one, but he knew that he was going to have to get to the lake. His father had taken the car, and that left only the hated bicycle. He took it down from where it hung on two rusty nails on the garage wall, noticing with a mixture of anger and fear that Rachel's bike was missing from its usual spot next to the lawn mower. Then he pedaled through the humid August night as fast as he was able. They lived less than half a mile from Deer Lake, but he was perspiring freely by the time he got there. There was a road that circled the lake but it didn't hug the shore, and trees hid the water from view even during the day. There was a narrow path that followed the waterline. It was rutted and root-veined and it was impossible to ride a bicycle on it. But he stuck to his bike as long as Rachel had stuck to hers. He saw the moon glinting redly off the reflector of her bicycle where she had parked it neatly against a tree trunk just off the path, and he let his fall to the ground next to it and ran on down the path on foot.

"*RACHEL?*" he called.

Crickets shrilled in the grass and the water splashed on the rocks. There was a pale moonlight, and he searched the waters off the shoreline with his eyes.

"*RA-A-CHEL. . . .*"

Somebody laughed from under a nearby tree and he thought

for a moment that he had found her. But then he made out three figures, two men in bathing suits and a woman who wasn't many years older than himself. She wore a halter and a cotton skirt, and she sat with her back to a tree, her knees in the air. The moon shone softly on her thighs.

She laughed again. "Lost your girl, sonny?"

"My sister," Max said. "Did you see a little girl? Eight years old."

All three of them held opened cans of beer. The woman tipped hers to her lips and swallowed, her white throat moving as she drank. "Ah, that's all right," she whispered.

"We ain't seen a kid," one of the men said.

He crashed along down the trail. The other man said something as he ran away, and the three under the tree laughed.

He remembered that two summers before he had been swimming in this part of the lake one afternoon when a drowned man had been discovered. The man's hair had streamed when they pulled him out of the water and his flesh had been like dough. Rachel could dogpaddle for about five feet and when she tried to do the dead man's float she got water in her nose.

"Please, God," he said. "Oh, God, please, please, please." He ran on and on, stumbling on the rough trail, too winded now to call out, praying soundlessly and without end.

The boat was about two hundred feet offshore when he saw it. It was an old skiff. It looked black in the moonlight, and it was pointed the wrong way, its nose toward the near shore. A small figure in white pajamas sat in one corner of the stern.

Max kicked off his sneakers and skinned out of his pants. The chinos, crumpled into a ball when he threw them from him, dropped over the slight bluff that was the shoreline and fell into the water, but he didn't bother about them. Instead he threw himself into the lake. The water was shallow near shore, with a rocky bottom five or six feet out, where he landed in his shallow dive. His chest scraped lightly against the rocks and then he rose and started to swim, his legs kicking him swiftly toward the boat. He reached it and heaved himself aboard.

"Hi, Max," Rachel said dreamily. She was picking her nose. He sprawled spread-eagled in the bottom of the boat and panted for breath. There was a lot of dirty water in the skiff, which was very old and very leaky.

"Momma's over there," she said.

Max stared at the network of yellow lights at which Rachel pointed. They were on the far shore, a quarter of a mile away. He moved over to his sister and took her into his wet arms. The two of them sat that way for several minutes, looking at the hospital lights. They didn't speak. It was very quiet. Every now and then a burst of music from the dance at the barn drifted across the water. Closer, a girl began to laugh shrilly, then to scream. The beer-drinkers, Max thought.

"Where are the oars?" he said finally. "The two oars?"

"There was only one, but I lost it. I think it sank. Why are you wearing your BVD's? They look funny, sticking to you that way."

He had been watching the water in the skiff's bottom for some time, and now it was unmistakably clear that it was rising. "Rachel," he said, "this boat is sinking. I'm going to have to swim you to shore."

Rachel looked at the black water. "No," she said. "I don't want to."

He had often towed her during horseplay in the water, but he was tired and he doubted his ability to get her to shore if she fought him. "Rachel, if you let me swim you to shore, I'll give you half a dollar," he said.

She shook her head. "I'll do it on one condition."

He watched the water. It was beginning to rise swiftly.

"*What?*"

"You let me use your harmonica for two whole days."

"Come on," he said. He slipped over the side of the skiff and treaded water while he held up his arms to receive her. She squealed as she entered the water, but she was quiet and good as he lay on his back, his hand under her chin, and pulled her ashore.

His sneakers were where he had left them, but his chinos could not be seen. He stepped off the bluff into a deep ooze and felt around in the water with his hands.

"What are you looking for?"

"My slacks."

"See if you can find my oar."

He searched fruitlessly for ten minutes, treating his sister to several additions to her vocabulary, and then he gave up.

He held her hand all the way back to the bicycles, keeping an eye peeled for the two men and the woman, but the only sign of them was a six-pack of empty beer cans under the tree where they had drunk.

They took a long time cycling home. Max's BVD's didn't come equipped with zipper fly. He chose the darkest streets he could find, and twice he dived for nearby bushes to escape the beams of approaching automobiles.

Finally, tired and scratched, he stood in the darkness of the garage and put the bikes away. He did not turn on the lights. There were no curtains on the garage windows.

"I won't spit in the harmonica, Max," Rachel said. She stood outside in the driveway, scratching herself. "Hurry up," she said, yawning. "I want a glass of milk."

Max had half turned to go when the sound of footsteps approaching the driveway froze him in his tracks. They were light, feminine steps, and he had guessed whose they were even before he heard Dessamae Kaplan's voice.

"Rachel? What are you doing out here? Where's Max?"

"We been swimming and riding our bikes. I got on my p.j.'s and Max is wearing his underwear. See?"

Her thumb tripped the light switch, and Max stood in his muddy yellow BVD's as if rooted to the oil-spotted garage floor, his hands cupping his crotch, while the love of his life shrieked and fled into the darkness.

All this Max told to Rabbi Kind on the following Friday evening as they walked together to the *shabbos* service at the temple.

And three months later Michael thought of his son's birthday as he sat, his own birthday letter, cards, and gift spread in front of him, and wrote a letter to his wife in the hospital overlooking the shore where his son had found his God and lost his pants.

CHAPTER THREE

On a dark night, when snowflakes as large as feathers fled on a horizontal line before the northeast wind, he carried three armloads of wood in from the back shed and made a fire in the fireplace, building it too high so that it roared its heat into the room. Then he made himself a large whiskey and soda and picked up the tractate *Berakoth*, slipping into the Babylonian Talmud's intricacies like a man escaping into a dream.

It was the kind of evening he hadn't spent in too long; he read until after eleven o'clock, rising from his chair only to add more wood to the fire and to say good night to his children.

Then, yawning and stretching, he sat down to consider the day's correspondence.

Young Jeffrey Kodetz had requested a character reference to go with his application to M.I.T. It was the kind of thing he tended to let slide if he waited to dictate it to Dvora Cantor, his secretary; he sat down and wrote a first draft that he could hand her in the morning for retyping.

There was also a letter from the Columbia College Alumni Association, informing him that in eighteen months he and his classmates would be celebrating their twenty-fifth reunion; in addition to planning to attend, would he forward to them within the next three months an autobiography for inclusion in the Quarter-Century Class Book?

He read it again, shaking his head in bewilderment: a quarter of a century?

He felt too tired to do anything but write to Leslie. When he had sealed the envelope he found that he was out of stamps; this was a problem, since he mailed her letter each morning on the way to early services, before the post office was open.

He remembered that Max usually carried a book of stamps in his wallet. When he entered Max's room the boy was sound asleep, sprawled across the bed and snoring gently. One leg spilled from the blanket onto the floor. His pajamas were too short, and Michael saw with amusement that his feet were becoming enormous.

His slacks were hung by their cuffs with careless efficiency in the top drawer of his dresser. Michael tugged the wallet from the pocket. It was fat with all manner of strange, tattered papers. His fingers, searching for the book of stamps, closed around something else. It was small, oblong, aluminum-foil covered. Unable to believe his fingertips, he carried it to the doorway and read the printing by the light of the hall bulb:

"Trojan-Enz are individually water-tested on our special machines. Young Rubber Corporation Manufacturer, Trenton, N.J., New York, N.Y."

At his age, he asked himself fearfully, this adolescent, this ball-bouncer who only this morning had called him Daddy? And with whom? Some bored, possibly diseased slattern? Or worse, that clean-limbed red-haired child, God forbid? He held the thing up to the light. The foil was worn and cracked. He reminded himself that once long ago he had considered it a mark of juvenile maturity to carry if not to use a similar contrivance.

Returning it, he replaced the wallet in Max's pants, dislodging a jangle of coins from the side pocket. They clattered on the floor, rolling and skittering about the room. He held his breath, waiting for the boy to stir and waken, but Max slept as though drugged.

Drugged? That's next, he told himself grimly. He got down on his hands and knees, not to pray like a Christian but to sweep the floor with his fingers. Under the bed he found two nickels, a quarter, a penny, three socks and a great many dust curds. He located most of the coins and returned them to the pants pocket. Then he went downstairs, washed his hands, and put on coffee to perk.

Listening to the midnight news over the second cup, he heard the name of one of his people. Gerald I. Mendelsohn was on the critical list at Woodborough General Hospital. His right leg had been caught between two pieces of heavy machinery during the night shift at the Suffolk Foundry.

The Mendelsohns were a new couple in town, with probably few friends as yet, he thought wearily.

Luckily he had not yet changed into pajamas. He put on his

tie and jacket and coat and hat and six-buckle arctics and let himself out of the house as quietly as possible. The streets were bad. Wheels spinning, he drove the car at crawling speeds past dark houses whose sleeping occupants he envied.

Mendelsohn was unshaven, his pale face like something from a crucifixion painting. He lay in a hospital bed in a room off the Emergency Ward, drugged to unconsciousness but groaning loudly.

His wife was suffering. She was a small, attractive woman with brown hair and large eyes and a flat chest and very long red fingernails.

He concentrated desperately and came up with her name: Jean. He seemed to remember her delivering children to the temple for Hebrew classes.

"Is there anyone at home with the kids?"

She nodded. "I have very good neighbors. Lovely Irishers." She sounded like New York. Brooklyn?

She was from Flatbush. He sat with her and talked of the neighborhoods he remembered. The man on the bed groaned regularly, as if the sound were mechanically timed.

At two-fifteen they came and took him away and Michael and the woman waited in the corridor while the leg was amputated. After that, she seemed relieved. When he finally said goodby her swollen eyes were sleepy and calm, like the eyes of a passionate woman after love.

It stopped snowing as he drove home. The stars hung low in the dark sky, ripe and bright.

In the morning, gazing at his reflection in the process of shaving, he discovered that he was no longer young. His hair was thin, his nose was growing hawkish and hooked, like that of the Jew in the anti-Semitic cartoons, his flesh sagged, and his jowls jiggled under the blanket of shaving cream. He was like a leaf that felt itself turning brittle and cracking, he thought. Some day it would fall from the tree and the world would go on, scarcely noticing its disappearance from the scene. He realized that he barely remembered what the spring of his life had tasted like, but now it was unmistakably autumn.

When the telephone rang he turned from the mirror in relief.

It was Dr. Bernstein. It was the first time the psychiatrist had called him in the four weeks Leslie had been receiving electro-shock, and he felt a concern Dan immediately dispelled.

"She can go home for a visit if she wants to," he said casually.

"When?"

"Any time you say."

He canceled two appointments and drove straight to the hospital. She was seated in her tiny room when he came in. Her blonde hair was pulled flat back and held with a thick, ugly elastic band in a ponytail style he hadn't seen her wear for years. Instead of being youthful, it made her look matronly. She had on a clean blue cotton dress and her lipstick had been freshly applied. She had gained a lot of weight, but it was becoming.

"Hello," he said.

At first he was afraid it was going to be the way it had been in the early days of her illness. She looked at him and didn't make a sound. But then she smiled and began to cry. "Hello," she said.

She felt soft and familiar in his arms. He filled his nostrils with the Leslie-smell he had missed so long, a combination of Camay soap and Paquin's Hand Cream and warm flesh, and he held her close.

Thank you God. Amen.

They kissed clumsily, suddenly very shy, and then they sat on the edge of the bed, holding hands. The room smelled of a strong disinfectant.

"The children?" she said.

"Fine. They want to see you. Any time you say."

"I've changed my mind. I don't want to see them. Not here, not like this. I want to go home as soon as I can."

"I've just talked to Dr. Bernstein. You can go home for a visit, if you'd like."

"Oh, yes."

"When?"

"Now?"

Michael got Dan on the telephone and it was arranged. Five minutes later he was helping her into the station wagon and then they drove away from the hospital grounds like two youngsters out on a date. Leslie was wearing her old blue coat and a white kerchief. She had never looked more beautiful, he thought; her face was alive and excited.

It was shortly after eleven o'clock. "It's Anna's day off," he said.

She looked at him out of the corners of her eyes. "Anna?"

He had written to her about Anna half a dozen times. "The housekeeper. Shall we stop someplace nice for lunch?"

"Un-huh. Home. I'll find something on the shelves I can fix."

When they got there he left the car in the driveway and they went in through the back door. She wandered through the kitchen, the dining room, and the parlor, straightening pictures and pulling open curtains.

"Take your coat off," he said.

"The kids will be so surprised." She looked at the mantel clock. "They'll be here in about three hours." She shrugged out of her coat and he hung it in the hall closet. "You know what I want? A deep, hot bath. I want to soak in it for a long time. I don't care if I never have another shower as long as I live."

"Coming up. The way you like it." He went upstairs and ran the bath for her, sprinkling into it some of the bath salts that hadn't been used since she had left them behind. While she bathed he took off his shoes and lay on the brass bed listening to the occasional splash noises and the snatches of songs she hummed and sang as she washed. It was a beautiful sound.

She came out in his robe, running through the chill room to the closet, where she began shoving hanger after hanger along the pole, searching for a dress to wear.

"What will I put on for this afternoon?" she said. "Come and help me decide."

He walked to her. "The green knitted jersey," he said.

She stamped a bare foot. "I couldn't get it on my nose. Oh, I've grown so fat in that place."

"Let me see." He swung the robe, and she stood still and let him look at her.

She threw her arms around him and pressed her head to his chest. "Oh, Michael, I'm freezing."

"Come, I'll warm you." She waited while he hurried out of his clothes and then they shivered together on the cold sheet, arms wrapped around one another and her toes digging into his calves, holding him fast. Over her shoulder he saw their images captured in the large vanity glass that leaned against the wall. He gazed at their white bodies in the yellow glass, and he began to grow young. The leaf no longer was cracked and crumbling. It was full of summer instead of autumn. In a few moments they stopped trembling and grew warm and he stroked her and touched all the richness of her moist, soft body, and she was crying soundlessly in a way that broke his heart, sadly and without hope. "Michael, I don't want to go back there," she said. "I can't go back."

"It will only be for a little while," he told her. "A little while only. I promise you." She covered his mouth with her own, alive and loving and tasting of Ipana.

Afterward with the sheet she dried his eyes, then her own. "What a couple of fools," she said.

"Welcome home."

"Thank you." She propped her head on her hand and looked at him for a moment, then she grinned, the same grin he saw every day on his daughter's face, but this one riper, knowing. He bounded out of bed, jumping to the dresser to grab a comb and brush and bounding back beneath the covers again while she giggled at the sight, then he took the ugly elastic band away and let her hair fall free and beautiful around her neck while she sat up in bed with the comforter pulled up to her chin. He brushed her hair and parted it carefully, the way he did for Rachel, then he threw the elastic band against the far wall and she was once more the wife he knew completely.

Max and Rachel said very little that evening but they stayed by her like twin shadows.

After supper they sat and listened to records, Leslie in a chair with Max at her feet and Rachel in her lap, while Michael stretched out on the couch, smoking.

Telling the children that she would go back to the hospital was difficult, but she did it herself, matter-of-factly and with the kind of efficiency he had always admired in her. Rachel went to bed at nine o'clock and at Leslie's insistence Max kissed her and went up to do his homework.

She was silent during much of the ride back. "It was a day," she said. She took his hand and held it for a long time. "You'll come tomorrow?"

"I'll be here."

He drove home very slowly. Max was playing his harmonica, and for a while Michael smoked and listened. He went upstairs finally and kicked Max into bed, then he took a long shower and changed into pajamas. He lay in the dark. The wind blew in gusts that shook the house until the windows rattled. The brass bed seemed as big and empty as the whole world outside. He stayed awake for a long time, praying.

Soon after he fell asleep, Rachel cried out in terror and then sobbed. She called out a second time and this time he heard and he slid out of the bed and hurried across the cold floors in his bare feet to her room, picking her up and moving her to the far side of the bed against the wall to make room for him.

She continued to sob in her sleep, her face wet with tears.

"*Shah,*" he said, taking her in his arms. "*Shah, shah, shah,*" gently rocking his shoulders as he held her in the dark.

Her eyes opened, white slots in her heart-shaped face. She smiled suddenly and pressed close to him, and he felt her wet face on his neck.

Feigileh, he thought, little bird. He could remember when he was her age, the problems he had had when his own father was forty-five. My God, he could remember his *zaydeh* when the old man was not much older than that.

He lay very still in the dark, trying to remember it all.

Brooklyn, New York
September 1925

CHAPTER FOUR

His grandfather's beard must have been black when Michael was a little boy. But he remembered it only the way it was when he was a young man—a full, white bush that Isaac Rivkind shampooed with care every third night and combed with love and vanity, so that it lay smooth and soft-looking beneath his tough and swarthy face down to the third button of his shirt. His beard was the only soft thing about him. He had a rapacious hawk's nose and the eyes of a disgusted eagle. The top of his head was bald and as shiny as polished bone, set in a circlet of frizzled hair that never achieved the whiteness of the beard but remained a dark gray until the day of his death.

The truth about Michael's grandfather was that he was as tender toward the world as a mother nursing her fatally ill child. What covered his love with a thick veneer was an overwhelming fear of the Gentiles. He had gained that fear in the Bessarabian town of Kishinev, where he was born.

There were 113,000 people in Kishinev. Almost 80,000 of them were Jews. Another few thousand were gypsies. The remainder were Moldavian Rumanians. Although they were the majority in the town, the Jews of Kishinev submitted with resignation to the curses, sneers, and scorn of the Moldavians, knowing that Kishinev was an island ghetto surrounded by a sea of hostility. Even if a Jew wanted to leave the town to work as a fruit-picker or a grape-treader in the vineyards and wineries of the countryside, he was forbidden by the government to do so. The administration taxed the Jews heavily, confined them closely, and supported a daily newspaper—the *Bessarabetz*—edited by an anti-Semitic fanatic named Pavolachi Krushevan, whose sole goal was to incite his readers to the shedding of Jewish blood.

Michael became familiar with Krushevan's name while he was still a little boy, learning on his *zaydeh*'s knee to hate it with the same feeling the name of Haman inspired. Instead of fairy tales or nursery rhymes, when he crawled up on Zaydeh's lap in the mysterious gloominess of the tiny grocery store, he heard the legends of how his grandfather had come to America.

Isaac's father had been Mendel Rivkind, one of the five blacksmiths of Kishinev, a man with the stink of horse-sweat always in his nostrils. Mendel was more fortunate than most of his fellow Jews; he was a man of property. Against the north wall of the poor, sagging wooden structure he called his house were two homemade brick forges. In them he burned charcoal which he made himself in an earthen pit, blowing his fire with an enormous leather bellows fashioned from the hide of a huge bull.

There was great unemployment in Kishinev. No one could afford to pay much to have his animals shod, and the Rivkind family was as poor as its neighbors. It was hard merely to exist, and saving money was something the Jews of Kishinev never considered because there was no spare money to save. But a month before Isaac was born, two of Mendel Rivkind's cousins were savagely beaten by a crowd of drunken Moldavian youths. The blacksmith decided that somehow, some day, he and his family would escape to a better part of the world.

If they had been poor before, the decision rendered them impoverished. They denied themselves a single luxury and eliminated expenses they had thought of as necessities. Ruble by ruble, a tiny hoard of money grew behind a loose brick at the base of one of the forges. Nobody but Mendel and Sonya, his wife, knew of its existence; they told no one because they did not wish to be murdered in their sleep some night by a beer-smelling peasant who came in search of their nestegg.

The years passed, and each year the pile of money was increased by a painfully small amount. After Isaac was *bar mitzvah* his father took him out to the forge on a dark and frosty night and, prying the brick away, allowed him to feel the accumulated rubles, telling him of the dream.

It was hard to build the freedom fund fast enough to keep ahead of their family. First Isaac had arrived, then three years later a daughter, whom they had named Dora after her grandmother, *aleha hasholom*, she should rest in peace. By 1903, a sufficient number of rubles had been saved to pay for three steerage passages to the United States. But by this time Dora was eighteen and Isaac was twenty-two and had been a married man for more than a year. His bride, the former Itta Melnikov, already was feeling life in her womb, a child who would require more rubles to be placed behind the brick in the years to come.

The times grew worse. Krushevan grew more clamorous. A Christian girl who was a patient in the Jewish hospital of Kishinev committed suicide. In a nearby *shtetl* the uncle of a small boy beat him to death in a fit of drunken rage. Krushevan seized upon both incidents eagerly. Each of the victims had been killed by the Jews, who practiced the loathsome ceremony of ritual murder, his paper reported.

Clearly it was time for those who could to depart. Mendel told Isaac to take the money and go; the rest of the family could follow later. Isaac had other ideas. He was young and strong, and his father had taught him the blacksmith's trade. He and Itta would remain in Kishinev and continue to save rubles toward the day they could leave. Meanwhile, Mendel, Sonya, and Dora could go to the United States and save money to help bring Isaac, Itta, and their child to the New World. When Mendel objected, Isaac reminded him that Dora was of a marriageable age. Did her father want her to marry a poor Jew of Kishinev and face the kind of life that went with such a marriage? She was a beautiful girl. In America a *shidduch,* a match, could be made that would give her a wonderful future—and even help the whole family.

Mendel agreed with reluctance; the necessary applications were filled out laboriously and forwarded with the help of the Jewish tax collector, who accepted with protest the six rubles Mendel forced into his hands, but who made no move to return the money. They were to leave on May 30. Long before the precious passports arrived, to be placed behind the brick with the freedom money, Sonya, Itta, and Dora set to work making feather beds and goose-down pillows, sorting through the few pieces of personal property again and again, trying to decide what should be taken and what should be left behind.

Early in April the men began to run out of charcoal with which to stoke the forges. Mendel obtained his wood in the forest twenty kilometers away from Kishinev, hard chestnut logs which he bought cheap from peasants clearing the woods for farming. He hauled, sawed, split, and burned the charcoal himself. It was an unending chore. Although Jews were confined to the ghetto, the government recognized the importance of keeping animals in working condition, and blacksmiths were given permits allowing them to leave the town to purchase wood. Since Isaac was to be the new head of the business, he decided that he should buy the wood this time. When she heard, Itta pleaded that she be allowed to go along. They left the next morning, sitting happy and proud on the high seat of the flat bed wagon behind the two old horses.

It was a marvelous trip. Spring was in the air. Isaac allowed the horses to set their own slow pace, and the couple enjoyed the scenery as it slowly rolled by. When they arrived at the woodland which was being cleared it was already afternoon. The peasants were happy at the prospect of unexpected extra money to help ease the debts they had incurred at Easter. They allowed Isaac to walk through the woods and mark the trees that would best suit his purpose. He chose young wood that would be easiest for him to saw up when he took it back home. That evening he and Itta ate sumptuously from the kosher lunch Sonya had packed for them. The peasants were accustomed to this, and understood. That night they slept in a small hut near the fields, excited and happy with the novelty of being away from home together, her head on his shoulder and his hand on her swollen belly. In the morning Isaac worked in his shirtsleeves with the peasants, chopping down the trees and trimming the branches, then loading the trunks onto his wagon. When they were through, the sun stood high in the sky. Isaac paid the farmer eight rubles for the wood, thanked him with warmth and received equally sincere thanks, and then sprang to the high seat next to Itta, clucking to start the horses pulling the heavy load.

The sun was setting as they approached Kishinev. They had realized that something was wrong while they were still miles from the town. A pig farmer who was a longtime customer at the blacksmith shop came riding toward them on a mare that wore shoes which Mendel's hammer had fashioned only the week before. When Isaac hailed him gaily the man's face became pale. He kicked his heels savagely into his horse's flanks and pounded away over the fields.

As they drew closer they saw the first fires, the smoke smudging skyward in long columns that swirled purple in the setting sun. In a little while they heard the wailing. They didn't speak to one another, but Isaac could hear his wife's ragged breath, loud and terrified, a half-sobbing sound, as the horses pulled the loaded wagon down streets which on both sides were long rows of still-burning buildings.

At the blacksmith shop only the brick forges remained whole, blackened now outside as well as within. The house was three-quarters gone, a charred, roofless shell. Near it waited Itta's brother, Solomon Melnikov. He gave a shout of joy when he saw them alive and safe. And then, like a child, he put his head on Isaac's shoulder and began to cry.

Isaac and Itta stayed with the Melnikovs during the funeral and the seven days of mourning. All of Kishinev sat *shiva*. Forty-seven Jews had been killed in the pogrom. Almost six hundred were injured. Two thousand families had been utterly ruined by the crazed mob that had swept through the town, raping and mutilating before they had slit throats and crushed skulls. Seven hundred houses had been destroyed. Six hundred stores were pillaged.

On the last night of the mourning week Isaac walked alone to the ruined blacksmith shop through the dark streets, noting burned shells of houses like missing teeth in a jaw. The loose brick at the base of the forge came out almost too easily, and for a dull moment he was sure the passports and the money would be gone. But they were there. He put them in his pockets, for some reason replacing the brick so that it neatly closed the hole at the bottom of the forge.

He gave his mother's passport to the Melnikovs; he never knew whether anyone used it to leave Kishinev. They said good-by only to the Melnikovs and to his father's cousins, who had also survived the terror.

The Melnikov family was wiped out by the influenza epi-demic which swept Bessarabia in 1915. But, as Michael's *zaydeh* used to say, that is another story, all of the facts of which are not known.

His grandfather related these events time and time again, until his mother, who always squirmed throughout the more horrible portions of the tale and whose patience was worn thin by the presence in her home of an old and cantankerous man, would snap, "We *know*. You told us already. Oy, to the children he tells such things!" This is why most of the stories he heard from his *zaydeh* were in the confines of Rivkind's Grocery Store, a place full of the wonderful smells of garlic and farmer's cheese and smoked fish and half-sour pickles. His grandfather smelled good, too, when Michael crawled into his lap. His beard gave off a fragrance that was a mixture of Castile soap and the strong Prince Albert pipe tobacco he smoked six days a week, and his breath always carried faint traces of sugared ginger and rye whiskey, to both of which he was addicted. He was that rarity, a Jew who was a dedicated drinker of alcohol. Liquor was a luxury to which he had succumbed in his loneliness and single affluence following the death of his wife. He allowed himself a shot every couple of hours from the bottle of Canadian V.O., procured from a friendly Prohibition-hating druggist, which he believed he kept a secret in a barrel of lima beans.

Michael had no need for stimulation from paper-and-ink heroes. He had a living stalwart who was a combination of Don Quixote, Tom Swift, Robinson Crusoe carving a new life out of a strange world. "Tell me the *meiseh* about the border, Zaydey," he would beg, burrowing his face into the soft beard and closing his eyes.

"Who has time for such foolishness," Isaac would grumble, but they both knew that he had more than enough time. The old rocking chair that he kept behind the grocery counter would start to move back and forth, creaking like a cricket, and Michael would settle his face even deeper into the beard.

"When I left Kishinev with my Itta, *aleha hasholom*, she should rest in peace, we traveled by train northward, around the mountains. We had no trouble getting into Poland. It was part of Russia then. They didn't even check your passport.

"I was nervous about my passport. It was my father's, he should rest in peace. I knew they wouldn't bother Itta. She had my dead sister's papers. But I was a young man carrying an old man's passport.

"Our troubles began when we got to the border between Poland and Germany. It was a time of *tsorris* between the two countries. There always is trouble between Poland and Germany. But this time the *tsorris* was worse. When we got to the border the train was stopped and everyone had to get out. We were told that only a certain number of persons were allowed to cross, and that the quota had just been filled."

At this point the rocking of the chair would cease, a signal that Michael should ask a question in order to build up the suspense. So he spoke into the beard, feeling its hairs tickling his lips and surrounding his nose. Every once in a while the beard into which he leaned his face would become damp from his breathing, forcing him to choose a dry spot. "What did you do, Zaydey?"

"We were not alone. There were perhaps a hundred others in the same trouble. Poles, Germans, Russians, Jews. Some Rumanians and a few Bohemians. Some of them went outside the railroad station, looking for a place where they could run across the border. There were people from the little town who approached us and told us that for money they would show a safe way across. But I didn't like their looks, they looked like criminals. And besides, your grandmother, *aleha hasholom*, had a big belly. Like a watermelon. She was pregnant with your father. I was afraid to try a long trip by foot. So all day long we waited by the border gate. The sun was hot, like a fire, and I worried that your grandmother would become sick. We had some bread and cheese and we ate it, but a little later we became hungry. And we were very thirsty. There was nothing to drink. All day we waited. When the sun went down we stayed because we didn't know where else to go."

"Who saved you, Zaydeh?"

"Also waiting near the gate were two beautiful *Yiddisheh* girls. *Shayneh maydlach*. And behind the border gate were two red-faced German soldiers. The *maydlach* went to the soldiers and whispered and laughed with them. And they opened the gate to let the girls in. And then all of us, Jews and Poles and Germans and Russians and Bohemians and Rumanians, your grandmother and her big belly and I—all of us together, like the cattle that you see running in the moving pictures—we shoved and pushed through the gate until we were across the border, and then we kept mixing, mixing with the crowds in the station until we were lost to the soldiers. And in a little while a train came and we got on and it took us away."

Michael wriggled, because the best part was yet to come. "And why did the soldiers open the gate for the girls, Zaydey?"

"Because they promised the soldiers something."

The taste buds in his mouth began to manufacture saliva. "What? What did they promise the soldiers?"

"Something sweet and warm they promised them. Something the soldiers wanted very much."

"What was it, Zaydey?"

His grandfather's belly and chest would begin to tremble. The first time he had told the story Michael had asked the same question, and searching desperately for a suitable answer to give a small boy, he had hit upon exactly the right one. "Candy. Just like this!"

In his pocket he always carried a wrinkled brown paper sack, and in the sack, inevitably, was candied ginger. The fiery root was sugar-coated. Until you sucked through the sugar it was sweet, but then it was so strong it made your eyes water. Michael loved it as much as his grandfather did, but whenever he ate too much of it he suffered on the following morning, his *tush* burning so badly when he went to the bathroom that he sat there and wept in silence, afraid to let his mother hear lest she forbid Zaydeh to give him any more ginger.

As he ate the ginger in the store he would beg for another story. "Tell me about what happened after the train, Zaydey."

And Isaac would tell him how the train had taken them only as far as Mannheim, where again they had waited, sitting in the hot spring sun. The railroad yard was on the Rhine River. Isaac had struck up a conversation with a Dutch bargeman who with his stout, broad-shouldered wife was loading his barge with bags of coal. The bargeman had refused when Isaac had asked to buy passage for two down the river. Itta, sitting on a tree stump nearby, her skirts dragging in the gritty mud, had burst into tears. The riverman's wife had looked at the Jewish girl's swollen belly and pale face. She had spoken sharply to her husband, and although his eyes were annoyed he had motioned them aboard with a silent movement of his coal-blackened thumb.

It was a strange way to travel, for them, but they found it very good. Despite the coal cargo, the living quarters were very clean. The bargeman's mood changed as soon as he saw that Isaac was willing to work as well as pay for his passage. The days were sunny, the river flowed green and clean. Isaac saw color come back into Itta's cheeks.

In the morning he would stand alone on the dew-covered deck next to the bags of coal with his *tallis* wrapped around his shoulders and his phylacteries on his forehead and bared arm, softly chanting, while the quiet barge floated past great stone castles that turreted into the blue-white sky, past gingerbread houses in which Germans slept, past villages and cliffs and rolling pasturelands. On the fourth morning he finished intoning the prayers and looked up to see the Dutchman leaning against the rail, watching him. The man smiled respectfully and filled his pipe. After that Isaac felt at home on the barge.

The castles of the middle Rhine disappeared. When they reached Bingen Isaac worked like a deckhand, obeying the bargeman's shouted commands as the boat hurtled through the rapids. Then the river turned into a sluggish stream, and for two days they drifted slowly. On the ninth day the Rhine turned westward into the Netherlands. Presently the river became the Waal. Two days later it carried them to the waterfront of Rotterdam. The boatman and his wife went with them to the wharf where the transatlantic steamers docked. The Dutch customs man looked closely at the young emigrant when he saw the age—fifty-three—listed on his passport. Then he shrugged and stamped it quickly. Itta wept when the Dutch couple walked away. "They were like Jews," Michael's *zaydeh* told him every time he related the story.

Unless a customer came into the grocery, Isaac would next tell Michael the story of his father's birth on the high seas during a wild Atlantic storm, with waves "high like the Chrysler Building," and of how the doctor on the ship had selected that night to get sodden drunk, so that his trembling grandfather pulled the baby from Itta's body with his own hands.

A customer during one of the stories was a catastrophe, but if the shopper were Italian or Irish and they were close to the end, Isaac kept him waiting and finished the narrative. The Borough Park section of Brooklyn was predominantly Jewish, but there were whole blocks of Irish and whole blocks of Italians. Their Jewish block was set between two such Christian nests. There was a market run by a man named Brady in the Irish block and Alfano's Grocery in the Italian block, and for the most part each ethnic group traded with its own supplier. Occasionally, however, one of the groceries was out of an item, forcing the customer to go to one of the other two, where he was waited on politely but without warmth by a proprietor who knew that the custom was temporary and born of emergency.

Michael's grandfather had bought his Borough Park grocery after his Itta had died, when the boy was three years old. Before that Isaac had owned and operated another tiny grocery in the Williamsburg section of Brooklyn, where he and his wife had settled upon coming to the United States. The block in which he had lived in Williamsburg was a cockroach-infested slum, but it was as Orthodox as any European ghetto, and probably for that reason he loved it and didn't want to leave. But to Michael's father the thought of his aging parent living alone and untended had been intolerable. At Abe Rivkind's insistence Isaac sold the Willamsburg store and came to live in Borough Park with his son's family. He brought with him his prayer books, four bottles of whiskey, a feather bed made by Itta's own hands, and the great brass bed that had been their first purchase in America, and in whose gleaming surfaces, he convinced his grandchildren, they might see their souls if they were free from sin.

Isaac could have retired at that time, since Abe Rivkind was making a fine living as a small manufacturer of ladies' corsets and girdles. But he wanted to buy his own whiskey and his son and daughter-in-law gave in before his fierce eyes; he bought the small grocery around the corner from their Borough Park apartment.

For Dorothy Rivkind, the day her father-in-law moved into her home must have been an unhappy one. She was a plump, peroxide-blonde woman with placid eyes. In theory she kept a kosher home, serving neither pork nor scaleless creatures of the sea, but her conscience never kept her awake nights if by mistake, while cleaning up after dinner, she slipped a meat dish into a pile of dairy china in the cupboard. Isaac, on the other hand, was a man to whom the Law was the law. Beneath the counters of his store he kept a stack of dog-eared and annotated commentaries, and he observed the religious statutes just as he breathed, slept, saw, and heard. His daughter-in-law's infractions at first filled him with horror and then with wrath. None of the family was spared. The neighbors grew accustomed to the sound of his voice, thundering in righteous and indignant Yiddish. On the day he moved in with the family, Michael and his sister Ruthie came to the dinner table, on which lay a roast of beef, carrying pieces of bread-and-butter which hunger had dictated that they make for themselves in the kitchen.

"*Goyim!*" their grandfather screamed. "To a *fleishig* table you bring butter?" He turned to their mother, who was growing pale. "What kind of children are you raising?"

"Ruth, take the bread-and-butter from Michael and throw it away," Dorothy said quietly.

But Michael was a little boy, and he liked what he was eating. He struggled as his sister tried to remove the bread from his grasp, and a lump of butter fell upon his plate at the table. It was a meat plate, and their grandfather's fresh bellows sent Ruth racing with him to his room. They fearfully hugged one another and listened in fascination to the magnificence of their grandfather's rage.

The experience set the pattern for life in the Rivkind household with Zaydeh. Each day he spent as many hours as possible in the grocery. He prepared his own lunch, over Dorothy's protests, on a small electric hotplate in the back room. When he came back to the apartment in the evening, the hawk's eyes would catch them in tiny ritual transgressions, and the eagle's cry, ancient and fierce, would destroy the peace of their home.

He knew that he made them unhappy, and the knowledge made him sad. Michael realized this, because he was his grandfather's only friend. For several weeks after he came to live with them, Michael lived in fear of the bearded old man. And then one night, when the others slept while Isaac could not, he came into his grandson's room to make sure the boy was covered.

Michael was awake. When Isaac saw this he sat on the edge of the bed and stroked the boy's head with a hand made horny by years of carrying crates of canned goods and bushels of vegetables.

"Did you talk with God tonight?" he whispered hoarsely. Michael hadn't prayed, but sensing that it would please his grandfather he nodded shamelessly, and when Isaac kissed his fingers he could feel the old man's lips smiling. With his thumb and the knuckle of his forefinger Isaac pinched the young cheek.

"*Dos is gut,*" he said. "Talk with Him often."

Before he crept back through the silent house to his own room he reached into the pocket of his faded flannel robe. Paper rustled and then the blunt fingers held the bit of ginger to young lips. Michael fell asleep in bliss.

The bond between Michael and his *zaydeh* grew stronger during the early fall, when the days began to shorten and the autumn feast of Sukkos drew near. Each autumn during his four-year stay with the Rivkinds Zaydeh built in their postage-stamp back yard a *sukkah,* or ceremonial hut. The *sukkah* was a small house of wooden planks covered with boughs and sheaves. It was hard work for an old man to build it, especially since hayfields, corn shocks and trees were not plentiful in Brooklyn. Sometimes he had to go deep into Jersey for raw materials, and he badgered Abe for weeks until he was driven to the country in the family Chevrolet.

"Why do you bother?" Dorothy asked him once when she brought a glass of tea to where he strained and perspired to raise the hut. "Why do you work so hard?"

"To celebrate the harvest."

"What harvest, for God's sake? We're not farmers. You sell canned goods. Your son makes corsets for ladies with big behinds. Who has a harvest?"

He looked pityingly at this female his son had made his daughter. "For thousands of years, since the Jews emerged from the Wilderness, in ghettos and in palaces they have observed Sukkos. You don't have to raise cabbages to have a harvest." His big hand grasped Michael behind the neck and pushed him toward his mother. "Here is your harvest." She didn't understand,

and by then Zaydeh had been living with them long enough not to expect understanding from her.

But if his mother wasn't gladdened by the *sukkah*, Michael was thrilled. Zaydeh ate his meals within its thatch walls, and when the weather permitted he slept there, too, in a folding cot placed on the dirt floor. That first year Michael begged so hard that his parents gave in and let him sleep with his grandfather. It was Indian summer, a time of warm days and crisp nights, and they slept under a thick feather bed that had come with Zaydeh from Williamsburg. Years later, when Michael slept out of doors in the mountains for the first time, that night came back to him vividly. He remembered the sound of the wind rustling the dry corn stalks in the *sukkah* roof, the patchwork pattern made by the light of the harvest moon shining through the network of boughs and casting their shadows on the dirt floor. And, incongruously but somehow beautiful, the traffic noises, muted and fairylike, floating into their back yard from 13th Avenue, two blocks away.

It was the only night they had like that, an unhappy old man and a wondering small boy huddling warmly together against the night air and pretending they were in another world. They tried to sleep outside once more that Sukkos but it rained. And every other year until his *zaydeh* went away, his mother decided it was too cold.

It was inevitable that Isaac should leave. But when it happened, his grandson couldn't quite understand. The final straw was a nine-year-old Italian named Joseph Morello. He was in the fifth grade at P.S. 168 with Ruthie, and she was in love with him. She came home from school one afternoon ecstatic with the news that Joey had asked her to his birthday party on the following Saturday. Unfortunately, she made the announcement to Michael at a moment when Zaydeh was at the kitchen table having a glass of tea and reading the *Jewish Forward*. He looked up and pushed his steel-rimmed spectacles to his forehead.

"On *shabbos*? On *shabbos* this boy has a party? What's the matter with his people?"

"Oh, Zaydey," Ruthie said.

"What's his father's name, this Joey?"

"His name is Morello."

"Morello? An *Italiana?*" He moved his glasses back to his nose and shook the *Forward.* "You don't go."

Ruthie's anguished wail split the air, bringing her mother hurrying in from her bedroom, bandanna around her head and drymop in hand. She listened as her daughter sobbed and then she put the mop on the floor. "Go to your room, Ruth," she said.

When the girl had gone Dorothy looked at her father-in-law, who was looking at the *Jewish Forward.* "She is going to the birthday party," she said.

"Not on *shabbos.*"

"You want to stay home on *shabbos,* you stay home, or go to *shul* with the other old men. She is a little girl who has been invited to a birthday party. She is going to sit around a table with other little girls and boys and have some cake and ice cream. There is no sin in that."

He turned his eagle's eyes on her. "With *shkotzim?* Christians?"

"With boys and girls."

"The first step," Isaac Rivkind said. "The first step, and you push her into it. And when she is just a little older and has breasts, and an *Italiana* comes one day and puts a cross on a cheap gold chain between them, what will you say then?" He folded the paper and stood up. "What will you say then, my fancy daughter-in-law?"

"For God's sake, it's a birthday party for children, not a wedding," Dorothy said. But he was already leaving the kitchen.

"She does not go," he said as he slammed the door.

Dorothy stood in the middle of the kitchen, white-faced. Then she ran to the window and threw it open. Two stories below, Isaac was just walking through the front door to the sidewalk.

"*SHE'S GOING,*" she screamed at him. "*DO YOU HEAR ME, YOU OLD MAN? SHE IS GOING!*" Then she banged the window shut and started to cry.

That night Michael's *zaydeh* stayed late in his store, keeping it open long after the usual closing time. When Michael's father came home from the factory he and Dorothy talked for a long time in their bedroom. Ruth and Michael could hear them arguing. Finally their father came out, his round face twisted, like a child who wants to weep but can't. He fixed a plate of cold cuts from the refrigerator and took it to Zaydeh. The children fell asleep before they returned.

It was Ruthie who told her brother on the following day what their parents had been arguing about. "That stinkin' old man isn't going to be around here much longer," she said.

He felt a sudden tightness in his chest. "What do you mean?" he asked.

"He's going away to a place where there are only old men and old ladies. Momma said so."

"You're a liar."

He went to her and kicked her shins. She screamed, slapping his face and digging her nails into his arm. "Don't you call me a liar, you little brat!" Although she had tears in her eyes she wouldn't give him the satisfaction of seeing her cry. But she had hurt him and he knew that he would cry if he stayed, so he ran out of the house. He went downstairs and out the front door, around the corner and to Rivkind's Grocery Store. Zaydeh was sitting in his rocker, not reading or doing anything. Michael climbed into his grandfather's lap and put his face in the beard. Every time Zaydeh's heart beat, a tendril of beard tickled the boy's ear.

"Are you going away, Zaydey?"

"No, no. It is foolishness."

His breath was strong with Canadian V.O. "If you ever go away, I'm going with you," Michael said.

Isaac held the small head into his beard with his hand and began to rock, and Michael knew that everything had to be all right. In the middle of the one about the customs inspector, fat Mrs. Jacobson came into the store. Michael's *zaydeh* looked up at her.

"Go away," he said.

Mrs. Jacobson smiled politely, as if at a joke she didn't understand. She just stood there, waiting.

"Go away," his grandfather said again. "I don't want to wait on you. You have a fat ass."

Mrs. Jacobson's face seemed to break up in disbelief. "What's the matter with you?" she said. "Are you crazy?"

"Just go away. And don't pinch the tomatoes with your thick fingers. I've been wanting to tell you for a long time."

Half a dozen times during the afternoon he said similar things to customers and sent them hurrying angrily from his door.

Finally, during the story of how he had bought his first grocery, Michael's father came into the store. He stood and looked at the two of them, and they looked at him. Michael's father was only medium-tall but he had a well-proportioned body that he kept hard and taut at the YMHA. In his bedroom he kept a set of weights and sometimes Michael sat and watched his biceps roll and swell as he performed curl after curl with a 25-pound dumb-bell in each hand. His thick black hair was cropped short and kept carefully combed and his skin was deeply tanned, in the summer from the sun and in the winter from the lamp at the Y. Men liked him well enough, but he was very successful with the women buyers of the foundations business. He was a handsome man with blue eyes that seemed always to be full of laughing light.

Now his eyes were serious. "It's time for dinner. Let's go home," he said.

But Michael and his grandfather just sat there.

"Papa, did you have your lunch?" his father asked.

His *zaydeh* frowned. "Of course I had my lunch. What do you think, I'm an infant? I could be taking care of myself like a lord in Williamsburg if you and your fine wife hadn't stuck in your noses. So you took me away from there, and now you want me to go to a museum."

His father sat down on an orange crate. "Papa, I went to the Sons of David Home today. It's a wonderful place. A real *Yiddisheh* place."

"I wouldn't consider it."

"Papa, please."

"Listen, my Abe, I'll stay away from your fine wife. She can serve *trafe* every Monday and Tuesday, I still won't say a word."

"Mr. Melnick is there."

"Reuven Melnick from Williamsburg?"

"Yes. He sends you his regards. He says he loves it there. The food is like in the Catskills, he says. And everybody speaks

Yiddish, and they've got a *shul* right in the building, with a rabbi who comes in, and a cantor every *shabbos*."

His *zaydeh* lifted Michael off his knee and stood him on the floor. "Abe, you want me to leave your house? You *want* me to leave?" He spoke in Yiddish in a low voice, so that Michael and his father could hardly hear him.

His father's voice wasn't loud, either. "Papa, you know I don't want it. But Dorothy wants us to be alone. She's my wife, Papa—" He looked away.

His *zaydeh* laughed. "All right," he said almost gaily.

He took a cardboard Wheaties carton and into it he packed his volumes of the commentaries, his pipes, six cans of Prince Albert, some writing tablets, and a package of pencils. He went to the lima-bean barrel and burrowed in it until he brought out the bottle of V.O. and added it to the things in the box. Then he walked out of Rivkind's Grocery Store without a backward glance.

The next morning Michael and his father went with him to the Sons of David Home for Aged and Orphans. In the Chevrolet his father kept up an animated stream of chatter. "You'll love your room, Papa," he said. "It's right next to Mr. Melnick's."

"You're a fool, Abe," his *zaydeh* said. "Reuven Melnick is an old *yenteh* who gabs, gabs, gabs. You will have to get the room changed."

His father cleared his throat nervously. "All right, Papa," he said.

"What about the store?" Zaydeh asked stonily.

"Don't worry about the store. I'll sell it and deposit the money in your account. You've been working long enough. You deserve a rest."

The Sons of David Home was a long yellow-brick building on Eleventh Avenue. There were some chairs outside on the sidewalk, and when they drove up three old men and two old women were sitting in the sun, not reading or talking, but just sitting there. One of the old ladies smiled at his *zaydeh* when they got out of the car. She wore a cinnamon-colored *sheitel*, a wig that fit her badly; her face was very wrinkled.

"*Shalom*," she said, as they went inside, but they didn't answer her. In the admitting office a man named Mr. Rabinowitz held his *zaydeh*'s fingers in both hands. "I've heard a lot about you," he said. "You're going to have a wonderful time here."

His grandfather smiled strangely, shifting the Wheaties box in his arms. Mr. Rabinowitz peeked inside.

"Oh, but we can't have this," he said, reaching in and pulling out the whiskey. "It's against the rules, unless you have a doctor's prescription." The smile on his *zaydeh*'s face grew wider.

Mr. Rabinowitz showed them around the Home. He took them to the chapel, where a lot of candles burned in glasses for the dead, and to the hospital, where half a dozen old people were in bed, and to the therapy room, where a few old people played checkers or knitted or sat reading the Jewish paper. Mr. Rabinowitz talked a lot. His voice was husky, and he kept clearing his throat.

"We have an old friend who's waiting for you," Mr. Rabinowitz told Zaydeh as they came to one room. Inside was a short, white-haired man who threw his arms around Isaac's neck. "It's wonderful to see you!" he said.

"Hello, Reuven," his grandfather said.

"You have a nice room here, Mr. Melnick," his father said. The room was very small. There was a bed, a table and a lamp, and a dresser. On the wall was a Morrison & Schiff Jewish calendar. On the dresser was a Bible, a pack of cards, and a bottle of brandy. Reuven Melnick noticed Isaac's eyebrows go up when he saw the liquor.

"I have a prescription. From my son Sol the doctor," he said.

"A wonderful boy, your Solly. I want him to examine me. You and I are going to be next-door neighbors," Michael's grandfather said.

Abe Rivkind opened his mouth, remembering that Isaac had ordered him to have the room changed, but then he looked at the brandy bottle and he closed his mouth again. They went next door and unpacked Zaydeh's suitcase and put the things from the Wheaties box on the dresser. Then they stood together for a few minutes in the corridor outside. The floor was covered with shiny brown linoleum. Everywhere you looked there were old people, but Michael was surprised to see three boys about his own age running and playing tag in and out of two rooms. A woman in a white uniform came by and told them to cut it out, but they just laughed at her and lip-farted. He tugged at his father's sleeve.

"What are they doing here?" he whispered.

"They live here," Abe said. "They're orphans."

Michael remembered that he had told his *zaydeh* that if Isaac was going away he would go with him and he became very frightened. He took his father's hand and held it tightly.

"Well, Papa, we'd better go now," his father said.

His grandfather smiled the same smile. "You'll come to see me, Abe?"

"Papa, you'll see so much of us you'll tell us not to bother you so much."

His grandfather reached into his pocket and pulled out the wrinkled paper sack full of candied ginger. Isaac took out one piece and put it in his mouth, then he took Michael's hand and closed it around the neck of the paper bag. "Go home, *mine kind*," he said. Michael and his father walked quickly away, leaving him standing alone on the shiny brown linoleum.

On the way home his father didn't speak. As soon as they were in the Chevrolet Michael lost his fright and he missed his *zaydeh*. He felt sad because he hadn't placed his arms around the old man and kissed him good-by. He opened the paper bag and began to eat the ginger. Even though he knew that the next day his *tush* would burn he ate it all, piece by piece. He finished the whole bag, partly because of Zaydeh and partly because he had the feeling he wasn't going to get much ginger from then on.

CHAPTER FIVE

At Joey Morello's party his sister Ruthie got into a fight with an Italian girl and came home scratched up and crying. Michael felt glad and angry, all at the same time. He was glad that she got what was coming to her, and angry that his grandfather had had to go away because of a birthday party she didn't even enjoy.

Within a week his father had sold the grocery to a young German immigrant who installed lighting and a line of non-kosher meats. The lights turned the store from a mysterious cave into a drab and shabby food outlet, and Michael never went there unless ordered to do so. Not only the store was affected by Zaydeh's departure, however. In the Rivkind home the change was even more pronounced. Dorothy went around humming and pinching her children's cheeks. Glorying guiltily in her new freedom, she no longer separated milk dishes from the meat ones. She stopped lighting candles at dusk on Friday and instead scheduled a weekly canasta game for that evening.

Abe Rivkind apparently approved of the new atmosphere. His separation from his father's accusing gaze allowed him to do several things he had been thinking about for some time. His corset business was flourishing ("Knock wood, girdles are expanding rapidly and bras are holding up"), and he had reached a point in his business life where it was advantageous to take a customer to a fine Manhattan restaurant for lunch if you were trying to nail down an order. He enjoyed the experience, and sometimes when he came home in the evening he would tell his wife and children of the strange and wonderful things he had eaten. He became enamored of lobster, and his descriptions of the flavor of the sweet pink flesh dipped in melted butter exceeded their imaginations.

"Does it taste like chicken?"

"A little bit. But not really."

"Does it taste like fish?"

"A little."

"What does it *really* taste like?"

Finally one Saturday afternoon he came home carrying a large, damp paper bag. "Here," he said to Dorothy. "*Ess gezunteh hait.*"

She took the bag and then squealed as she dropped it onto the kitchen table. "There's something *alive* in there," she said.

He tore open the bag and roared with laughter as he watched his wife's face when she saw the lobsters. There were three of the creatures, large and green, with small dark eyes that protruded, raising gooseflesh on Dorothy's arms. When it was time to drop them into the pot of boiling water it became apparent that Abe was more than a little afraid of the waving tentacles and the cruel claws himself, and it was her turn to laugh. She would have none of the lobster meat. Although she had rebelled against her father-in-law's sternness and had started the family's insurrection against the things he stood for, there was a great deal of difference between mixing dishes in the cupboard and actually chewing and swallowing flesh which all her life she had been told was forbidden and disgusting. Shuddering, she ran out of the room. But she came to like crisp bacon when Abe brought it home and fried it for her himself, and soon she was serving it with eggs at breakfast several times a week.

Michael's father was one of the first of the girdle-makers to package his product in colorful narrow tubes, and the enthusiasm with which his customers greeted the innovation made him dream of expansion and a highly upgraded line. One day he came home and made Dorothy take off her apron and sit down.

"Dorothy," he said, "what would you think if I changed your name?"

"*Mishugineh*, you did that fourteen years ago."

"Dorothy, I'm serious. I mean change it from Rivkind. Legally."

She looked at him in alarm. "To what? And what for?"

"Rivkind's Foundations, Inc., that's what for. It sounds like just what it is. A loft outfit that will never be a leader in the corset industry. These new packages deserve a classy name."

"So change the name of the company. What does that have to do with our name?"

"Look. All you have to do is cut our name in half." He showed her the slogan typed on a piece of stationery. "*Be KIND To Your Figure*." She looked at him and shrugged. So because the word fit into an advertising slogan on a slim tube, but most important, because something within Michael's father made it imperative that he be Mr. Kind of Kind Foundations, the Rivkind family's name was legally changed by the courts.

Reform, even in personal matters, is difficult to contain in tight bounds. Several of their neighbors had moved to new sections of Queens, and finally Abe listened to Dorothy's urging and they bought an apartment in a yellow-brick building that had just been raised in Forest Hills.

When Isaac heard that they had moved away from Brooklyn to a neighborhood that was miles from the Sons of David Home he appeared unaffected by the news. Their visits to him had become less and less frequent, and when on occasion Abe, haunted by a sudden storm of conscience, took Michael to see his *zaydeh,* the three of them had little to talk about. Zaydeh had succeeded in having Mr. Melnick's Solly examine him and write a prescription, and Abe gladly paid for the bottle of medicinal Canadian V.O. that occupied a place of honor on his father's dresser at all times. Rye whiskey and the deep study of the Torah now filled Isaac Rivkind's life, and the visitors soon ran out of conversation about both of these subjects.

One visit they made to the Home soon after their exodus to Queens provided Zaydeh with something to talk about, however. *Sukkos* was approaching, and as always at that season Michael thought a great deal about his grandfather. He had begged his father for weeks to take him to see Zaydeh, and when the day arrived he had a bundle of crayon drawings that were his special gift to the old man.

When Isaac sat on his bed and looked at the pictures, one in particular caught his eye. "What is this, Micheleh?" he asked.

"That's our building, where we live," Michael said as he pointed to a tall blob of color. "And that's a tree with chestnuts on it, and a squirrel. And that's the church on the corner." It was the latter, adorned with a cross that was the drawing's most lifelike representation, that had captured Isaac's interest. The cross, and Michael's carefully printed new signature.

"Don't you know how to spell your name?" he asked.

"Papa," Abe said quickly, "he's spelled it right. I had it legally changed." He expected a burst of the old thunder, but Isaac scarcely blinked.

"Your name isn't Rivkind any more?"

He listened without comment to his son's long explanation about the business reasons for the change, and then to an enthusiastic description of the new line of girdles and bras. When it was time for them to go, Isaac kissed Michael on the cheek and shook his son's hand.

"Thank you for coming, Abraham." Then he stopped short. "Your name still is Abraham?"

"Of course it is," Abe said. All the way home he snarled at Michael whenever the boy opened his mouth.

Two days later Abe received a letter from his father. It had been written on lined paper in smudged, penciled Yiddish by a hand made tremulous by age and alcohol. It took Abe hours of cudgeling his memory to translate the letter, and much of it turned out to be pure Talmudic reference that meant nothing to him. But the main message in the letter came through. Isaac indicated to his son that he had given up hope for everyone in the family save his grandson, Micheleh. Two-thirds of the letter was a fervent plea that Michael should be given a Jewish education.

Dorothy laughed and shook her head when her husband read her as much of the letter as he could turn into English. But to Michael's unpleasant surprise his father seemed to take the request more seriously.

"It's time. He's of an age for *chedar*," he said. And so, the chosen person, Michael began to attend Hebrew school every afternoon following his release from public school. He was in the third grade at P.S. 467 and he had absolutely no desire to learn Hebrew. Nevertheless he was enrolled in the Talmud Torah of the Congregation Sons of Jacob Synagogue. Sons of Jacob was located half a mile from the public school. It was an Orthodox synagogue, but this played no part in the choice of its school. He would have been enrolled had it been Conservative or Reform. It happened to be the only Hebrew school to which he could walk from P.S. 467 every day. The fact that the walk to Hebrew school would take him through one of the toughest Polish neighborhoods in New York had been given no consideration by the adults who controlled his destiny.

On the third day of Hebrew school he met Stash Kwiat-kowski as he walked homeward. Stash was in his class at P.S. 467. This was his third year in the third grade. He was at least two years older than Michael, a broad-faced blond boy with very large blue eyes and a half-ashamed grin that he wore like a mask. Michael knew him in class as a boy who made a lot of humorous mistakes during recitation, and when he saw Stash he grinned.

"Hi, Stash," he said.

"Hi, kiddo. What you got there?"

What he had there were his three books, an *"aleph-bez"* from which he was learning the Hebrew alphabet, a notebook, and a storybook history of the Jews.

"Just some books," he said.

"Where'd you get 'em. The lib'ry?"

"Hebrew school."

"What's that?"

He could see that the idea intrigued Stash, so he explained that it was a place to which he went when all the others in their class were released from public school for the day.

"Let me see 'em."

He looked dubiously at Stash's hands, which were grimy with the dirt of three hours of after-school play. His books were new and immaculate. "I'd better not."

Stash's grin grew wider as he clamped a hand on Michael's wrist. "Come on. Let's see 'em."

He was at least four inches shorter than Stash, but the other boy was slow-moving. Michael tore out of his grasp and leaped away. Stash chased him a surprisingly short distance and then dropped out of the race completely.

But the following evening as Michael walked homeward he suddenly appeared, stepping out from behind a billboard where he had set his ambush.

Michael tried smiling at him. "Hi, Stash."

This time Stash made no pretense at friendliness. He grabbed the books, and the *aleph-bez* fell to the ground. One of the things that had made an impression upon Michael a few days earlier was the sight of a young rabbi who had dropped a pile of prayer books to the floor, reverently kissing each book as he picked them up. A short time later he was to learn to his deep embarrassment that the practice was reserved for books containing the word of God, but at the time he thought that it was something which Jews did to any volume printed in Hebrew. Some perverse stubbornness caused him to pounce upon the alphabet book and press it to his lips while Stash stared.

"What did you do that for?"

Hoping that a glimpse into another way of life would ease Stash's belligerence, he explained that the book was printed in Hebrew and therefore had to be kissed whenever it hit the ground. It was a mistake. Recognizing a source of endless amusement, Stash dropped the book to the ground as fast as he could pick it up and kiss it. When his hand closed into a fist Stash whipped it behind his back and twisted it until he cried.

"Say 'I'm a dirty Yid.'"

He was silent until he thought his arm would break, and then he said it. He said that Yids gobble shit, that Yids killed Our Saviour, that Yids cut the ends off their pricks and ate them in stew on Saturday night.

For good measure Stash tore the first page out of his alphabet book and rolled it into a ball. When he stooped to pick up the crumpled paper Stash kicked him in the buttocks with stunning force that made him whimper in pain as he ran away. That night in the privacy of his bedroom he smoothed the page out as best he could and taped it back into the book.

In the days that followed, the inquisition in Queens became a routine. Stash largely ignored him in school, and he was free to laugh as loudly as any of the others when the older boy made a shambles of a recitation. When the final bell rang Michael dashed out in order to get through Stash's neighborhood before he arrived. And on the way home from Hebrew school he tried varying his route in an effort to evade his tormentor. But if Stash missed him for a couple of days the big boy would move out a block or two, trying a different position each afternoon until inevitably Michael walked into one of his traps. Then he would add a little extra torture, to make up for the fun Michael had made him miss through his evasive tactics.

But he had problems other than Stash. The Hebrew school had turned out to be a place of no fun and swift discipline. The teachers were laymen who were given the honorary title of *reb*, a word that gave them status approximately halfway between that of the rabbi and the janitor. The reb who taught his class was a thin young man with spectacles and a brown beard. His name was Hyman Horowitz, but he was never called anything but Reb Chaim. The gutteral *ch* of his Yiddish first name fascinated Michael, who mentally dubbed him Chaim Chorowitz the Chunter, because he habitually sat back in his seat behind the desk, his eyes closed and his fingers forever wandering through his bushy beard, as if continually chunting, chunting for cooties. Chooties?

There were twenty boys in the class. As a new boy Michael was given a seat directly in front of Reb Chaim, and he soon learned that this was the worst seat in the room. A pupil never stayed in it for any length of time unless he was stupid or an archcriminal. It was the only seat in the room in which the victim could be reached by Reb Chaim's rattan. Slender and supple, a cross between a switch and a bastinado, it lay before him on his desk. Any infraction of civilized behavior, from whispering to poor recitation, brought it whistling through the air to land— *whomp!*—on offending shoulders. Despite underwear, shirt, and sweater to cushion the effect of the blow, the rattan was as wicked a weapon as any of the pupils had ever met, and they held it in justifiable awe.

Chaim the Chunter gave Michael a taste of the rattan at the end of the first lesson, when he saw him glancing around the battered old classroom instead of paying strict attention to his studies. One moment the teacher leaned back in his chair, apparently about to doze off with his eyes closed and his fingers chunting, chunting through his beard. And the next moment, a brief whistle like the sound of a dropping bomb compressed into one-tenth of a second's time, and then—*whomp!* He didn't even open his eyes, but the rattan hit Michael dead center on the left shoulder. He was too overcome with admiration for the Reb's performance to cry, and the sound of the muted ripple of laughter which swept his classmates took some of the personal tragedy away from the punishment.

The blow had been standard operating procedure, and he did not become listed as a Public Enemy until his fifth day at Hebrew School. Reb Chaim was charged with teaching his pupils religion as well as Hebrew language, and on that day he had just finished telling them the story of Moses and the burning bush. God, he informed them solemnly, was all-powerful.

Michael was seized by a fascinating thought. Before he knew what he was doing he had raised his hand. "Do you mean that

God can do anything at all?"

Reb Chaim stared at him impatiently. "Anything," he said.

"Can He make a great big rock? One so heavy that a million men can't move it?"

"Of course He can."

"And can He move it?"

"Of course."

Michael became excited. "Then can He make a rock so heavy that He can't move it Himself?"

Reb Chaim beamed, happy to have stimulated so much zeal on the part of his new pupil. "Certainly," he said. "If He wanted to."

He was so excited that he shouted. "But if He can't move it Himself, then He can't do everything! So He's not all-powerful!"

Reb Chaim opened his mouth and then closed it. His face grew flushed as he looked at Michael's triumphant grin.

Whomp! Whomp! Whomp! The rattan fell on both of the boy's shoulders in a shower of blows that must have been as exciting to watch as a tennis match, but which was terribly painful to receive. This time he did cry, but nonetheless he had become a hero to his class and Public Enemy Number One to his Hebrew teacher.

It was very discouraging. Between Stash and Reb Chaim his life became a series of nightmares. He tried playing hooky. In the afternoon when he got out of P.S. 467 he went to a bowling alley four blocks from the school and sat for three hours on a wooden bench, watching the players. It wasn't a bad place to wait. He did this for four days, and on each day he sat behind the alley used by the same fat woman with massive breasts and great haunches. She raised the big bowling ball as though it were a bead, and she moved forward on the tips of her toes in mincing steps that caused her to shake and tremble so that you knew she could profit immensely by wearing some of his father's products. She chewed gum steadily and without expression, and when she released the ball and sent it cannoning down the alley she suspended chewing until the pins were exploded and had stopped falling. Usually this meant that she stood on one foot with her mouth open, like a statue made with too much clay by a mad sculptor. She was interesting and educational to watch, but his nerves gave out, and besides, when she sat down on the bench in front of him, her body odor nauseated him. On the fifth day he returned to Hebrew school, having forged a note from his mother saying that he had had an attack of sinus trouble, the symptoms of which he knew because his sister Ruthie suffered them vociferously most of the year around.

The pressure began to tell on him. He grew increasingly tense and nervous and he lost weight. At night he thrashed in his bed, unable to sleep. When he did sleep he dreamed of being beaten by Reb Chaim, or he dreamed that Stash waited for him outside the door, his figure rising three feet taller than his actual height.

One afternoon while he was in Hebrew class the boy behind him handed a piece of paper over his shoulder. Reb Chaim's back was turned to the class as he wrote the next day's grammar lesson on the blackboard, so Michael glanced at the paper without worry. It was a crude caricature of their teacher, unmistakable because of the beard, the glasses, and the skullcap. Grinning, Michael added a wart to his nose—he actually had one there—and drew in an arm with the hand hunting, hunting in the beard, neatly printing *Chaim Chorowitz the Chunter* beneath the picture.

The fact that the Reb was standing above him and gazing down at the paper on which he wrote was conveyed to him by the awful stillness of the classroom. It was a stillness that transcended the quiet demanded even by Reb Chaim. No pencil moved, no foot shuffled, no nose was blown. Only the ticking of the clock was heard, loud and slow and grimly portentous.

He sat and waited for the rattan to descend on his shoulders, refusing to look up into the brown eyes behind the shiny spectacles. Reb Chaim's hand slowly came into range of his downcast eyes. It was a long-fingered, slender hand with freckles and crisp black hairs on the wrist and below the knuckles. The hand picked up the piece of paper and took it out of his sight.

And still the rattan did not strike.

"You will remain after school," Reb Chaim told him quietly. There were eighteen minutes until the lesson was over, and each one stuck to the afternoon as if fastened with glue. Finally they were gone, however, and the class was dismissed. He could hear the other boys running and yelling as they left the building. The room was very quiet. Reb Chaim arranged some papers and put an elastic band around them and put them away in his second drawer. Then he walked out of the classroom and down the corridor to the teachers' john. He shut the door behind him but the building was so quiet that Michael could hear him urinating, a drumming like a tiny machine gun over in another sector of the front.

Michael left his seat and walked up to the teacher's desk. The rattan lay there. It was brown and varnished-looking, but he knew that the gleam was a polish that had been achieved through constant application to the tender skin of young Jewish boys. He picked up the rattan and flexed it. It took surprisingly little effort to make it cut viciously through the air, making a noise like corduroy knickers rubbing together. Suddenly he began to tremble, and to cry. He knew that he could not take any more pain either from Reb Chaim or from Stash Kwiatkowski, and he knew that he was going to quit Hebrew school. He turned on his heel and walked out of the room, still holding the rattan and leaving his books on his desk. He left the building slowly and walked home, planning how he would take the rattan to his mother and pull off his shirt to show her the mottled marks on his shoulders, the way Douglas Fairbanks had lowered his shirt to show his sweetheart the marks of her father's lash in the picture he had seen the preceding Saturday afternoon.

He was relishing the way his mother would cry over him when Stash stepped from behind the billboard and blocked his way. "Hello, Mikey," he said softly.

Michael didn't know that he meant to hit Stash until the rattan sang through the air with the sound of bees and caught him across his right cheek and his lips.

He let out an astonished yelp. "You little kike!"

He rushed blindly and Michael hit him again, reaching up to get his arms and shoulders.

"Stop that, you little bastid," Stash screamed. Instinctively he raised his arms to protect his face. "I'm going to kill you," he raged, but as he half turned to evade the zipping switch Michael cut the rattan across his fat, fleshy behind.

He heard the sound of someone crying and realized incredibly that it was not himself. Stash's face was screwed up until his chin looked like a wrinkled potato, and tears mingled with the blood that trickled from his lip. Every time Michael hit him he let out a little scream, and Michael hit him again and again as they ran, until finally he stopped chasing him because his arm was tired and Stash ran around a corner and was gone.

He spent the rest of the walk home thinking about how he should have handled the situation better, how he should have stopped hitting him long enough to make him say that Jews didn't kill Christ or gobble shit or cut off their pricks and eat them in stew on Saturday night.

When he got home he hid the rattan behind the furnace in the apartment house basement instead of taking it up to his mother. The following morning he took it from its hiding place and brought it to school. Miss Landers, his teacher at P.S. 467, noticed it and asked him what it was, and he told her it was a pointer his mother had borrowed from the Hebrew school. She stared at it and opened her mouth, but then she closed it again as if she had changed her mind. After public school he ran to Hebrew school until he was out of breath and had a stitch in his side, and then he walked as fast as he could.

He got there fifteen minutes before class. Reb Chaim was alone in the classroom, correcting papers. He kept his eyes on Michael as he walked toward him holding the rattan. Michael handed it to him.

"I'm sorry I borrowed it without your permission."

The Reb turned it over in his hands, as if seeing it for the first time. "Why would you borrow it?"

"I used it. On an anti-Semite."

Michael could swear that his lips twitched behind the camouflage of beard. But he was not a man to be diverted from the business at hand. "Bend over," he said.

Reb hit him six times across the behind. It hurt a lot and he cried, but all the while he was thinking that he had hit Stash Kwiatkowski a lot harder than Reb Chaim was hitting him.

By the time the rest of the class came in and sat down he wasn't crying any more, and a week later he was moved out of the front seat and Robbie Feingold took permanent possession because he was a silly kid who always got the giggles during recitation. Reb Chaim never hit him again.

CHAPTER SIX

At 3 A.M. on the day he was to be *bar mitzvah*, nervous and unable to sleep, he sat in the kitchen of the apartment in Queens and touched the imaginary fringes of an imaginary *tallis* to an imaginary Torah and then to his lips.

"*Borchu es adonoi hamvoroch*," he whispered. "*Boruch adonoi hamvoroch l'olom voed.*"

"Michael?" his mother shuffled groggily into the kitchen, her eyes slitted against the light, one small white hand to her hair. She wore a blue flannel robe over pink cotton pajamas that were too short. She had recently begun to have her hair dyed a passion-red that made her look like a fat female clown, and even through his nervousness he felt embarrassment and love wash over him in successive waves as he looked at her.

"Are you sick?" she asked anxiously.

"I wasn't sleepy."

The truth was that while lying awake in his bed he had run through his part in the *bar mitzvah* ceremonies, as he had been doing at least fifty times a day for the past few months, and he had found to his horror that he could not say the *brocha*, the short blessing that preceded the longer Torah reading called the *haftorah*. He knew the *brocha* as well as he knew his own name, but some part of his mind, tired of being hammered at by a single set of sounds, had rebelled and had wiped his memory clean of the words.

"You've got to get up in a few hours," she whispered fiercely. "Go to bed."

More asleep than awake, she turned and shuffled back to

her mattress. He heard his father question her as the spring creaked under her descending weight.

"What's the matter?"

"Your son is crazy. A real *mishugineh.*"

"Why doesn't he sleep?"

"Go and ask him."

Abe did, walking barefoot into the kitchen, his uncombed black hair dropping over his forehead. He wore only pajama bottoms, as he did throughout the year because he was proud of his body. Michael noticed for the first time that the curling hair on his chest was beginning to be frizzled with gray.

"What the hell?" he said. He sat down on a kitchen chair and dug into his scalp with both hands. "How do you expect to be *bar mitzvah* tomorrow?"

"I can't remember the *brocha.*"

"You mean you can't remember the *haftorah?*"

"No, the *brocha.* If I remember the *brocha* the *haftorah* comes out fine. But I can't remember the first line of the *brocha.*"

"Jesus Christ, son, you knew the damn *brocha* when you were nine years old."

"I can't remember it now."

"Look. You don't have to remember it. It will be up there in the book. All you have to do is read it."

Michael knew that this was true, but he didn't feel any better. "Maybe I won't be able to find the place," he said weakly.

"There'll be more old men on the platform with you than you'll want to look at. They'll show you the place." His voice grew crisp. "You get to bed, now. That's enough of this *mishu-gahss.*"

Michael went back to bed but he lay awake until the shades on his window were rimmed with gray light. Then he closed his eyes and drifted off, only to be awakened by his mother after what seemed a split second of sleep. She peered at him anxiously.

"Are you all right?"

"I guess so," he said. He stumbled off to the bathroom and threw cold water on his face. He was so tired he hardly knew what was happening as he dressed, ate a hasty breakfast, and accompanied his parents to the synagogue.

His mother kissed him good-by at the door and hurried upstairs to the women's section. She looked frightened. He accompanied his father to a place in the second row. The synagogue
was crowded with their friends and relatives. His father had
few kinfolks, but his mother came from a great and sprawling
clan, and it seemed as though they were all there. Many men
whispered hello as they walked to their bench. His lips moved
in response, but his voice said nothing. He was encased in a
suit of fright that moved with his body when he moved and from
which there was no escape.

Time passed. Dimly he was aware that his father had been
called to the *bema,* and from far away he heard Abe's voice reciting in Hebrew. Then his own name was called in Hebrew—
Mi-cha-el ben Avrahom—and on legs that had no feeling he
mounted the platform. He touched his *tallis* to the Torah and
kissed the fringes, and then he stared at the Hebrew letters on
the yellowed parchment. They wriggled like snakes before his
eyes.

"Borchu!" hissed one of the old men by his side.

A quavering voice that couldn't have been his picked up the
chant.

"Borchu es adonoi hamvoroch. Borchu—"

"Boruch." The old men all grunted or growled the correction
at the same time, the brusque chorus of their voices slapping him
across the face like a wet towel. He looked up dazedly and saw
that his father's eyes were desperate. He began the second sen-
tence again.

*"Boruch adonoi hamvoroch l'olom voed. Boruch ahtoh
adonoi, elohainu melech hoalom."* Huskily he finished the *brocha,*
ploughed blindly through the Torah reading and the subsequent
blessings and began the *haftorah.* For five minutes he quavered
on, the thin piping of his voice sounding hollowly in a silence
which he knew was caused by the congregation's conviction that
any second now he was going to get hopelessly lost in the complexities of the Hebrew passage or in the ancient tune. But like a
wounded matador whose training and discipline refuses to let
him squirm into merciful oblivion beneath the horns of the bull,
he refused to die. His voice steadied. His knees ceased their
trembling. He sang on and on, and the congregation sat back

in their seats, half-disappointed in the knowledge that he was not going to create a fiasco for their diversion.

Soon he had even forgotten the ring of bearded critics who surrounded him, and the large audience of friends and blood relations. Caught up in the melody and in the tone poem of the wildly beautiful Hebrew, he swayed to and fro in rhythm to his own chanting. By the time the passage was finished he was enjoying himself immensely, and it was with regret that he drew out the last note as long as he dared.

He looked up. His father's face looked as though the First Lady had just told him personally that he was official bra-maker to the White House. Abe started toward his son, but before he could reach him Michael was enclosed in a forest of hands, all reaching to grip his wet palm, while a chorus of voices wished him *mazel tov*.

He walked with his father up the central aisle toward the back of the synagogue, where his mother waited at the foot of the balcony stairs. As they walked they shook hands with a dozen people, and he accepted envelopes containing money from men whose names he didn't know. His mother kissed him tearfully and he hugged her fat shoulders.

"Look who's here, Michael," she said, pointing. He looked up to see his grandfather making his way down the aisle of the synagogue toward them. Isaac had slept at the nearby apartment of one of Abe's pressers, in order to be able to walk to the synagogue and thus avoid violating the Sabbath law prohibiting riding.

It wasn't until years later that it occurred to Michael how shrewdly his grandfather had waged his war against Dorothy or how victorious he had been. His strategy had required patience and the passing of time. But having utilized these, without once having raised his voice, he had vanquished his daughter-in-law and turned her household into the observant place he wanted it to be.

Michael had been his agent, of course.

The overthrowing of Stash Kwiatkowski had provided him an impetus that for months made him eager to walk to Hebrew school and back each day. By the time this pleasure had worn thin and he no longer felt like Jack the Giant Killer, he had been caught up in the rhythm of a learning process. Reb Yossle followed Reb Chaim and Reb Doved followed Reb Yossle, and then for two ecstatic years he bathed each afternoon in the warmth emitted by the electric blue eyes of Miss Sophie Feldman, pretending to soak up knowledge and trembling every time she spoke his name. Miss Feldman had honey-colored hair and a sprinkling of freckles across the bridge of a deliciously retroussé nose, and during each class she sat with her ankles crossed, the toe of her right foot turning, turning in a lazy circle which he watched with a fascination that somehow allowed him to recite when he was called upon.

By the time she had become Mrs. Hyman Horowitz, and had waddled pregnantly from the classroom for the last time, he had little leisure to waste in such luxuries as jealousy, because he was in his thirteenth year and the *bar mitzvah* loomed before him. He spent each afternoon in the special *bar mitzvah* class of Reb Moishe, the school principal, studying his *haftorah*. Every couple of Sundays he took the subway to Brooklyn and sang the *haftorah* for his grandfather, sitting in Isaac's room next to him on the bed, both of them wearing skullcaps and *tallises*, tracing the words in the book with a perspiring finger as he chanted them slowly and with far too much self-importance.

His grandfather would sit with his eyes closed, not unlike Reb Chaim, and when Michael made a mistake he would spring to life and sing the correct word in an old weak voice. After Michael had recited Isaac would ask subtle questions about life at home, and what he heard must have filled him with satisfaction. Michael's exposure to the environment of the Sons of Jacob Synagogue had turned the tables on the spirit of reform that had permeated the Kind household.

Dorothy Kind was not suited to be a revolutionary. When Michael began to question the presence in their home of meats and seafood which his rebs at the Hebrew school told him were forbidden to good Jews, his mother seized upon the excuse to ban them from the house. Challenged by her father-in-law, she had fought wildly for her right to be a free thinker. Questioned innocently by her son, she conformed with meekness and a quickened conscience. The *shabbos* lights came to be kindled in the apartment each Friday evening once more, and milk was milk and meat was meat, the two were not to be mingled.

Now, when his grandfather had made his slow way to them through the crowded synagogue, Dorothy amazed him by kissing him with affection. "Wasn't Michael wonderful?" she demanded.

"A good *haftorah*," he conceded gruffly. He kissed Michael on the head. The service was over and the congregation began to pour toward them. They accepted the congratulations until the last person had shaken their hands and departed for the vestry, where tables were laden with chopped liver, pickled herring, kichles, and bottles of bootleg Scotch and rye.

Before they joined the guests his grandfather removed the boy-sized prayer shawl from around Michael's neck. Isaac took the *tallis* from around his own shoulders and wrapped the silken folds around his grandson. Michael was familiar with this *tallis*. It was not the one Isaac wore every day. This prayer shawl he had bought soon after coming to America, and he wore it only on the high holidays and other special occasions. It was carefully cleaned each year and wrapped and stored away after each wearing. The silk was slightly yellowed but well preserved, and the blue stitching was still strong and bright.

"Papa, your good *tallis*," his mother protested.

"He'll take care of it," his *zaydeh* told her. "Like a *shayneh Yid.*"

CHAPTER SEVEN

On a bright, cold Saturday morning in the winter of his thirteenth year he became a member of the working masses. He drove into Manhattan with his father, leaving the house before the rest of the family was out of bed. They breakfasted on orange juice, cream cheese, lox, and crusty rolls, dawdled pleasantly over thick mugs of coffee, and then left the cafeteria and crossed the street to the old loft building, the fourth floor of which contained Kind's Foundations.

The dreams Abe had enjoyed when he had changed the firm's name, and their own, had never materialized. Whatever constitutes the ingredient that transforms a healthy business into a rich enterprise had eluded Abraham Kind. But while the business had not mushroomed it continued to supply them with a good living.

The plant consisted of sixteen machines bolted to an oily wooden floor and ringed by wooden tables bearing supplies of cloth, cups, stays, garters, and the other bits of materials that went into corsets, garter belts, girdles, and bras. Most of his father's employees were skilled workers who had been with him for many years. Michael knew many of them, but his father took him from machine to machine and introduced him gravely.

A white-haired cutter named Sam Katz removed the stumpy cigar from his mouth and patted his round belly.

"I'm the shop steward," he said. "You want I should negotiate union business with you or with your father, Sonny?"

Abe grinned. "You *gonif*, stay away from this boy with your union propaganda. If I know you you'll put him on the negotiating committee."

"It ain't a bad idea. Thanks, I think I will!"

His father's grin faded as they walked away together toward the front office. "He makes more money than I do," he said.

There was a wall separating the front office from the machines. The reception room was carpeted, softly illuminated, and had been furnished well in the days when Abe had still had grandiose illusions about the future. By the time Michael started working there the furniture was shabby but still attractive. A glass cubicle in the corner contained two desks, one for his father and one for Carla Salva, the bookkeeper.

She was seated behind her ledgers, doing her nails. She flashed them a smile with her "Good morning." She had incredibly white teeth and a mouth that nature had made thin-lipped and Max Factor had redesigned in red lushness. Next to her thin, flared nostrils was a large brown birthmark. She was a large-bosomed, slim-hipped Puerto Rican girl with creamy skin.

"Any mail?" Abe asked. She jabbed the freshly carmined

nail of her forefinger, as sharp and red as a bloody stiletto, at a pile of papers on the far side of her desk. His father picked them up and carried them to his desk and began to separate the orders from the bills.

Michael stood there for a few minutes and then cleared his throat. "What do you want me to do?" he asked.

Abe looked up. He had forgotten that the boy was there. "Oh," he said. He took him to a small closet and showed him where a battered Hoover vacuum cleaner squatted. "Clean the rugs."

They needed cleaning badly. When the carpets had been vacuumed he watered the two large elephant-ear plants and then polished the metal ashtray stand. He was doing this at ten-thirty when the first customer came in. Abe moved out of the glass cubicle as soon as he saw him.

"Mr. Levinson!" he said. They shook hands warmly. "How are things in Boston?"

"Could be better."

"Here, too. Here, too. But let's hope things will start to hum soon."

"I've got a reorder for you." He handed Abe an order blank.

"You didn't come in to New York just to reorder? I have some beautiful things to show you."

"The price would have to be very good, Abe."

"Mr. Levinson, you and I can worry about price later. All I ask you to do is sit with me and enjoy these new things."

He looked toward the cubicle. "Carla. The new line," his father said.

She nodded and smiled at Mr. Levinson. She went into the stock room and in a few minutes carried two boxes into the dressing room. When she came out she was wearing only a corset.

Michael's hands froze to the ashtray stand he was polishing. He had never seen so much of a woman's body before. The cups of the corset pushed Carla's breasts into two high balls of flesh that made his knees weak. She had a birthmark on the inside of her left thigh that matched the one on her face.

His father and Mr. Levinson didn't seem to know that she existed. Mr. Levinson looked at the corset and his father looked at Mr. Levinson.

"I don't think so," the buyer said finally.

"You don't even want to know how cheap you can pick these up?"

"It would be an extravagance at any price. I've got too much in the store now."

His father shrugged. "I won't argue."

Carla returned to the dressing room and changed into a panty girdle and a black bra. The girdle was cut low enough so that her navel winked at Michael secretly as she walked to and fro in front of the two men.

Mr. Levinson didn't seem any more interested in the panty girdle than he had in the corset, but he leaned back and closed his eyes. "How much?"

He winced when Abe told him. They argued heatedly for several minutes and then his father shrugged his shoulders and made a face as he agreed to Mr. Levinson's last offer.

"Now, how much for the corsets?"

His father grinned and the bargaining began again. When the deal was concluded both men looked satisfied. Three minutes later Mr. Levinson was gone and his father and Carla were back at their desks. He sat there polishing vigorously and sneaking peeks at Carla's bored face, his mind commanding the next customer to walk through the door.

He liked working with his father. When they closed up Kind Foundations at 5 P.M. on Saturdays the two of them would go to a restaurant for dinner and then to a movie or perhaps to the Garden to watch a basketball game or the fights. Several times they went to the YMHA and worked out together and then sat in the steam room. His father could breathe steam indefinitely and emerge pink-cheeked and bright-eyed. Michael had to leave the room after five or ten minutes, his knees weak and the vitality drained from his body.

One night they sat on the bench in the steam room, the vapor wisping around their faces.

"Hit my back, will you?" his father asked.

He went to the tap in the wall and soaked a towel with icy water, then he shivered while he slapped Abe's body. Grunting with pleasure, Abe took the towel and wiped his own face and legs.

"Want me to hit you?"

Michael declined with thanks. Abe turned the steam spigot and clouds of fresh steam began to pour into the tiny room. His son's breath became labored, but his own breathing remained slow and easy.

"I'm going to get you a set of weights," he said. He was lying on his back on a bench with his eyes closed. "I'll get you a set of weights and the two of us will work out together."

"Great," Michael said without enthusiasm. The truth was, he couldn't lift most of the weights his father had in his bedroom, nor did he particularly want to. At thirteen he had already begun to grow, and he was tall and very skinny. He looked at his father's splendid physique and thought of his short fat mother and wondered about the incredible tricks nature plays.

"What's the matter, you don't want weights?"

"Not very much."

"You want something else?"

"Nothing special."

"You're a funny kid."

It didn't seem to require an answer so he continued to sit there, gasping.

"I've been meaning to have a talk with you."

"What about?"

"Sex."

He was embarrassed, but he tried not to show it. "You got a problem, Pop?"

Abe sat up on the bench, grinning. "Don't be a fresh kid. I've never had that kind of problem, *boychik*. Now. . . . How much do you know?"

He couldn't meet his father's amused eyes. "I know all about it."

For a moment there was no sound but the hissing steam. "Where did you get your information?"

"The guys. We talk."

"Do you have any questions?"

He had several fine points that he had been wondering about for some time. "No," he said.

"Well, if you do, you come to me. You hear?"

"I will, Pop," he promised. He waited another two minutes and then fled to the shower room. Pretty soon Abe came out and soaked under the cold spray while Michael dawdled under the hot, and they harmonized on "The Sheik of Araby." Abe had a lousy voice, gravelly and uncertain.

Abe enjoyed having his son at the plant, but he treated him just like any of the other help. When Michael started to work his father paid him three dollars for Saturday. After he had been there a year he asked Sam to negotiate a raise for him. The union steward was delighted. He and Abe got a great deal of *nachus* out of a session they dragged out for twenty minutes, and the result was an increase of a dollar.

After he got his raise he saved for a couple of weeks and took his father to a play. It was Maxwell Anderson's *Mary of Scotland,* starring Helen Hayes and Philip Merivale. His father fell asleep in the middle of the second act. The following week Abe took him to the Yiddish theatre to see a review called *The Greeneh Cozineh,* about an American family that was transformed by the arrival of an immigrant cousin. He didn't understand all the Yiddish, but the jokes that came through to him made him laugh until his cheeks were wet.

They grew closest through the Friday evenings they spent together. Just before the *bar mitzvah* Abe had begun to worry a little about whether his own Hebrew was sharp enough to allow him to make a good showing when he was called to the *bema,* so at his suggestion they attended a Friday-night service at Sons of Jacob Synagogue. The service was not too long and to Abe's surprise he found that he remembered most of the Hebrew he had learned as a boy. The following Friday they went again, and soon it was a weekly habit. Together they stood and greeted the Bride of the Sabbath. Soon the synagogue "regulars" began to count on their presence. Michael was proud of Abe as he stood next to him, a tough, muscular man with eyes that smiled, singing the praises of God.

When he was fifteen be became a freshman at the Bronx High School of Science, gratefully making the long underground trip from Queens each morning. He was conscious that it was the most competitive secondary school in New York. His first term paper worried him. It was in biology, and it dealt with the massive reproductivity of Trypedita, the family of which the fruit fly was a member. When he was unable to find enough reference material in the public library his biology teacher managed to get him special permission to use the library at New York University, and several evenings a week he rode the subway into Manhattan and took copious notes, some of which he understood.

One night, conscious of the fact that the research paper was due in ten days, he sat at a table in the N.Y.U. library and worked feverishly, in more ways than one. He was tired and he felt as though he was coming down with a cold. His head felt warm and his throat was beginning to hurt when he swallowed. He sat and took notes about the prodigious reproductive efforts of the fruit fly and some of its competitors:

According to estimates by Hodge, the San Jose scale insect produces 400 to 500 young. The Dobson fly lays 2,000 to 3,000 eggs. Social insects are heavy egg-layers. The queen honeybee may lay 2,000 or 3,000 eggs a day. The queen hermit is able to lay 60 eggs per second until several million are laid.

Reading about all that laying made him feel a little horny. The only girl within examining distance had bad teeth and a thick layer of dandruff on her shapeless black sweater. Discouraged, he took more notes:

Herrick has reported that a pair of flies beginning in April, would by August have produced 191,010,000,000,000,000,000. If all of the offspring were to survive through some freak of nature, allowing one-eighth of a cubic inch per fly, there would be enough of them to cover the earth 47 feet deep.

He sat and thought of what it would be like to have the world covered by forty-seven feet of flies, all buzzing and spreading germs and screwing so that the tide of flies would continue to rise. Or do flies screw? It took him twelve minutes to look up the fact that the females laid eggs and the males fertilized them. Was that kind of sexual arrangement fun? Was there joy in the act of fertilization, or was the male fly a kind of sexual milkman, making his regular deliveries as expected?

He tried to find out in the index of the reference book. He looked under SEX, under INTERCOURSE, under MATING and even, although without much hope, under PLEASURE. But he found nothing which shed enlightenment. The process took until ten o'clock, however, and as the library closed at that hour he turned in the book and took the elevator down. The weather was foul; a light drizzling rain had melted the piles of dirty snow along the curb until they were shallow humps, more dirt than snow. Evening classes had let out, and he was moved toward the subway kiosk by a surging human tide. It pressed toward the narrow subway entrance, crowding and pushing. He stood on the fringes of the mob, crushed chest to chest against an attractive chestnut-haired girl in a brown suede coat and a beret. For a moment he forgot his cold. It was a nice situation to be in. She looked into his eyes and then at the books he clutched.

"What are you, a child prodigy?"

Her voice was amused. He leaned back, trying to avoid contact with her, hating her suddenly for not being three years younger. The mob surged, but they got no closer to the subway entrance. From the corner of his eye he saw the Fifth Avenue bus approaching less than a block away. He elbowed aside a fat, bearded young man and dashed for the bus, thinking to take it to 34th Street, where the subway station was sure to be less crowded.

But as they passed 20th Street and out of habit he glanced up at the loft which housed Kind Foundations, he saw that the two front windows were lighted. It could mean only that his father was working late, and his hand shot up and pulled the buzzer cord, happy to exchange the prospect of a long standing subway ride for a relaxed trip in the Chevrolet.

The building was oppressively hot, as it always was in winter. The elevator was turned off, and by the time he had climbed the three steep flights of stairs to the fourth floor he was perspiring heavily and his throat felt sore. He pushed open the door to Kind Foundations and stood in the threshold and watched his father, naked except for a tee shirt, making love to Carla Salva on the worn couch he vacuum-cleaned so industriously every Saturday morning. One of Carla's long thin feet was on the floor, resting on the crumpled silk of her panties. The other

foot moved gently against the back of his father's calf. Her Max
Factor mouth was slightly open and her thin nostrils were dilated.
She made no sound under his father's athletic efforts. Her eyes
were closed. She opened them lazily, looked straight at Michael,
and screamed.

He turned and crashed down the dark hallway to the stairs.
"Who was that?" he heard his father's voice demand.

And then: "Oh, my God."

He was on the second floor landing when Abe began to
shout down the stairwell. "Mike. Mike, I've got to talk to you."

He continued to crash down the stairs until he was out of the
hot building and into the icy rain. Then he ran. He sprawled on
the ice as a taxi horn blared and a driver cursed him in Southern
tones, and he got to his feet and began running again, leaving his
books and his notes where they had fallen.

When he reached 34th Street he was sick and out of breath
and he stumbled toward the subway kiosk.

He didn't remember how he got home. But he knew that he
was in bed. His throat felt as though it had been rubbed with a
potato grater, his head throbbed, and he burned. He felt like a
bunsen burner; when they turn me off, he thought, nothing will
be left but the container.

Sometimes he dreamed of Carla, of her open mouth, slack
and wet, and of the thin nostrils dilating in passion like the slow
motion of butterfly wings. He was conscious that he had imagined
her that way recently, and he was ashamed.

Sometimes he dreamed of the fruit fly, reproducing with
magnificent ease, gaining far more efficiency out of the mating
procedure than man, but no ecstasy, poor thing.

Sometimes he heard a drum, beating up into his ear through
his hot pillow.

Two days after he became ill he came to his senses. His
father was sitting on a chair next to the bed. Abe was unshaven
and his hair wasn't combed.

"How do you feel?"

"All right," Michael said hoarsely. He remembered everything as if the scenes were sculpted in blocks of crystal and set
before him in a row.

Abe looked at the door and wet his lips with his tongue.

In the kitchen Michael could hear his mother doing the dinner dishes.

"There are lots of things you don't understand, Michael."

"Go play with your weights."

The hoarseness made him sound on the verge of tears. The fact that this was so filled him with rage. What he felt was not sorrow but icy hate, and he wanted his father to know.

"You're a kid. You're a kid, and you shouldn't judge. I've been a good father and a good husband. But I'm human."

His head hurt and his mouth was dry. "Don't you ever try to tell me what to do," he said. "Never again."

His father leaned forward and looked at him piercingly. "Some day you'll know. When you've been married twenty years."

They could hear his mother put down her dish and start toward his bedroom. "Abe?" she called. "Abe, he's up? How is he?" She came hurrying into the room, a fat woman with sagging breasts and thick ankles and ridiculous red hair. Just to look at her made everything worse.

He turned his face to the wall.

CHAPTER EIGHT

The girl in the apartment across the hall was Miriam Steinmetz. One spring evening during his last year at the High School of Science Mimi and he lay together on the thick rug of the Steinmetz living room and read the Summer Help Wanted columns of *The New York Times.*

"Wouldn't it be nice if we could find jobs at the same resort?" Mimi asked.

"Yeah."

Actually, the thought made him want to shudder. He felt the necessity to go someplace new that summer, but more than that he felt the need to meet new people, to look at faces that were unfamiliar. Mimi's face, although pretty and vivacious, was hardly unfamiliar. The Steinmetzes had been living in apartment 3-D when the Kinds had moved into apartment 3-C; she largely ignored Michael until when he was sixteen he accepted an invitation to join the Mu Sigma high school fraternity. She was an Iota Phi girl and the advantages were obvious, so she adopted him. She took him to sorority dances and he took her to fraternity dances and after some of their dates they necked with an almost asexual casualness. The trouble with his relationship with Mimi was that he knew more about her than he knew about his sister Ruthie. He had seen her with her hair just washed and ratty looking, with salve all over her face to fight acne, and with one foot immersed in steaming water to cure an infected toe. She could never be Cleopatra to his Mark Antony. There wasn't a shred of mystery left to nurture such an arrangement.

"This one looks good," she said.

The ad was for kitchen help at a hotel in the Catskills. He was more interested in the advertisement directly below it. It was for kitchen help at a place called The Sands, outside of Falmouth, Massachusetts.

"Shall we both answer this one?" Mimi asked. "It would be fun to spend the summer in the Catskills."

"Okay," he said. "You write down the ad number and I'll take the paper home."

She scribbled the symbols on a pad at the telephone stand and then came to him and kissed him lightly on the mouth. "I enjoyed the movie."

Gallantry forced him to take the initiative. He tried to kiss her with as much abandon as Clark Gable had kissed Claudette Colbert in the picture they had just seen together. Involuntarily his hands became interested in her sweater. She offered no resistance. She had breasts like small pillows that would some day grow up to be large pillows.

"That scene where they hung the blanket between them in the motel was a riot," she said in his ear.

"Would you sleep with a guy if you loved him?"

She was silent for a moment.

"You mean really *sleep* with him? Or make love?"

"Make love."

"I think it would be very foolish. Certainly not until you were engaged to be married. . . . And even then—why not wait?"

Two minutes later he was letting himself into his own apartment across the hall. Careful not to make any unnecessary noise that might waken the family, he got out pen and stationery and wrote a letter of application to The Sands.

There was a car waiting at the bus station in Falmouth. The driver was a dour, white-haired little man who said his name was Jim Ducketts.

"Expected you in on the other bus," he said accusingly.

The Sands Hotel was on the waterfront, a large meandering white structure ringed by wide porches facing landscaped lawns and a white-sanded private beach.

There was a bunkhouse at the rear of the hotel property for the hired help. Ducketts pointed to a rickety iron cot.

"Yours," he said. He went out the door without saying good-by.

The bunkhouse was built of bare lumber planks nailed to two-by-fours and covered with tarpaper. Michael's cot was in a corner. The corner was also inhabited by a huge spiderweb containing, like an iridescent jewel in its very center, a large hairy-legged black spider with blue and orange markings.

His skin crawled. He looked around for something with which to slay the monster, but nothing he saw seemed to lend itself to the task.

The spider didn't move. "All right," he told it. "You stay off my back and I'll stay off yours."

"Who you talkin' to, man?"

Michael whirled and then grinned sheepishly. The other boy stood in the doorway and regarded him with suspicion. He was a blond, crewcut youth with a tan almost as deep as Abe Kind's. He was dressed in sneakers, jeans, and a tee shirt that had YALE printed across the front in large blue letters.

"The spider," Michael said.

He was puzzled but Michael decided that the more he explained the more ridiculous it would sound. The other boy stuck out his hand and introduced himself. He was a hand-pumper. "Al Jenkins," he said. "You got anything to eat?"

Michael had a candy bar he had been saving, but he handed it to him in a burst of community spirit. He lay on Michael's mattress and bit off half the bar after throwing the wrapper under Michael's cot.

"You go to school?" he asked.

"I'm starting Columbia in the fall. How long have you been at Yale?"

He threw back his head and hawed. "Hell, I don't go to Yale. I go to Northeastern. That's in Boston."

"Why do you wear the Yale shirt?"

"That's Ivy League cover, man. For the quiff."

"The quiff?"

"The quail, the cunt, the poon tang, the broads. This your first season working a summer place?"

Michael confessed that it was.

"You've got an awful lot to learn, fella." He finished the candy bar. Then remembering, he sat up suddenly in Michael's bed.

"Were you really talking to this goddam spider?"

They got up at 5:30 A.M. There were twenty of them in the bunkhouse. The busboys and beachboys groaned and cursed the kitchen help for waking them hours before they had to go to work, and after the first few mornings the kitchen help didn't bother to curse back.

The chef was a tall, spare man named Mister Bousquet. Michael never heard his first name, nor did it ever occur to him to ask what it was. Mister Bousquet had a long face with veiled eyes and immobile features, and he spent his time tasting and giving infrequent orders in an unemotional monotone.

On the first morning they were taken into the kitchen by the hotel personnel manager. Michael was handed over to a Korean of indeterminate age who was introduced as Bobby Lee.

"I am pantry man," he said. "You are pantry boy."

There were three crates of oranges stacked on a table. Bobby Lee handed him a crowbar and a knife. He opened the crates and cut oranges in half until he had filled three large earthenware tubs.

To his relief he found that the juicer was automatic. He held half an orange against the whirling core until there was nothing left inside the orange but white skin, then he threw it into a basket and picked up another half. An hour later he was still pressing oranges against the juicer. The muscles in his arm were knotted and his fingers were so stiff he was sure he would go through life looking as if his right hand were poised to grasp the chest of any female foolish enough to stray within range. When the orange juice was done there were melons to be cut and grapefruits to be sectioned, cans of kadota figs to be opened, and serving stands to be filled with crushed ice and juice and fruits. By the time the cooks came in at seven-thirty Bobby and he were cutting vegetables for the luncheon salad.

"We have breakfast pretty soon," Bobby said.

By facing the pantry door as he worked he was able to see the waitresses when they bustled back and forth through the swinging door between the dining room and the kitchen. They ranged from plain to flashily beautiful. He enjoyed watching one girl in particular. She had a good, strong body that moved under her uniform when she walked, and thick yellow hair worn in a coil that made her look as though her picture belonged in an ad for Swedish beer.

Bobby saw him watching her and grinned.

"Do we eat with the waitresses?" Michael asked.

"They eat in zoo."

"In the *zoo*?"

"What we call dining room for the help. We eat right here in pantry."

He saw Michael's disappointment and his grin widened. "Be happy. Food in zoo not fit for animals. We eat same as guests."

He proved his words a few minutes later. Michael breakfasted on kadota figs and clotted cream, fluffy scrambled eggs and link sausages, sugared strawberries the size of pingpong balls, and two cups of strong hot coffee. He went back to work in a haze of dreamy contentment.

Bobby watched approvingly as he sliced cucumbers. "You work good. You eat good. You fine young sonabitch."

He agreed modestly.

That evening he sat on a rain-warped piano stool outside the bunkhouse door. He was tired and very lonesome. Inside, someone played haltingly on a banjo, alternating between "On Top of Old Smoky" and "All I Do the Whole Night Through Is Dream of You." He played each of them four times.

Michael watched the merging of the male help and the female help. They had been warned against socializing with the guests, but he observed immediately that the management need have no fears. Most of the hired hands seemed to be veterans of previous summers who had come back to Cape Cod to pick up amorous connections where they had been broken off by the previous Labor Day. He was an envious witness to reunion after reunion.

The bunkhouse was separated from the female quarters by a deep pine grove. The grove was veined with paths leading into the woods. The pattern inevitably was the same. Boy and girl would meet at the grove, chat for a few minutes and then stroll down one of the paths together. He didn't see the girl with the Swedish braids. There must be somebody, he thought, who isn't half of a couple.

Just as it was growing dark a girl came up the path toward him. She was a tall, assured brunette wearing a Wellesley sweatshirt. The first and the last ls in WELLESLEY were at least a foot closer to him than the rest of the letters.

"Hi," she said. "I'm Peggy Maxwell. You're new this season, aren't you?"

He introduced himself.

"I saw you in the pantry today," she said. She leaned forward. She was very impressive when she leaned.

"Would you do me a favor? The food in the zoo is awful. Could you bring me something from the pantry tomorrow night?"

He was about to pledge his foraging services for the entire summer when the banjo inside the bunkhouse fell silent and Al Jenkins stood in the doorway. He was wearing a sweatshirt with Princeton markings.

"*PEG-LEGS!*" he shouted exultantly.

"*ALLIE POOPOO!*"

They fell into one another's arms, laughing and swaying, with much laying-on of the hands. Within seconds, palms clasped,

they had disappeared down one of the wooded paths. Michael
watched them turn a leafy corner, wondering if Peggy Maxwell
really went to Wellesley or if the sweatshirt was Ivy League
cover for the studs. She could starve, for all he cared.

He sat on the piano stool until it was dark and then he went
into the bunkhouse and turned on the naked bulb. He had a
book in his bag: *The Writings of Aristotle.* He pulled it out and
flopped down on his bed. Two flies buzzed over a piece of
chocolate that that slob Al Jenkins had dropped on his mattress
when he ate the only candy bar. Michael swatted them with the
book and dropped the carcasses into his friend's web. A small
moth had flown into the web and lay in stiff, imprisoned death
near the spider. "Listen:

*People who fall short with regard to pleasures and delight
in them less than they should are hardly found; for such insensi-
bility is not human. Even the other animals distinguish different
kinds of food and enjoy some and not others; and if there is any
one who finds nothing pleasant and nothing more attractive than
anything else, he must be something quite different from a man;
this sort of person has not received a name because he hardly
occurs."*

By the time he finished the paragraph the two flies had disappeared and the spider was motionless again. The moth was
still untouched. "You listen good. You eat good. You fine young
sonabitch," he said. The spider didn't deny it.

He snapped out the light, stripped down to his underwear,
and got into bed. They fell asleep, the spider and he.

For three weeks he worked in the pantry, he ate, he slept,
and he was lonely. After Al Jenkins saw him reading Aristotle
he couldn't withhold the news that Michael also talked to spiders,
and within five days he was branded as the hotel queer. He didn't
give a damn. There wasn't one of those cretins he wanted to
engage in a five-minute conversation.

The name of the girl with the braids was Ellen Trowbridge.
He found out by swallowing his pride and asking Jenkins.

"She's not your lollipop, Sonny boy," Jenkins said. "She's

a frigid Radcliffe bitch who's strictly no-score. Ask the man who knows."

She had Tuesday afternoons off. He bribed the information from Peggy Maxwell with a lamb chop. He had Thursdays, but Bobby Lee agreed without hesitation to let him switch.

That evening he went to the girls' bunkhouse, knocked at the door and asked for her. When she came out she looked at him with a little frown that furrowed two wrinkles in her forehead.

"I'm Mike Kind. We both have tomorrow afternoon off, so I wondered if you might like to join me in a picnic."

"No, thank you," she said clearly. Somebody inside the bunk-house giggled.

"At the town beach," he said. "It's a little crowded, but it's not bad."

"I'm not dating this summer."

"Oh. You're sure?"

"I'm sure," she said. "Thank you for asking me."

She went inside. As he started to walk away Peg Maxwell and a little redhead who was sort of cute came out.

"Would you like some other company tomorrow afternoon?" Peggy asked.

The other girl giggled, but his guard was up anyhow. She had asked much too sweetly.

"No, thank you," he said.

"I was going to suggest Aristotle. Or your spider. Is it a female spider, or is your relationship homosexual?" They both doubled over with laughter.

"Go to hell," he said. He turned on his heel and started up the path.

"Mr. Kind!" It was Ellen Trowbridge's voice. He stopped and waited for her, but he didn't say anything when she reached him.

"I've changed my mind," she said.

He knew she had overheard his exchange with Peggy. "Look, don't do me any favors."

"I'd like to go with you tomorrow. I really would."

"Well, then—sure, fine."

"Shall I meet you in the grove? At three o'clock?"

"I'll pick you up at your bunkhouse."

She nodded and smiled, and they both walked down the path in different directions.

Bobby Lee had packed him a generous picnic basket and he watched with awe as she ate her way through it.

"Is the food in the zoo that bad?"

"Worse." She stopped gnawing at a chicken leg. "Am I making such a pig of myself?"

"No, no. You're just so—hungry."

She smiled and resumed her gnawing. He was glad that she kept herself involved with the food. It gave him a chance to study her. She was generously made, her body trim and firm-looking in a white one-piece bathing suit. As she finished the last crumb of lunch he looked at her thick blonde braids and made himself a bet.

"Svenska?" he asked, touching one of the braids lightly. "Right?"

She looked puzzled, then she understood and she laughed.

"Wrong. Scotch-German on my mother's side and English-Yankee on my father's." She studied him. "You're Jewish."

"According to sociologists, you're not supposed to be able to tell that by looking. How did you know? My nose? My face? The way I talk?"

She shrugged. "I just knew."

She had very white skin. "You're going to burn," he said anxiously.

"My skin isn't used to the sun. By the time I finish work the sun's gone down." She took a bottle of lotion from her bag.

"Would you like me to put that on for you?"

"No, thank you," she said politely. Her fingernails were short and she used colorless polish. When she put the lotion on the inside of her thighs he couldn't breathe.

"Why did you tell me yesterday that you weren't dating this summer? Do you go steady? With a Harvard boy?"

"No. I'm just a freshman. I haven't even begun at Radcliffe yet. I mean, no; there isn't anybody."

"Then why?"

"I accepted four dates with four different boys my very first week here. Do you know what happened each time we took a dozen steps into those damn woods? With four boys I hadn't known for five minutes?"

She had stopped rubbing lotion but she sat with her right palm suspended a few inches above her left calf, her body frozen, her eyes staring straight into his. Her irises were actually green. He wanted to look away but there was no where else to look.

She looked away and poured more lotion into her palm. She kept her face down, but he could see the blood rising pink on the back of her white neck. The sun was very hot. The beach was crowded and noisy with children, and not far offshore a motor launch whined; but they sat on an island of silence. She must have poured too much lotion into her hand. When she went back to rubbing it on her calf it made an intimate, liquid sound against her flesh. He ached to put his hand on her, anywhere, just to make contact. She had legs that were long and slender but very muscular.

"Are you a dancer?" he asked.

"Ballet. Very amateur." She placed a palm beneath each calf. "Aren't they awful. It's the price you pay."

"You know they're not. Why did you change your mind and go out with me?"

"I could tell you were different."

His knees trembled with desire. "I'm not," he said fiercely.

Startled, she looked up, and then she began to roar with laughter. For a moment he was ashamed and angry, but her amusement was infectious. Despite himself, he grinned. Soon he laughed with her and the tension drained away, carrying with it, regrettably, the voluptuousness.

"Let's just say," she said, fighting for breath, "that you looked nice but lonely like me and I figured it was safe to come to this deserted stretch of beach with you."

She got up and held out her hand and he grabbed it as he got to his feet. Her fingers were strong but soft and warm. They picked their way through the beach blankets and the sprawled clumps of humanity.

At the water's edge out of the corners of their eyes they watched a fat brown-skinned woman enter the sea. She walked into the water until it touched the bottom of her pendulous breasts. With her hands she scooped small chunks of ocean and

let them dribble and splash into the top of her bathing suit.
When her chest was wet she rose and fell, now stretching high,
now submerging slightly, going deeper each time, until the
vastness was gone and nothing was left above the water but her
round head.

"Come on down the beach," he said. "We've got to do that."

They walked far enough to be hidden from the fat lady's
sight and then imitated her performance. The girl even splashed
water into the bra of her suit. He was careful not to smile. It was
a serious business and, they found, very enjoyable. When nothing
remained above the ocean but her head and his, they moved
together until their mouths were a foot apart on the surface of
the sea.

She had grown up on a turkey farm in Clinton, Massachusetts.

She hated turkey and any other kind of fowl.

And eggs.

She loved red meat.

And Utrillo.

And Gershwin.

And Paul Whiteman.

And Sibelius.

She hated all Scotch.

She loved good sherry.

And ballet, but she wasn't enough of an artist to be professional.

She wanted to go to Radcliffe and then become a social
worker and a wife and a mother, in that order.

The water was warm but finally their lips turned blue.
People started to leave the beach but they sat in the water.
letting waves moving toward the beach pull them in and those
washing back pull them out. Every so often they had to move
a little to stay at the depth they wanted. She began to ask him
questions.

Where was he going to school? Columbia.

What was he going to major in? Physics.

What did his father do for a living? Supports bosoms.

Did he like New York? I suppose so.

Was he a religious Jew? I don't know.

What was a synagogue service like? Like a church service performed in Hebrew, perhaps. But he couldn't really tell because he never had seen a church service.

What did it mean when something was Kosher?

"Jesus Christ," he said. "You don't have to study to become a social worker. You already work up an efficient ethnic case history."

Her eyes became cold. "I told *you*. Anything you asked. I would have answered any of your questions. You fool, you've ruined everything." She started out of the water but he put his hand on her arm and apologized.

"Ask me anything you want," he said. They hunkered down in the water again. Her lips were almost white. Her face was sunburned.

Did he have any brothers or sisters? An older sister. Ruthie.

What was Ruthie like? A pain in the ass. She was spending the summer in Palestine.

Did he have to be vulgar? Sometimes it feels good.

Didn't he love Ruthie though, deep down? He didn't really think so.

Where did they live? Queens.

Did the apartment have a dumbwaiter? Yes.

Did he ever ride in it when he was a kid? Of course not. Your mother keeps it locked so you won't fall in and kill yourself.

Did he like opera? No.

Did he like ballet? He had never seen one.

Who was his favorite writer? Stephen Crane.

Were New York girls really fast? Not the ones he met.

Had he ever been in love? Not till now.

"Don't be a wise guy," she said. "I couldn't stand it. I mean it."

"I'm not a wise guy." Maybe it was shock, but she stopped asking questions and by mutual agreement they left their ocean. The beach was almost deserted. The sun was setting and the air had turned chill enough to raise goose bumps on their arms and legs. When they started to run in an attempt to warm up, the stones made a little pogrom for the benefit of their soles.

She lifted a foot and bit her lip as she examined a stone

bruise. "Damn rock quarry," she said. "Give me the beach at the hotel anytime. The sand feels like silk."

"You're joking," he said. The hotel beach was reserved for guests. They were told constantly that if they were discovered using it the consequence would be instant dismissal.

"I swim there at night. When the hotel and the rest of the world is asleep."

His skin prickled. "Can I join you sometime?"

She looked at him and then grinned. "You think I'm crazy? I wouldn't go within miles of the hotel beach." She picked up her towel and began to rub herself dry. Her face was very sunburned.

"Give me your lotion," he said. She submitted while he spread the stuff on her forehead and cheeks and neck. Her flesh was warm and resilient and he rubbed it with his fingertips long after the lotion had disappeared.

They walked back to The Sands slowly, getting there with dusk. At the grove she gave him her hand. "It was a wonderful afternoon, Mike."

"Can I see you tonight? Maybe for a movie in town?"

"I have to be up early in the morning."

"Then we can just take a walk."

"Not tonight."

"Tomorrow night."

"No night dates," she said firmly. She hesitated. "I'm off again next Tuesday. I'd love to go back to the beach with you."

"It's a date." He stood and watched her walk up the path until he couldn't see her any longer. She had a wonderful walk.

He couldn't wait a week. On Wednesday he asked her out again and received a firm refusal. On Thursday, when she gave him a short "No!" that had tears as well as anger in it, he went away and sulked like a child. That night he couldn't sleep. Something she had said two days before—about swimming at the hotel beach when everyone else was asleep—kept returning to claw at his imagination. He tried to dismiss the thought by remembering that she had turned the remark into a meaningless joke, but that bothered him even more. The joke had no meaning, and Ellen Trowbridge wasn't the kind of girl who babbled.

About one o'clock he got out of bed and put on a pair of

jeans and some sneakers. He left the bunkhouse and walked down the path, past the hotel to the dark beach. At the edge of the beach he pushed off his sneakers and carried them. She was right; the sand was like silk.

The night was overcast but very hot and muggy. If she comes, he thought, it will be to the far end of the beach, away from the hotel. He walked to the lifeguard stand in that area and sat down in the soft sand behind it.

The Sands was a family hotel with a minimum of night people. There were still a few lights showing yellow through the hotel's windows, but as he watched they blinked out, one by one, like eyes closing in sleep. He sat and listened to the water hissing on the sand and wondering what he was doing there. He wanted a cigarette badly but he didn't want anyone to see the match or the glowing tip. A couple of times he fell asleep, only to jerk himself into annoyed wakefulness.

Pretty soon he stopped being impatient. It was pleasant there, digging into the silken sand with his toes. It was the kind of night when the air was silken, too, and he knew the water would feel the same way. He thought a lot, not about specific things, but about life and himself and New York and Columbia and the family and sex and books he had read and pictures he had seen, in a relaxed way that was peaceful and pleasing. It was very dark. After he had been sitting there a long, long time he heard a small noise at the water's edge and he was afraid that she was there and he didn't know it. He got up and walked toward the noise and almost stepped on three sand crabs. He curled in his toes, but they were more disturbed by his presence than he was by theirs, and they scuttled into the blackness.

She came up to the water's edge only twelve or fifteen feet from where he was kneeling and watching the crabs go away. The sand had muffled her footsteps so that he hadn't heard her until she had crossed nearly the entire beach. He was afraid to call out for fear of startling her, and then when he made up his mind to, it was too late.

He heard the sound of a zipper, and then the rustle of clothing. In only a couple of seconds there was the whisper of the clothing hitting the sand and he could see the faint white blur of her. He heard the rasp-rasp of her nails on her skin as she

scratched herself; he couldn't see where she was scratching but
it was an intensely personal sound and he knew that if Ellen
Trowbridge were to discover him now, kneeling in the sand like
some filthy peeping tom, she would never speak to him again.

She went into the water with a splash like a dropped rock.
After that there wasn't a sound. It was then that he should have
gone, as quickly and as quietly as possible. But he grew afraid for
her. Even the best of swimmers don't jump into the ocean alone
in the middle of the night. He thought of cramps and undertows
and even of the sharks that every couple of years are reported to
attack swimmers. He was about to call out to her when he heard
her splashing in and saw her whiteness as she left the water.
Guiltily, he took advantage of the sound of an incoming wave to
drop prone, his face in his arms and his stomach in the sand,
while the sea hissed along his legs, wetting his jeans to his crotch.

He could no longer see her when he looked up. She must
have been standing not far away, letting the warm breeze dry
her body. It was very dark and very quiet except for the Atlantic
Ocean. Suddenly she slapped herself on the buttock. Then he
could hear her running and jumping, running and jumping. A
couple of times she came dangerously close to where he lay, a
white shape that rose in the air and dropped like a playful
seagull. Although he had never seen a ballet on the stage, he
knew that she was dancing to music that played only in her mind.
He listened to the quick pant-pant of her breathing as she leaped,
and he wanted to be able to throw a switch that would turn on
bright lights, so he could see her in her dance, her face, her body,
the jiggling of her breasts as she jumped, the place she had
slapped and the places she hadn't. But there was no switch to
throw and soon she grew tired and stopped leaping. She stood for
another minute or two, breathing hard, and then she picked up
her clothing and walked naked back where she had come from.
There was an open shower just off the beach where guests could
wash off the sand and salt. He heard the serpent's hiss as she
stood under it and pulled the cord, and then the night was quiet.

He waited for another little while, just to make sure she
was gone, and then he went back to the lifeguard stand and
picked up his sneakers. When he returned to the bunkhouse he
took off his wet jeans and hung them up to dry. By the light of a

match his watch said ten minutes after four. He lay down on his bunk and listened to the ugly snores of too many males sleeping under the same roof. His eyelids burned but he was desperately awake.

Dear God, he thought, please help me. I'm in love with a *shickseh.*

CHAPTER NINE

The following Tuesday it rained. He awoke that morning and listened to the drumming on the tarpaper roof with a sense of doomed resignation. He hadn't tried to see his blonde pigeon, his naked Amazon, his dancer in the dark—his Ellen—since he had spied on her at the beach. Instead he had spent his time dreaming about what Tuesday afternoon would be like. And now he knew: wet.

Bobby Lee looked at him for a long moment when he asked if he could have a picnic lunch.

"Where are you going to picnic today?"

"Maybe it'll stop."

"Not stop." But he packed the lunch. When Michael got through at noon the rain had changed in character, turned finer and gentler, but it fell with discouraging regularity and the skies were a uniform heavy gray.

He had planned to pick her up at two. But there seemed to be no point. There was no place to take her. "To hell with it," he told the spider, and reached for Aristotle. It was quiet in the bunkhouse. There was only the spider and he and Jim Ducketts, the gray-haired old driver who lay on his bunk near the door looking at the pictures in a girlie magazine. Ducketts was on call, and when the knock sounded about three o'clock he jumped up and answered the door. A second later he dropped down on his bunk again.

"Hey," he said. "It's for you."

She was wearing a red raincoat and a floppy rainhat and rubbers. Her cheeks were wet with rain and there were tiny drops on her eyelashes and brows.

"I waited and waited," she said.

"The beach would be pretty wet." He felt foolish but very glad that she had come to him.

"We could go for a walk. Do you own a raincoat?"

He nodded.

"Put it on."

He did, and grabbed the lunch on his way out. They walked along in silence.

"You're angry," she said.

"No, I'm not."

They turned down a path leading through the grove to the forest. Unable to help himself, he said, "Aren't you afraid?"

"Of what?"

"To come in here alone? With me?"

She looked at him sadly. "Don't be angry. Try to understand how things are."

They were stopped in the middle of the path. Water from overhanging limbs dripped on their heads. "I'm going to kiss you," he said.

"I want you to."

It was strange. Her face was wet and slightly cold, the flesh firm and clean-tasting when he put his mouth to her cheek. Her mouth was soft and slightly open. She kissed him back.

"I may be in love," he said. It was the first time he had ever said that to a girl.

"Aren't you sure?"

"No. But—it scares me a little. I never felt this way before. I don't even know you."

"I know. I feel the same way." She put her hand into his as if she were giving him something and he held it even in places where the path narrowed so they had to walk single file. They came to an enormous pine tree whose branches made an umbrella. The needles under it were thick-fallen and dry, and they sat there and ate their lunch. They talked very little. After lunch she lay back in the needles and closed her eyes.

"I'd love to put my head in your lap."

She undid the hooks of her raincoat and threw it open. She wore shorts and a jersey. He put his head down cautiously.

"Too heavy?"

"No." Her hand came down and began to stroke his hair. Her lap was warm and yielding. Around them the world dripped. When he rolled his head his cheek fell on the incredible skin of her thigh.

"You aren't cold?" he asked guiltily. Her hand left his hair and gently covered his mouth. It was slightly salty to his tongue.

All during the next morning as he made his juice and cut and sliced his fruits and vegetables he sat so he faced the swinging doors in order to catch a glimpse of her. The first time she came through the doors she smiled, for him alone. After that she didn't have time to notice him. The waitresses worked like frantic slaves, practically roller-skating through the swinging doors with their order and then, tray held high above their heads on the fingertips of one hand, using their hips as bumpers to open the doors the other way and roller-skate out again.

She came into the pantry from time to time and, while she picked up salads or grapefruit, he managed to get in a few words.

"Tonight?"

"I can't," she said. "I go to sleep right after dinner." She bustled away again, leaving him there like a pot on the stove.

He began to simmer. What the hell is this, he thought. Yesterday we were talking about love, and today she's worried about sleep.

He was sullen next time she came in. She leaned over him as he sat and sliced lemons. There was a soft line of what looked like the last of her baby fat under her chin.

"I go to sleep early so I can get up before dawn and go swimming at the hotel beach. Want to come?" Her eyes were excited with the secret.

He could have eaten her up.

"I guess so," he said.

There was an insect buzzing in his ear and no matter where he moved his head it wouldn't go away. He opened his eyes.

The bunkhouse was dark. He slipped his hand under the pillow. The alarm clock was wrapped in two undershirts and a towel and its buzz had been muffled by several pounds of feathers, but after he silenced it he lay and listened to see if it had awakened anyone else. There were only sleep-noises.

He slipped out of bed. He had hung his bathing trunks over the front rail of his cot and he found them in the dark and carried them outside before putting them on. It was very quiet.

Ellen was waiting for him at the grove. They held hands and ran toward the water.

"Don't splash too much or shout," she said in a half-whisper.

They went in like thieves, making the Atlantic Ocean their private swimming pool, nobody else allowed. They swam straight out, side by side, then he turned on his back and so did she and they floated and held hands and looked at the dark sky and the quarter moon that had about an hour to live.

When they left the water they stood and wrapped their arms around each other, shivering in the breeze. He began tugging at her head with his fingers.

"What are you doing?"

"Letting down your hair." There was an incredible number of both hairpins and bobby pins. Some of them fell to the sand.

"Those things cost money," Ellen said. He didn't answer her. Soon the coiled braids were free. The thick blonde ropes fell and, when she shook her head, loosened into a mane that reached below her white shoulders. He held two handfuls of thick hair as he kissed her. Soon he let go of her hair. When he touched her she pulled her mouth away.

"Stop that," she said. Her fingers closed around his hand.

"I wonder who's going to say it first?"

"Say what?"

"I love you," he said.

Her hands dropped to her sides. But only temporarily.

And so the days passed. He made mountains of fruit salad and oceans of juice. After supper they took walks into the woods and then went to bed early, to wake while the world slept and swim and kiss and caress and tease each other unmercifully with mutual desire that Ellen savagely refused to allow them to fulfill.

They saw Cape Cod on their days off. One Tuesday they hitchhiked all the way to the Canal and back, finishing the last leg of the trip in the back of a Portuguese vegetable peddler's open horsedrawn cart, in a drenching rain, with Ellen huddled against him and his hand between her warm thighs underneath a tarpaulin that smelled of damp manure and the toilet water she wore.

They didn't escape unnoticed. One evening as he exchanged his white work-ducks for jeans Al Jenkins stopped by his bunk for a neighborly chat.

"Hey, spider man. You actually makin' it with that Radcliffe icicle?"

Michael just looked at him.

"Well," he said loudly, "how is it?" One of the busboys dug another one in the ribs. Michael felt taut and ready. He hadn't hit another human being since he was a small boy, but now he knew what he had been saving up for. He closed the top snap in the jeans and walked around the bunk.

"Just one more word," he said.

Jenkins had started to grow a mustache, and Michael knew that he would hit him there, on the light blond fuzz between his nose and the smirking lips. But Jenkins disappointed him.

"Shit," he said as he walked away. "People around here are gettin' mighty friggin' sensitive."

The busboys hooted, but there was no mistaking the fact that it was not Michael they were hooting at.

He should have felt fine, but a couple of minutes later he found himself walking in the direction of town in a black humor. The mood hadn't dissipated by the time he got to the drugstore. There was a skinny, pimpled girl behind the counter, and a gray-haired man waiting on trade at the other end of the store.

"Can I help you?" the girl said.

"I'll wait for him."

She nodded coolly and walked away.

"Three or a dozen?" the man asked calmly.

The season still had three weeks to go. "A dozen," he said.

That night when he went to meet Ellen he carried a small blue zipper bag.

"Do you plan to run away from home?"

He turned it over so she could hear the gurgle. "Sherry, my love. For thee and me. After the sea."

"You are my genius."

They swam and they stood in the water while they kissed and touched one another and murmured of their love; then they moved up onto the beach. He had counted on the wine, but he found himself removing her bathing suit without resistance and the zipper of the bag hadn't been opened.

"No, Michael, don't," she said dreamily as the suit descended over her hips.

"Please," he whispered. "Please." Her hand stopped his. Her fingers were determined. She kissed him and the tips of her breasts touched his skin.

"Oh my God," he said. He held one of her breasts, soft and warm. "Let's just undress," he said. "Nothing else. I just want to be naked with you."

"Don't beg me," she said.

He grew angry. "What do you think I'm made of?" he said. "If you *really* loved me—"

"Don't you dare put that kind of price on us."

But she was doing something with her hands at her hips, and the bathing suit fell on the sand around her feet.

With numb fingers he pulled off his trunks. They sank together on the soft sand. In the darkness her body was full of tiny shocks and little surprises. Her buttocks sat in his hands, smooth and firm. They were much smaller than he had imagined. She flexed them and he gasped into her mouth.

He couldn't speak. He reached to touch her, but she held him off. "Not now. Please, not now."

He couldn't believe it. He wanted to howl. He wanted to smash her in the mouth and violate her. His fingers dug into her shoulders. "Not *now*? Well, when? *When*, for Christ's sake?"

"Tomorrow night."

"What's different about tomorrow?"

"Try to understand. Please."

He gave her shoulders a little shake. "What the hell is there to understand?"

"I don't know anything about sex. Hardly anything."

Her voice was so low he could barely make sense out of what she was saying. Under his hands he could feel a steady shivering that made him want to hold her close until it went away, and he felt ashamed and oddly afraid. He pulled her face into his shoulder.

"Honestly, Ellen?"

"I want you to tell me about it. Everything. Exactly how it will be. Don't leave anything out. I want to think about it and think about it, every second from now until tomorrow. Then I'll be ready."

He groaned. "Ellie."

"Tell me," she said. "Please."

So they lay there together, naked in the dark, with her lips on his shoulder and his hand moving in small circles in the beautiful hollow at the small of her back, which was the least inflammatory place he could find to touch. He closed his eyes and began to talk. He talked for a long time. When he had finished they lay without moving for a couple of minutes. Then she kissed him on the cheek and picked up her bathing suit and ran.

He stayed stretched out on the sand long after the shower had ceased its hissing. Then he took the wine out of the bag, opened it and waded into the surf. The sherry tasted of cork. He wanted to say a *brocha,* but he suspected it would be sacreligious. The warm tide pulled at his unprotected genitals and made him feel very pagan. He took a long drink from the bottle and then poured some into the sea, a libation.

She had been right. Thinking about what was going to happen that night was a torture, but it was pain of the most pleasurable variety. He lived in a state of ecstatic anxiety while he waited to catch his first glimpse of her from the pantry.

Had she been disgusted by his little recitation? Had it added to her fears?

The moment he saw her he knew that everything was all right. She came bustling in for a tray of orange juice and just stood there and looked at him. Her eyes were very soft and very

warm and her lips granted him a small, secret smile before she
fled with the juice.

Suddenly he became aware that there was blood all over
the avocado he was slicing.

The next few minutes were confused. The cut was in the
fleshy part of the index finger of his left hand. He felt little pain,
but he grew faint at the sight of blood, even other people's. He
could feel his face becoming pale.

"I take care of it," Bobby Lee said. He stuck Michael's hand
under the tap and then poured half a pint of peroxide into a
bowl and kept the hand in it until a scum of tiny bubbles formed
over the cut.

The kitchen phone rang. A second later Mr. Bousquet stuck
his head through the door.

"What the hell?" the chef said, surveying the carnage.

"Just a cut. Clean as a baby's ass. I diaper now," Bobby Lee
said.

"Long distance for you, Mr. Kind," Mr. Bousquet said
courteously.

At that time in his life a long-distance call was guaranteed
to mean something very important. He jumped up and walked
quickly to the telephone that hung on the white-tiled wall,
trailing several drops of bright blood and Bobby Lee, who was
saying things he didn't understand, probably Korean swear
words.

"Hello?"

"Hello, Michael?"

"Who is this?"

"Michael, it's Dad."

Bobby Lee stuck a basin under his hand and went away.

"What's the matter?" he said into the phone.

"How are you, Michael?"

"I'm fine. Is there anything wrong?"

"We would like for you to come home."

"Why?"

"Michael, I think you're going to be needed here."

He held the receiver tightly and looked into the mouth-
piece. "Look, Dad, you tell me just what the hell is going on."

"It's your grandfather. He broke his hip. He fell down at the home."

"What hospital is he at?"

"He's at the home's infirmary. They have everything, even an operating room. I called in a big specialist. He put in a pin. Like a nail to hold the bone together."

Bobby Lee was back, carrying iodine and bandages.

"Well, that's not good, but that doesn't sound too serious." He knew that Abe wouldn't have called long distance if the situation were not serious, but a gigantic overriding selfishness had assumed command. "I can't come today, but I can take the first bus out tomorrow."

"Today," his father said loudly.

"There are no buses," he said. It was not until later, following the sorrow, that he felt the shame and guilt.

"Rent a car or something. He's calling for you."

"How bad is he? Really." Bobby Lee held the basin under his hand and poured iodine into the cut.

"He has pneumonia from lying on his back for so long. He's eighty-seven years old. The lungs fill up with fluid when they're that old."

He felt the sharp bite of remorse and the tearing pain of the iodine at almost the same instant, and he drew his breath with a sibilance that his father heard in New York.

Strange noises answered him from the receiver, and in a moment he realized that it was a sound he had never heard before. The rough, hoarse grunting was Abe Kind, weeping.

CHAPTER TEN

Night was falling on the Borough of Brooklyn by the time he left the taxi and ran up the yellow-brick stairs of the Sons of David Home for Aged and Orphans. A nurse took him down the

shiny brown linoleum to the infirmary, where in a small private
room his father sat in a chair next to the bed. The shade was
pulled to the bottom of the window and only a small nightlight
burned to dispel some of the darkness in the room. An oxygen
tent covered the upper half of the bed. Through its transparent
plastic windows he could see his *zaydeh's* shadowed face and
white beard.

His father looked up at him. "*Nu*, Michael?" Abe was unshaven and his eyes were red, but he seemed in perfect control.

"I'm sorry, Dad."

"Sorry? We're all sorry." He sighed heavily. "Life is a *cho-
lem*, a dream. Before you know it, it's over."

"How is he?"

"He's dying." Abe's voice had its normal loudness, and the
words ground down on them like the heel of doom, causing Michael to look in fright at the figure in the bed.

"He'll hear you," he whispered.

"He hears nothing. He hears nothing and he knows nothing."
His father said this resentfully, his inflamed eyes glaring.

He walked to the bed and put his face to the celluloid window. His *zaydeh's* cheeks were sunken and the hair in his nostrils was untrimmed. His eyes were unseeing. His lips were dry
and cracked. They were moving, but Michael couldn't make out
the words they shaped.

"Is he trying to tell us something?"

His father's head made a tired movement of denial. "He
babbles and burbles. Sometimes he thinks he's a boy. Sometimes
he talks to people I never heard of. Mostly he sleeps. Longer and
longer, now, he sleeps.

"Yesterday he called you a lot," Abe said after a moment.
"Me he didn't call at all."

They were thinking about this when his mother came back
from supper with a clatter of high heels. "Have you eaten?" she
said as she kissed him. "There's a good delicatessen next block.
Come on, I'll go back with you. They have good soup."

"I ate," he lied. "Just a while ago."

They talked briefly, but there was nothing to say, nothing
that compared with the old man in the bed. There was another
chair near the window; his mother sat in this and he stood, now

on one foot and now on the other. His father began to crack his knuckles.

First one hand.

Pop.

Pop.

Pop.

Pop.

Pop.

Then the other.

Pop.

Pop.

Pop.

Pop.

Abe's thumb would not make a noise. He struggled with it valiantly.

"Oy, *Abe*," Michael's mother said with a shudder. She looked at her son's hands and gasped, for the first time noticing the bandaged finger. "What did you do to yourself?"

"It's nothing. Just a cut."

But she insisted upon seeing it and then fussed until he accompanied her in meek obedience down the corridor to the office of one Benjamin Salz, M.D., a balding middle-aged man with a British mustache who was lying in his shirtsleeves on a couch, reading a tattered copy of *Esquire*.

The doctor struggled wearily to his feet after Dorothy had explained their errand, glanced indifferently at Michael's finger and then took two neat stitches in his flesh. The pain had by that time dulled to a familiar ache, but following the stitches it leaped into life with new enthusiasm.

The doctor looked longingly at *Esquire* while Dorothy questioned him first about Michael and then about his grandfather. Hot epsom salt soaks for Michael, he said. No telling how long for Mr. Rivkind. "He's a tough old man. I've seen them hang on."

When they got back his father had fallen asleep, his mouth open and his face gray. An hour later Michael asked his mother to take a taxi home, convincing her to do so by telling her that he wanted to stay and that he needed her chair. She left at ten-thirty, and he pulled the chair close to the old man's side and sat there, watching him. His finger throbbed with regularity, his father snored, the oxygen hissed gently in the tent, and the liquid bubbled in his *zaydeh's* lungs, drowning him with infinite slowness.

At midnight he dozed and was awakened by a voice weakly calling his name in Yiddish: "Micheleh? Micheleh?" And again, "Micheleh?"

He knew that Isaac was calling little Micheleh Rivkind and, more asleep than awake, he knew that he was Michael Kind and could not answer. Finally, coming to with a start, he bent forward and looked through the celluloid window.

"Zaydeh?" Michael said.

Isaac's eyes rolled wildly in his head. Would he go, Michael asked himself, with only me to watch? He thought of waking his father, or running for the doctor, but instead he pulled the zipper in the corner of the oxygen tent and opened it. He pushed his head and shoulders inside and took his grandfather's hand. It was soft and warm, but light and dry as rice paper.

"Hello, Zaydeh."

"Micheleh," he whispered. *"Ich shtarb."*

His eyes were filmed. He was saying that he was aware he was dying. How much of the earlier conversations had he heard? Michael grew angry with his snoring father, cloaking himself so selfishly in guilty grief that he had invented the certainty that the old man was already dead, a corpse without ears that could hear the words of the living.

Behind the film Isaac's eyes contained something, a flicker, a light—what was it? And then he knew with a certainty: fear. His grandfather was afraid. Despite a lifetime spent in search of God, now that he stood on the brink he was filled with terror. Michael tightened his grip on his grandfather's hands until he felt the bones, brittle as old fishbones, and he slackened his hold for fear that they would snap.

"Zaydeh, don't be afraid," he said in Yiddish. "I'm here with you. I'll never leave you."

The eyes were already closed. His mouth worked like a child's. "I'll never leave you," Michael said, knowing as he repeated the words that they couldn't erase the long years of the old man's walking alone up and down the long corridors of polished brown linoleum, a bottle of whiskey his most comforting relative.

Michael held his hand as he hallucinated, talking to some of the people who had left footprints on his memory when they had walked across his life. Sometimes he sobbed. The boy let his wrinkled cheeks stay wet with his tears; somehow it seemed as though to wipe them would be to invade his privacy. He was reliving the argument with Dorothy which had led to his leaving their household. He ranted and raved about Michael's sister Ruthie and a little *skotz* named Joey Morello. Suddenly he squeezed his grandson's fingers hard. His eyes opened wide and they stared. "Have sons, Micheleh," he said. "Many *Yiddisheh* sons." He closed his eyes and for five minutes or so he appeared to be sleeping peacefully, his breathing regular and the color high in his cheeks.

Then he opened his eyes wide and half-started out of his bed in rage. He tried to scream, but he didn't have the strength; instead his words came out in a cracked whisper. "Not a *shick-seh!*" he said. "*Not* a *shickseh!*" His fingers dug into Michael's hand like wire claws. His eyelids slammed shut and his face twisted into an almost-comical grimace. Then the blood flooded into his cheeks, turning them gray-black underneath the transparent skin. He fell back heavily, no longer breathing.

Michael pried his fingers away from his *zaydeh*'s hand one by one and got his head out of the oxygen tent. He stood in the middle of the floor, trembling and rubbing his bandaged finger. Then he walked over to where his father sat snoring with his head against the wall. He looked defenseless in his sleep. For the first time Michael noticed how like Zaydeh Abe was in appearance, his nose hooking into prominence as he aged and his receding hairline already showing bald skull. The stubble on his face was more white than gray; if he didn't shave during the week of *shiva* he would have a beard.

He reached out his hand and touched his father's shoulder.

CHAPTER ELEVEN

The funeral was held in the chapel of the Sons of David Home, with a eulogy by an elderly, asthmatic Orthodox rabbi and a long limousine ride to the crowded cemetery in Long Island. Many of the old men from the Home came along. On the way, seated between his father and mother in the rented car that smelled of floral offerings, Michael watched the neighborhoods roll past and wondered how many times his grandfather had made the trip to say good-by to friends.

Isaac was buried in the plain wooden box of the devout Jew, along with a new prayer book with ivory covers and a handful of earth from *Eretz Yisroel*, the Promised Land. Michael would have buried him with the tattered old *siddur* he had prayed from for so many years, and he would have enclosed a sack of candied ginger and a bottle of booze. When the rabbi shoveled in the first spadeful of earth, stones clattered down on the lid of the box and his father's knees sagged. He and his mother had to hold Abe up while the rabbi cut the black ribbon pinned to his lapel. He said the *kaddish* through gulping sobs, while Dorothy turned her head and cried like a little girl.

They held the seven days of *shiva* in the apartment. On the second night of mourning, his sister Ruthie returned from Palestine. They hadn't wired her, and she took one look at the covered mirrors and went into hysterics that started his mother and father weeping again. But gradually things quieted down. There were always too many people in the apartment, and too much food. Every day people brought gifts of food, and every day a lot of yesterday's food was thrown out. Most of Zaydeh's real friends were dead. The people who visited the Kinds were their friends, neighbors, and customers and employees of Abe's. They brought cakes and fruit and cold cuts and chopped liver and nuts and candy. Mimi Steinmetz came in and squeezed Michael's hand while her father told his father to sign up for perpetual care of the grave, because then you didn't have to worry about details every year, you could just forget about it.

Michael thought a great deal about the things his grandfather had said before he had died. He knew they were the kind of things he might have expected Zaydeh to say, and that his warning had nothing to do with Ellen Trowbridge. But he was troubled that Isaac had died full of fear of death and the gentile, even though the first was inevitable and the second wouldn't bother him ever again. He tried to tell himself that Zaydeh was an old man from a world that no longer existed. On the fifth night, while his parents and their visitors sat in the living room and listened to Ruthie describe orange-picking in Rehovob, he went into the kitchen and took the phone off the hook. He dialed operator. The line buzzed twice and the operator came on. "I want to call long distance," he said.

"What is the number of the party you wish to reach?"

His mother came into the kitchen. "I'll put on some tea," she said. "Ah, I'll be glad when this is over. People every day and people every night."

He replaced the receiver in the cradle.

The night after the week of mourning ended, they went to a restaurant for dinner. Halfway through the steak he was eating, he couldn't swallow. He excused himself and walked out of the dining room. He gave the cashier three dollars and took the change in quarters, dimes, and nickels. Then he went into the telephone booth. He sat on the little seat and pressed his head against the glass, but he didn't place the call.

The next day when his mother asked him to stay home instead of returning to The Sands, he felt relieved. "It will help your father to have you around," she said.

He called the hotel's New York booking office and they said they would send him a check. He had four hundred and twenty-six dollars and nineteen cents coming.

His father went back to work and Michael saw very little of him. He took long walks and he started going to small theaters that showed old movies. When the time came, he registered at the university. On his third day as a student he went to his mailbox on campus and found a letter from Ellen Trowbridge. It was a short letter, friendly but a little formal. She didn't ask why he hadn't gotten in touch with her. She just said that she was living at a place called Whitman Hall if he wanted to write to her at school, and she said she was sorry about his grandfather. He put the letter in his wallet.

Two nights later he went to a prepledge stag at a fraternity house on 114th street. He had four drinks and decided he didn't want to join, because he would be living at home and anyway the fraters didn't look particularly interesting. He left the party and walked until he came to a small bar and he went inside and ordered a straight shot of V.O. He had two more, remembering Zaydeh's bottle in the lima-bean barrel. Then he wandered outside and walked until he was on the campus. He circled the Butler Library and sat down on a stone bench next to a splashing fountain. All the buildings were dark except the library behind him and the journalism building. Below him the statue of John Jay loomed like a *golem*. He took the letter from his pocket and tore it carefully in half, then in quarters, then into little pieces that lay on the cement at his feet. Somebody was sobbing. Pretty soon he realized it was he. Two girls came walking down the library stairs. They stopped and goggled at him.

"Is he sick?" one of them asked. "Shall I go for a cop?"

The other one came toward him. "Evelyn," the first one said. "Be careful." How embarrassing, he thought.

The girl stuck her face into his. She wore glasses. She had buck teeth and freckles. Her sweater was blue and fuzzy. She sniffed and then grimaced. "Drunk as a skunk," she said. "A crying jag." Their heels clicked righteously into the darkness.

He knew she was right. There were no tears on his cheeks. He did not weep because Zaydeh was below the ground or because he was afraid to love Ellen Trowbridge. He gulped and sobbed because he wanted the wind to blow the scraps of letter toward Amsterdam Avenue, and instead they were being blown toward Broadway. Then the wind changed and the scraps fluttered quickly in the right direction. But he kept on sobbing. It felt so good.

BOOK II:

Wandering in
the Wilderness

Woodborough, Massachusetts
November 1964

CHAPTER TWELVE

Mary Margaret Sullivan, R.N., eased her huge hips into the chair behind the desk in the head nurse's office and sighed. She reached over and took a metal-covered file from the records stand. For several minutes her pen scratched, recording a disturbance in Templeton Ward caused by a Mrs. Felicia Serapin, who had struck another woman in the face with the heel of her shoe.

When she was through she gazed thoughtfully at the coffee kettle and the hotplate on top of a file cabinet across the room. She had decided that coffee would not be worth the effort required to heave her body from its resting place when Rabbi Kind stuck his head through the door.

"Ah, the Jewish padre," she said.

"How are you doing, Maggie?" He came into the office and stood there with a pile of books in his hands.

She stood with great effort and walked to the cabinet for two cups, plugging in the hotplate as she passed it. She set the cups on her desk and spooned in brown powder from a jar she kept in the top drawer.

"I can't have coffee. I want to give these to my wife."

"She's over at occupational therapy. Most of them are." She sat again joltingly. "We've got a new Jewish patient here in the ward you might try saying hello to. Her name is Hazel Birnbaum. Mrs. Birnbaum. Poor thing thinks we're all conspiring to get her. Schiz."

"Where is she?"

"Seventeen. Don't you want some coffee first?"

"Thanks, but I'll look in on her. If there's time afterwards you can sell me a cup."

"It'll be gone. See the chaplain."

Smiling, he walked through the nearly deserted ward. Everything was so depressingly clean: the mark of patient labor.

In room seventeen a woman lay on the bed.

Her hair splashed dark and tangled against the white pillow. My God, he thought, this one looks very much like my sister Ruthie.

"Mrs. Birnbaum?" he said, smiling. "I'm Rabbi Kind."

Large blue eyes flicked at him for one damning moment and then switched their gaze back to the ceiling.

"I just wanted to say hello. Is there anything I can do for you?"

"Go away," she said. "I won't bother anybody."

"All right, I won't stay. I come through the ward regularly. I'll see you again."

"Morty sent you," she said.

"No. No, I don't even know him."

"Tell him to leave me *ALO-O-ONE!*"

No screams, he thought, I am defenseless against screams. "I'll see you again soon, Mrs. Birnbaum." Her legs and feet were bare and the ward was chilly. He took the gray blanket at the foot of the bed and covered her, but she kicked it off like a petulant child. He left hurriedly.

Leslie's room was down the corridor and around the corner. He put the books in the middle of the bed and then ripped a page from his notebook and printed a note: *I'll come back this afternoon. You were at O.T. I hope what you're making is useful, like a pair of men's socks with no holes.*

On the way out he looked into Maggie's office to say good-by. But the head nurse was gone. The water in the kettle was sending a pillar of steam to wet the ceiling. He pulled the hotplate plug and, deciding that he had time, poured water into one of the cups.

Drinking the coffee slowly, he wrote a list:

THINGS TO DO

At Woodborough General Hosp—

    Susan Wreshinsky in maternity (boy, gl?) Wish mazel tov.

    Lois Gurwitz (Mrs. Leibling grnd-dtr), apndx.

    Jerry Mendelsohn, leg

At public libr—

    Order Bialik biog

    Microfilm of NY Times stories on Jewish vigilantes in racially-torn nbrhoods, for sermon.

His eyes saw his wife's name on one of the metal covers in the records rack and of their volition his hands lifted the file. He hesitated only a moment and then he opened it. Shuffling through the papers, he took another swallow from the coffee cup and began to read.

Woodborough State Hospital
Patient: Mrs. Leslie (Rawlings) Kind
Case history presented at
Staff Conference
Dec. 21, 1964
Diagnosis: Involutional Melancholia

The patient is an attractive, well-formed white female, forty years of age, who has the appearance of good health habits. Her hair is dark blonde. Her height is 5′ 7″, her weight is 143 lbs.

She was brought to the hospital August 28, 1964, by her husband. Pre-admission symptoms were those of a "neurasthenic" state, during which she complained that things had been too heavy for her, that she was easily tired both mentally and physically, that she was irritable, restless, and unable to sleep.

For the first eleven weeks of hospitalization the patient remained mute. Frequently she had the appearance of wanting to weep without being able to achieve relief by doing so.

Speaking was resumed at the conclusion of the second in a course of twelve electroconvulsive treatments, nine of which have been administered to date. Thorazine seems to have given her good symptomatic relief. Its use is being supplanted with Pyrrolazote in a gradually increasing dose up to 200 mg. q.i.d.

Amnesia resulting from the treatment appears to be minimal. In interviews with her psychiatrist during the past week the patient has told the therapist that she recalls maintaining silence because of a disinclination to share with anyone her guilt arising from an estrangement from her father and from the supposition that she was an unfit wife and mother because of a premarital sexual experience while she was a college student more than two decades ago. Her husband was made aware of this experience before their marriage, and the patient does not remember being bothered by any further remorse—or even thinking about the incident—until several months ago. While she clearly recollects the recent advent of guilt feelings regarding both the youthful sexual incident and the loss of her father's love, these feelings of guilt no longer plague her. The patient now appears calm and optimistic.

She described her sexual relationship with her husband as a good one. Her menstrual cycle has been irregular for almost a year. Her present illness apparently is an anxious, agitated delusional depression of the menopause.

The daughter of a Congregational minister, the patient converted to Judaism prior to her marriage to her rabbi husband eighteen years ago. Her commitment to the Jewish religion appears strong, and her guilt feelings appear not to be centered upon her abandonment of her Christian beliefs, but rather upon what she considered as the betrayal of her father. The patient, reared in a home where biblical lore was an integral part of the environment, since her marriage has become a Talmudic student who has the friendship and admiration of recognized authorities at the rabbinical schools, according to her husband.

Their life has been the intermittently transient existence of the family of a clergyman with somewhat rigid ideas concerning the behavior of his congregation. This apparently has placed certain emotional burdens upon both the patient and upon her husband.

Despite these burdens the prognosis in this case is good.

I would recommend that the patient be considered for release from the care of the hospital following the twelfth electroconvulsive shock treatment. It is recommended that treatment be continued by a psychiatrist from whom she can receive intermittent psychotherapy, possibly with supportive therapy to be arranged for her husband.

(signed) Daniel L. Bernstein, M.D.
Senior Psychiatrist

He was beginning the next psychiatric report when he saw Maggie standing in the doorway looking at him.

"You walk as if you're wearing sneakers," he said.

She moved heavily to her desk and took Leslie's file from his hands and returned it to the rack.

"You know better, Rabbi. You want to know something about your wife's condition, you ask her psychiatrist."

"You're right, Maggie," he said. She nodded silently when he said good-by. He put his notes into his pocket and left her office, walking quickly down the hollow-sounding, too-clean corridor.

The letter came four days later.

My Michael,

When you visit the chaplain's office again, you will notice that your copy of the Cabala is missing from your desk. I talked Dr. Bernstein into utilizing a passkey so that he could open the door and get it for me. He did the actual stealing, but I'm the brains of the mob. Dear Max Gross always insisted that a man should be 40 years old before attempting to assimilate the cabalistic mysticism. How shocked Max would be to know that I have been struggling with it for ten years now—I, a mere woman!

I have been meeting regularly with Dr. Bernstein for what you used to call "pscho-shmyko" sessions. Alas, I will never again feel so smug as to be able to sneer at psychotherapy. Oddly, I remember almost everything about the period of illness. I want very strongly to tell you about it. I think that it would be easiest to do so in a letter—not because I don't love you enough to discuss these things while looking into your eyes, but because I'm such a coward that I don't know if I would speak all the necessary words.

So I will write them, now, before I lose my courage.

As you know too well, for the past year I have been in trouble. What you could not know, because I could not tell you, was that for almost a month before you took me to the hospital I slept scarcely at all. I was afraid to sleep, afraid of two dreams that I had over and over again, as if I were on one of those amusement park rides through some mad House of Horrors and couldn't get off.

The first dream took place in the parlor of the old parsonage on Elm Street, in Hartford. I saw every detail as clearly as if I viewed it on a television screen. I saw the worn heavy plush scarlet sofa and the two matching cut-velour chairs, with the tatted antimacassars that Mrs. Payson donated yearly with regularity and belligerence. I saw the threadbare Oriental rug and the varnished mahogany coffee table bearing two chipped china canaries under a glass dome. I saw the things on the walls; a Wallace Nutting hand-tinted photograph of a tired little brook gamely struggling through a mustard-colored meadow, the Currier & Ives ice-skaters, a framed bouquet of artificial flowers made by my grandmother from the curls and clippings of my first haircut, and over the huge marble fireplace in which a fire never burned, a small-stitched sampler:

The Beauty of the House is Order
The Blessing of the House is Contentment
The Glory of the House is Hospitality
The Crown of the House is Godliness

The ugliest room ever put together by God-fearing but miserly parishioners.

And I could see the people.

My Aunt Sally, thin and gray-haired and worn from the task of taking care of us after my mother died, and full of so much love for her dead sister's husband that everybody knew it except him, poor thing.

And my father. His hair was white even then, and he has always had the smoothest pink jowls of any man I've ever seen. I have never seen him needing a shave. I could see his eyes, light blue, that could bore their way right through you to the lie you were hiding in the middle of your head.

And I could see me, about twelve, my hair in long braids, gawky and skinny and wearing wire-framed spectacles because I was near-sighted until the year I entered high school.

And in every dream my father stood in front of the fireplace and looked me right in the eye and said the words that he must have said eight hundred times to us in that ugly room on Saturday evenings after supper.

"We believe in God, the Father, infinite in wisdom, goodness and love, and in Jesus Christ, his son, our Lord and Savior, who for us and our salvation lived and died, and rose again and liveth evermore, and in the holy spirit, who taketh of the things of Christ and revealeth them to us, renewing, comforting and inspiring the souls of men."

Then the dream would fade into black as if my father were
a TV preacher who had been interrupted for the commercial,
and I would wake up in our bed, my body tingling and goose-
fleshed the way it always got whenever my father looked right
through my eyes and talked about how Jesus had died for me.

I didn't think anything about the dream at first. Everybody
has dreams, all sorts of dreams. But I began to have it every
couple of nights, the same dream, the same room, the same words
spoken by my father as he looked into my eyes.

It never shook my Jewishness. That was settled a long time
ago. I converted for you, but I was one of the lucky ones and
found something else besides. I don't have to go into all that.

But I started thinking about what it must have been like
for my father when I threw aside the things he had taught me
and became a Jew. I began to think about how it would be for
you if one of our children should decide to convert, to become
Catholic, for instance. I would lie there and stare up at the
dark ceiling and remember that my father and I were almost
strangers. And I would remember how I had loved him when
I was a little girl.

The dream lasted for a long time, and then I began having
another one. This time I was twenty years old. I was in a convertible parked on a dark dirt road off the Wellesley campus,
and I didn't have any clothes on.

As in the first dream, every detail and impression came
through to me clearly. I don't remember the boy's last name—
his first name was Roger—but I saw his face, excited, young
and a little frightened. He was a crewcut boy who wore a blue
Leverett House football jersey with white numerals: 42. His tennis shorts and his underwear lay in a heap with my clothing on
the floorboard. I looked at him with great interest; his was the
first male body I had ever seen. What I felt was not love, or
desire or even affection. The reason I had needed absolutely no
persuasion to let him park his car in this dark place and undress
me was that I felt a great curiosity and the conviction that there
were things I wanted to know. And as I lay with my head jammed
against the car door and my face pressed into the back of the
cracked leather seat, and as I felt him engaging me with the
same stupid diligence he would have used in an intramural foot-

ball game, and as I felt myself painfully split open like a pod, my curiosity was satisfied. Somewhere far-off a dog barked, and in the car the boy made a noise like a sigh and I could feel myself become a receptacle. And all I could do was listen to the faraway barking in the knowledge that I had been cheated, that this was nothing but a sad invasion of personal privacy.

And when I awoke in our dark room and found myself lying in our bed next to you, I wanted to wake you and ask your forgiveness, to tell you that the stupid girl in the convertible is dead and that the woman I have become had known only you in love. But instead I lay there through the long night, sleepless and trembling.

The dreams came again and again, sometimes one, sometimes another, so often that they became all mixed up with my wakeful life and at times I couldn't tell what was dream and what was not. When my father looked into my eyes and talked of God and Jesus, even though I was only twelve years old I knew that he was seeing me as an adultress and I wanted to die. My period was five weeks late and one afternoon when I started to flow I locked myself in the bathroom and sat on the edge of the tub and trembled because I couldn't cry, and I didn't know whether I was a college girl welcoming the curse or a fat, forty-year-old woman happy because I was not going to have a baby that didn't belong to you.

During the day I could no longer meet your eyes or let the children kiss me. And at night I would lie rigid in bed, pinching the flesh of my arms to keep myself from falling asleep and dreaming.

And then you took me to the hospital and left me and I knew that it was as it should be, because I was evil and should be shut away and put to death. And I waited for them to kill me, until the shock treatments began and the fuzzy lines of my world began to snap into place once more.

Dr. Bernstein advised that I tell you about the dreams if I really wanted to. He believes that once I have done so they may never bother me again.

Don't let them cause you pain, Michael. Help me wipe them from our world. You know that your God is my God, and that I am your wife and your woman, in body and mind and

*fact. I spend my time lying on my bed with my eyes closed,
thinking about how it will be when I leave this place, about the
so many good years that I have left with you.*

Kiss my children for me. I love you so much.

Leslie

He read it many times.

It was remarkable that she had forgotten the boy's last name.
It was Phillipson. Roger Phillipson.

She had said it to him only once, but he had never forgotten
it. Seven years ago, awaiting dinner at the home of a rabbinical
colleague in Philadelphia, he had chanced to look through the
tenth yearbook of his host's Harvard class. The name had flown
out of the page at him from beneath a picture that smiled with
insurance-man sincerity. Partner, Folger, Phillipson, Paine &
Yeager Insurance Agency, Walla Walla, Wash. Wife, the former
something or other of Springfield, Mass. Three daughters, nordic
names, ages 6, 4, 1½. Hobbies, sailing, fishing, hunting, statistics.
Clubs, University, Lions, Rotary, two or three others. Life's goal,
to play touch football at the fiftieth class reunion.

A few weeks later, during Yom Kippur services at his own
temple, he had repented, seeking atonement in his empty belly
and asking God's forgiveness for the feeling he had experienced
toward the smiling picture. He had prayed for Roger Phillipson,
wishing him long life and short memory.

CHAPTER THIRTEEN

The letter heightened the concern he felt for Max.

That night he lay in the brass bed, trying to remember what
his son had looked like as a baby and as a little boy. Max had
been a plain child, escaping ugliness only when he smiled. His
ears had sprung from his head like—what were those things,

sonar receivers?—instead of lying flat. His cheeks had been full and soft.

And today, Michael thought, you go to his wallet to borrow a stamp and you discover that he's a hulking male with sexual desires. He brooded.

His imagination was not dampened by the fact that Max and Dessamae Kaplan had entered the house twenty minutes before and were making noises in the living room. Low laughter. And a variety of other sounds. What is the sound of a wallet leaving a pocket? He found himself straining his ears to catch it. Keep your wallet in your pocket, my son, he pleaded silently. And then he started to perspire. If you must be that stupid, my son, he thought, be sure and take your wallet out of your pocket.

Sixteen, he thought.

Finally he got up and put on his robe and slippers. He started down the stairs. He could hear them plainly now.

"I don't want to," Dessamae said.

"Come on, Dess."

He stopped, halfway down, and stood on the dark stairs, frozen. In a second he could hear a small sound, regular and rhythmic. He wanted to run away.

"That feels so good. . . . Ah, that's good."

"Like this?"

"Uh-huh. . . . Hey—"

She laughed, a throaty sound. "Now you scratch my back, Max."

Ah, you dirty old man, he told himself. You filthy middle-aged voyeur. He hurried down the stairs, stumbling a little, and pushed into the living room, blinking against the light.

They sat cross-legged on the rug in front of the fireplace, Dessamae holding the ivory Chinese backscratcher.

"Hello, Rabbi," she said.

"Hi, Dad."

He said hello. He couldn't look at either of them. He went into the kitchen and brewed some tea. They came in and joined him for the second cup.

When Max left to take her home he went up the stairs and crawled into the brass bed, falling into sleep like a man dropping into a warm bath.

The telephone woke him. He recognized Dan Bernstein's voice.

"What's the matter?"

"Nothing. That is, I don't think so. Is Leslie there with you?"

"No," he said, unpleasantly awake.

"She walked out of here a couple of hours ago."

He sat up on the edge of the bed.

"There was a disturbance. A patient named Mrs. Serapin cut up a patient named Mrs. Birnbaum with one of those tiny pocket knives. Lord knows where she got it. We're trying to find out." Dr. Bernstein paused and then said quickly, "The incident has nothing to do with Leslie. But it was the only time she could have gotten out; it must have been then."

"How's Mrs. Birnbaum?"

"She'll be all right. These things happen."

"Why didn't you call me right away?" he asked.

"Well, they just now discovered she was missing. She'd have been there by now if she had headed home," the psychiatrist said thoughtfully. "Even if she walked."

"Is she in any danger?"

"No, I don't think so," Dr. Bernstein said. "I saw her today. She is absolutely not suicidal. Or dangerous to anybody. She's a pretty healthy woman, in fact. She would have been sent home in two or three weeks."

He groaned. "When she comes back, will this mean a longer hospitalization?"

"Let's wait and see," Dr. Bernstein said. "Sometimes patients take French leave for healthy reasons. Let's see what she had on her mind."

"I'd better go look for her."

"I have a couple of attendants out. Of course, by now she may be on a bus or train."

"I don't think so," he said. "Why would she want to do that?"

"I don't know why she *left*," Dr. Bernstein said. "We'll see. We notify the police as a routine procedure."

"Whatever you say."

"I'll call you when we have word," Dan said.

When he had hung up Michael dressed warmly and took the large flashlight down from the closet shelf.

Rachel and Max were asleep in their beds. He walked into the boy's room. "Son? Wake up," he said. He touched Max's shoulder and the boy opened his eyes. "I'm going out. On temple business. Take care of your sister."

Max nodded, half-comprehending.

Downstairs, the hall clock said twelve-thirty. He put on his arctics on the front porch, then he walked around the front of the house to the car, the boots making little squeaking noises in the crisp snow.

There was a sound.

"Leslie?" he said. He switched on the flash. A cat sprang from the trash barrel and fled into the darkness.

He backed the car out of the driveway and drove the entire route between the house and the hospital, very slowly, stopping three times to beam his light at shadows.

He passed nobody walking, and only two cars. Somebody might have given her a lift, he thought.

When he reached the hospital he parked overlooking the lake and floundered through the snow to the shore and then onto the ice. Two winters before, two college boys on a fraternity initiation had wandered blindfolded across the lake and had crashed through soft ice and one of them had died; Jake Lazarus' nephew, he remembered. But the ice seemed hard and thick; he played the electric torch across the white expanse and saw nothing.

On a sudden hunch he returned to the car and drove into town to the temple. But Beth Sholom was without light. The sanctuary was empty.

He went home.

In the house he looked through every room, one by one. In the living room he picked up the backscratcher. We were never that young, he thought wearily.

The telephone didn't ring.

The letter from Columbia was on the mantel. It reminded him of Phillipson's Harvard yearbook but he picked it up anyway and read it through, then he sat down at his desk and in a little while he began to write. It was something to do.

Columbia College Alumni Association
116th Street and Broadway
New York, New York 10027

Gentlemen:

   The following is my autobiographical contribution to the
Quarter-Century Book of the class of '41:

   It is incredible to think that almost twenty-five years have
vanished since we all left Morningside Heights.

   I am a rabbi. I have filled Reform pulpits in Florida, Arkan-
sas, Georgia, California, Pennsylvania and Massachusetts, where
I now live in Woodborough with my wife, the former Leslie
Rawlins (Wellesley, '46) of Hartford, Connecticut, and our son
Max, 16, and our daughter Rachel, 8.

   I find myself looking with surprising anticipation toward the
twenty-fifth reunion. The present is so busy, we do not often
enough have opportunity to look back at the past. . . .

Queens, New York
February 1939

CHAPTER FOURTEEN

One wintry afternoon during Michael's sophomore year at Columbia his mother gave careful instructions to Lew, her beauty
operator of many years service, and he applied foul-smelling
liquids which changed her hennaed hair to gray. Her entire life
took a subtle shift. Perhaps Abe Kind subsequently gave up
chasing other women because he was putting his youth behind

him; Michael preferred to think it was because his mother had come to terms with herself. For one thing, she used less makeup, the gray hair surrounded a face instead of a mask. She learned to knit, and the whole family began to wear cashmere sweaters and argyle socks. Both Abe and Dorothy started to go to services with their son on Friday nights. The Kinds became, for the first time in any real sense, a family.

One Sunday morning while his parents slept late Michael dragged himself out of bed to find his sister, still in her pajamas and robe, curled up on the living-room sofa eating a bagel and cream cheese while she did *The New York Times* puzzle. He took the book section and the News of the Week in Review and fell into a chair. For ten minutes they sat and read and he listened to Ruthie eat the bagel and cheese. Then he couldn't stand it any longer and he got up and brushed his teeth and spread cheese on a bagel of his own. She looked at him while he ate and ignored her. Finally he looked up. She had his mother's eyes, but they contained his father's intelligence.

"I almost didn't come back from Palestine," she said.

"What do you mean?" he asked warily.

"I met a boy there. He asked me to marry him. I wanted to, very much. Would you have missed me, if I hadn't come back?"

He took another bite and studied her. She was telling the truth, he decided. If she had been giving him the business she would have done it more dramatically.

"If you wanted to, why didn't you?"

"Because I'm no good. Because I'm a spoiled, middle-class bag from Queens instead of a pioneer woman."

He asked what the Palestinian was like. She got up and padded to her room in her bare feet. Michael heard the click of her purse opening. When she came back she held a snapshot of a young man with wavy brown hair and a crisp brown beard. He wore only khaki shorts and sneakers and he stood next to a tractor, one hand on it and his head cocked to one side, his eyes half-closed against the sun. He wasn't smiling. His body was tanned and muscular, a little on the skinny side. Michael didn't know whether he liked the man in the picture or not.

"What's his name?" he asked.

"Saul Moreh. It used to be Samuel Polansky. He's from London, England. He's been in Palestine four years."

"He changed his name; he's not in the foundations business?"

She didn't smile. "He's very idealistic," she said. "He wanted a name that would mean something. He chose Saul because when he first got to Palestine he spent three months as a soldier fighting off Arab raiders. And Moreh because it means teacher and that's what he wanted to be, that's what he is."

Michael looked at the tractor. "Not a farmer?"

She shook her head. "He teaches in the *kibbutz* school. The settlement is called Tikveh le' Machar. It's in the middle of the desert with only a few friendly Arabs for neighbors. The sun is so strong it hurts your eyes. The sky hardly ever has clouds in it. The desert is nothing, just bleached sand and baked rocks, and the air is very dry. The only green is inside the irrigation ditches. If they stop flowing, the plants shrivel and die."

There was a silence. He saw how serious she was, and he didn't know what to say to her.

"There's one telephone, located in the *kibbutz* office. Sometimes it works. You should see the toilets. Like something out of ancient American history." She picked a flake of bagel crust from her robe and turned it over and over, studying it. "He asked me to marry him, and I wanted to so badly. But I couldn't stand the toilets, so I came home." She looked at him and smiled. "Isn't that a hell of a reason for turning down a proposal?"

"What are you going to do?" She had quit school after studying merchandising for two and a half years at N.Y.U. Now she was working as a secretary at the Columbia Broadcasting System.

"I don't know. I'm so mixed up. For more than a year he's been writing to me. I answer all his letters. I can't stop." She looked at him. "You're my brother. Tell me what to do."

"Nobody can tell you what to do, Ruthie. You know that." He cleared his throat. "What about all the guys you date all the time? Isn't there anybody who . . . ?"

Her grin was sad. "You know most of the boys I date. I'm destined to marry someone who writes commercial continuity. Or a customer's man. Or somebody with a father who owns an automobile agency. Somebody with heartburn, somebody who can give me a toilet that plays Brahms when you sit on the

Church seat and sprays Chanel when you turn the golden knob to flush it."

He stared at his sister, seeing her for a moment as she appeared to other men. A clear-eyed brunette with a nice smile that showed even, white teeth. A high-breasted girl with a good body. A beautiful woman. He sat down next to her and for the first time since their childhood he put his arm around her. "If you do," he said, "I'll come over all the time, to use the john."

His own romantic life was scarcely more auspicious than Ruthie's. He dated Mimi Steinmetz because she was there, right across the hall. Every once in a while they engaged in schoolboy-schoolgirl sexual play, her hands holding him away, but reluctantly, pleading to be overruled. He did no overruling, sensing that what she was experiencing was not so much desire to have him as it was desire to own him. He had no wish to own or to be owned.

His sexual energy had no real outlet and he became restless and nervous. Sometimes while he studied late at night he paced. The Friedmans, who lived in the apartment directly below the Kinds, complained hesitantly to Dorothy. So Michael started taking long outdoor walks. His feet ate up the pavement near the campus, block after block of Manhattan. He walked in Queens. One day he took the elevated into Brooklyn, at first thinking to get off at the old Borough Park neighborhood but instead remaining glued to his seat until the train was well past it, getting off in Bensonhurst and walking past block after block of old attached houses. Walking became like liquor and he became a drunkard, spending time at the secret vice when his friends were sleeping or listening to music or studying or trying to make a girl.

One January night after studying until ten o'clock he left the Butler Library and started to walk to the subway. It was snowing, fat white flakes that masked the world. He walked past the subway kiosk like a man in a dream. In ten minutes he was lost but he didn't care. He turned a corner into a dark, narrow street, too wide to be an alley but a place of no light, broken tenements on both sides. A cop stood in the single island of light under a corner street lamp, big and blue-shouldered with his chapped red face turned up at the falling snow. He nodded as Michael walked by.

Halfway down the block Michael heard quick, light steps
following him. His heart began to hammer and he turned, sorry
he had been foolish enough to walk alone at night in Manhattan,
then the man passed, quickly but close enough for Michael to
barely see him. A short man, big-headed and bearded, snow
sticking to his beard, large-nosed, eyes unseeing and half-closed,
dark coat unbuttoned despite the temperature, ungloved hands
clasped behind his back while he muttered softly to himself.
Praying? Michael thought he heard Hebrew.

In a few seconds Michael could no longer see him. He heard
the attack rather than saw it: the sound of blows, the grunt of
expelled air as they hit him in the stomach, the smack of fists.

"*POLICE!*" Michael yelled. "*POLICE!*" Far down the street,
the cop under the lamp turned and began to run. He was very
fat and he lumbered with infinite slowness. Michael wanted to
run to him and lead him by the hand, but there was no time.
He ran forward instead, practically stumbling over them, two
of them, kneeling over a still form.

One of the kneeling figures rose silently and ran into the
darkness. The other, closer, came at Michael, whose right fist
rasped on the man's cheek-stubble. Michael saw eyes full of hate
and fear, a mashed nose, a thin mouth. Young, a black leather
jacket. Leather gloves. One smashed into his mouth and he felt
it with relief: no knife. In his left hand was Ferguson and Bruun's
Survey of American Civilization, weighing at least four pounds.
He shifted it to his right hand and swung as hard as he could.
The book smacked solidly and the assailant sprawled in the
snow. "Prick!" he whispered in a half-sob. He scuttled a few feet
on his hands and knees, rose and ran away.

The short, bearded man on the ground was sitting up. His
wind had been knocked out of him and his breath rattled in his
throat as he sucked air. Finally he breathed deeply, and grinned,
ducking his head at the textbook. "The power of the printed
word." His words were thick with accent.

Michael helped him to his feet. A dark blob in the white
snow turned out to be a *yarmulka*. It was full of snow. Snow and
all, he stuffed it into his coat pocket with an embarrassed nod
of thanks. "I was saying *Shema*. The evening prayer."

"I know."

Panting horribly, the police officer arrived. Michael told him what had happened, drinking the blood from his smashed mouth. The three men walked back into the pool of light beneath the street lamp. "Did you see their faces?" the policeman asked.

The short man shook his head. "No."

Michael had seen a few features, blurred by motion. The cop asked if he could pick the man from a lineup. "I'm sure I couldn't."

The officer sighed. "Might as well forget them, in that case. By now they're far away. Probably from some other part of town. They get anything?"

The bearded man had a dark bruise below his left eye. He reached into his trousers pocket and pulled out his fist. When he opened it, his palm contained a half-dollar, a quarter, and two nickels. "No," he said.

"That's all you're carrying?" the cop asked gently. "No wallet?"

He shook his head.

"They'd kill you for your last nickel," the policeman said.

"I'm taking a cab home," Michael said to the bearded man. "Let me drop you."

"No, no. It is only two short blocks. On Broadway."

"I'll walk with you then, and take my cab from there." They thanked the policeman and walked through the snow in silence, feeling their bruises. When finally the man stopped it was in front of an old brick building with an unreadable wooden plaque on the door.

He grasped Michael's hand. "I thank you. I am Gross, Max Gross. Rabbi Max Gross. Will you join me, please? A cup of tea?"

Michael was curious and he agreed, introducing himself. As they entered Rabbi Gross stood on his toes in order to touch a *mezuzah* placed high on the doorframe, then he kissed his fingertips. From his pocket he took the *yarmulka*, now sodden with melted snow, and clapped it on his head. A small cardboard carton contained a heap of other skullcaps, and he pointed to them. "This is God's house." Michael put one on, thinking that if it were so, God needed a handout. The room was small and narrow, more of a hallway than a room, wide enough to accom-

modate only ten rows of attached wooden folding chairs set
before the altar. A crumbling linoleum covered the floor. At one
end of the room a tiny vestry contained a battered office table
and some scarred cane chairs. Gross removed his coat, dropping
it on the table. He wore an unpressed suit of navy blue. Michael
couldn't tell if there was a tie beneath the beard. The rabbi was
very clean, but Michael got the impression that if he had no
beard he would walk around all the time needing a shave.

There was a rumble that shook the whole building and the
naked yellow bulb at the end of its striped cord leaped, sending
large shadows swaying on the ceiling. "What's that?" Michael
gasped.

"Subway." At the soapstone sink he filled a dented aluminum
pot with water and set it to boil on an electric hotplate. The
mugs were thick and cracked. He colored both cups of water
with one tea bag. They used lump sugar. He said a *brocha*. They
sat on the cane-bottomed chairs and sipped.

The bruise on the rabbi's face was turning purple. His eyes
were large and brown and soft with innocence, like a child's or
an animal's. A saint or a fool, Michael told himself.

"Have you been here long, Rabbi?"

He blew on his tea. He thought a long time. "Sixteen years.
Yes, sixteen."

"How many members do you have in your congregation?"

"Not many. A few. Old men, mostly old men." He simply
sat and drank. He showed no curiosity about Michael, asked him
no questions. They finished the tea and shook hands, and Michael
put on his coat. At the doorway he turned and looked back.
Rabbi Gross seemed unaware that he was not alone. His back
to his visitor, he swayed and bobbed, finishing the evening
Shema that had been interrupted on the street: *Hear O Israel,
the Lord our God, the Lord is One.* The subway rumbled. The
building shook. The lightbulb leaped. The shadows swayed.
Michael fled.

One night just before midterms he sat in the Student Union
drinking coffee with two other students, one of whom was a
desirable woman. All three of them were having just a little
trouble with American Philosophy. "What about Orestes Brown-

son and his disillusionment over the Enlightenment?" Edna Roth
asked. She had a small pink tongue that flickered as she licked
Danish-roll stickiness from her fingertips.

"My God, all I remember about him is that he converted to
Catholicism," he said, groaning.

"I've been thinking about your father," Chuck Farley said
out of the blue. "Small capitalists like your father are the work-
ingman's greatest enemies."

"Most weeks my father has trouble meeting his payroll,"
Michael said shortly. Farley had never met Abe Kind. A couple
of times he had asked about Kind foundations and Michael had
answered his questions. "The union is giving him an ulcer. What
has that to do with American Philosophy?"

Farley raised his eyebrows. "Everything," he said. "Can't
you see that?" Farley was very ugly, with a prominent, freckled
nose and ginger-colored hair, lashes, and brows. He wore octag-
onal frameless glasses and was a fussy but drab dresser. Whenever he gave a talk in class he pulled from his pants an enormous
cartwheel of a gold watch and set it on the desk in front of him.
Michael drank a lot of Student Union coffee with him because
Edna Roth was always sitting by his side.

Edna was a soft, dark brunette with a beauty mark high on
her left cheekbone and a slight swell to her underlip that made
Michael want to try it between his teeth. A trifle fat, just slightly
dowdy, neither pretty nor unpretty, she wore her femaleness
comfortably in her brown eyes and she exuded a bovine heat
and a faint, puzzling smell like milk.

"From now on no happy little drunkies," she said, although
Michael had never bar-hopped with them. "No forty winks, no
tiddlywinks, no Cecil B. De Mille's extravaganzas. We need a lot
more studying for that exam." She blinked at Farley anxiously.
She was nearsighted; it gave her face a dreamy, slightly out-of-
focus look. "Will you have enough time to study, honeybun?"

He nodded. "On the train." He was commuting to Danbury,
Connecticut, where he was helping to picket the hat industry.
Edna was very understanding about these activities. She was a
widow. Her late husband, Seymour, had also been a Party member. She knew all about picketing.

Farley left, after touching his thin lips to her full mouth.

Michael and Edna finished their coffee and retired to a cubicle
on the third floor of Butler, where until closing time they wrestled
with Brownson and Theodore Parker, the transcendentalists, the
cosmic philosophers, the radical empiricists, Calvinism, Borden
Parker Browne, Thoreau, Melville, Brook Farm, William Torrey
Harris. . . .

On the stairs outside, he blinked his burning eyes. "There's
too much, too many details."

"I know. Look, honeybun, want to come to my place and
study for another hour or two?"

They took the subway. She lived in an old red-brick apartment building in Washington Heights. She opened the door with
her key, and he was surprised to see a thin young Negro girl
seated by the radio, doing her math homework, which she started
to gather together as soon as she saw them.

"How is he, Martha?" Edna asked.

"Fine. He's just a darling boy."

The girl left, carrying her books. He followed Edna into the
small bedroom and bent with her over the crib. He had thought
that all Seymour had left her was enough money to return to
Teachers College to pick up her meal ticket. But here was a different legacy.

"He's a handsome guy," Michael said when they had returned to the living room. "How old is he?"

"Thank you. Fourteen months. His name's Alan." She went
into the kitchen and started putting on a pot of coffee. He looked
around. There was a picture on the mantel. He knew without
asking that this was the late Seymour, a somewhat handsome
man wearing a ridiculous mustache and a strained smile. The
furniture was Colonial borax. With luck it would last until she
began to teach or remarried. When he looked out the window
he saw the river. The building was nearer to Broadway than the
Drive, but the land dropped away sharply toward the Hudson,
and Edna's apartment was on the eighth floor. Warm little lights
that were boats crawled slowly over the water.

They had coffee in the tiny kitchenette and then they studied
without moving from their places at the table, his knee finding
her thigh. Before forty minutes had passed he was through and

she had closed her book, too. It was warm in the kitchen. Her milky smell was there again, faint but distinct.

"Well, I guess I'd better be going."

"You can stay if you want, honeybun. I mean tonight."

He used the telephone while she cleared the coffee dishes. His mother answered, her voice foggy with sleep, and he told her he was studying late and would sleep with a friend. She thanked him for calling so that she wouldn't worry.

The bedroom adjoined the baby's, and the door was open. They undressed back to back by the light of the baby's night-light. He caught her underlip gently between his teeth, the way he had promised himself. In the bed, close to her, the faint, milky smell was very real. He wondered if she could still be nursing the baby. But her nipples were dry, hard little buds. Everything else was soft and warm, no shocks or surprises, a gentle rising and falling, the steady rocking of a cradle. She was kind. When he fell asleep, her palm was holding the back of his head.

The baby started to cry at four A.M., a thin rope of sound that pulled them into wakefulness. She yanked her arm from beneath his head, leaped out of bed, and ran to heat a bottle. Viewed naked from the back her buttocks were large and slightly drooping. When she took the bottle from the pan of hot water the milk-smell mystery was solved, she shook a white jet into the soft, sensitive flesh in the bend of her elbow. Satisfied that the temperature of the milk was all right, she put the nipple into the baby's mouth. The wailing stopped.

When she had re-entered the bed he leaned over her body to kiss the place where the milk had fallen. It was still damp and warm. He let the tip of his tongue explore the softness inside her elbow. The milk was sweet. She sighed deeply. Her hand reached for him. This time he was more confident, she less maternal. When she slept he got out of bed carefully, dressed in the dark and let himself out of the apartment. Downstairs, outside, it was dark; a wind blew from the river. He turned up his coat collar and began to walk. He felt weightless and happy, relieved of the burden of innocence. "Finally," he said aloud. A kid pedaling by in the gutter, his deep bicycle-basket loaded with packages, shot him a look hard and shining as a marble.

Any other place in the world would still be sleeping at 5:05 A.M.
Manhattan was alive. People on the sidewalk, taxis and cars in
the street. He walked for a long time. It had been light for several
minutes when he recognized one of the buildings he was passing.
It was the little *shul* where the subway shook the lights, the
synagogue of Rabbi Max Gross.

He approached the door and put his eyes inches away from
the almost-obliterated lettering of the small wooden plaque. In
the gray light of dawn the faded Hebrew letters seemed to twist
and squirm, but with difficulty he made them out. *Shaarai
Shomayim*. The Gates of Heaven.

CHAPTER FIFTEEN

By the time he was four years old in the Polish town of Vorka,
Max Gross could read portions of the Talmud. At the age of
seven, when most of his small friends still were mastering language and the stories of the Bible, he had plunged deep into the
complexities of the law. His father, Chaim Gross the wine merchant, rejoiced that his storekeeper's seed had produced an *ilui*,
a Talmudic prodigy who would bring the blessings of God on
the soul of Soreleh, his late wife, who had been sent to Paradise
by influenza while her son still crawled. From the time Max
could read he accompanied his father and the other Chassidim
when they gathered before their leader, Rabbi Label. Each Sabbath evening, the Rabbi of Vorka "presented his table." The pious
Jews would dine early in their own homes, knowing that their
leader awaited them. When they had gathered around his table
the elderly Rabbi would begin to eat, from time to time handing
a tidbit—a piece of white chicken, a sweet marrow bone, a small
portion of fish flesh—to a deserving Jew who nibbled it blissfully,
aware that food from the Rabbi's hand was food that had been
touched by God. Max the prodigy sat in the midst of his elders

wearing a white velvet *caftan*, skinny and large-eyed, even then small for his years, with a perpetual frown on his face as he tugged at one of his earlocks while he strained to hear the Rabbi's words of wisdom.

He was a boy in addition to being a prodigy, and he gloried in the festivals. On the evening of any holiday the Chassidim gathered to celebrate. The tables would be covered with bowls of the boiled chickpeas called *nahit*, platters of cakes and kugels, and bottles of schnapps. Women, being lesser creatures, did not intrude on the scene. The men ate sparingly and drank frequently. Aware that evil could be overcome only by joy and not by sorrow and believing that ecstasy brought them close to God, they allowed happiness to flood their souls. Soon one of the bearded Chassids would rise and beckon to a comrade. Hands on each other's shoulders, they would start to dance around the floor. Others would pair off and begin to dance, until the floor was filled with bearded couples. The tempo was swift and triumphant. The only music was the voices of the dancers, chanting over and over again a single biblical phrase. Someone would give Max a swallow of fiery schnapps as a joke, and someone would choose the little boy for his dancing partner, perhaps even the Rabbi himself. Head light and feet unsteady, propelled by large hands which gripped his shoulders, he would whirl around the room in breathless joy, his small feet flying in imitation of his partner's kicking and stamping, while the deep voices of the bearded men boomed a rhythmic repeated chorus: *"V'tahhair libanu l'avd'choh be-ehmess"*—"Purify our hearts to serve Thee in truth."

He became a community legend years before he was *bar mitzvah*. As he plunged deeper and with increasing power into the sea of Talmud, he was singled out frequently for choice morsels at the Rabbi's table, and his father's friends would stop him in the street to pat his back or touch his head. At the age of eight he was taken from the *chedar* where the rest of the boys went to school and placed for private instruction with Reb Yankel Cohen, a tubercular scholar whose eyes shone with sick brilliance. It was almost like studying alone. The boy recited for hours on end while the gaunt man sat and coughed endlessly into a large rag. They did not converse. When Max's tired voice strayed into false philosophy or faulty interpretation, the man's clawlike hand would dart out and fingers like pincers would squeeze the flesh in his forearm. His arms wore purple splotches until after Reb Yankel had been buried. Four months before the teacher died he informed Chaim Gross that he had taught the ten-year-old all that he knew. From that day until Max was *bar mitzvah* he went each morning to the community Study House, where he sat around a table with men, some of them graybeards. Each day they studied a different portion of the Law, arguing hotly about interpretation. After Max had assumed Jewish manhood at thirteen, Rabbi Label himself undertook the responsibility for the prodigy's education. It was a singular honor. The only other student in the Rabbi's home was his son-in-law, a man of twenty-two who was awaiting ordination as a rabbi.

Chaim Gross thanked God daily for the benediction he had received in his son. The boy's future was assured. He would become a rabbi and his brilliance would enable him to gather around him a distinguished rabbinical court, bringing him wealth, honor, and fame. This, from the son of a seller of resinous wines! Dreaming of Max's future one winter night, Chaim Gross died of heart failure, smiling.

Max didn't question God for having taken his father. But standing at the open grave in the little Jew's Cemetery, saying the *kaddish*, he felt for the first time the cut of the wind and the gnawing of the cold.

At the advice of Rabbi Label he hired a Polish clerk named Stanislaus to tend the wine shop. Once a week Max carelessly checked the books in order to keep Stanislaus' stealing at a reasonable level. The shop gave him far less money than his father had earned, but it enabled him to continue his life of study.

He was twenty years old, preparing to be a rabbi and keeping his eyes open for a suitable wife, when hard times began to grind Poland. The summer that year was fiercely hot, with no rain. In the fields, the peasants' wheat and barley burned in the sun until the plants cracked instead of bending when the wind blew. The few sugar beets that were harvested that fall were soft and wrinkled, and the potatoes were small and bitter. With the first snows the peasants flocked to the textile mills and the glass and paper factories, where they competed to work for lower and lower wages. Soon savage fighting marked the changing of work shifts, and mobs with hungry bellies began to form in the streets, listening to sullen men who waved their fists when they shouted.

In the beginning, only a few Jews were beaten. Soon, however, regular raids were made on the ghettos, the Poles forgetting their children's hunger cries in the momentary thrill of striking down the men who had killed the Saviour. In Vorka, Stanislaus realized that as manager of a Jew's shop it would be difficult to convince a marauding mob that he was not a Jew. He fled the shop one afternoon without bothering to lock the door, taking with him a week's receipts in lieu of notice. His exit was timely. The following evening a laughing pack of drunkards swept into the Vorka ghetto. In the streets blood flowed like wine; in the shop of the late Chaim Gross wine spilled like blood. What they could not drink or carry away they wasted and smashed. The next day, while Jews tended their wounds and buried their dead, Max realized that the shop was gone. He accepted the loss with a feeling of relief. His real work lay with his people and with God. He helped the Rabbi conduct four funerals and he prayed with his brethren for God's help.

After the crisis had passed, Rabbi Label supported him for two months. He was ready to become a rabbi with his own flock. But when he began to look for a congregation, it became clear that the Jews of Poland had no need for new rabbis. Jews by the tens of thousands were leaving the country, mostly for England and the United States.

Rabbi Label tried not to show his worry. "So, you will be my son. What we eat, you will eat. Times will grow better."

But every day Max saw more Jews leaving. Who would help them find God in strange surroundings? When he asked Rabbi Label the teacher shrugged.

But the pupil already knew the answer.

He arrived in New York during an August heat wave, wearing his long, heavy gabardine and a round black hat. For two days and two nights he stayed in the two-room flat of Simon and Buni Wilensky, who had left Vorka with their three children six weeks before he had left for America himself. Wilensky had a job in a loft factory where small American flags were made. He was a stitcher. He assured Max that as soon as Buni stopped crying she would like America, too. When Max had listened to Buni cry for two days and could no longer stand the sounds and the smells of the Wilensky children he walked out of the tenement and wandered through the East Side until he came to a synagogue. Inside, a rabbi listened to him and then put him in a taxi and took him to the Union of Orthodox Rabbis. They had no congregations open at the moment, a Union rabbi told him sympathetically. But there were many requests for cantors to sing the High Holiday services. Was he a *chahzen,* a cantor? If so, they could send him to Congregation Beth Israel in Bayonne, New Jersey. The *shul* was willing to pay seventy-five dollars.

The moment he began to sing in Bayonne the worshipers looked at him in amazement. He had committed the service to memory while a young boy, and he knew each note of the melody like a friend. In his mind the music ran true and clear, but what came from his mouth could not be called singing. He had the voice of a learned frog. Following the first service, a stern congregation treasurer named Jacobson beckoned him with an imperious finger. It was too late for the *shul* to get another *chahzen.* But in a brief conversation Max was informed that he would not get seventy-five dollars for singing during the holidays. He would get ten dollars and a place to sleep. For ten dollars, nobody could demand a nightingale, Jacobson said.

His performance as a cantor was so wretched that most of the people in the synagogue avoided him. But Jacobson grew friendlier. He was a fat bald man with pale skin and a gold front tooth. From the lapel pocket of his checkered suit three cigars always peeped. He asked a lot of personal questions and Max answered them politely. Finally the *Amerikaneh* revealed that he was a *shadchen,* a marriage broker.

"The answer to your troubles is a good wife," he said. " 'For created He both male and female.' And said he, 'Be fruitful and multiply and replenish the earth.' "

Max was receptive. As a young scholar of reputation he had expected to marry into one of the wealthy Jewish families in Vorka. With a pretty girl to make him a home, and with influential in-laws to provide a large dowery, life in America would be much more pleasant.

But Jacobson looked at him closely and spoke aloud in English, which he knew Max did not yet understand. "You greenie you, you dress like you're inviting a pogrom. You ain't a giant, no girl is going to feel small next to you." He sighed. "Your face ain't pocked, that's the nicest thing a person can say." In Yiddish he explained that in America the market for Polish Jews was not nearly so good as in Poland.

"Do your best," Max said.

Leah Masnick was five years older than Max. An orphan, she lived with her uncle Lester Masnick and his wife Ethel. The Masnicks conducted a kosher chicken business. They treated her tenderly, but the girl imagined that their bodies smelled of blood and feathers even when they were freshly bathed. A second-generation American, she would never have considered marrying an immigrant if it were not for the fact that it had been years since a man had asked her anywhere. She was not ugly, although her eyes were small and her nose was long, but she lacked femininity; she did not know how to smile at a man, or how to make him laugh. Of late, she had felt even less like a woman. Her pancake breasts seemed to her to be growing flatter. Her periods became irregular and she skipped several months; sometimes she imagined wildly that her tall, slender body was turning into a boy's for lack of use. She had twenty-eight hundred forty-three dollars in the New Jersey Guarantee Trust Company. When Jacobson came to her uncle's house one evening and smiled at her over his coffee cup she knew that whoever he had for her would be all right, that she could not afford to waste any chance. When she heard that the man was a rabbi she felt a thrill of hope. She had read English novels about ministers and their wives, and she pictured her future life in a small but neat English parsonage with *mezuzahs* on the doors. When she saw him, a little shrimp of a man, bearded and wearing funny unpressed clothes, with odd, girl-like curls dropping in front of his ears, she forced herself to talk pleasantly to him, her eyes bright with tears.

Even so, she became hysterical ten days before the wedding and screamed that she would not marry him unless he got an

American haircut. Max was shocked, but he had noticed that the American rabbis he had met did not wear earlocks. Resignedly he sat in a barber's chair and let an Italian get the giggles as he slashed off the *payehs* Max had worn all his life. Without the earlocks he felt naked. When Leah's Uncle Lester took him into a department store and bought him a gray double-breasted suit with square padded shoulders, he felt that he could now pass as a genuine *goy*.

But his appearance caused no undue excitement when he returned to the office of the Union of Orthodox Rabbis. His visit was fortunately timed, they told him. A new congregation was being started in Manhattan, and its members requested that the Union obtain the services of a rabbi for them. *Shaarai Shomayim* was small, with only a few members and one rented room in which to hold services, but it would grow, the Union rabbis assured him. Max was overjoyed. He had his first rabbinate.

They rented a four-room flat two blocks from the *shul*, spending a large portion of the dowry on furniture. It was here they came on the night they were married. Both were tired from the overexcitement of the day and weak from lack of food, having been unable to eat the wedding chickens cooked by Aunt Ethel Masnick. Max sat on his new sofa and fiddled with the dial of his new radio while his new wife disrobed in the next room and got into the new bed. When he lay down next to her he was aware that the top of his head touched her ear while his cold toes rested on her trembling ankles. Her hymen was tough as leather. He strove mightily, muttering quick prayers, intimidated by the fact that it would not give and by the shrill little cries of fright and pain which came from his bride. At last he succeeded and the membrane tore, accompanied by a piercing shriek from Leah. When it was over she lay alone at the far edge of the bed and wept, partly because of the pain and humiliation and partly because her strange little husband lay sprawled naked on two-thirds of the bed singing triumphant songs in Hebrew, a language she did not understand.

At first everything pressed on Max Gross, threatening him. The sidewalks were filled with unfamiliar people who pushed and shoved, forever hurrying. In the streets, motor cars and

buses and trolleys and taxicabs blared their horns and filled the
air with the stink of gas exhausts. Everywhere there was noise
and dirt. In his own home, where there should have been peace,
there was a woman who refused to speak Yiddish to him, although she was his wife. He never spoke anything but Yiddish
to her; she never answered in anything but English: it was a
tie. Amazingly, she had expected conversation during meals,
weeping when he insisted on studying while he ate. One night
soon after the wedding he told her gently that she was the wife
of a rabbi who had been raised by the Chassidim. A Chassid's
wife, he explained, must cook and bake and sew and clean and
pray and *bench licht* instead of forever talking, talking, talking
about nothing and everything.

Each day he went to *shul* early and stayed late, finding
peace. God was the same as He had been in Poland, the prayers
were the same. He was able to sit all day and study and pray,
losing himself in contemplation while the shadows of the day
grew longer. His congregation found him learned but aloof. They
respected his knowledge but they did not love him.

When they had been married almost two years, one afternoon Leah packed her clothing in an imitation-leather valise
and wrote a note telling her husband that she was leaving him.
She took a bus to Bayonne, New Jersey, where she moved into
her old room in the Masnick's house and once more began to
keep her Uncle Lester's books at the chicken market. After she
left, Max found that he had to get up half an hour earlier every
morning in order to get to the *shul* in time for *kaddish*. He
ignored the apartment. Ropes of dust grew on the floor and
dishes piled up in the sink.

Leah had forgotten about the blood-and-feathers smell of
the chicken shop. Her uncle's books had been kept haphazardly
in her absence and the ledgers were hopelessly in error; they
gave her migraine headaches as she sat at the old desk in the
rear of the shop and struggled to balance the accounts while
the hens cackled and the roosters crowed. At night she could
not sleep. The strange bearded bantam she had married was
strong and lusty and for two years he had used her body at will.
She had thought that she would feel free without him. But now
she lay in the bed of her former maidenhood and discovered to

her amazement that when she dozed her hand found its way
between her legs and she dreamed of the small tyrant in shock-
ing detail.

One morning, her fingers flying busily over the keys of the
adding machine while she tried to ignore the odor of chicken
droppings, she began to vomit. She was ill for hours. That afternoon a doctor told her that her baby would arrive in seven
months. When Max returned from the synagogue late the following evening he found his wife working in the kitchen. The apartment had been cleaned. Alluring smells came from pots that
bubbled and steamed on the stove. Supper was almost ready,
she told him. She would see to it that nothing disturbed his
study afterward, but during the meal there were to be no books
on the table or she would go back to Bayonne immediately.

He nodded happily. At last she was talking to him the way
a Jewish wife should, in Yiddish.

Congregation *Shaarai Shomayim* did not grow into a large,
powerful synagogue. Max was not an administrator, nor was he
the kind of rabbi who saw the synagogue as a social institution.
Shaarai Shomayim had neither a Brotherhood nor a Sisterhood. It
held no annual picnic. It showed no movies. Families which
sought this kind of synagogue were quickly disappointed. When
several other congregations were founded in nearby neighborhoods most of these families one by one transferred their alle-
giances and their annual dues. Eventually what remained in his
flock was a handful of men who wanted their religion undiluted.

Most of his life was spent in the small, dark room with the
Torah. The prophets were his family. Leah had given birth to
one child, a son they had named Chaim. He lived for three years
before being killed by a ruptured appendix. Holding the boy in
his arms during the final hours, feeling the life fluttering away
as the small face burned under his lips, Max had told his wife
that he loved her. He never said it again, but Leah would
remember always. It was not enough to make up for the loneliness that never left her, for the grief, for the emptiness of her
days, for the realization that she could not compete with God;
but it was something.

As the years passed and the *shul* grew shabby and then

decrepit, the old men of the congregation came to regard him with a loyalty that surprised him because it contained love. He never thought of seeking a more prosperous pulpit. The pittance they raised for his annual salary satisfied him. Twice he infuriated Leah by refusing small increases, telling the *shul* president that all a Jew needed was food and a fringed garment. Finally Leah went to the congregation and accepted the increase for him.

He felt loneliness only when he thought of the Chassidim. Once he heard of some families from Vorka who were living in Williamsburg. He took the long subway ride and sought them out. Happily, they remembered him, not as a face or as a person but as a legend, the *ilui*, the prodigy who had been the favorite of Rabbi Label, may he rest in peace. He sat with them and the women served *nahit* and some of the men still wore beards, but they were not Chassidim. They lacked a leader, a great rabbi at whose table they could gather to hear wisdom and eat tidbits of holy food. They did not dance man with man, or feel joy, but simply sat and sighed, talking of how it had been in *der alte hame*, in the old home they had abandoned long ago. He never visited them again.

Sometimes he argued spiritedly over the Law with the old men of the congregation, but he held his best debates when he sat alone in the shadowy little *shul*, a bottle of whiskey uncorked on the table by his open books. By the third or the fourth drink he would feel his spirit lighten and his mind would rise happy and unleashed. Presently he would begin to hear the voice. His opponent always was Rabbi Label. Max never would see the great man, but the wise, slow voice was there, in his mind if not in the room, and together the two of them pitted their intellects in the old way, the voice supplying parry and riposte for each philosophical lunge by Max, complete with biblical sources and legal precedents. When he was thrilled but exhausted by the argument the voice would fade away and he would drink until the room began to spin and whirl, and then he would lean back in his chair and close his eyes and become once again a small boy, feeling large grown-up hands grasping his shoulders as he flung himself around the room to the quick thunder of a biblical chant. Sometimes the music in his mind would put him to sleep.

One afternoon, opening his eyes after just such a slumber,

he thought with a surge of joy that for the first time he could see the presence of Rabbi Label in the room. Then he realized that it was a tall young man standing over him, someone he had met before.

"What do you want?" he asked. There was something about the boy's eyes. The boy's eyes could pass for the eyes of the Rabbi of Vorka. He stood in front of Max's table, holding out a cake in a box from a kosher bakery as if it were a ticket of admission.

"Tell me about God," Michael said.

CHAPTER SIXTEEN

In the small empty hours of the morning Michael had begun to have doubts about God's existence, at first idly and then with a wondering desperation. Tossing and thrashing until the sheets were twisted, he lay and blinked into the blackness. Since his childhood he had prayed. Now he wondered where his prayers were directed. What if he prayed only to the singing quiet of the sleeping apartment, spoke his ambitions and fears into millions of miles of nothing, or gave thanks to no greater power than the cats that made soft, shuffling sounds as they scraped their claws against the clothesline posts in the alley beneath his window?

After his questions had grown too persistent and the sleeplessness had driven him to Max Gross, he fought bitterly with the rabbi, hating his calm certainty. The two of them sat at the scarred table and stared at one another over steaming glasses of tea, aware of impending combat.

"What is it you want to know?"

"How can you be sure that man didn't imagine God, because he was afraid of the dark and the lousy cold, because he needed the protection of anything, even his own stupid imagination?"

"What makes you think this is what happened?" Max asked calmly.

"I don't know what happened. But I do know that for more than a billion years there's been life on this earth. And always, if you look into every rude culture, you find something to be prayed to, a mud-smeared wooden statue, or the sun, or a mushroom, or a big stone whang."

"*Vos ment* whang?"

"A *potz.*"

"Ah." To a man who argued with the voice of Label of Vorka, this was hardly an exercise. "Who made the people that worshiped the obscene idols? Who created life?"

A physics major at Columbia could answer that one easily. "A Russian named Oparin says life could have begun with the accidental generation of carbon compounds." He looked at Gross, expecting to see the annoyance of the nonscientist being dragged into a scientific discussion, but all he saw was interest. "In the beginning, the atmosphere of the earth lacked oxygen, but it had plenty of methane, ammonia, and water vapor. Oparin believes that bolts of lightning sent electricity through these things, creating synthetic amino acids, the stuff life is made of. Then organic molecules developed in ancient pools for millions of years, and natural selection resulted in complicated creatures, some that wriggled, some that had webbed feet, some that invented God." He looked defiantly at Rabbi Gross. "Do you understand what I'm talking about?"

"I understand enough." He stroked his beard. "Let us assume that this is so. Then let me ask you: Who furnished the—what do you call it—the methane, yes; and the ammonia and the water? And who sent the lightning? And the world in which this marvelous thing could take place, where did it come from?"

Michael was silent.

Gross smiled. "Oparin, oshmarin," he said softly. "You really don't believe in God?"

"I think I've become an agnostic."

"What is that?"

"Someone who is uncertain whether or not God exists."

"No, no, no, then call yourself an atheist. Because how can anyone be certain that God exists? By your definition we are all agnostics. Do you think I have scientific knowledge of God? Can I go back in time and be there when God speaks to Isaac or delivers the Commandments? If this could be done there would be only one religion in the world; we would all know which group is right.

"Now it happens to be the way of all men to take sides. A man has to make a decision. About God, you don't *know* and I don't *know*. But I have made a decision in favor of God. You have made a decision against Him."

"I've made no decisions," Michael said a bit sullenly. "That's why I'm here. I'm full of questions. I want to study with you."

Rabbi Gross touched the books piled on his table. "A lot of great thoughts are contained here," he said. "But they don't hold the answer to your question. They can't help you decide. First you make a decision. Then we will study."

"No matter what I decide? Suppose I decide that God is a fable, a *bubbeh-meisir.*"

"No matter."

Outside, in the dark hallway, Michael looked back at the closed door of the *shul*. Goddam you, he thought. And then, in spite of everything, he smiled at his choice of words.

CHAPTER SEVENTEEN

Michael's sister Ruthie turned into someone with whom he could no longer exchange verbal torturings. At night the sound of her pillow-muffled weepings became almost a routine background noise, like the hum of the refrigerator motor. Her parents tried tempting her with subsidized ski week ends, psychiatry, and the handsome sons and nephews of friends, to no avail. Finally Abe Kind sent a money order and a long letter to Tikveh le'Machar, Palestine, and six weeks later Saul Moreh walked into the commercial continuity department of the Columbia Broadcasting

System, causing Ruthie to rise up, scream, and faint with great sincerity. To the family's disappointment Saul turned out to be a foreigner; he was smaller than they had imagined from his pictures, very British with briar pipe, heavy tweeds, accent, and University of London B.A. and M.A. But they liked him well enough as they grew accustomed to him, and Ruth lost her wilt and regained her bloom. On Saul's second day in New York he and Ruth told her family they would be married. There was no question of their staying in the United States. German Jews who could afford to escape were finding their way into Palestine. It was not a time for a Zionist to desert *Eretz Yisroel*, Saul said; they would return to the *kibbutz* in the desert in three weeks.

"So, the American success story," Abe said. "I work hard all my life, I save my money, and in my middle age I buy my daughter a peasant."

He gave them a choice of a large wedding or a small family *chupeh* plus three thousand dollars with which to start their married life in Palestine. Saul took visible pleasure in refusing the money. "Everything we ever need will be given to us by the *kibbutz*. Everything we have will be owned by the *kibbutz*. So save your dollars, please." He would have preferred a *chupeh* to a formal ceremony but Ruthie overruled him, accepting a wedding at the Waldorf, small but very elegant, as a last wallowing in luxury. It cost twenty-four hundred dollars. Saul agreed to accept the other six hundred dollars in the name of the *kibbutz*. It became the basis of a larger fund that grew out of wedding presents which either came in as cash or were exchanged, since there are not many gifts suitable for a bride and groom about to start their life together in a socialized desert village. Michael gave Ruth an antique chamber pot and added twenty dollars to the *kibbutz* fund. At the wedding he drank too much champagne and danced a medley of numbers with his right leg between Mimi Steinmetz's thighs, bringing a flush into her high-boned cheeks and a sparkle into her kitten's eyes.

The ceremony was performed by Rabbi Joshua Greenberg of Sons of Jacob Synagogue. He was a spare, well-dressed man with a carefully trimmed goatee, a silky declamation style, and a habit of rolling his *r*s in moments of high emotion, as when he asked Ruthie if she would love, honor-r-r, and obey. In the middle

of the ceremony Michael found himself comparing Rabbi Greenberg to Rabbi Max Gross. Both of them were Orthodox, but there
the similarity ceased with an almost comical abruptness. Rabbi
Greenberg enjoyed a salary of thirteen thousand dollars a year.
His services were attended by well-dressed middle-class men
who grumbled when it came time to make donations to the *shul*
but who made them nevertheless. He drove a four-door Plymouth
sedan which he traded for a new car every two years. He and
his wife and their plump daughter spent three weeks every
summer at a kosher resort in the Catskills, where he paid their
bill in part by conducting services on *shabbos*. When they enter-
tained in their Queens apartment, which was in a new co-
operative building, the linens were snowy and the silver service
was sterling.

Let's face it, Michael told himself, watching as the Rabbi
gave the nuptial cup of wine first to Ruthie and then to Saul,
compared to Rabbi Greenberg, Rabbi Gross is a shabby bum.

And then the glass, wrapped in a napkin to catch the flying
shards, was shattered under Saul's piledriver heel and his sister
kissed the stranger and people surged forward. *Mazel tov!*

Not content with killing Michael's people, Hitler succeeded
in ruining his sex life. The hat industry began to manufacture
military caps for the Army and the Navy and the union ejected
the Communists and refused to picket defense plants, so Farley
no longer traveled to Danbury and Edna never again invited him
to her apartment. Finally, at their request, on a cold Friday morning he accompanied them to City Hall and witnessed their marriage. He gave them a sterling tray he couldn't afford, with a
small card on which he had written "Knowing you has meant
one of the most important experiences in my life." Farley raised
his bushy eyebrows and said Michael would have to come to
dinner. Edna blushed and frowned and crushed the tray against
her breasts. After that he saw very little of the Farleys, even in
the Student Union. Eventually the episode in Edna's bed became
like an incident he had read in a book and he was once more a
virgin, restless and desiring.

One of his friends, a fellow named Maury Silverstein, was

trying for a place on the Queens College boxing team. One evening Michael went to the gym with him and sparred. Maury was
built like Tony Galento, but he was no wild-swinging ox, his
left flickered in and out like the tongue of a snake and his right
was a rocker. The idea of Michael's putting the gloves on with
him was to give him practice against a taller boxer with a lot
more reach. Silverstein treated Michael carefully at first, and
for several minutes it was an enjoyable experience. Then Maury
became overenthusiastic; the rhythm of the thudding gloves carried him past his restraints. All at once Michael was aware of
leather slamming into his body from all directions. Something
exploded on his mouth. He raised his gloves and another explosion in his midriff sent him crashing to the mat.

He sat there and gasped. Above him, Silverstein rocked on
the balls of his feet, his eyes veiled and his gloved hands still
raised. Then slowly the veil lifted and his hands were lowered;
he looked down at Michael in astonishment.

"Thanks, killer," Michael said.

Silverstein knelt, babbling apologies. In the shower Michael
felt sick, but afterward, toweling in the locker room, he caught
sight of his face in the mirror and felt a thrill of strange pride.
He had a fat lip and a red welt under his left eye. At Maury's
insistence they went to a walkdown cellar joint not far from the
campus, a place called The Pig's Eye. Their waitress was a skinny
redhead with improbably tilted breasts and slightly buck teeth.
As she served them she looked at Michael's battered face and
shook her head.

"Some ape made a pass at a lovely waitress and I flattened
him."

"Oh, sure," she said wearily. "Anyway, he should have murdered you, buttinsky. Can't waitresses have any fun?"

When she brought the second round of beers she dipped
some foam from the top of his glass and touched her cold, wet
fingertip to the bruise on his cheek.

"What time do you finish work?" he asked.

"In twenty minutes." They watched her little behind waggle
as she walked away.

Silverstein was trying not to reveal that he was excited.
"Listen," he said, "my folks are visiting my sister in Hartford.

The apartment's empty, the whole apartment. Maybe she can get another pig for me."

Her name was Lucille. While Michael telephoned to tell his mother that he would not be home, Lucille got another girl for Maury, a short blonde named Stella. She had thick ankles and she chewed gum, but Maury appeared to be eminently satisfied. In the taxi on the way to the apartment the girls sat in their laps and Michael noticed a small wen on the back of Lucille's neck. In the elevator they kissed and when she opened her mouth he tasted onion on the tip of her tongue.

From a closet Maury produced a bottle of Scotch and after two drinks together they separated, Maury and his girl going into what Michael assumed was the bedroom of the elder Silversteins, since it was adorned with a large double bed. Lucille and Michael settled down on the living-room couch. He became conscious of blackheads on her chin. The girl lifted her face for his kiss. In a little while she clicked off the light.

From the other room there came the sound of Silverstein's groan and a rush of giggling.

"Now, Lucille?" Stella shouted.

"Not now," Lucille called irritably.

He found that he had to think of other women, Edna Roth, Mimi Steinmetz, even Ellen Trowbridge. Throughout the entire subsequent act she lay motionless, nasally humming. April in Paris, he thought in bewilderment as he labored. When it was over they lay half-dozing until Lucille wriggled from under him.

"Now," she called gaily, walking naked toward the bedroom. As she entered, Stella slipped out. The maneuver was accomplished with the ease of practice at many similar parties, he realized suddenly. The switching excited him. But as the short, plump Stella came to him his fingers touched doughy flesh and he was struck by odor, not of woman but of unwashed flesh, and he was suddenly impotent.

"Wait a minute," he said. His clothes were in heap on the carpet at the foot of the couch. He picked them up and walked carefully through the dark apartment until he came to the foyer, where he dressed quickly, not bothering to lace his shoes.

"Hey," the girl called as he let himself out of the apartment. He took the elevator down and walked quickly away from the building. It was 2 A.M. He saw no taxis until he had walked more than half an hour; by that time he was only two blocks from home, but he took the cab anyway.

Happily, his parents were sleeping when he let himself into the Kind apartment. In the bathroom he brushed his teeth for a long time and then took a scalding shower, using a great deal of soap.

He felt no urge to sleep. In pajamas and robe he crept out of the apartment and as softly as a thief climbed the stairs to the roof. Walking on tiptoe in order not to wake the Waxmans, who lived in the top rear apartment, he went to a chimney and sat down with his back to the bricks.

He could taste spring in the wind. The sky was studded with stars and he held his head back and stared at them until the breeze made his eyes fill and the glowing white points of light circled and swam in his vision. There *has* to be more to it than that, he told himself. Maury had called the girls pigs, but if so he and Maury had been pigs, too. He swore that he would have no more sex until he fell in love. The stars were unusually bright. He smoked a cigarette and watched them, trying to imagine how they looked without the interfering lights of a city. What held them up there, he wondered, and then the automatic answers came; he remembered vaguely about mutual attractions, the force of gravity, Newton's First and Second Laws of Motion. But there were so many thousands, scattered at such vast distances, and so balanced, behaving so steadily, circling precisely in their orbits like the works of a giant, beautifully constructed clock. The laws in the textbooks weren't enough, there had to be something else, otherwise for him the beautiful complexity was meaningless and without passion, like loveless sex.

He started another cigarette with the old one and then flipped the butt over the edge of the roof. It glowed like a nova as it fell but he didn't notice it. He stood with his head thrown back, looking at the stars, trying to see something far beyond them.

That afternoon when he opened the door of the *Shaarai Shomayim* Synagogue an old man was talking quietly with Max Gross at the study table. Michael sat on a wooden folding chair in the rear row and waited patiently until the old man sighed, patted the rabbi's shoulder, struggled to his feet and left the *shul.* Then Michael walked to the table. Rabbi Gross peered up at him. "So?" he said. Michael said nothing. The rabbi continued to stare. Then he nodded in satisfaction.

"So." He reached into the mound of books on the table and selected a Gemara and the Pentateuchal commentary of Rashi. "Now we will study," he said kindly.

CHAPTER EIGHTEEN

It was five months before he broke his vow of chastity. Accompanying Maury to a *bar mitzvah* in Hartford—the *bar mitzvah* of Maury's brother-in-law's sister's son—he met the sister of the confirmee, a slim girl with black hair and very smooth white skin and thin, waxy nostrils. When they danced at the party that evening he noticed that her hair smelled sweet and clean, like soapy water that had dried in the sun. The two of them left the house and he drove Maury's Plymouth into a country road off the Wilbur Cross Parkway. He pulled the car under a huge chestnut tree whose lowest branches brushed the car roof and they kissed a lot until things happened without plot or plan. Afterward, sharing a cigarette, he told her that he had broken a promise to himself that this would never happen again until it was with a girl he loved.

He expected her to laugh but the girl seemed to think this was very sad. "You mean it?" she said. "Really?"

"Really. And I don't love you," he said, adding hastily, "how could I? I mean, I hardly know you."

"I don't love you, either. But I like you a lot," she said. "Won't that do?" They both agreed it was the next best thing.

That summer, the summer of his junior year, he worked as

an assistant in a laboratory on campus, washing glassware, wiping down and storing microscopes, setting up equipment for experiments whose purposes or outcome he never learned. At least three times a week he studied with Rabbi Gross. Abe questioned him eagerly when he came home from work. "So, how's Einstein?"

His answers failed to disguise his lack of enthusiasm, his disappointed disinterest toward physics and science in general. Several times on these occasions he felt that Abe had something to say to him, but his father always stopped before he began and Michael didn't press him. Finally, on a Sunday morning two weeks before school reopened, at Abe's suggestion they drove to Sheepshead Bay, where they rented a boat and bought a shoebox full of wicked-looking seaworms. When Michael had rowed out far enough to satisfy his father they dropped bottom rigs and the flounders cooperated with Abe's desire to talk by not even nibbling.

"So what's going to happen next year at this time?"

Michael opened two bottles of beer and handed one to his father. They were not very cold and the foam spilled over. "To whom, Pop?"

"To you, that's to whom." He looked at Michael. "You spent three years studying physics, all about how everything is made up of little pieces that you can't see. And now you're going back for another year. But you don't like it. I can tell." He drank some beer. "Right? Or Wrong?"

"Right."

"So, what will it be? Medicine? Law? You got the marks. You got the brains. I got enough money to make a doctor or a lawyer. Take your pick."

"No, Pop." Two desperate jerks pulled the line in his hands and he hauled dripping lengths of it into the boat, glad for something to do.

"Michael, you're older now. Maybe you understand certain things better. Have you forgiven me?"

Damn it, he thought savagely. "For what?"

"You know very well what I'm talking about. For the girl." There was nowhere to look but the water, with the bright sun reflecting to hurt his eyes. "Forget that. It doesn't do any good to hang on to things like that."

"No. I must ask you. Have you forgiven me?"

"I've forgiven you. Now—*let it go.*"

"Listen. Listen to me." He could hear the relief in his father's voice, the excitement and the rising hope. "This shows how close we really are, you and me, to be able to survive something like that. We got a business in our family that's always given us the best of everything. A good business."

At the end of the line was a fish the size of a dinner plate. When Michael hauled it into the boat it thrashed, knocking over the bottle of beer and sending foaming liquid spilling onto one of his sneakers.

"Once I thought I could do it," Abe said. "But I'm of the old school, I don't know big business. I got to admit it. But *you*—you could go to Harvard Business for a year, come back full of modern methods, and Kind Foundations could be a leader in the industry. What I always dreamed of."

To control the flopping of the fish Michael placed the foot with the beer-wet sneaker on the flounder's mottled brown flatness, feeling the fluttering spasms through the thin rubber sole. The fish was hooked deeply. Its white, blind side was down, and both dark goggle-eyes looked up at him, still bright and unglazed.

Michael spoke the words quickly. "Don't Pop. I'm sorry." He started to twist out the hook, hoping that it wouldn't hurt but feeling the tearing of the flesh as the barb pulled free.

"I'm going to be a rabbi," he said.

CHAPTER NINETEEN

Temple Emanuel of Miami Beach was a large brick building with white Georgian columns and wide steps of white marble. Over the years the crystals in the marble had been worn by the feet of worshipers until they were highly polished, causing the stairs to glitter in the strong Florida sun. Within the building there was air conditioning that was almost noiseless, a sanctuary of seemingly endless rows of red plush seats, a soundproofed ballroom, a complete kitchen, an incomplete library of Jewish reading, and a small but carpeted office for the assistant rabbi.

Michael sat in misery behind a polished desk that was only a few square inches smaller than the desk in the larger office down the hall, the domain of Rabbi Joshua L. Flagerman. He frowned as the telephone rang. "Hello?"

"May I speak to the rabbi?"

"Rabbi Flagerman?" He hesitated. "He isn't here," he said finally. He gave the caller the rabbi's home telephone number. The man thanked him and hung up.

He had been on the job for three weeks, or just long enough to ascertain that he had made a mistake in becoming a rabbi. His five years as a rabbinical student at the Jewish Institute of Religion had sadly misled him.

He had shone at the rabbinical school. "Like a jewel among the Reform pebbles," Max Gross commented bitterly on one occasion. Gross didn't try to hide his sense of betrayal over the fact that Michael had chosen Reform as the vehicle for his rabbinate. They remained bound by spiritual ties, but their relationship never became what it might have been if Michael had become an Orthodox rabbi. He had found it difficult to explain his choice. He knew only that the world was changing quickly and Reform seemed to him the best available way to handle the change.

During the summers he worked in a settlement house in lower Manhattan, trying to throw straws of faith to children who were drowning in invisible seas. Some of them were kids whose fathers were away in the military and whose mothers worked double shifts in war plants or brought home a variety of unfamiliar, very temporary "uncles" in uniform. He learned to recognize the bouncy walk and the dilated pupils of the teenage junkie who was high, and the spastic limb control and the jerky gum-chewing of the tortured juvenile who was hung up without a supply. He watched childhood being ground down by ugliness. Once in a very great while he was conscious that he had helped someone in a very small way. The realization prevented him from quitting in favor of a counseling job at a summer camp.

He had finished three semesters at the rabbinical school when the Japanese attacked Pearl Harbor. Most of his friends enlisted or were quickly sucked into the funnel of Selective Service. Theological students were exempted from the draft; half a dozen boys resigned from the school and got into uniform. The others, Michael among them, were convinced by their advisors that rabbis would be needed more than ever in the days ahead. For the most part he felt regret, as if he had been cheated out of an adventure that was rightfully his. In those days he believed in death but not in dying.

Nevertheless, when he received occasional letters from places with names that were unfamiliar and sometimes unpronounceable they seemed exciting and romantic. Maury Silverstein kept in touch. He had entered the Marine Corps as an enlisted man slated for Officer Candidate School at Quantico as soon as he finished boot training. He boxed a little at Paris Island, and during one bout he and his drill instructor somehow became entangled in a grudge feud, the details of which never were described to Michael. What Maury did say in a letter was that several weeks later he and his enemy met with bare knuckles outside the ring. As a matter of fact it was outside the gymnasium, or to be more exact, behind it, with his entire squad yelling approval as he broke the jaw of the other man, who was a corporal. The corporal had removed the shirt that bore his stripes and no formal disciplinary action was taken, but from then on the other DIs bore down heavily on the trainee who had made one of their number useless as a molder of men. Silverstein was placed on report at the slightest hint of a rules infraction, and his expectations of becoming an officer soon vanished. When he left boot camp he received a few weeks of instruction as a mule skinner and then he was placed in charge of a short-legged mule with a fat behind. He named the animal Stella for sentimental reasons, he told Michael in the last letter he wrote in the United States. He and Stella were shipped out together to an unnamed and presumably mountainous Pacific island where he languished, hinting by V-mail of phenomenal lechery with native women. Respect for the cloth, he wrote, prevented him from revealing these exploits in their fullest detail.

During Michael's last year at the Institute he was assigned to assist in the high-holiday ceremonies at a temple in Rockville, Long Island. The services went without a hitch and he felt that at long last he was truly a rabbi. He began to ooze a cocky self-confidence. Then, three weeks before graduation and ordination, the Institute placement service arranged for him to be interviewed by Temple Emanuel in Miami, where they were looking for an assistant rabbi. He preached a guest sermon at a Friday-night service. He had written the sermon carefully and polished his delivery in front of his bedroom mirror. It had been praised by his faculty advisor; he knew that the sermon had power and style. When he was introduced in Miami, he felt ready. He greeted Rabbi Flagerman and the congregation in a strong voice. Then he gripped the speaker's platform with both hands and leaned forward slightly.

"What is a Jew?" he began.

Upturned faces in the front of the hall looked at him with such mute expectancy that he found it necessary to shift his glance. But wherever he looked, in every row, there were faces turned up at him. Some were old, some were young, some were unmarked, some were furrowed by experience. He was paralyzed by the realization of what he was doing. Who am I, he asked himself, to tell them anything, anything at all?

The pause grew into a silence, and still he could not speak. It was worse than the day he was *bar mitzvah*. He grew numb. His tongue clove to the roof of his mouth. In the back of the hall a girl tittered, the small sound causing people to shuffle their feet.

Through sheer will power he forced himself to talk. Stumbling several times, he hurried through the sermon. Afterward he made desperate small talk and then took a taxi to the airport. Stolid with despair, he looked out the window most of the way back to New York, merely grunting his refusals when the red-haired stewardess offered coffee or liquor. That night, travel-weary, he found escape in sleep, but the next morning he lay in bed and wondered how he had become trapped in a calling for which he had no shred of talent.

During the next week he reviewed the alternatives to the rabbinate. The war with Germany had already ended and Japan could not hold out very long; it would be sheer anticlimax to enlist now. He could teach; but the prospect made him melancholy. That left only Kind Foundations. He was screwing up sufficient courage for a talk with Abe when a wire came from the hiring committee of the Florida congregation. They were not quite sure; would he be willing to visit them again at their expense and preach another sermon on the coming week end?

Queasy of stomach, filled with self-loathing, he made another trip to Miami. This time, although his knees trembled and he was certain his voice quavered, he reeled off the sermon on schedule.

Two days later the call came.

His duties were uncomplicated. He conducted the children's service. He assisted the rabbi on the Sabbath. He read the back issues of the temple bulletin. At the request of Rabbi Flagerman he worked on a catalog of rabbinical literature. During the day, when both the older rabbi and his secretary were present, Michael did not answer the telephone, which rang simultaneously on all three of their lines. But if he was in the office in the evening, when they were not there, he took the calls. If someone wanted the rabbi, he gave out Rabbi Flagerman's home number.

He made some pastoral visits to members of the congregation who were ill. Because he didn't know Miami, members of the Temple Youth Group drove him. One afternoon his chauffeur was a blonde sixteen-year-old named Toby Goodman. Her father was a wealthy meatpacker with his own herds in the grazing country around St. Petersburg. She was very tanned and she wore white shorts and halter and drove a long blue convertible. She asked him wide-eyed questions about the Bible which he answered with great seriousness, even though he knew that she was laughing at him. While he made his calls she waited patiently in the car, parking in the shade when it was available and eating melting candy bars and reading a paperback whodunit with a sexy cover. When the calls were completed they headed back toward the temple in silence. He watched her while she tooled the car slowly through the crowded streets.

Everywhere there were uniforms. Miami was full of overseas veterans attending the rest and rehabilitation centers in the famous hotels that lined the beach. They filled the streets, strolling singly or in groups and marching loosely in double files to attend a lecture or a movie.

"Get out of the way," the girl muttered. She threw the shift into neutral and gunned the motor, causing three Air Force men to leap aside hurriedly.

"Take it easy," Michael said mildly. "They didn't make it home just to be run down by a rabbi making pastoral calls."

"All they do is lie around in the sun and whistle and make remarks about how they just saw you in a film." She giggled. "I have a boy friend in the Navy, you know? He was home last month. He never wore anything but civvies. We drove these guys nuts."

"How?"

She appraised him, narrow-eyed. Then, making up her mind, she braked swiftly and leaned past him to fumble in the glove compartment. When she straightened up, she held a half-filled gin bottle in her hand. Forty feet away, a double line of men, many of them wearing Combat Infantry Badges, filed slowly by in the hot sun. They looked up when she whistled shrilly. Before Michael knew what she was doing, she had thrown one arm around his shoulders, the hand at the end of it waggling the bottle enticingly.

"*He's* 4-F!" she called mockingly at the marching men. Then she kissed the top of his head.

The convertible jolted so hard he was thrown back against the seat as the car roared away. Even so, he preferred the rough ride to the alternative. The file of GIs had broken at once. Some of them chased the long blue car for half a block. The girl shook with laughter, appearing not to hear the words shouted by the running men.

He sat in silence until she pulled the car to a halt in front of the temple.

"You're mad, huh?"

"That doesn't quite describe it," he said carefully. He got out of the car.

"Hey, that's my bottle." He was holding it by the neck, having picked it up from the seat where she had dropped it.

"You can claim it when you're twenty-one." He marched up the stairs and into the temple. The telephone was ringing. When he answered it a woman asked to speak to the rabbi and he gave her Rabbi Flagerman's home number.

There was a package of paper cups in the bottom drawer of his desk. Pouring a stiff shot, about three fingers, from the girl's bottle, he swallowed the drink in a gulp, then he stood with his shoulders slumped and his eyes closed.

It was warm water.

Two nights later, Toby Goodman telephoned and apologized. He accepted her apology but refused her offer to drive for him the next day. A few minutes later the telephone rang again.

"Rabbi?" The voice was strangely hoarse.

When Michael gave Rabbi Flagerman's number, a panting like the sound of a tired dog came from the phone.

He began to smile. "Whom do you think you're kidding, Toby?" he said.

"I'm going to kill myself."

The voice was male.

"Where are you?" Michael asked.

The address was garbled. Michael made him repeat it. He knew the street, it was only a couple of blocks away.

"Don't do anything. I'll be right there. *Please.*" He ran outside and stood on the marble stairs, praying while he tried to hail passing taxis. When he found one that was empty he sat on the edge of the seat and tried to think of something, anything, to say to a man who was afraid to live. But his mind was a blank when the cab pulled up in front of a stucco bungalow. He handed the driver a bill and without waiting for change ran across a parched and sandy lawn, up three steps and through a screened porch.

The sign over the bell said Harry Lefcowitz. The door was open and the screen door was unlocked.

"Mr. Lefcowitz?" he called softly. There was no answer.

He pushed the door open and went inside. The living room smelled of sourness. Opened bottles and half-filled glasses of beer were on the window sills. Bananas rotted in a glass bowl on the table. The ashtrays were filled with cigar stubs. An Army shirt hung over the back of a chair. There were sergeant's chevrons on the sleeves.

"Mr. Lefcowitz?" There was a small sound behind one of the doors leading off the living room. He pushed it open.

A short, slight man in khaki pants and a tee shirt sat on the bed. His feet were bare. He had a thin mustache that was almost lost in the stubble of his unshaven face. His eyes were red and sad. In his hand was a small black pistol.

"You're a cop," he said.

"No. I'm not. I'm a rabbi. You called me, remember?"

"You're not Flagerman." There was a loud *click* as the pistol's safety was released.

Inwardly Michael groaned, realizing that he had confirmed his knowledge of his rabbinical ineptness. He had not called the police. He had not even left a note at the temple to inform anyone of his whereabouts.

"I'm Rabbi Flagerman's assistant. I want to help." The pistol came up slowly until it was pointed straight at his face. The round opening at the end was obscene. The man played a game with the safety, clicking it off and on. "Get your ass out of here," he said.

Michael sat down on the unmade bed, trembling only slightly.

Outside it was dark.

"What would it solve, Mr. Lefcowitz?"

The man looked at him narrowly. "You think I won't kill you, hero? Why, it should bother me, after what I've seen? I'll kill you and then I'll kill myself." He looked at Michael's face and laughed. "You don't know what I know. It won't make any difference. The world will still go on."

Michael leaned toward him. His outstretched hand was a gesture of compassion, but the man saw it as a threat. He jammed the muzzle of the pistol into Michael's cheek. It was bruising and painful.

"You know where I got this gun? I took it off a dead German. His head was half shot off. It can do the same to you." Michael said nothing. In a few minutes the man took the gun out of his cheek. With his fingertips Michael could feel the little ○ the muzzle had indented in his flesh. They sat and looked at one another. Michael's watch ticked loudly.

The man began to laugh. "That was a lot of crap, what I just said. I seen plenty of dead Germans, and I spit on some, but I never took anything from their bodies. I bought the gun for three cartons of Lucky Strikes. I wanted to have something to give the kid, something he could keep." Lefcowitz scratched his foot with his free hand. His feet were long and bony, with crisp black hairs on the knuckles of his big toes.

Michael looked into his eyes. "A lot of this little act is a lot of crap, Mr. Lefcowitz. Why should you want to hurt me? I simply want to be your friend. And it would be even worse to do harm to yourself." He tried a smile. "I think it's a joke of some sort. I think the gun isn't even loaded."

The man raised the pistol and, in the same split second that the report sounded monstrously loud in the small room, his hand jumped slightly and a small black hole appeared in the white ceiling over their heads.

"There were seven," Lefcowitz said. "Now there are six. More than enough. So don't think, Sonny. Sit there and keep your mouth shut."

Neither spoke for a long time. It was a quiet night. Michael could hear an occasional automobile horn and the slow, steady sound of the surf on the nearby beach. Someone must have heard the shot, he assured himself. They are bound to come soon.

"Do you ever get lonesome?" Lefcowitz asked suddenly.

"All the time."

"Sometimes I get so lonesome I could bawl."

"We're all that way sometimes, Mr. Lefcowitz."

"Yeah? Then why not?" He looked at the pistol and shook it. "When you come right down to it, why not?" He grinned mirthlessly. "Now's your chance to talk about God, or guts."

"No. There's a simpler reason. That"—Michael touched the gun with his fingertips, moving it slightly so that it no longer pointed at him—"is final, irreversible. There would be no chance to decide that you had been wrong. And although there is a lot of ugliness in the world, there are times when it's wonderful to be alive. Just getting a drink of water when you're very thirsty, or seeing something beautiful, anything at all that's beautiful. The good times make up for the bad times."

For a moment Lefcowitz looked less certain. But he moved the pistol so that it once more was aimed at Michael. "I don't get thirsty very often," he said.

He was silent for a long time and Michael didn't try to make him talk. Once two boys ran by the house, hooting and shouting, and the man's face worked curiously.

"Are you a fisherman?"

"Not a very active one," Michael said.

"I was just thinking that I've had good times, like you said, while I was fishing. With the water and sun and all."

"Yes."

"That's why I came here in the first place. I was a kid, working in a shoe store in Erie, P-A. I drove down to Hialeah with a bunch of guys and won forty-eight hundred dollars. The money was nice, but what did I know from money, I had no responsibilities in those days. It was the fishing. I caught sea trout all day long. Those guys thought I was nuts when I wouldn't go back with them. I got a job tending bar in a joint on the Beach. I had fishing and sun and broads in bathing suits, and I knew I was in paradise."

"You were a bartender when you were drafted?"

"Had my own place. There was this guy who worked with me. Nick Mangano. He had a few tips put away, and with what I had we took over a clam bar with a liquor license on that fishing wharf they call Murphy's Pier. Do you know it?"

"No."

"We saved our dough and a few years later we spread out, a larger joint with some booths and a piano player. It worked out very nice. I was married by then and I took the day shift. All day long I got fishermen, mostly old men. There are a lot of old people here. They make a very good brand of customer, a couple of quiet jolts every day and never any trouble. And at night Nick would be here with another guy we hired, to take care of the swinging crowd."

"It sounds like a good business."

"You married?"

"No."

Lefcowitz was silent for a moment. "I married a *shickseh*," he said. "An Irish girl."

"Are you still in the Army?"

"Yeah, I got rest and rehabilitation coming, and then a discharge." His mouth worked slightly. "See, when I was drafted I gave Nick power of attorney. He's got a funny heart, it kept him out. So for four years he's been running the joint alone, keeping open twenty-four hours a day."

He began to droop. His voice became furry around the edges. "See, I expected to walk into that joint and get at least a little coming-home party from my pal Nick. It's funny, in Naples I even treated the wop babes with respect. I figured Nick would like that when I tell him. So the whole place is closed, boarded up. Everything's cleaned out of the bank." He looked at Michael and grinned, his eyes full and his lips trembling. "But that's the *funny* part.

"Right here he was living, all the time I was overseas. Right here in this house."

"Are you sure?"

"Mister, I've been *told*. And told. At a time like this, you'd be surprised at how many talkative friends you have. They come out of the cracks."

"Where are they now?"

"The boy's missing. She's missing. He's missing. The money's missing. No forwarding address. Everything clean as a picked bone."

Michael fought for words that might help but he could think of nothing.

"See, I knew she was a bimbo when I married her. I figured, so who's an angel, I've lived too, maybe we can make it brand-new together. So we didn't, that's life, about her I don't care. But the kid was named Samuel. *Shmuel*, after my father, *alev hasholom*. They're both Catholics. That's one kid who will never be *bar mitzvah*."

He groaned, and it was like the breaking of a dam. "My God, I'm never going to see that kid again." He threw himself forward, his head striking Michael's shoulder and almost knocking him off the bed. Michael held him tightly and rocked, saying nothing. After a long while he reached down and with great gentleness removed the gun from the slack fingers. He had never held a gun before. It was surprisingly heavy. Over the man's head he read the raised printing on the barrel: SAUER U. SOHN, SUHL, CAL 7.65. He set it down on the bed beside them. He continued to rock. With his right hand he held the man's head to his shoulder, stroking the matted hair. "Cry," he said. "Cry, Mr. Lefcowitz."

When the Military Police let him off at the temple it was still dark. He found that he had left without locking the door or shutting the lights and he was glad he had come back instead of going straight to his roominghouse; Rabbi Flagerman might have been annoyed. In his office the air conditioner was still going at full speed. The night air was chill and the temperature in the room was uncomfortably low. He switched the air conditioner off.

He fell asleep at his desk, his head in his arms.

When the telephone jolted him awake the clock on his desk said eight-fifty-five. His bones ached and his mouth was dry. Outside, the sun was hot and yellow. Already the humidity was uncomfortable. He switched on the air conditioning before he lifted the telephone.

It was a woman. "May I speak to the rabbi?" she asked.

He stifled a yawn and sat up straighter.

"Which one?" he said.

CHAPTER TWENTY

Not quite a year after he had come to Miami, Michael flew to New York to help Rabbi Joshua Greenberg of Sons of Jacob Synagogue officiate at the marriage ceremony of Mimi Steinmetz and a certified public accountant who had just been made a junior partner in her father's firm. As the marriage was made and the couple kissed he felt a flash of regret and desire, not for the girl but for a wife, someone to love. He danced the *kezatski* with the bride and then drank too much champagne.

One of his former professors at the Institute, Rabbi David Sher, was now with the Union of American Hebrew Congregations. Two days after the wedding Michael paid him a visit.

"Kind!" Rabbi Sher said, rubbing his palms briskly. "Just the man I'm looking for. I have a job for you."

"Good job?"

"Lousy job. *Miserable.*"

What the devil, Michael thought, I'm awfully tired of Miami. "I'll take it," he said.

He had thought that circuit-riding ministers were an oddity out of the Protestant past.

"Hebrew hillbillies?" he exclaimed.

"Jews in the Ozarks," Rabbi Sher said. "Seventy-six families in the mountains of Missouri and Arkansas."

"There are temples in Missouri and Arkansas."

"In the lowlands and in the larger communities. But nothing in the region I'm talking about. The rough country, where an occasional lone Jew keeps a general store or runs a fishing camp."

"But you said lousy. It sounds wonderful."

"You'll travel a twisting circuit five hundred miles through the hills. There aren't going to be hotels wherever you need them, you'll have to live off the land. Most of your congregation will welcome you with open arms, but some of them will

send you away, some of them don't care. You'll be on the road all
the time."

"A portable rabbi."

"A rabbinical hobo." Rabbi Sher went to a filing cabinet
and took out a manila folder. "Here's a list of things to buy;
you can charge it all to the Union. A station wagon goes with
the job. You'll need a sleeping bag and other camping equipment." He grinned broadly. "And, Rabbi—when you get the car,
have them put on the heaviest shock absorbers made."

Four weeks later, he was in the mountains, having driven
the sixteen hundred miles from Miami in two days. The station
wagon was a year old, but it was a big rugged green Oldsmobile,
and he had had it outfitted with heavy-duty shocks that looked
strong enough to support a tank. Thus far Rabbi Sher's gloomy
portents had not materialized; the roads were good and easy to follow on his map and the weather was so mild that he continued to
wear his Florida clothing, ignoring the mounds of winter gear piled
high in the back of the car. The first name on his list was George
Lilienthal, a lumber operations manager whose address was
Spring Hollow, Arkansas. As he drove through the foothills and
the roadway's angle of elevation became more marked, his
spirits rose. He traveled slowly, enjoying the scenery: hard-
scrabble farms with log cabins, houses with silvery plank ex-
teriors, rail fences, an occasional mining town or factory building.

At four in the afternoon it began to spit snow and he felt
cold. He stopped at a filling station—a farm barn with two
pumps—and changed into warmer clothing in the barn while an
old man with a wrinkled face filled his gas tank. The notes
Michael had made in the Union office said that Spring Hollow
was seventeen miles by dirt road beyond Harrison. But the old
man shook his head when Michael tried to confirm this.

"No. You want to take sixty-two up beyond Rogers and then
cut east a few miles beyond Monte Ne. Gravel road. If you'uns
get lost, just ask a person."

By the time he turned off the highway beyond Rogers he
could only guess that the new road was gravel-covered, since its
surface was hidden by snow. The wind blew in gusts that rocked
the station wagon and sent icy pockets of air in through the tops

of the windows. The clothing that had been on Rabbi Sher's list was adequate, he observed thankfully. He wore heavy boots, cord slacks, woolen shirt, sweater, lined suede jacket, gloves, and a cap with ear flaps.

The heavy snow came just as darkness fell. Sometimes on curves he could see his headlight beams shine straight ahead into dark emptiness. He was conscious that he knew nothing about the mountains or how to drive over them at night. At first he pulled over to the side of the road and parked, thinking to sit the storm out. But it grew very cold. He started the car's motor and turned the heater to high, only to find himself wondering whether there was enough ventilation, whether next morning his stiff body might be found within the car (*motor still running, State Police said*). In any event, it occurred to him, the parked car was a prime obstacle for any vehicle that might come rolling out of the dark and the snow. So he drove, very slowly, until he topped a rise and in the distance saw a yellow square of light that subsequently proved to be the window of a farmhouse. He parked the car under a large tree and knocked at the farmhouse door. The man who answered looked nothing like Li'l Abner. He wore jeans and a heavy brown work shirt. When Michael explained his predicament the man asked him in.

"Jane," he called. "Man here needs a bed for the night. Can we he'p?"

The woman came slowly into the cabin's front room. Beyond her, Michael could see yellow light through the chinks of a pot-bellied stove in the kitchen. The house was very cold. There was a lantern hung from a nail.

"You bring a deck of cards?" Her hands pinched together the buttonless coat sweater she wore.

"No," he said. "I'm sorry. I don't have playing cards."

Her mouth was severe. "This is a good Christian home. We don' allow no cards 'r no whiskey."

"Yes, ma'am."

In the kitchen he sat at a rickety table that looked hand-hewn and she warmed up a plate of stew. The meat tasted strange and strong, but he lacked the courage to ask what it was. When he had eaten, the man took the lantern and led him into a pitch-black back room.

"Hyah, get out there," the man grumbled. A large yellow dog, yawning, reluctantly left the narrow cot. "She's all yours, Mister," he said.

When he had closed the door behind him, taking with him all light, Michael decided against removing his clothes. It was very cold. He unlaced and slipped off his boots and then he settled into the bed under covers that were ragged and did not hold enough warmth. They smelled very heavily of dog.

The mattress was thin and packed into bumps and furrows. He lay for several hours without sleeping, tasting the greasiness of the stew, cold and unable to believe where he was. At midnight, there was a scratching at his door. The dog, he thought, but it opened under a human hand and he saw with some alarm that it was his host.

"Hsst," the man said, his finger to his lips. In his other hand he carried a jug. He left it and disappeared without a word.

It was the worst drink Michael had ever had, but strong as an explosion and very warming. It took only four swallows to make him sleep as though he were dead.

When he awoke in the morning neither man, woman, or dog was in the house. He left three dollars at the foot of the bed. His head ached and he no longer wanted the jug but he was afraid that the woman would find it. He carried it into the woods beyond the cabin and left it in the snow, hoping the man would come across it before it was discovered by his wife.

The car started with a minimum of coaxing. Before he had driven a mile he saw how wise he had been to have stopped for the night. The road grew progressively narrower. It climbed. On the left of the car there was always the side of the mountain, studded with outcroppings of rock. On the right the drop from the shoulder was sheer, offering a swooping view of a snow-covered valley with peaks thrusting beyond and ridges on both sides. The hairpin turns were slushy and covered by melting ice in spots. He made them gingerly, certain that beyond each bend the road ended in a cliff over which he and his car would fall a great distance.

It was mid-afternoon before he drove into Spring Hollow.

George Lilienthal was out in the woods with the lumbering crews, but his wife, Phyllis, greeted Michael like a newfound relative. They had been watching for the rabbi's arrival for days, she told him.

The Lilienthals lived in a three-bedroom house owned by the Ozarks Lumber Corporation. It had a good hot-water system, a refrigerator and freezer, and a hi-fi set they claimed to be wearing out. By the time George Lilienthal came home for supper the rabbi had soaked in a hot bath for an hour, had shaved, and changed his clothing; glass in hand, he was listening to Debussy. George was thirty-seven, a big, beaming man who had done graduate work at Syracuse in reforestation. Phyllis was an immaculate housekeeper whose soft spreading hips advertised that she liked her own cooking. Michael said the blessings during the meal. Afterward he led them in prayer, sharing a *siddur* with Bobby, their son. The boy was already eleven years old; he had only twenty months before his *bar mitzvah*; yet he could not read a Hebrew word. Michael spent the entire afternoon with him on the following day, teaching him the Hebrew alphabet. He left an *aleph-bez* with Bobby, and a lesson assignment to be completed before his next visit.

Next morning George started him down a logging road that would take him toward his next stop.

"You shouldn't have a hard trip," the lumberman said anxiously as he shook hands. "Of course, you'll have to ford two or three streams and the water's kind of high this time of year. . . ."

At a place called Swift Bend the general store overlooked the river, which flowed cold and fast, flecked with ugly gray chunks of ice. A bearded man wearing a brown plaid mackinaw was unloading bundles from the back of a 1937 Ford coupé. The bundles were composed of stacked and cord-tied pelts of some kind of small, furry animal, or perhaps several kinds. The pelts were stiff with cold, and the man was arranging the bundles in piles on the porch of the general store.

"Is this Edward Gold's store?" Michael asked.

The man continued to work. "Yep."

Inside, there was a stove and it was warm. Michael waited

while the woman behind the counter dipped three pounds of unbleached flour into a brown paper sack for a young girl. When she looked at him he saw that she was a mountain woman, or rather a girl, skinny and freckled, but with rough skin and chapped lips.

"Is Edward Gold around?"

"Who is wantin' to know?"

"I'm Rabbi Michael Kind. Mr. Gold got a letter telling him that I would be coming by to see him."

She looked at him coldly. "You are talkin' to his woman. We got no use for no rabbi."

"Is your husband here, Mrs. Gold? Could I talk with him for a few moments?"

"We got no need for no religion of your'n," she said fiercely. "Can't you understand?"

He tipped his cap and left.

As he got into the station wagon he was hailed softly by the man who was piling skins on the porch. He sat and let the motor warm as the man approached.

"You the rabbi?"

"Yes."

"I'm Ed Gold." The man pulled the leather mitten from his right hand with his teeth and dug into his pants pocket beneath the mackinaw. He pressed something into Michael's hand.

"That's the best I can do," he said as he pulled the mitten back on. "You better not come back here anymore." He walked quickly to the Ford and drove away.

Michael sat there and looked after him. In his palm were two one-dollar bills.

He mailed them back to the man when he got to the next town.

When he had completed the circuit he had nineteen Hebrew students, ranging in age from seven to sixty-three, the latter a trailer-camp operator who hadn't been *bar mitzvah* as a boy and who wanted to be before he was sixty-five. Wherever Michael found a Jew who was receptive, he conducted religious services. Great distances separated the members of his "congregation."

In one long haul he had to drive eighty-seven difficult miles between one Jewish home and another. He learned to get off the road at the first sign of snow, and he found shelter in a variety of mountain homes. One night when he mentioned this to Stan Goodstein, a miller whose family was one of his regular stops, Goodstein gave him a key and some road directions.

"Whenever you pass Big Cedar Hill, stay at my hunting lodge," he said. "It's stocked with plenty of canned food. The only thing you must remember there is that if it snows, get out fast or settle down to stay until the snow melts. You have to drive over a suspension bridge. Once snow piles up on the bridge it's an impossibility to get a car over."

Michael stayed at the cabin on his next trip around the circuit. The bridge spanned a deep chasm cut over the years by a stream of racing white water. He sat stiffly when he drove across, gripping the steering wheel until his knuckles protruded and hoping that Goodstein had had the bridge inspected lately. It stood the test with no signs of weakness. The cabin was at the top of a worn-down mountain. The kitchen and the cupboard were complete and he made himself a very adequate meal, finishing off with three cups of strong, hot tea which he drank in front of a roaring fire he made in the stone fireplace. At dusk, dressed warmly, he walked through the nearby forest, preparing to say the *Shema*. The huge trees that gave the place its name rustled and sighed as the wind moved through their great branches. The foliage rose and fell as if the trees were old men, praying. Walking under them, praying aloud, he felt not in the least bit strange.

In the cabin he found half a dozen new corncob pipes in a bowl and a humidor of stale tobacco. He sat in front of the fire and puffed and thought. Outside, the wind began to pick up a bit. He felt snug and warm, at peace. When he grew sleepy he banked the fire and pulled the bed close to it.

Something dragged him awake just after 2 A.M. When he glanced out the window he knew at once what it was. The snow was light but driving. It could grow heavier within minutes, he knew. He lay back in the bed and groaned. For a moment he was tempted to close his eyes and return to sleep. If he were snowed in he could rest until the snow melted in three or four days. The prospect was tempting; the cabin had plenty of food and he was tired.

But he knew that if he were going to succeed in the mountains he would have to become a familiar figure to the people he visited. He forced himself to leave the warm bed and dress quickly.

When he reached the bridge it was already covered with a thin layer of white. Holding his breath and praying without words, he drove the car slowly onto the span. The wheels held; in a few moments he was across.

Twenty minutes later he came to a cabin with lights in its windows. The man who answered his door was dark and spare, with thinning hair. He listened impassively to Michael's statement about not wanting to drive in the snow and then held the door wide and motioned him in. It was now almost three o'clock in the morning, but three lanterns hung in the cabin's front room, a fire roared in the fireplace and a man, a woman, and two children sat around it.

Michael had hoped for a bed. They offered him a chair. The man who had answered the door introduced himself as Tom Hendrickson. The woman was his wife. The little girl, Ella, was their daughter. Tom's brother Clive sat with his boy Bruce. "This here's Mr. Robby Kind," Hendrickson told the others.

"No, that's *Rabbi* Kind," Michael said. "My first name is Michael. I'm a rabbi."

They stared. "What's that?" Bruce asked.

Michael smiled at the adults. "What I do for a living," he told the boy. They settled back in their chairs. From time to time Tom Hendrickson threw a pine knot at the fire. Michael glanced at his watch and wondered what was going on.

"We're sittin' up with our Maw," Hendrickson said.

Clive Hendrickson picked a violin and a bow from the floor by his chair. He leaned back, eyes closed, and began to fiddle softly, his foot tapping. Bruce whittled on a piece of soft pine, sitting close to the fire so that the thick, curling shavings fell into the flame. The woman was teaching her daughter a knitting stitch. They bent over their needles, talking in whispers. Tom Hendrickson stared into the fire.

Feeling more alone than he had when he had been in the

woods by himself, Michael slipped a small Bible from his jacket pocket and began to read.

"Mister."

Tom Hendrickson was looking at the Bible intently. "You a preacher?" The fiddling, the whittling, and the knitting stopped; five pairs of eyes stared at him.

He realized that they didn't know what a rabbi was. "You might say that," he said. "A kind of Old Testament preacher."

Tom Hendrickson took down one of the lanterns and motioned with his head. Mystified, Michael followed. In a small room at the rear of the cabin it became suddenly apparent why no one in that house slept. The old lady was long and spare, like her sons. Her hair was white, carefully combed, and tied in a bun. Her eyes were closed. Her features were composed, at least in death.

"I'm sorry," Michael said.

"She had a good life," Hendrickson said in a clear voice. "She was a good mother. She lived seventy-eight years. That's a long time." He looked at Michael. "Thing is, we got to get her buried. It's been two days. Preacher we used to have hereabouts died a couple of months ago. Clive and me were figuring on driving her clear over the mountain in the morning."

"She wanted to be buried here. I'd sure appreciate it if you could see your way clear to preach over her."

He felt impelled to laugh and cry, both at the same time. He did neither, of course. Instead, in a dry, matter-of-fact voice, he said: "You understand that I'm a *rabbi*? A Jewish rabbi?"

"Denomination don't matter. You're a preacher? A man of God?"

"Yes."

"Then we'd appreciate your help, Mister," Hendrickson said.

"I'm honored," Michael said helplessly. They returned to the front room.

"Clive, you're the best carpenter. There's everything you need in the shed for makin' the box. I'll go down to the buryin' ground." Hendrickson turned to Michael. "Will you be needin' anythin' special?"

"Just some books and things in my car." He spoke with more confidence than he felt. He had assisted at two funerals, both of them Jewish. This would be his first as officiating clergyman.

He went out of the station wagon and returned with his bag. Then he sat in front of the fire once again, this time alone. Bruce had gone with his father to make the coffin. Ella and her mother were mixing up a cake in the kitchen, for the funeral breakfast. Michael riffled through his books, seeking passages that would be appropriate.

From somewhere outside came the muffled thump of an instrument striking frozen earth.

He read the Bible for a long time without making up his mind. Then, drawn by the digging sound, he closed the book and put on his jacket and cap and boots. Outside, he followed the sound until he saw the glow of Hendrickson's lantern.

The man stopped digging. "Something you need?"

"I came to help. I'm not much of a carpenter, but I can dig."

"No, sir. No need of that." But when Michael took the pick from his hands he gave it up.

He had already removed the snow and the top frozen layer. The earth beneath it was soft but full of rocks. Michael grunted, lifting out a large one.

"Chert soil," Hendrickson said softly. "Full of flint. Best crop we got is stone."

The snow had stopped, but there was no moon. The lantern flickered but continued to glow.

Within a few minutes Michael was breathing hard. A band of pain stretched across his back and gripped each biceps. "I forgot to ask you," he said. "What was your mother's religion?"

Hendrickson moved down into the grave and motioned him out. "She was Methodist, Godfearing but not much of a churchgoer. My pap was raised a Baptist, but he hardly ever went that I can recollect." He pointed with the shovel to a grave a few feet away from the hole they were digging. "There he is over there. Died seven years back." For a while he dug in silence. A crow cawed and he straightened up and shook his head in disappointment. "That's a rain raven. Means we'll have moisture in the morning. I sure do hate a wet funeral."

"So do I."

"I was her second-to-least boy. The least one was named Joseph. He died when he was three years old. Fell out of a tree we was climbin' together." He looked at his father's grave. "He wasn't even at the funeral. See, he left us for a spell back there. Was gone fourteen months. Just up and went off one mornin'.

"She took care of us just as if he was here. She shot rabbits and squirrels so we always had meat. And kept a good garden. Then one day he came back, as nat'ral as though he never went. Till the day he died, we never did find out where he spent those fourteen months."

They swapped again. They were deeper now and there was less stone, Michael found.

"Mister, you one of them preachers dead set against drinkin'?"

"No, I'm not. Not at all."

The bottle had been set in the shadows just beyond the lantern's light. Hendrickson politely gave him first swallow. He was sweating from the work but a fresh breeze had begun to blow off the mountain and the liquor felt good.

The darkness was diluting when Michael helped Hendrickson clamber out of the completed grave. From far off the high, clear bell of a hound floated to them. Hendrickson sighed. "Gotta get me a good dog," he said.

The woman had heated water and they washed and changed their clothing. Perhaps the rain raven had been correct but premature; low gray clouds scudded across the mountaintops, but no rain fell. While they brought the pine box in from the shed, Michael selected his texts, marking the pages in the Bible with bits of torn newspaper. When he was ready he placed a *yarmulka* on his head and threw his coat around his shoulders.

The crow cawed again as they carried the box to the grave. The two sons lowered the coffin, and then the five of them stood there and looked at him.

"The Lord is my shepherd," he said. "I shall not want.

"He maketh me to lie down in green pastures: He leadeth me beside the still waters. He restoreth my soul. He guideth me in the paths of righteousness for His name's sake."

With her toe, the little girl moved a clod of earth until it disappeared into the grave. She jumped back, her face ashen.

"Yea, though I walk through the valley of the shadow of death, I will fear no evil; for Thou art with me; Thy rod and Thy staff, they comfort me. Thou preparest a table before me in the presence of mine enemies; Thou hast anointed my head with oil; my cup runneth over.

"Surely goodness and mercy shall follow me all the days of my life, and I will dwell in the house of the Lord for ever."

The little girl was holding her mother's hand.

"A Virtuous Woman who can find?" Michael asked. "For her price is far above rubies.

"The heart of her husband trusteth in her, and he shall have no lack of gain. She doeth him good and not evil all the days of her life. She seeketh wool and flax, and worketh willingly with her hands. She is like the merchant ships, she bringeth her food from afar. She riseth also while it is yet night, and giveth meat to her household, and their task to her maidens."

Clive Hendrickson looked down into his mother's grave. His arm was around his boy. Tom Hendrickson's eyes were closed. He pinched a fold of the flesh on his forearm between the tips of his fingers and the edge of his horny thumbnail.

"She considereth a field and buyeth it: with the fruit of her hands she planteth a vineyard. She girdeth her loins with strength, and maketh strong her arms. She perceiveth that her merchandise is profitable: her lamp goeth not out by night. She layeth her hands to the distaff, and her hands hold the spindle. She spreadeth out her hand to the poor; yea, she reacheth forth her hands to the needy.

"Strength and dignity are her clothing; and she laugheth at the time to come. She openeth her mouth with wisdom; and the law of kindness is on her tongue. She looketh well to the ways of her household, and eateth not the bread of idleness."

The first raindrop struck like an icy kiss on Michael's cheek.

"Her children rise up and call her blessed; her husband also, and he praiseth her: 'Many daughters have done virtuously, but thou excellest them all.' Favour is deceitful, and beauty is vain: But a woman that feareth the Lord, she shall be praised. Give her of the fruit of her hands; and let her works praise her in the gates."

It was beginning to spatter now, the drops smacking into the wet ground. "Let us each pray according to his own

fashion for the soul of the departed, Mary Bates Hendrickson,"
Michael said.

The two brothers and the woman sank to their knees in the
mud. Exchanging a frightened glance, the two children did like-
wise. The woman wept as she bowed her head. Standing over
them Michael spoke in a loud, clear voice the ancient Aramaic
words of the Hebrew prayer for the dead. Just before he finished,
drops the size of half-dollars began to drum steadily from the
heavens.

While the woman and the children scampered, softly
screeching, Michael stowed the Bible in his jacket pocket and
then helped the brothers pack the stones and wet earth back
into the hole, mounding the grave high against the pull of time.

After breakfast Clive began to play light airs on his fiddle
and the children laughed. They seemed relieved to say good-by.

"That was a fine funeral," Tom Hendrickson said. He held
out a dollar and one-half. "This is what we used to pay our
preacher, the one who died. Is it all right?"

Something in the man's eyes prevented Michael from
refusing the money. "It's generous. Thank you very much."

Hendrickson walked him out to the car. While the motor
warmed up he leaned on the half-open window. "This fella
I worked with one time on a big farm in Missouri?" he said.
"He told me Jews had nigger hair and two little horns growin'
up the tops o' their head. I always knew he was a dumb liar."
He shook hands hard.

Michael drove away slowly. The rain had melted the snow.
He reached a town in about forty minutes, stopping by the
single gas pump in front of Cole's General Merchandise (SEEDS,
FEEDS, DRY GOODS, GROCERIES) to fill the tank because he knew
the next pump was almost three hours away. Beyond the town
was a wide river. The ferryman took his quarter when he had
driven his car onto the raft and shook his head when Michael
asked about road conditions up ahead.

"Don't know," he said. "Ain't no one come over from there
yet today." He smacked his lead mule across the rump with
a willow switch and both his animals strained, turning a winch
which pulled the cabled raft into the stream.

He had driven for twenty minutes on the other side when he stopped and turned the car around. Back at the ford the man came out of his little shelter and stood in the rain. "Road out up there?"

"No," Michael said. "I forgot something."

"Won't be able to give you your money back."

"It's all right." He paid another quarter.

Back at Cole's General Merchandise he parked the car and entered the store. "Do you have a pay phone?"

It was located on the wall inside the door of a storeroom that smelled of moldy potatoes. He dialed for the operator and gave her the number. He had a lot of silver but not quite enough and he had to change the dollar bill that Hendrickson had given him, then he fed coins into the slot.

Outside, it began to pour; he could hear the rain thrumming on the roof.

"Hello? Hello, it's Michael. No, nothing's wrong. I just wanted to speak to you.

"How are you, Momma?"

CHAPTER TWENTY-ONE

Since the Arkansas mountains could not be visited from Massachusetts over long week ends and Hartford was only two hours away from the Wellesley campus, Deborah Marcus had gone home to Connecticut with Leslie Rawlins half a dozen times during their three-year friendship. At a New Year's party in Cambridge during their senior year, while kissing the man she loved and simultaneously on another level of consciousness worrying whether her parents would like him, Deborah had conceived the idea that Leslie could accompany her to Mineral Springs during their spring vacation, to lend her moral support while she told her mother and father about Mort.

Five weeks later, toweling her long bronze hair in the shower room of the deserted dormitory on a Saturday night when she should have had a date but didn't, Leslie noted that someone had blocked up the toilet again, causing it to overflow. This circumstance, although hardly a rare one, enraged her sufficiently to make a break in routine eminently attractive, and the next morning, while sleepily handing sections of the Boston Sunday *Herald* back and forth between their beds, she told her roommate that she would go with her to the Ozarks.

"Oh, Leslie!" Deborah stretched and yawned, then smiled radiantly. She was a large-boned girl, slightly topheavy, with pretty brown hair and dark features that were plain until she smiled.

"Will we have Passover?" Leslie asked.

"With all the trimmings. My mother's even going to have a rabbi, this year. You'll be a real Jew by the time vacation's over."

Ugh, Leslie thought. "Many are called but few are Chosen," she said, rattling the comics.

Mineral Springs proved to be just that—three springs that bubbled out of the earth at the top of a hill, over which Nathan Marcus, Deborah's father, had built a bathhouse adjoining their small inn. A limited but regular clientele composed mostly of arthritic Jewish ladies from the large cities of the Midwest came to the inn annually for the waters, which smelled like rotten eggs and brimstone and tasted only slightly better than they smelled. But Nathan, a graying kewpie doll of a man, assured the city folks with great sincerity that the waters contained sulphur, lime, iron, and other things that would cure anything from sciatica to puppy love, and the ladies were always certain that their pains were fewer following a ten-minute immersion. Anything that smelled that bad, they remarked to him archly and often, had to be good for you.

"Temperature of the springs is going up," Nathan told the young rabbi as they sat on the lawn in wooden-slat chairs with Deborah and Sarah, Nathan's wife. Leslie, wearing jeans and a blouse, lay on a blanket at their feet, gazing into the meadow and woodland that fell away below them in the dusk.

"How long has the temperature been rising?" the rabbi

asked. He looked a little like Henry Fonda, Leslie decided, but not as big in the shoulders as he might be, and somewhat thinner. He needed a haircut dreadfully. When she had seen him yesterday for the first time, climbing out of that dirty station wagon wearing high boots and rumpled clothes that had never seen a dry cleaners from their looks, she had thought that he was some kind of mountain man, a farmer or a trapper. But now he wore a sports coat and slacks and he looked more acceptable and just as interesting. Only, the hair was too long.

"Been going up every year for six years, about half a degree annually. Up to seventy-three degrees now."

"What is it that warms the water up?" she said lazily, looking up at them. He could be Italian. Or Spanish, she thought, or even Black Irish.

"There are several theories. Maybe way underground the water is meeting molten rock or hot gases. Or some chemical reaction down below may be heating the water. Or radioactivity."

"Wouldn't it be nice if the water became real hot," Sarah Marcus said hopefully.

"Make us rich as kings. Nothing like that anywhere between here and way out to Hot Springs. And the government owns those. With hot mineral water on our ground, this would be *some* health resort. As it is, you have to heat the water before these damn women will get into it. Don't know why. Over two hundred years ago the Indians were using these springs to cure whatever was wrong with 'em. Quapaw tribe. Used to camp here for a couple of weeks every summer, I'm told."

"What finally happened to them?" his daughter asked innocently.

"Died out, mostly." He frowned at her. "Got to take the temperature," he said, and got up and walked away.

Sarah was shaking with laughter. "Oh, you mustn't tease your father," she said to Deborah. She pushed herself out of the chair. "They didn't ship out enough matzo meal. If we're going to have matzo-meal pancakes tomorrow, I'd better crumble up a lot of matzos."

"I'll come and help you," Deborah said.

"No, you stay here with the other young people. I don't need any help."

"I want to talk to you." She rose. "See you later," she said, and she winked to Leslie.

When they were gone the girl on the ground chuckled. "Her mother wanted her to stay with you. Mrs. Marcus is a real matchmaker, isn't she? But her daughter's engaged. I imagine that's what Deb is going to tell her now, while they're sitting there making matzo crumbs."

"Wow," he said. He took a cigarette and handed it to her, then took one himself and struck his lighter. "Who's the lucky man?"

"His name is Mort Beerman. He's a graduate student in architecture at M.I.T. He's coming here in a couple of days. They're sure to like him."

"How do you know?"

"He's very nice. And he's Jewish. Deb has told me several times that they feel guilty and afraid about having raised her out here, away from young Jews." She rose from the blanket, rubbing her goose-fleshed arms. When he took off his coat she allowed him to place it around her shoulders without thanking him. She sat in the chair next to his, the one Deborah had sat in, tucking her legs under her.

"It must be hard for you here," she said. "There can't be many Jewish girls around."

From the kitchen of the inn ripped a short scream, followed by a delighted babbling.

"*Mazel tov*," Michael said, and the girl laughed.

"No," he said, "there aren't many Jewish girls here. There aren't any the right age for dating."

Her eyes mocked him. "What is the word you people use? For a gentile female?"

"We people? You mean *shickseh*?"

"Yes." She paused. "Am I a *shickseh*? Is that the word you think of when you look at me?"

Their glances locked. They stared at one another for a long time. Her face was pale in the gathering darkness and he noticed the smooth flesh planes under her high cheekbones, and her mouth, full-lipped but not slack, perhaps a little too large for beauty.

"Yes, I guess it is," he said.

He left after the *seder* the next day, not intending to return to the Marcus inn for four or five weeks. But three days later he found himself turning the car back in the direction of Mineral Springs. He tried to tell himself that he was curious to see Mort Beerman and then he grew angry and thought to hell with excuses, I haven't had a real day off since I began this crazy hillbilly existence, or talked to a woman like a human being instead of a rabbi. Anyhow, maybe she had a boy friend who was driving up with Beerman or perhaps she had already cut her visit short.

But when he got to the inn she was still there and there was no boy friend in sight, only Beerman. He had thinning hair and a sense of humor and a second-hand Buick, and the proud Marcuses had made him their son upon introduction. That night Leslie and Michael played bridge against the engaged couple, and Michael bid very badly, even getting his counting all mixed up, but nobody cared because they were drinking good brandy that Nathan Marcus had brought up out of his cellar, and laughing a great deal about things they couldn't recall an hour later.

Next morning when he appeared for breakfast, the girl was eating alone. She was wearing a cotton skirt and an off-the-shoulder peasant blouse that made him look away as if by reflex.

"Morning. Where is everybody?"

"Hi. Mrs. Marcus is training a new housekeeper. Mr. Marcus is off in the pickup, buying vegetables."

"And your hostess and her beau?"

"They vant to be ah-lone," she whispered.

He grinned. "Can't say that I blame them."

"Not at all." She applied herself to her grapefruit.

"Hey. Would you like to go fishin'?"

"Really?"

"Sure. I've been giving Hebrew lessons to a little boy and he's been giving fishing lessons to me. It's opened up a whole new world."

"I'd love to."

"Fine." He threw another brief glance at her blouse. "Better wear old clothes. In places this country's rough as a cob, as we people say."

He drove slowly toward Big Cedar Hill, making one stop at a river landing to buy a bucket of chub shiners. He had rolled all the windows down, and the warm spring air, exciting with the smell of melted ice, poured over them. The girl had changed into sneakers, jeans, and an old gray sweatshirt. Sitting beside him she yawned and stretched, grunting in unashamed pleasure.

He drove over the suspension bridge and then parked. She carried a blanket and he took the bait and the fishing rod, walking after her along the narrow path that followed the stream-cut gulley. The path was lined with flowering shrubs, heavy with small red blossoms and larger white ones. Her jeans were faded from repeated washing until some of the threads were almost white, and they were very tight; he could imagine her wearing them while hunched over the handlebars of a bicycle, riding around the campus. The dappled sun set off little lights in her hair.

They followed the path until the gulley's sides leveled off and disappeared and the river widened and slowed in tempo, then finally they found a spot and spread the blanket on a grassy bluff overlooking a deep, clear pool at the foot of a riffle caused by drift logs. She watched in silence as he palmed a shiner from the bucket and plunged the hook in one side of its body and out the other, careful to place the hook above the spinal column so the bait would stay alive.

"Does that hurt the minnow?"

"I don't know." He swung it out into the center of the pool and they watched it for a few moments as it wriggled deeper, to where the water was slightly green and cold-looking and they could no longer see it.

A blossom floated at the water's edge and she leaned over the bluff to pick it up. Her sweatshirt rode up, revealing two inches of lower-back flesh and the first sweet spreading hint of hips above the top of her beltless jeans, then dropped back as she sat up holding the dripping flower, large and creamy-white but with one of its four petals broken. "What is it?" she asked, and looked at it with wonder when he told her it was dogwood.

"My father used to tell me stories about the dogwood," she said.

"What kind of stories?"

"Religious ones. It was dogwood from which the Cross was fashioned. My father is a minister. Congregational."

"That's nice." He tugged experimentally on the line.

"That's what you think," she said. "He was my minister, just as he was everybody's, but he was so busy serving God and the people he never found time to be a father. If you ever have a daughter, Rabbi, watch out for that."

He started to reply but then he held up his hand and pointed to the floating line that was beginning to disappear beneath the surface, a few feet at a time, tugged by something unseen. He stood, reeling hard, and the fish broke the water, a good brassy-green fish about a foot long with a white belly and a broad tail that it walked on twice before shaking off the line and disappearing in the pool. He reeled in. "Hit it too soon and forgot to set the hook. My teacher would be ashamed."

She watched him rebait and cast. "I'm almost glad," she said. "If I tell you something will you laugh?"

He shook his head.

"From the time I was fourteen until my senior year in high school, I was a vegetarian. I just decided that it was wicked to eat living things."

"What made you change your mind?"

"I didn't, really. But I began to go out with boys and a whole crowd of us would go out for dinner all the time and people would eat steak and I would munch salads and the smell would drive me out of my mind. So finally I ate meat, too. But I still hate the thought of living things suffering."

"Sure," he said. "I understand. But you'd better hope that *that* living thing bites again, or one of his cousins. Because that fish is your lunch."

"Didn't you bring us any other lunch?" she asked.

He shook his head again.

"Is there a restaurant around?"

"Nope."

"My God," she said, "you're crazy. Suddenly I'm famished."

"Here, you try," he said, handing her the rod. She stared into the water.

"Kind is a funny name for a rabbi, isn't it?" she said after a while.

He shrugged.

"I mean, it's not very Jewish."

"It used to be Rivkind. My father changed it when I was a little boy."

"I like originals. I like Rivkind better."

"So do I."

"Why don't you change it back?"

"I'm used to it. That would be just as silly as his changing it in the first place, wouldn't it?"

She smiled. "I understand what you mean." About two feet of the floating line went under suddenly and she placed her hand on his arm. But it was a false alarm, nothing else happened.

"It must be very uncomfortable being Jewish, far worse than being a vegetarian," she said, "with all those people hating you and knowing about the death camps and the ovens and all that."

"If you're in the ovens or a concentration camp, yes, it must be uncomfortable," he said. "Outside, anywhere else, it can be marvelous or I imagine it can be uncomfortable if you let it, if you let people ruin a good day for example by talking when they should be concentrating on filling their beautiful but hungry and rumbling bellies."

"My belly isn't rumbling."

"I heard it distinctly, a most animal-like noise."

"I like you," she said.

"I like you, too. I have so much confidence in you I'm going to take a nap." He lay back on the blanket and closed his eyes and amazingly, although he had not at all intended to do so, he fell asleep. When he awoke he had no idea how long he had slept, but the girl was sitting there in the same position, looking as though she hadn't moved except that her sneakers were off. Her feet were well shaped but there were two little yellow callus ridges on her right heel and a small corn on the pinky of the same foot. She turned her head and caught him looking at her and she smiled and just then the fish struck and the reel gave a loud whir.

"Here," she said, shoving the rod toward him, but he pushed it back into her hands.

"Count to ten, slowly," he whispered. "Then give the rod a good jerk to set the hook."

She counted aloud, her voice shaking with nervous laughter after she reached four. When she said ten she yanked, hard. She began to reel in but the fish ran back and forth across the pool, not breaking water but fighting all the way, and in her excitement she dropped the rod and hauled the line in hand over hand until she had the fish out of the water, a beautiful bass, better than the first one, deep and broad and about fifteen inches long. The fish bounced and flapped on the blanket, trying to get back into the pool, and they both tried to grab it until it was trapped between them and his arms went around her and her hands were in his hair and he felt her breasts separate and alive against his chest and the fish even more alive between her breasts, while as he kissed her the laughter bubbled into his mouth from hers.

He was afraid that Leslie would be angry with him when she saw Stan Goodstein's hunting lodge at the top of the hill, but she began to laugh again when he showed her the shelves full of canned food. He set her to heating baked beans in the cabin while he took the carcass of the fish out to the pump behind the house. This was the part he had forgotten about when he had planned the day. Except for one small bass he had hooked with little Bobby Lilienthal two weeks before, the only fish he had ever caught were flounders which he and his father were accustomed to hand triumphantly to a neighborhood fish market clerk for conversion into food. He had watched Phyllis Lilienthal prepare her son's catch for their supper and now, armed with a rusty scissors, pliers, and a dull butcher knife, he tried to remember what she had done, step by step.

With the knife he made two deep but shaky incisions along each side of the spiny dorsal fin, then he used the pliers to yank it out. When Phyllis Lilienthal had done this the fish had proven to be still alive and it had leaped almost out of her hands. Recalling that, Michael had smashed the head of this fish against a rock with enough force to decapitate a man, but nevertheless the remembrance of the other fish's gory revival made him shudder. He used the scissors to slit the white belly from the anal opening to the jaw. Then he peeled the skin off with the pliers and was amazed at the ease with which the viscera popped out, with very little tearing. He had trouble cutting off the head. As he strug-

gled and sawed the knife back and forth the red eyes seemed to
stare accusingly, but then the head dropped off and he ran the
blade down the backbone and over the rib cage. If the resulting
fillets were a bit ragged, they were nevertheless fillets. He rinsed
them under the pump and carried them inside.

"You look a little pale," she said.

Bobby's mother had dipped her fish in beaten egg and
cracker crumbs and then fried it in vegetable shortening. There
was no egg and no shortening, but he found cracker crumbs and
a bottle of olive oil. He was somewhat dubious about the omis-
sion and the substitution, but the fish came out looking like a
Crisco ad in the *Ladies' Home Journal*. She watched and listened
intently when he said the *brocha*. The beans were good and
the fish was flaky and wonderful, and she had opened another
can on her own and heated its contents, zucchini, which he usually hated but now ate with relish. For dessert they opened a can
of Elberta peaches, drinking the juice.

"You know what I'd love to do?"

"What?"

"Give you a haircut."

"What else would you like to do?"

"No. Really. You need one so badly. And the way your hair
is, somebody who doesn't know you might think you're . . . you
know."

"I *don't* know."

"Queer."

"You hardly know me. How do you know I'm not?"

"I know," she said. She continued to tease and in a few
moments he gave in and moved one of Stan Goodstein's maple
chairs outside into the sunshine. He removed his shirt and she
went and got the scissors and began to snip and then he sniffed
a couple of times and became angry.

"For Christ's sake, didn't you wash it? It's all fish." He was
ready to quit right there but she went back to the pump and
rinsed the scissors and wiped them on the taut seat of her jeans
and he told himself, I've never before had this much fun in all
my life.

He sat back in the chair and closed his eyes and enjoyed

the warmth of the sun while the rusty scissors went snip-snip, snip-snip.

"I'm very grateful to you," she said.

"What for?"

"I responded when you kissed me. I responded very strongly."

"Is that so unusual?"

"It is for me ever since I had an affair last summer," she said.

"Hey." He leaned forward so that she had to stop cutting his hair. "You don't want to be telling me about something like that."

She grabbed him by the hair and pulled his head back. "Yes, don't you see, I haven't been able to tell anybody, but this is so safe. This is practically made to order. You're a rabbi and I'm a . . . a *shickseh,* and we'll probably never see each other again. It's even better than if I were a Catholic telling it to a priest hidden behind a screen in a confessional, because I *know* the kind of person you are."

He shrugged and sat quietly while the scissors snipped and the hair fell on his bare shoulders.

"It was with this Harvard boy I didn't even like. His name is Roger Phillipson, his mother went to school with my aunt, and to please them we went out a couple of times so we could both write home about it. I let him make love to me in his car, only once, just to see what it was like. It was simply awful. Nothing. Since then I haven't enjoyed kissing a boy and I've never been able to feel passionate. I was very worried. But when you kissed me after I caught the fish I felt as passionate as anything."

He felt both flattered and extremely annoyed. "I'm glad," he said. They were both silent.

"You don't like me as much as you did before I told you that," she said.

"It isn't that. It's simply that you caused me to feel like something that made the right color on your litmus paper."

"I apologize," she said. "I've wanted to tell somebody about that ever since it happened. I grew so disgusted with myself afterwards, and so sorry that I had let my curiosity get the better of me."

"You shouldn't let that single experience make a great big difference in your life," he said carefully. His back was beginning to itch, and several clumps of hair had worked their way down into his trousers.

"I don't intend to," she said in a low voice.

"None of us can go through life untouched. We all hurt ourselves and others. We feel boredom and we put a small creature on a hook, we feel hunger and we eat flesh, we feel desire and we make love."

The girl burst into tears.

He turned to look at her, touched and amazed that his words should have so profound an effect, but she was staring at his head as she wept.

"It's the first time I ever cut anybody's hair," she said.

They drove slowly over the mountain roads, talking quietly, until it was dark. Once Leslie covered her face with her hands and slumped down in the seat, but this time he knew she was laughing. When they arrived at the inn he kissed her good-by in the car.

"It was a day," she said.

He sneaked up to his room without being seen. Next morning he got up and out very early, having instructed Leslie to make his excuses. In order to find a barber—one he had been avoiding for weeks because the man was careless and unskilled —he had to drive thirty miles beyond his next scheduled stop.

The old man kept shaking his head as he cut his hair. "Have to get it down mighty close to even it off," he said.

When he finished, a *yarmulka* would not hide the fact that all that was left was a sort of brown fuzz. In a general store next to the barber shop Michael bought a khaki hunting cap, which during the next few weeks he wore even when the days became hot, feeling fortunate that he did not have to remove his hat to pray.

CHAPTER TWENTY-TWO

When summer actually came he stopped seeking shelter at night and unrolled the sleeping bag that had been one of the items on Rabbi Sher's good list, finding it slightly mildewed but very serviceable. At night he lay under the stars waiting to be eaten by a wolf or a bobcat and listening to the wind sliding over the mountain tops and making restless noises in the trees. On afternoons when the distant hills shimmered blue in the hot sun he stopped the car and imitated the fishes instead of trying to catch them, sometimes lying naked and alone in a shallow, tumbling stream and shouting and laughing aloud at the icy cold, and once in his BVD's joining a bunch of gawking, silent mountain boys in a river swimming hole. His hair grew, and as it did he soaked it with water every morning and brushed it straight back, getting rid of the part he had had before his short haircut. He shaved regularly and used the tub or shower wherever he made a stop. His congregation kept him too well fed, everyone planning large meals on the occasion of the rabbi's visits, and he stopped doing his own laundry after receiving four offers from housewives along his route; he let them take turns.

Bobby Lilienthal was learning enough Hebrew to begin working on his *haftorah* in preparation for his *bar mitzvah*. Stan Goodstein's mother died and he had his first Jewish funeral in the congregation and then Mrs. Marcus reserved his services for August 12 and he had his first wedding.

It was a good-sized wedding, almost but not quite taxing the facilities at the inn, and surprisingly formal for the Ozark Mountains. Marcus and Beerman relatives came from Chicago, New York, Massachusetts, Florida, Ohio, and two towns in Wisconsin. Mort's male friends were not there but four of Deborah's classmates were, including Leslie Rawlins, who was maid of honor.

Before the ceremony Michael sat for almost an hour in an

upstairs bedroom with Mort and his younger brother, who was
to be the best man. Both brothers were extremely nervous and
had been nibbling on the contents of a pinch bottle in search of
ease. Michael took the bottle with him when he left the room.
He stood at the top of the stairway, wondering where he could
dispose of the Scotch. In the room below him a crowd had
gathered, the men in white jackets and the women in gowns that
obeyed the New Look commandment of Dior. In their long
gloves and big floppy hats and *peau de soie* dresses of lovely
pastels, viewed from the top of the stairs the women looked more
like flowers than females, even the fat ones. Obviously, he decided, he couldn't walk down among them carrying a bottle of
booze. He disposed of it finally in an upstairs hall closet, standing
it behind a vacuum cleaner and in front of a large can of floor
wax.

When the ceremony began everything went as rehearsed.
Mort was sober and serious. Deborah's white net cloud, topped
by a halolike wreath of white blossoms, created the standard
gasps when she entered on her father's arm, her eyes demure
and doe-like behind the full veil. Only the tightness with which
she held her floral prayerbook denied her tranquility.

When it was over and he had congratulated everybody,
Michael found himself reaching for champagne while Leslie
Rawlins' eyes stared at him over the rim of her glass.

She swallowed and smiled at him. "My," she said, "you're
an impressive fellow."

"Was it all right?" he asked. "I'll let you in on a secret if you
don't tell anyone. It's the first one I've ever handled alone."

"Congratulations." She held out her hand and he shook it.
"Wonderful, honestly. You sent chills up and down my spine."

The champagne was dry and icy cold, exactly what he
wanted now that the ceremony was over. "You're the one to be
congratulated," he remembered presently. "You and Deborah
were graduated in June, weren't you?"

"Oh, yes," she said. "As a matter of fact, I have a job. After
Labor Day I'm going to be a researcher at *Newsweek*. I'm quite
excited. And somewhat frightened."

"Just remember to count ten and then set the hook," he said,
and they both laughed. Her dress and accessories were the color

of cornflowers, the exact shade of her irises. The bridesmaids, who were the other three Wellesley girls plus one of Deborah's cousins from Winnetka, wore rose. Blue made her bronze hair blonder, he decided. "I like you in blue. But you're thinner."

She made no effort to hide her pleasure. "I'm so glad you noticed. I've been dieting."

"Don't be a fool. You said *Newsweek,* not *Vogue.* You were perfect before." He took her empty glass and returned a moment later with two full ones. "I'm looking forward to November. Three weeks vacation. I'll be going to New York myself. I can hardly wait."

"I don't have an address yet. But if you get bored call me at the magazine. I'll take you fishing."

"Okay," he said.

Rabbi Sher was very pleased. "*Very* pleased," he repeated. "I can't tell you how happy I am that your traveling circus has worked out. Perhaps this will lead to circuit-riders being sent to other remote areas."

"Next time I'd like a jungle," Michael said. "Some place with swamps and lots of malaria."

Rabbi Sher laughed, but he looked at Michael keenly. "Tired?" he said. "Want to give somebody else a shot at it?"

"I've got two boys almost ready for *bar mitzvah.* I've learned to find my way over a lot of mountains. I'm working on plans for a communal *seder* next Passover, with perhaps forty families taking part at Mineral Springs."

"The answer, I take it, is *no.*"

"Not yet."

"Well, just remember that I never envisioned this as your life's effort. Temples all over America are trying to hire rabbis. Outside of the country, too. When you get tired of pioneering, let me know."

Each of them was content when they shook hands.

New York, New York was somewhat dirtier than he had remembered it but far more exciting. The preoccupied pace of Manhattan; the unheeding way people banged shoulders on the sidewalks; the bitchy loveliness of the smart women along Fifth Avenue and upper Madison; the sophistication of a white French poodle squatting to defecate in the gutter on 57th Street off the Park, while a gray-haired Negro doorman flicked his cuffs and looked the other way, holding the leash slack—all these things appeared new to him, although he had seen them most of his life and had thought nothing of them.

On his first day in the city, after talking with Rabbi Sher, he walked a lot, and then he took the subway back to Queens.

"Eat," his mother said.

He tried to explain to her that he had been well fed, but she knew that he lied to spare her.

"So what do you think of the kids?" his father asked.

Ruthie's son was seven years old. His name was Moshe. The girl, Chaneh, was four. Their maternal grandparents had visited them for two months on the previous year, despite Arab raids and the British blockade, through which they had sailed with their hands on their American passports. They had a dress box full of snapshots of two little tanned strangers to show him.

"Imagine," his mother said, "so young to sleep all alone away from the mother and father. In a separate building with only other *pitzilehs*. What a system."

"Socialists, the whole *kibbutz*," his father said. "And outside, Arabs that look daggers. Can you imagine your sister driving a truck with a gun on the seat?"

"A bus. For the children," his mother said.

"A truck with seats in back," his father said. "I'm glad here I'm a Republican. And those British soldiers, everywhere inspecting with long noses. And no food. Did you know it's impossible to buy a dozen eggs there?"

"Eat," his mother urged.

On his third night home he started thinking about some of the girls he had known. He could remember only two who he had not heard were married. He called the first one; she was married. The other girl's mother informed him that her daughter was a Ph.D. candidate in clinical psychology at the University of California. "At Los Angeles," she emphasized. "Don't write to her at the other one or it may not reach her."

He called Maury Silverstein, who had his own apartment now in the village. Maury had majored in chemistry at Queens but he was a television agent, having joined one of the largest agencies as a trainee directly from the Marine Corps. "Listen, I'm going to California in about forty minutes," he said. "But I'll be back next week. I must see you. I'm giving a party at my place on Thursday. I want you to come. Lots of wonderful people I want you to meet."

He called Mrs. Harold Popkin, née Mimi Steinmetz. She had just received word that a rabbit test had proved positive. "You should be flattered," she said. "My mother doesn't even know. Only Hal. I'm telling you because you're an old flame." They chatted about pregnancy.

"Say," he said finally, "do you know a nice girl I can date while I'm home? I seem to have lost touch."

"See what happens to old bachelors?" She was silent for a moment, savoring what he had become without her. "How about Rhoda Levitz? We've grown to be very good friends."

"She was a very heavy girl? With a lot of acne?"

"She's not that heavy," Mimi said. "Look, I'll think about it. I'm sure I can come up with somebody else. New York is full of single girls."

The telephone operator at *Newsweek* didn't know how to find Leslie, but when he told her that Miss Rawlins was a new employee and in the research department, she checked a list and located the extension.

He waited for her outside the building on 42nd Street and at five-ten she came down, looking lovely and just excited enough.

"So that's another thing about you," he said, taking her hand. "You're late for appointments."

"So that's another thing about you. You're a clock-watcher."

He looked for a cab, but then she asked where they were going and when he suggested Miyako she wanted to walk. They strolled the fourteen blocks. It was not very cold but the wind blew in gusts, whipping open the lower flaps of her coat and plastering her skirt against her fine legs. When they got to the restaurant the blood was marching through their veins and they were ready for martinis. "To your job," he said as they touched glasses. "How's it going, anyway?"

"Ah." She wrinkled her nose. "It's not as exciting as once it sounded to me. I spend a lot of time in libraries and poring over dramatic volumes like the Ashtabula telephone directory. And I clip newspapers from towns you've never heard of."

"Going to try something else?"

"I don't think so." She ate her olive. "Everybody said I did a very good job as editor of the Wellesley *News*. One story I wrote—about the hoop race being won by a married woman—was picked up by the Associated Press. I think I'd make a pretty good news writer. I'll hang on until they give me a chance to see."

"What's a hoop race?"

"At Wellesley the senior girls roll hoops every year in their caps and gowns. It's a very old tradition. The winner is supposed to be the first girl in the class to snag a husband. That's what made it so funny our year. Lois Fenton had been secretly married for six months to a boy at Harvard Medical. When she won she became so flustered that she burst into tears and blurted out everything, and that's how they announced their marriage."

The food came, tempura and a clear delicately flavored soup garnished with thin slices of vegetables cut in intricate patterns, followed by sukiyaki cooked at the table by a deft, theatrical waiter. Michael ordered a stone jug of saki but she didn't care for it because it was heated and he drank it alone, quickly losing all feeling in his toes.

Afterward, while he was helping her on with her coat, the heels of his palms touched her shoulders lightly and she turned her head and looked at him. "I didn't think you would call me," she said.

Perhaps it was the liquor, but he felt a great urgency to be completely honest with this girl. "I didn't want to," he said.

"Rabbis shouldn't date gentile girls. I know that," she said.

"Then why did you accept my invitation?"

She shrugged, then shook her head.

Outside, he hailed a taxi, but she didn't want to go anywhere else.

"Look, this is silly. We're adult and we're modern. Why shouldn't we be friends? It's so early," he said. "Let's go somewhere and listen to good music."

"No," she said.

They talked hardly at all until the cab pulled up at her address, a red-brick roominghouse far west on 60th Street.

"Please don't get out," she said. "Sometimes it's awfully hard to get another cab on this block."

"I'll get one," he said.

She lived two flights up and the hallway was a bleak brown. She stood in front of her door. He felt that she did not want to go into the room.

"Let's start fresh tomorrow night," he said. "Same time, same place?"

"No," she said. "Thank you." She looked at him and he knew that she would probably cry when she was alone.

"Look," he said, leaning forward to kiss her, but she turned and their heads bumped.

"Good night," she said and went inside.

He found a taxi without any trouble, as he had known he would.

He slept late the next morning, consuming an enormous brunch when he finally did leave his bed after eleven o'clock.

"You're appetite's improved," his mother said happily. "You must have had a good time with all your old friends last night."

He decided to call Max Gross. He had not studied with a fine Talmudic scholar in two years and this is how he would spend the rest of his vacation, he told himself.

But when he went to the telephone he dialed the magazine's number and asked for her.

"This is Michael," he said when she answered.

She was silent.

"I would like very much to see you tonight."

"What is it you want from me?" she asked. Her voice sounded strange, and he realized she must be cupping her hand over the speaker of the telephone in an attempt to keep the conversation private from someone in the proximity of her desk.

"I just want to be your friend."

"It's because of what I told you last spring, isn't it. You have some sort of a social-worker complex. You consider me a case history."

"Don't be a fool."

"Well, if that's not the case you must consider me a push-

over. Is that what you want, Michael? A little secret sex before
you return to the hills?"

He became angry. "Look. I offer you my friendship. If you
don't want it, to hell with you. Now, shall I be there at five or
not?"

"Be there," she said.

They had dinner again, this time at a Swedish restaurant,
and then they had the music, Eddie Condon's in the Village. At
her door she shook his hand and he kissed her cheek.

The following night was Friday and he went to the synagogue with his parents, gritting his teeth throughout the *oneg
shabbat* while his mother introduced him to half a dozen people
he already knew: "This is my son the rabbi," just like in the
jokes.

On Saturday he started to call her and then, after he had
dialed only the first two digits of her number, he stopped and
asked himself what he was doing, like a man suddenly awakened
from a dream.

He got into the car and drove for a long time, and when he
thought to look around he was in Atlantic City, and he parked
the car and turned up his coat collar and walked along the beach
close to the edge of the water. He played the game he always
played while walking along a beach, letting the water hiss up to
his feet until the very last minute and then stepping away very
quickly in order not to get his shoes filled. Eventually the sea
would win if he kept it up long enough; it was a fool's game, he
knew, like the game played by a rabbi who would date a minister's daughter. The way to win at both games was to step far
away, and permanently. No more dinner engagements, no more
jokes, no more secret studying of her profile or longing for her
flesh. He would not contact her again, would not see her, would
not talk to her, would thrust her out of his mind. The decision
filled him with relief and he stepped away from the water with
a kind of sad pride, lengthening his stride and filling his lungs
with salt air as he marched over the hard-packed sand. The wind
drove spray into his face and eventually cut through the protection of the coat and he quit the beach after a while and had a
tasteless shore dinner in a restaurant full of conventioneers,

either refrigeration people or frozen foods, he couldn't make out which.

He drove around New Jersey some more and it was almost midnight by the time he got back to New York and he stopped and called her from a telephone booth in an all-night drug store, feeling the dream quality catch him up again as she answered the insistent ringing.

"Did I wake you?" he asked.

"No."

"Want a cup of coffee?"

"I can't. I just started to wash my hair. I thought you weren't going to call tonight."

He was silent. "I'm not working tomorrow," she said. "Would you like to come here for lunch?"

"What time?" he asked.

She lived in a large furnished room. "This is what they call an efficiency," she said as she took his coat. "What saves it from being a studio apartment is the small kitchen. Or maybe it's the other way around." She smiled. "I could have afforded something better if I had doubled up with one or two other girls, but after four years of dormitory life, privacy means a lot to me."

"It's nice," he lied. It was a gloomy room, with one large but solitary window which she had tried to make attractive with bright curtains. There was an Oriental rug, not quite threadbare; ugly old lamps; one beaten-looking stuffed chair; a painted table and two straight-backed chairs; a good mahogany desk that she had probably bought herself; and two bookcases containing college texts as well as a good number of novels, none of them historical. The kitchen was tiny, with barely enough room for the person doing the cooking on the two-burner range. The minuscule refrigerator was located under the sink. She gave him a martini and he sat on the hard convertible couch and drank it while she prepared the meal.

"I hope you like a large lunch," she said.

"I do. Then I can buy you a small dinner. Think of the money I'll save."

They had blue cheese and crackers and tomato juice and an antipasto with lots of anchovies, and veal cutlets parmigiana and lemon pie and black Turkish coffee. Afterward they started the *Times* crossword puzzle together and when they got stuck she washed the dishes and he wiped.

When the dishes were put away he sat on the couch and smoked and observed the way her breasts were mashed flat when she lay on her stomach chipping away at the puzzle.

He looked away, at her books. "Lots of poetry," he observed.

"I love it. I learned about poetry and about men and women from the same place, the place every minister's kid does."

"The Bible?"

"Mm-hmm." She smiled and closed her eyes. "When I was a young girl I used to daydream that on my wedding night my husband would recite the Song of Songs."

He wanted merely to touch her face with his hands, to push the hair back from the soft pink flesh of her ears and kiss her there. Instead he reached past her for an ashtray and tapped the dottle from his pipe. "I hope he does," he said gently.

On Monday she managed to leave the office early and they went to the Bronx Zoo and spent a lot of time laughing at the monkeys and at the horrible stink in the enclosure, which she swore turned his complexion an attractive light green. On Tuesday they went to *Aida* at the Metropolitan and then to Luchow's for a late supper. She exulted over the dark beer. "It tastes as though it were brewed from mushrooms," she said. "Do you like mushrooms?"

"Love, not like."

"Then you'll quit the rabbinate and I'll quit the magazine and we'll become farmers, we'll raise thousands and thousands of mushrooms in lovely steaming beds of manure."

He said nothing and she smiled. "Poor Michael. You can't even joke about leaving the rabbinate, can you?"

"No," he said.

"I'm glad. That's the way it should be. Some day when I am an old woman and you have become a great leader to your people I'm going to remember how I helped you spend your vacation when we both were young."

He watched her lips cover the rim of the glass and sip in the dark brew. "You'll make a beautiful old lady," he said.

On Wednesday they ate early and visited the Museum of Modern Art, looking and talking and walking until their spirits flagged. He bought her a small framed print to help the curtains fight the drabness of her room, three bottles done in orange, blue, and burnt umber by an artist neither of them knew, and they went to her apartment and hung it on the wall. Her feet hurt and he ran hot water into the bathtub while she removed her shoes and stockings in the other room and then gathered her skirt above her knees and stepped into the tub and sat on the edge. She waggled her toes in the hot water, making sounds of such pleasure that he took off his shoes and socks and rolled up his pants legs and sat next to her while she laughed, having to hold on to the edge of the tub to keep from falling in. Their toes began making underwater signals at one another, and his left foot went out to meet her right foot, and her right foot ventured out halfway, and their feet played together like children and then like lovers. He kissed her hard, and his right pants leg unrolled and slid down his shin into the water. She laughed some more when he became annoyed and hopped out to wipe his feet. When she came out, they had coffee together at the table while his tweed cuffs itched damply against his ankle.

"If you weren't a rabbi," she said slowly, "you would have made a serious pass at me long before this, wouldn't you."

"I am a rabbi."

"Of course. But I would just like to know. Wouldn't you? Even though the Jewish-Christian thing were there, if we had met before you were ordained?"

"Yes," he said.

"I knew that."

"Shall we stop seeing one another?" he said regretfully. "I've had a marvelous time with you."

"Of course not," she said. "It's been wonderful. There's no use denying the presence of physical attraction. But while this . . . chemical reaction . . . is a mutual compliment—that is, if you feel that way about me?"

"Yes, I do."

"Well, while this says something nice about our tastes in the opposite sexes, it doesn't mean that there has to be a physical affair, or anything like that. There's no reason why we can't rise

above the physical thing and continue a friendship I'm beginning
to value tremendously."

"I feel the same way. Exactly," he said eagerly, and they put
down their coffee cups and shook hands. They talked for a long
time after that, about many things. The cuffs of his trousers dried
and she leaned forward to listen to him with her arms flat on
the table, and as he talked he traced with a friendly fingertip
the lovely line of her forearm, his finger sliding over the outside
of her arm where there were short hairs so golden as to be almost transparent, passing the narrow bony wrist, then tracing
the promontories of her fingers, down and around and in and
out, and in and out, and in and out, and in and around the
thumb and then up along the soft warm inner part of her arm
while her face warmed with pleasure and she talked to him and
listened, laughing often at the things that he said.

On Thursday he took her to Maury Silverstein's party. The
station wagon had been left at a Manhattan garage for a tuneup
and he picked it up before he called for her. They were early so
he drove uptown first, toward Morningside Heights, but when he
came to the block in which the *Shaarai Shomayim* Synagogue was
located he parked the car and pointed out the *shul* to Leslie and
told her all about Max.

"He sounds wonderful," she said, and then was silent.
"You're a little afraid of him, did you know that?" she asked
finally.

"No," he said. "You're wrong." He felt annoyed.

"Have you seen him during the past ten days?"

"No."

"That's because of me, isn't it? Because you know he would
disapprove of your seeing me?"

"Disapprove? He'd have apoplexy. But he lives in his world
and I live in mine." He started the car again.

Maury's apartment was small and it was a large party when
they got there. They pushed through a forest of drinkers and
glass-holders, in search of the host. Michael recognized nobody
with the exception of a dark, molelike little man who was a
famous saloon-and-television comic; surrounded by a group of
laughing people, he was telling jokes as fast as they tried to
stick him with off-beat subjects.

"Here he is," Maury bellowed, waving, and they pushed their way to where he was standing with another man. "You son of a gun," Maury said, gripping Michael's arm with the hand that didn't have a drink in it. Maury was heavier and slightly pouchy under the eyes, but the stomach was smooth and hard-looking. Michael could imagine him going directly to the gym when he left the office every evening; or perhaps one of the closets of this apartment was full of Indian clubs and a set of barbells like the ones Abe Kind had used for so many years.

Michael introduced Leslie and Maury introduced his boss, Benson Wood, a smiling man with a large face and the heaviest horn-rimmed glasses Michael had ever seen. Wood ignored Michael, smiling drunkenly at Leslie and not letting go of her hand after he had shaken it. "Any friend of M. S.," he told her, pronouncing each syllable very distinctly.

"There's somebody here you've got to meet, one of my talents," Maury said to Michael, taking his arm and leading him back to the group around the man with the head like a mole. "Here he is, George," he told the comedian. "The fellow I told you about the other day. The rabbi?"

The comic closed his eyes. "*Rabbi. Rabbi.* Did you hear the one about the rabbi and the priest—"

"Yes," Michael said.

"—who were buddies and the priest says to the rabbi, Listen you really ought to try ham, it's delicious, and the rabbi says to the priest, Listen, you really ought to try girls, they're better than ham . . . ?"

"I did. Yes," Michael said again, while the group laughed.

"Yes?" The man closed his eyes and touched his fingers to his forehead. "*Yes. Yes.* . . . Did you hear the one about this fella takes this Southern loose lady to the drive-in movie and he asks for her favors, and by the time she could drawl Yes the picture was over and they had to move the car?"

"No," he said.

The man closed his eyes. "*No. No,*" he mused. Michael turned and went back to Leslie, who was glaring at Wood.

"Would you like to leave?" Michael asked.

"Let's have a drink first." They moved away and left Wood standing there.

The bottles were on a table next to the wall. Two girls were already there and Michael waited patiently while they made their drinks. They were tall girls, a redhead and a blonde, with exceptional figures and pert faces that carried too much makeup. Models or television actresses, he thought.

"He was a different man after he had the hernia fixed," one of them was saying.

"I should hope so," the redhead replied. "I couldn't stand taking dictation from him when he called the pool and the witch sent me. I don't know how you stood it all those months. Between his disposition and his breath I almost died."

A woman behind them screamed suddenly and they turned to see Wood spouting vomit, while people scrambled in the crowded room to create a clearing, spilling drinks as they fled. Maury emerged from nowhere. "It's okay, B. W.," he said. He grabbed his boss' body, his hand supporting the drunken man's forehead as Wood heaved. Maury looked as though he were accustomed to performing the service, Michael thought. The girl who had shrieked was holding her dress away from her bosom, making short sounds of disgust and outrage.

Michael took Leslie's hand and led her away.

Later, back at her apartment, they had their drink. "Ugh," she said, shaking her head.

"It was a mess. Poor old Maury Silverstein."

"That loud boor. And that ugly little man with the jokes. I'll shut off my television set next time he's on."

"You're forgetting the star."

"Indeed I am not. That horrible pigsty with the changed name."

His glass had been raised to his lips but he did not drink. Instead, he placed it on the table. "Changed name? Wood?" He stared at her. "You mean you think his name was once something like Rivkind?"

She was silent.

He stood up and reached for his coat. "He was a *goy*, sweetheart. A loud, sloppy, lecherous *goy*. A drunken Christian vomit-wallower. One of *yours*."

She sat there unbelieving as the door slammed behind him.

On Saturday evening Michael stayed home and played casino with his father. Abe was a good card player. He knew at all times how many spades were out and whether the good two and the ten of diamonds were still in the pack. In defeat he was the kind of opponent who slapped the cards on the table in frustration, but when playing against his son he seldom was forced to lose his composure.

"I got cards and spades. Count points," he said, puffing his cigar. The telephone rang.

"All I have is two aces," Michael said. "You get nine more points."

"A *shmeer*."

"Michael," his mother called. "It's Western Union."

He hurried to the telephone. His parents stood in the kitchen and waited as he said "Hello?"

"Rabbi Kind? I have a telegram for you. The message is 'I am ashamed. Thank you for everything. If you can comma forgive me.' Signed Leslie. Do you want me to repeat that?"

"No, thank you, I got it," he said, and hung up.

His parents followed him back to the card table. "*Nu?*" his father said.

"It was nothing important."

"So what's so unimportant that it requires a telegram?"

"One of my boys in Arkansas is going to be *bar mitzvah*. His family is a little nervous. They were just reminding me of some details."

"Can't they even let you alone on your vacation?" His father sat down at the table and shuffled the cards. "I don't think casino is your game. How about a little gin?"

At eleven o'clock his parents went to sleep and he went to his room and tried to read, first the Bible and then Mickey Spillane and finally his old Aristotle, but nothing worked and he noticed that the binding of the Aristotle was cracked and torn. He put on his coat and let himself out of the apartment and downstairs he unlocked the door of the station wagon and got in and drove, taking the Queensboro Bridge instead of the tunnel because he wanted to see the lights on the East River. He fought traffic in Manhattan and then, like a good omen, there was a parking space directly in front of her apartment house.

In the brown hallway he stood for a moment, uncertain, and then he knocked on the door and heard the whisper of her feet.

"Who is it?"

"Michael."

"Oh, God. I can't see you."

"Why not?" he said angrily.

"I look a mess."

He laughed. "Let me in."

The lock clicked free. When he was inside the room he saw that she was in faded green pajamas and a brown flannel robe so old that the edges of the sleeves were threadbare. Her feet were bare and her face was scrubbed free of makeup. Her eyes were slightly reddened, as if she had been crying. He put his arms around her and she leaned her head against him.

"Were you crying because of me?" he asked.

"Not really. I have a stomach ache."

"Can I get you something? Should you see a doctor?"

"No. It happens to me every time there's a new moon." Her words were muffled by his shoulder.

"Oh."

"Give me your coat," she said, but as she took it her features melted and she dropped the coat and began to cry with such intensity that he became frightened.

She lay down on the couch and turned her face to the wall. "Go away," she said. "Please."

But he picked up his coat and threw it over the top of a chair and then he stood and watched her. She had drawn up her knees and she was jiggling back and forth with insistent rhythm, as if trying to rock the pain to sleep.

"Can't you take something?" he asked. "Aspirin?"

"Codeine."

The bottle was in the medicine chest and he made her swallow one of the tablets with some water and then he sat at the foot of the couch. In a short time the codeine took effect and she stopped jiggling. His hand touched her foot and it was cold. "You should wear slippers," he said, taking a foot between his hands and kneading.

"That feels so good," she said. "Your hands are warm. Better than a hot water bottle." He continued to massage her feet.

"Put your hand on my stomach," she said.

He moved up on the couch and slipped his hand into the robe.

"That's nice," she said sleepily.

Through the cloth of the pajama bottoms his hand felt the smoothness of the skin of her belly, trisected by two harness straps. The tip of his middle finger lightly recognized that the well of her umbilicus was astonishingly wide and deep. She shook her head.

"Tickles."

"I'm sorry. Thy navel is like a round goblet, wherein no mingled wine is wanting."

She smiled. "I don't want to be your friend," she murmured.

"I know."

He sat looking at her long after she slept. Finally he removed his hand from her stomach and took the blanket from the closet and covered her, wrapping her feet well. Then he drove back to Queens and packed his bag.

At breakfast the next morning he told his parents that a congregation emergency had forced him to cut his vacation short. Abe cursed and offered him money. Dorothy complained and packed him a shoebox full of chicken sandwiches and a thermos of tea, wiping her eyes with her apron.

He pointed the station wagon southwest and drove steadily, eating the sandwiches when he got hungry but making no stops until four P.M. when he called Leslie from the telephone booth of a roadside diner.

"Where are you?" she asked when the chime of the last dropping coin had died away.

"Virginia. I think Staunton."

"Are you running away?"

"I need time to think."

"What is there to think about?"

"I love you," he said roughly. "But I like what I am. I don't know if I can throw it away. It's very precious to me."

"I love you, too," she said. They were silent.

"Michael?"

"I'm here," he said gently.

"Would marrying me mean definitely that you would have to throw it away?"

"I think it would. Yes, it will."

"Don't do anything yet, Michael. Just wait."

He was silent again. "You don't want to marry me?" he said finally.

"I do. God, if you knew how much. But I have some ideas and I have to think them out. Don't ask me any questions and don't do anything hasty just now. Simply wait and write to me every day and I'll write to you. All right?"

"I love you," he said. "I'll call you on Tuesday. Seven o'clock."

"I love *you*."

On Monday morning Leslie clipped the Boston and the Philadelphia newspapers and then she went to the magazine's library and withdrew six fat brown manila envelopes marked JUDAISM. She read the clippings in the envelopes during her lunch hour and that evening when she went home she took with her a bundle of selected clippings which she had wrapped in an elastic band and placed in her purse. On Tuesday morning she clipped the Chicago papers and then asked Phil Brennan, her boss, if she could have a couple of hours off to take care of some personal business. When he nodded she put on her hat and coat and took the elevator downstairs. In Times Square she waited under the billboard that blew real smoke rings, studying faces and trying to guess which ones were and which ones were not, until a Broadway bus came along and then she rode uptown until the bus came to the block in which was located the funny-looking little Jewish church; no, synagogue.

CHAPTER TWENTY-THREE

Max Gross looked at the girl in her stylish clothing and with her sleek legs and bold American eyes and he felt a surge of annoyance. Only four times during his entire rabbinate at *Shaarai Shomayim* had *goyim* sought him out and asked him to transform them into Jews. Each time, he reflected, the request had been made as if he were someone who could wave his hands in the air and—pouf!—in a cloud of smoke change the facts of their births. He had never seen fit to undertake a conversion.

"What do you see among the Jews that makes you want to be one of us?" he asked coldly. "Don't you realize that Jews are persecuted and alone in the universe? Don't you know that as individuals we are despised by the gentile and that as a people we are cut asunder?"

Leslie stood and collected her gloves and purse. "I didn't expect you to accept me," she said. She reached for her coat.

"Why not?"

The old man's eyes were bright and piercing, like her father's. The thought of the Reverend John Rawlins triggered relief that this rabbi was sending her away. "Because I don't think I could *feel* like a Jew. Not if I lived a million years," she said. "It's inconceivable to me that anyone could ever really want to harm me, to kill my future children, to lock me away from the world. I myself have had certain prejudices against the Jews; I must admit this. I feel unworthy to join a people who bear such a burden of mass hatred."

"You feel *unworthy?*"

"Yes."

Rabbi Gross stared. "Who told you to say that?" he asked.

"I don't know what you mean."

He stood up heavily and walked to the ark. Pulling aside the blue curtains and pushing open the sliding wooden door, he revealed two velvet-encased Torahs. "In these scrolls are the laws," he said. "We do not seek recruits to Judaism; we discourage them. It is written in the Talmud that rabbis must say specific things when apostates from other religions seek us out. The Torah says the rabbi must warn the gentile about the Jew's fate in this world. The Torah also is specific about another detail. If the gentile in effect answers 'I know all this yet I feel unworthy to be a Jew' he is to be accepted immediately for conversion."

Leslie sat down. "You mean you will take me?" she asked faintly.

He nodded. Ah, she thought, what can I do now?

She met with him on Tuesday and Thursday evenings. He talked and she listened, more carefully than she had listened in her most difficult lecture course at college, asking no idle questions, interrupting only when it was vital to get his explanation.

He outlined for her the fundamental principles of the religion. "I will not teach the language," he said. "New York is full of Hebrew teachers. If you wish, go to one of them." In *The Times* she saw an advertisement which brought her to the 92nd Street YMHA, and that took care of Wednesday evenings. Her Hebrew teacher was a worried-looking young Ph.D. candidate at Yeshiva University. His name was Mr. Goldstein and he ate his supper in the cafeteria below the classroom, always the same thing, she noticed, a cream cheese-and-olive on toast and a cup of black coffee. Total: thirty cents. The cuffs of his shirt were frayed and she knew that his supper was modest because he couldn't afford more. Her own well-filled tray by comparison always seemed gluttony to her, and for a couple of weeks she tried cutting down, but the class lasted two hours and then she went to another lecture down the hall, this one on Jewish history, and she found that unless she ate well she became dizzy with hunger.

Mr. Goldstein took his teaching seriously and the evening students were giving up valuable spare time, so they were well-motivated. One of the students, a middle-aged woman, came to only one session and then dropped out. The other fourteen members of the class learned the thirty-two-letter Hebrew alphabet in a week. By the third week they were taking turns saying aloud the silly short sentences of their limited Hebrew vocabularies.

"*Rabi ba*," Leslie read, and translated, "My rabbi is coming," with such exultation that the teacher and class stared.

But when it was again her turn to read aloud, the exercise was: *Mi rabi? Ahbah rabi.* "Who is my rabbi? My father is my rabbi," she translated. She sank quickly into her chair, and when she again glanced at the book it was as though she were looking at the page through milk glass.

Rabbi Gross was not an old man, she realized one evening as she listened to his voice tell her about idols and warn her that the Christian finds it extremely difficult to visualize a God without an image. But he looked and acted old. Moses himself could not possibly have appeared sterner. Now, as he glanced over her shoulder at her notebook, his mouth tightened.

"Never write the name of God. Always write G–d. This is very important. It is one of the commandments that His name should not be taken in vain."

"I'm sorry," she said. "There are so many rules." Her eyes filled. He looked away in disgust and resumed his pacing, his voice droning on, while the knuckles of his right hand gently slapped the palm of his left hand behind his back.

When she had been studying with him for thirteen weeks he told her one evening that she would be converted on the following Tuesday; unless, he suggested delicately, for any reason she could not undergo immersion in the ritual baths on that day.

"Already?" she asked wonderingly. "But I haven't studied for very long. I know so little."

"Young woman, I did not say that you were a learned scholar. But you have absorbed enough information to become a Jew. An ignorant Jew. If you want to be an educated Jew, that is something you will have to arrange by yourself as time goes on." His eyes softened and the tone of his voice altered. "You are a very hard-working girl. You did well."

He gave her the address of the *mikva* and some preliminary instructions. "Do not wear jewelry. No bandages, not even a corn plaster. Your nails should be cut short. Nothing, not even a wisp of cotton in your ear, should keep the waters from touching every outer cell of your body."

By Friday she had a continually nervous stomach. She didn't know how long the ceremonies would take, so she decided to plan on being away from the office the entire day.

"Phil," she said to Brennan, "I need Tuesday off."

He looked at her wearily and then at the pile of unclipped papers. "Holy Mother, our ass is dragging as it is."

"It's important."

He knew all the important reasons why female researchers needed the day off. "Grandmother's funeral?"

"No, I'm becoming a Jew and Tuesday is my conversion."

He opened his mouth to say something and then began to roar. "Jesus," he said, "I was going to say no, but how can I cope with a mind like that?"

Tuesday was gray. She had allowed too much time and she arrived fifteen minutes early at the synagogue where the *mikva* was located. The rabbi was a middle-aged man, bearded like Rabbi Gross but much gentler and very cheerful. He showed her a seat in his office.

"I was just having coffee," he said. "Let me give you a cup."

She started to refuse but then she smelled the coffee when he poured and it was good. When Rabbi Gross arrived he found them sitting and chatting like old friends. Another rabbi arrived a moment later, a younger man, unbearded.

"We will be witnesses to your immersion," Rabbi Gross said. He saw her face and laughed. "We will stay outside, of course. With the door open just a crack. So we can hear the splash when you enter the water."

They conducted her downstairs. The *mikva* was located in a one-story addition at the rear of the synagogue. In a dressing room they told her to make herself comfortable and to wait for someone named Mrs. Rubin. Then the rabbis went away.

Leslie wanted to smoke but she wasn't quite sure that it would be all right. The room was very depressing. It was small, with a wooden floor that creaked when you walked and a small braided rug that had been thrown in front of the little wooden dresser that stood against the wall. The dresser supported a mirror that had little yellow hemorrhages in the lower right corner and light blue hemorrhages in the upper right corner; it gave back a wavy, distorted image when she looked into it, like the mirrors in an amusement-park fun house. The only other furniture was a white-painted kitchen table and one kitchen chair, which she sat on. She was memorizing the nicks in the surface of the table when Mrs. Rubin came.

Mrs. Rubin was gray and plump in a dry, rather nice way. She wore a house dress and a blue apron, and her shoes were medium-heeled black with the leather in each stretched out into two big bumps by bunions. "Take off your clothes," she said.

"All of them?"

"Everything," Mrs. Rubin said without smiling. "Do you know the *brochas?*"

"Yes. At least I did a little while ago."

"I'll leave them. You can look them over." She took from her pocket a mimeographed slip of paper and placed it on the table, then she left the room.

There were no hangers. Leslie draped her clothing over the back of the chair and sat down to wait. The seat of the chair was very smooth. She picked up the paper and looked at it.

Blessed art Thou, O Lord our God, King of the universe, Who hast hallowed us with Thy commandments and commanded us concerning immersion.	ברוד אתה יי אלהינו מלד העולם אשר קדשנו במצותיו וצונו על הטבילה.
Blessed art Thou, O Lord our God, King of the universe, Who hast kept us in life and sustained us and enabled us to reach this significant moment. Amen.	ברוד אתה יי אלהינו מלד העולם שהחינו וקימנו והגיענו לזמן הזה.

She was reviewing the *brochas* when Mrs. Rubin returned and took a small pair of nail clippers from the pocket of her apron. "Your hands," she said.

"I clipped them close myself," Leslie said. She held them up with pride and Mrs. Rubin grasped them and from each finger snicked off another shaving of nail. She unfolded a clean bedsheet and draped it over Leslie's nakedness, then handed her

soap and a washcloth and led her through a door into a shower
room with seven stalls.

"Scrub, *mine kind*," she said.

Leslie hung the sheet from a hook on the wall and washed,
even though she had showered with equal thoroughness in her
own apartment the night before and then had soaked and
scrubbed in her bathtub only two hours before coming to the
mikva.

Through another doorway as she washed she could see the
surface of the pool, still and heavy as lead, gleaming under the
yellow light of a naked bulb. In one of his lectures Rabbi Gross
had told her that Jews had practiced ritual immersion for thousands of years before John the Baptist borrowed the rite. The
waters of the *mikva* had to be natural waters; originally the ceremony had been held in lakes and rivers. Since the modern need
for privacy had driven the pool indoors, rainwater was collected
in troughs on the roof and piped into a tiled tank. After a rela-
tively short while this inert water grew stagnant and unappetiz-
ing, so another tank adjoined the first. Into this second pool continually fresh water was drawn from the city water supply and
heated for comfort. A tiny plug in the wall separating the two
tanks was removed each time the second pool had been filled
with fresh water, allowing the waters in the pools to merge for
a fraction of a second before the plug was replaced. This sanctified the city water without raising its bacteria count, Rabbi Gross
had assured her. Nevertheless, glancing apprehensively at the
surface of the pool as she scrubbed her body, Leslie admitted
to herself that if the water appeared at all unclean she would
not be able to go through with it.

When she left the shower Mrs. Rubin was waiting. She
reached into her apron pocket again and this time took out a
small tortoise shell comb. She pulled it slowly through Leslie's
long hair, tugging gently when the comb hit a tangle. "There
mustn't be a single wet snarl to keep the water from your person,"
she said. "Lift your arms."

Leslie complied submissively and the woman stared at her
close-shaven armpits. "No hair," she said, like a merchant taking
inventory. Then Mrs. Rubin pointed with her forefinger and
handed Leslie the comb.

For a long moment, unbelieving, she could do nothing. "Is that really necessary?" she asked faintly.

Mrs. Rubin nodded. Leslie wielded the comb without looking, feeling the blood in her cheeks and the tears behind her eyelids.

"Come," the woman said finally, hanging the bedsheet around her shoulders again.

A black rubber runner led from the shower room to the pool. At the top of the three cement stairs leading down into the water, Mrs. Rubin stopped her. The old woman walked down the cement runway bordering the pool to the door at the far end of the tank. She opened it and stuck out her head. Leslie felt a draft from the door, which opened onto the back yard of the synagogue.

"*Yedst,*" Mrs. Rubin called. "She is ready."

Leslie could hear the sound of the rabbis conversing in Yiddish as they approached the doorway. The woman left the door open just a crack and came back to her. "Do you want the paper with the prayers?"

"I know the prayers," Leslie said.

"You must duck completely under the water and *then* say the prayers. It is the only time that a *brocha* is said after an act instead of before it. The reason is that the immersion cleanses you of all former religions, so that following it you are able to pray to God as a Jew. To make sure everything you got good and wet you will probably have to duck several times. You are not afraid of the water?"

"I'm not afraid."

"Good," Mrs. Rubin said. She took the sheet.

Leslie walked down the steps. The water was warm. In the middle of the pool it rose to a point just below the bottoms of her breasts. She stood for a moment and stared into it. It looked clean and clear, with a bottom of wavering white tile. She closed her eyes and sank down, holding her breath as she went to a sitting position and she felt against her haunches the crisscrossing grout lines of the tank's tile floor. Then she stood up, sputtering a little, and recited the prayers in a voice that trembled.

"*Oh-main,*" Mrs. Rubin chanted, and she could hear the

amens of the rabbis behind the almost-closed door. Mrs. Rubin
made a downward motion with both arms, like a football official
signaling to the crowd, and Leslie submerged again, this time
more confidently. It was so easy that she wanted to laugh. She
sat in the water, her hair floating, and miraculously she felt
purged of physical and spiritual weight, freed from the guilt of
having lived twenty-two years as a human being. Washed in the
blood of the Lamb, she thought giddily, and rose like a fish from
the bottom. Listen, my children, she thought, and I will tell you
the story of how Momma became a Jewish mermaid, and thereby
hangs a tail. She said the *brochas* this time with more assurance,
but Mrs. Rubin still wasn't satisfied. The arms dropped again,
and so did Leslie. On the third trip down she kept her eyes open,
peering up at the glowing bulb hanging over the pool, sending
its light through the waters to her warm and bright, like the
eye of God. She broke the surface and stood there, panting a
little, feeling her nipples grow in the cold draft that came through
the crack in the door where the rabbis listened, and this time
she said the prayers with gay certainty.

"*Mazel tov,*" Mrs. Rubin said, and as Leslie climbed out of
the pool, water streaming from her flanks, the old lady wrapped
her in the bed sheet and kissed her on both cheeks.

She stood in the rabbi's study with her makeup washed off
and her stringy hair coldly damp upon her neck, feeling as if
she had just gone ten laps in the Davenport Pool at the college.
The rabbi who had given her coffee smiled at her.

"Wilt thou love the Lord thy God with all thine heart, and
with all thy soul and with all thy might?" he asked.

"Yes," she whispered, no longer gay.

"And these words," he said, "which I command thee this
day, shall be upon thy heart: and thou shalt teach them diligently
unto thy children, and thou shalt talk of them when thou sittest
in thine house, and when thou walkest by the way, and when
thou liest down, and when thou risest up. And thou shalt bind
them for a sign upon thine hand, and they shall be for frontlets
between thine eyes. And thou shalt write them upon the door-
posts of thy house, and upon thy gates: that ye may remember
and do all my commandments, and be holy unto your God."

Rabbi Gross came to her and placed his hands upon her head.

"In token of your admission into the household of Israel," he said, "this rabbinical tribunal welcomes you by bestowing upon you the name of Leah bas Avrahom, by which you will henceforth be called in Israel.

"May He, Who blessed our mothers, Sarah, Rebecca, Rachel, and Leah, bless you our sister Leah bas Avrahom, on the occasion of your acceptance into the heritage of Israel and your becoming a true proselyte in the midst of the people of the God of Abraham. May you, under God, prosper in all your ways and may all the work of your hands be blessed. Amen."

Then the youngest rabbi handed her the conversion certificate and she read it:

IN THE PRESENCE OF GOD
AND OF THIS RABBINICAL TRIBUNAL

I hereby declare my desire to accept the principles of Judaism, to adhere to its practices and ceremonies, and to become a member of the Jewish People.

I do this of my own free will and with a full realization of the true significance of the tenets and practices of Judaism.

I pray that my present determination guide me through life so that I may be worthy of the sacred fellowship which I am now privileged to join. I pray that I may ever remain conscious of the privileges and the corresponding duties that my affiliation with the House of Israel imposes upon me. I declare my firm determination to live a Jewish life and to conduct a Jewish home.

If I shall be blessed with male children, I promise to have them brought into the Covenant of Abraham. I further promise to bring up all the children with whom God shall bless me in loyalty to Jewish beliefs and practices and in faithfulness to Jewish hopes and the Jewish way of life.

Hear, O Israel, the Lord our God, the Lord is One!
Blessed is His glorious sovereign Name forever.

And she signed it with a hand that trembled no more than was justified, and the rabbis signed it as witnesses, and Mrs. Rubin kissed her again and she kissed the old lady back and she thanked the rabbis and they shook her hand. The youngest

rabbi told her she was the best-looking conversion he ever
expected to participate in, and they all laughed and she thanked
them all again and left the synagogue. A wind blew and the sky
was still gray. She felt unchanged but she knew that her life
was going to be different from any existence she had ever
dreamed for herself. For a moment, but only for a moment, she
thought about her father and allowed herself to mourn the non-
existence of her mother. Then as she walked briskly down the
street she felt a mounting urgency, a need for a telephone booth
in which she could open her lips and whisper her earth-shaking
secret.

CHAPTER TWENTY-FOUR

Michael came to New York the next day, driving the station
wagon to Little Rock and then sitting in a pitching, tossing air-
liner that ploughed through a spring rainstorm all the way to
La Guardia. She was waiting for him at the airport and it seemed
to him as he hurried toward her that each time he saw her was
like the first time, that he would never become accustomed to
looking at her face.

"The thing I don't understand is the part about the *mikva*,"
he said in the taxi when he had stopped kissing her. "If you
had been converted by a Reform rabbi you would have skipped
all that."

"It was wonderful," she said shyly. "I wanted to do it the
most difficult way. So it would last."

But the next afternoon when they went together to the
Shaarai Shomayim, Max Gross grew pale.

"Why didn't you tell me?" he demanded of Leslie. "If I had
known that the man in your case was Michael Kind, believe me
when I say I never would have converted you."

"But you didn't ask me," she said. "I wasn't trying to deceive you."

"Max," Michael said. "I'm only doing what Moses did. She's a Jew. You made her a Jew."

Rabbi Gross shook his head. "You are not Moses. You are a *nahr*, a fool. And I have helped you to make this mistake."

"I want you to marry us, Max," Michael said quietly. "Both of us would like that very much."

But Rabbi Gross took a Bible from the table and opened it. Swaying, he began to read aloud, disregarding them as if he were alone in the *shul*.

Michael's mouth tightened as he listened to the Hebrew words. "Let's go," he said to Leslie.

When they were in the street she looked at him. "They can't . . . take it back or anything, can they, Michael?"

"You mean the conversion? No, of course not." He took her hand and pressed it. "Don't let him make you miserable, darling."

In the taxi going downtown she retained her grasp on his fingers. "Whom will you ask next? To perform the ceremony."

"One of my classmates at the Institute, I suppose." He thought for a moment and then decided. "Milt Greenfield has a congregation in Bethpage."

He called that afternoon, from a telephone booth in a Lexington Avenue drugstore. Rabbi Greenfield was warm and congratulatory and then silent and wary, in that order.

"You're *sure* it's what you want, Michael?"

"Don't be an ass. If I weren't sure I wouldn't be calling you."

"Well, then, I'm flattered you called *me*, you son of a gun," Greenfield said finally.

That night when Michael's parents were asleep he sat in his old room and searched through the *Modern Reader's Bible* for the English translation of the passage Max Gross had hurled at him to drive him from the synagogue. He found it after a while. Proverbs 5 : 3.

> . . . *The lips of a Strange Woman drop honey,*
> *And her mouth is smoother than oil:*
> > *But her latter end is bitter as wormwood,*
> > *Sharp as a two-edged sword.*

> *Her feet go down to death;*
> *Her steps take hold on Sheol;*
> *So that she findeth not the level path of life:*
> *Her ways are unstable and she knoweth it not.*

He thought that he would have trouble falling asleep. But he dropped off while praying. If he had dreams, he retained no memory of them when he awoke next morning.

At breakfast, he watched his mother uneasily. Leslie had telephoned her father and then had wept very quietly and for a long time. When Michael had suggested that they visit the Reverend John Rawlins and talk things over she had shaken her head. Feeling relief, he had not urged her to change her mind.

He did not want to tell his parents immediately, knowing that there would be a scene and preferring to postpone it.

As he was starting his second cup of coffee the telephone rang. It was Rabbi Sher.

"How did you know I was in New York?" Michael asked after the pleasantries had been exchanged.

"I happened to be talking to Milt Greenfield," Rabbi Sher said.

Good old Milt, Michael thought.

"Can you drop by the Union office for a chat?"

"I'll be there this afternoon," he said.

"I am certain that you've wrestled with this thing from every aspect," Rabbi Sher said with great gentleness. "I just want to be sure that you realize the probable consequences of such a marriage."

"I am marrying a Jewess."

"You are ruining what would certainly be a brilliant pastoral career. So long as you realize that, your decision is valid, if perhaps . . . unwise. I merely want to make sure that you have not overlooked the consequences in a state of—" He struggled for the words.

"Unthinking passion."

Rabbi Sher nodded. "Something like that."

"All our lives we insist, in the face of vicious filth spread in every society in the world, that Jews are as good as the next group, that as individuals all of us are equal in the eyes of God. In answer to the fairy tale about the Protocols of the Wise Men of Zion we carefully explain to our kids that we're Chosen only to carry the great burden of the Covenant between God and man. But deep down, fear has made us the most prejudiced people on the face of the earth. Why is that, Rabbi?"

From outside and far below the sound of horns drifted up to them. Rabbi Sher walked to the window and gazed down at the snarled traffic on Fifth Avenue. Taxicabs. Too many taxicabs. Except when you need one in the rain, he thought. He turned. "How do you think we've survived for more than five thousand years?"

"The girl I'm going to marry is a Jew. Her father is not. But is Judaism a blood line? Or an ethic and a theology and a way of life?"

Rabbi Sher closed his eyes. "Michael, no debates, if you please. Your situation isn't unique, you know. We've met it before this. It has always presented great difficulties." He turned away from the window. "You've made up your mind?"

Michael nodded.

"Then good luck to you." He held out his hand and Michael shook it.

"One more thing, Rabbi," Michael said. "You'd better find somebody else for the Ozarks."

Sher nodded. "With a new wife you won't want to be traveling every day." He made a pyramid of his fingers. "It raises the question of future employment. It might be interesting for you to try something academic. A Hillel chaplaincy, or a job with one of the cultural foundations. We have many requests for recommendations in these areas." He paused. "The campus mind is less apt to be a narrow one."

"I want a congregation." Michael met his gaze steadily.

Rabbi Sher sighed. "Temple boards are made up of parents. They are almost certain to see your marriage—however you see it yourself—as a bad example for their children."

"I want a congregation."

The older rabbi shrugged. "I'll do whatever I can to help you, Michael. Drop in with your wife when you can. I'd like to meet her." They shook hands once more.

When Michael had gone, Rabbi Sher lowered himself into his chair and sat for several minutes without moving, absent-mindedly humming the Toreador Song from *Carmen*. Then he pressed the buzzer on his desk.

"Lillian," he told his secretary when she appeared, "Rabbi Kind is going off the Ozarks circuit."

"You want me to put that card in the Positions Open file?" she asked. She was fading and middle-aged and he never stopped feeling sorry for her.

"Please," he said. When she left his office he sat and hummed all that he could remember of the Bizet music and then he punched the buzzer again.

"Hold that Ozarks card out for a while," he said when she came back. "We may not fill it at all unless we can find a married man to take the circuit."

She shot him a make-up-your-mind-boss look. "That isn't likely," she said.

"No," he agreed, "it isn't."

He walked to the window and leaned with his hands on the sill, looking down. The traffic on Fifth Avenue was a battle-field, with the horns sounding like the shrieks of wounded. Taxicabs, he thought, they're messing up the whole city.

CHAPTER TWENTY-FIVE

There was a time not so long ago when there was no Jewish congregation in Cypress, Georgia. Before the war—the second world war, that is, not the War Between the States—there were only a few dozen families of Jews in the whole town. Their leader was Dave Schoenfeld, the editor and publisher of the weekly Cypress *News,* and he was the great-great-grandson of Captain Judah Schoenfeld who took a Minié ball in the throat while commanding a troop under Hood at Peachtree Creek, so

Dave was more Southerner than Jew, almost like any hardshell Baptist in Cypress except perhaps a little more influential around election time.

Dave Schoenfeld was a lieutenant colonel in Intelligence at Sondrestrom in Greenland when the first Friday-night service was held back in his home town. A rabbi named Jacobs who was chaplain at Camp Gordon brought in a busload of Jewish infantrymen and officiated at a *Yom Kippur* observance in the First Baptist Church by special permission of the deacons. The service was attended by virtually all of the town's Jews and proved to be so popular that it was repeated the following year. On the *Yom Kippur* after *that* there was no rabbi to direct the service, Chaplain Jacobs having been shipped overseas before the arrival of his replacement. The High Holidays came and went without a service in Cypress, and the lack was noted locally and commented upon.

"Why don't we hold our own Sabbath service?" suggested young Dick Kramer, who had cancer and who did a lot of thinking about God.

Others were amenable, so on the following Friday fourteen of them got together in the rumpus room of Ronnie Levitt's house. They pieced together the service out of memory; Ronnie, who had studied voice in New York after World War I before he came home to go into his father's turpentine business, served as cantor. They sang remembered fragments of the service with enthusiasm and volume if not with harmony. In the kitchen upstairs, Rosella Barker, Sally Levitt's maid, lifted her eyebrows and grinned at her fourteen-year-old brother Mervin, who sat at the table drinking coffee and waiting to walk his sister home.

"Those people are born with rhythm, honey," she said. "Those white folks got music bustin' out all over 'em, even the way they walk." And she whooped silently at the expression on the boy's face.

Dave Schoenfeld was upped one grade on paper and was separated as a bird colonel in 1945. The Army had stolen his vintage years. His muscles had lost their tone, his step some of its spring. His hair had thinned and grayed and his prostate had gone bad, necessitating periodic attentions which, characteristically, he had obtained by having an affair with the most desirable nurse on the base. Two weeks after his return to civilian life he had received a note from a former fellow officer, informing him that the girl had taken an overdose of sleeping pills, had had her stomach pumped, and had been flown to Walter Reed Hospital for psychiatric observation. Schoenfeld had dropped the note into his wastebasket along with a large sheaf of unusable press releases and invitiations to social events he did not wish to attend.

He had come back to Georgia to find Cypress almost a thousand people bigger, with a lumber mill, a small electronics subcontracting plant, and the promise that a medium-size textile corporation was going to move out lock, stock, and looms from Fall River, Massachusetts. He was a rich, good-looking bachelor of forty-eight, and the many women he had known over the years and the many men who had benefited from his political influence at one time or another all flocked to greet him warmly. They made him feel glad to be home. He spent $119,000 to convert the *News* and its commercial printing shop from letterpress to offset, a process he had come to admire greatly in the military. He changed the paper from weekly to semiweekly to take advantage of the rise in potential circulation and hired an energetic young fellow fresh out of the Henry W. Grady School of Journalism to do the bulk of the new work, then he relaxed and resumed his twice-a-week poker games with Judge Boswell, Nance Grant, Sunshine Janes, and Sheriff Nate White.

For twenty years the five men had shared more than a love for poker. Together they controlled cotton, peanuts, law, power, and public opinion in Cypress. Their steadily growing syndicate holdings had long ago made each a wealthy man.

They welcomed Dave back into their midst.

"Well, how d'ya like it up in Green Land?" asked the Sheriff, pronouncing it as if it were two words.

"Like to froze my ass off," Dave said, shuffling the cards.

Sunshine cut. "Get your fill of that Eskimo nooky? Must be kind of fish-oily."

"Who, me?"

Sunshine guffawed and the other men smiled.

"Let's see if it changed my luck," Dave said as he started to deal.

He had taken a great many photographs and seven weeks after his return he was invited to give a talk before the men's club of the Methodist church. The color slides of the ice cap and the snow cliffs proved to be a great success, as did his anecdotes and funny stories about the lives of the Eskimos and the service men. On the following day Ronnie Levitt called him on the telephone and asked if he would repeat the talk after the *oneg shabbat* Friday night in the Levitt home.

The rumpus room was crowded with Jewish worshipers, not all of whom he recognized, he noted with surprise on Friday evening. Despite Ronnie's ragged leadership, the service was chanted enthusiastically. There was no sermon. His own talk afterward drew polite applause.

"How long has this been goin' on?" he asked.

"A long time," Dick Kramer said eagerly. "We just ordered prayer books. But you can see what we need. We should have a more suitable place to congregate, and a regular rabbi."

"I didn't think I'd been invited here because of a sudden burst of interest in polar bears," Dave said drily.

"We've got about fifty Jewish families in town now," Ronnie said. "What we need is a small frame house we can buy cheap and fix up to make a decent temple. A rabbi wouldn't cost a great deal. We can all pay dues."

"Can you raise enough from the membership to cover the entire program?" he asked, knowing that they couldn't or they wouldn't have been courting him.

"We need a few principal donors, people who can give substantial contributions for the first couple of years," Ronnie said. "I can help out in that respect. If you will assume a similar responsibility, we can get rolling."

"How much?"

Levitt shrugged. "Five-ten thousand."

Dave appeared to think carefully for a few moments. "I don't think so," he said finally. "I think services like these are fine and I'd like to join you again some time. But it doesn't pay to try to develop too fast. I think we should wait until there are more members, so everyone can feel he has an equal stake in the purchase of the buildin' and the hirin' of the rabbi."

They stood clustered around him, reluctant to turn away, with carbon-copy expressions of blank disappointment on their faces.

Saturday night Schoenfeld won one hundred thirty-one dollars playing poker. "What's this new industry doin' to our labor pool?" he asked.

"Nothin'," said the Judge.

"You let a few more factories into this town and labor's goin' to start grabbin' us by the short hair," Dave said.

Nance Grant bit the tip from a thick black cigar and spat the tatter to the floor. "Nobody else is comin' in. We let in just enough to help us a little with some of the chores."

Schoenfeld was puzzled. "Since when do we need help? And with what?"

The Judge rested a manicured hand lightly on his arm. "You've been away a while, Davey boy. Damn government's goin' to be givin' us more trouble than the five-year itch. Won't hurt us any to have some friends around to fight off the socialists."

"Our expenses goin' up all the time, too," Nance said. "Be kinda nice to share some of 'em."

"What kind of expenses?"

"Well, Billy Joe Raye, for one. He's a preacher. Fire an' brimstone an' the layin' on of hands."

"A faith healer?" Schoenfeld asked. "Why should we pay his way?"

The Sheriff cleared his throat. "Damned if he don't keep 'em in line for us better'n cheap whiskey."

Schoenfeld refused one of Nance's stogies with thanks and took a Havana from his inside pocket. "Well," he said, puffing on the match as he built the ash, "it can't cost us a hell of a lot for one preacher."

The Judge looked at him calmly. "Hundred grand."

They all grinned at the expression on his face.

"He's got an air-conditioned tent costs nearly that much alone," Sunshine said. "*An'* a radio program. *An'* tee-vee."

"What we gave him is just a grubstake. His collections are

already big enough to keep him just fine," Nance said. "And the
more this town builds a reputation as a religious, God-fearing
community, the better off we are."

"Goddam it, it don't have to *build* a reputation," the Judge
said. "This *is* that kind of community. Hell, now even the Jews
are holding prayer meetin's." There was a small silence. "I beg
your pardon," he said to Dave with courtly grace.

"No apology needed," Schoenfeld said easily.

That night he telephoned Ronnie Levitt. "I haven't been
able to get the temple out of my mind," he said. "What do you
say we get together again and talk it over?"

They found a small cottage in good repair and bought it,
Dave and Ronnie putting up five thousand dollars apiece for the
purchase of the building and the two-acre lot of land. It was
understood that the rest of the congregation would contribute a
sum sufficient to pay for renovations and the salary of the rabbi.

Ronnie Levitt hesitantly suggested that the temple be
named Sinai. Dave shrugged and nodded. There were no voices
of dissent.

"I'm goin' to New York next month to have a talk with the
paper's national reps," Schoenfeld said. "I'll see what I can do
about findin' us a rabbi."

He had exchanged correspondence with a man named Sher,
and when he got to New York he called the Union of American
Hebrew Congregations and invited the rabbi to lunch the next
day. Only after he said good-by did it occur to him that the
clergyman might be restricted to kosher food.

But when they met in the office of the Union of American
Hebrew Congregations, Rabbi Sher made no mention of where
they should eat. Downstairs, in the taxi, Dave leaned toward
the driver and said, "Voisin." He glanced quickly at Rabbi Sher
but saw nothing in his face but repose.

At the restaurant he ordered crêpes stuffed with lobster. The
rabbi ordered chicken *sauté échalote*, and Dave grinned and told
him that he had worried about not selecting a Jewish restaurant.
"I eat everything but shellfish," Sher said.

"Is there a rule?"

"No, no. Just the way I was raised. Every Reform rabbi makes up his own mind."

During the meal they spoke of the new temple.

"What will it cost us to hire a new rabbi?" Schoenfeld asked.

Rabbi Sher smiled. He spoke a name familiar to two-thirds of the Jews in the United States. "For him, fifty thousand dollars a year. Perhaps more. For a young fellow just out of rabbinical school, six thousand. For an older rabbi who has had many congregations without being kept on, six thousand. For a good man with a couple of years of experience under his belt, perhaps ten thousand."

"We can forget about the great man. Can you recommend a name or two from the other categories?"

The rabbi carefully broke his crusty roll. "I know somebody who is very good. He served briefly as an assistant in a large congregation in Florida and then he had his own circuit congregation in Arkansas. He's young and energetic and personable and extremely bright."

"Where is he now?"

"Here in New York. He is teaching Hebrew to children."

Schoenfeld shot him a keen look. "Full-time?"

"Yes."

"Why?"

"He's had some difficulty in finding a congregation. Several months ago he married a young woman who is a convert from Christianity."

"A Catholic?"

"I believe not."

"I don't think the marriage would bother us any," Schoenfeld mused. "We live very closely with our Christian neighbors. And as long as the man is in a tight spot, we should be able to get him for seven thousand, wouldn't you say?"

Something, Schoenfeld couldn't tell just what, flitted quickly across the rabbi's features and then was gone. "That will have to be between you and the young man," Sher said politely.

Schoenfeld took out a small leather-covered notebook and his pen. "What is his name?"

"Rabbi Michael Kind."

CHAPTER TWENTY-SIX

They bought a blue Plymouth convertible, two years old and with a set of almost-new tires, from a dealer in the Bronx. Then they drove back to the apartment on West 6oth Street and made arrangements to have Leslie's desk and their combined library of books sent to them Railway Express.

There was a last, uncomfortable dinner with his parents, an evening which dragged with the weight of things past said and unsaid. ("You damn fool," his father had cried when he had broken the news, "you don't *marry* them!" And he had seen sudden lights in Abe Kind's eyes behind the shadows of despair, the flickering of flame in coals of guilt that had been banked for years.) Throughout the evening Dorothy and Leslie chatted about recipes. When finally they kissed good-by, Dorothy was dry-eyed and preoccupied. Abe wept.

Next morning they drove to Hartford.

Inside the Hastings Congregational Church they sat in the gloom of a hallway on an old walnut bench until the Reverend Mr. Rawlins came out of his office, saying good-by to a young man and a young woman.

"Small weddings are the best kind," he was saying as he walked them to the door. "The warmest and the most sensible."

He looked at them, sitting there. "Well, Leslie," he said, his tone unchanged.

Michael and Leslie stood up. She introduced them.

"Will you have tea?"

He ushered them into his study and they sat and had tea and cookies served by a poker-faced middle-aged woman. They exchanged uncomfortable small talk.

"Remember the spice cookies Aunt Sally used to make?" Leslie asked her father as the tea things were removed. "Sometimes I think of her and I can taste them."

"Spice cookies?" he said. He turned to Michael. "Sally was my sister-in-law. A good woman. Died two years ago."

"I know," Michael said.

"She left Leslie one thousand dollars. Do you still have that money, Leslie?"

"Yes," Leslie said. "Yes, I do."

The minister wore rimless glasses; behind them his pale blue eyes observed Michael.

"Do you think you will like the South?"

"I've spent several years in Florida and Arkansas," Michael said. "I think that people are people, everywhere."

"As one grows older one begins to note significant differences."

They were silent. "Well," Leslie said, "we must be going." She kissed the smooth white cheek. "Take care of yourself, father."

"The Lord will take care of me," he said, showing them to the door.

"He will take care of us, too," Michael said. His father-in-law appeared not to have been listening.

Two days later Leslie and Michael drove into Cypress, Georgia, on a hot afternoon in early summer that foretold what the deep season in that town would be like. In the main square, the heat shimmered in visible waves from the bronze surface of the equestrian statue of General Thomas Mott Lainbridge. Michael idled the car next to the grassy rotary which bore the statue, and they squinted at it through the bright sunshine. They could make out only the name.

"Ever hear of him?" he asked Leslie.

She shook her head. He pulled over to the curb. Four teen-aged boys lounged outside the drugstore in the shade of the awning.

"Sir," Michael said to one of them. He stuck his thumb at General Thomas Mott Lainbridge. "Who was he?"

The boy looked at his friends and they grinned. "Lainbridge."

"Not his name," Leslie said. "What did he do?"

One of the boys left the shade and walked slowly to the statue. He pushed his face near the plaque at its base and paused, his lips moving soundlessly. Then he returned. "Commandin' General, Second Georgia Fusiliers."

"Fusiliers were infantry," Leslie said. "What's he doing on a horse?"

"Ma'am?"

"We thank you," Michael said. "Do you know where we can find Eighteen Piedmont Road?"

It was a three-minute drive. It turned out to be a small green house with a sagging porch and a weedy lawn. The windows were unwashed.

"It looks nice," she said uncertainly.

He kissed her cheek. "Welcome home." He stood in the front seat of the convertible and searched the street ahead, looking on the odd-numbered side because the temple was number 45. He was unable to guess which of the buildings down the street might be his new responsibility.

"Wait a minute," she said. She got out of the car and ran lightly up the steps. The front door was unlocked. "You go ahead," she said. "See it for the first time by yourself. Then come right back to me."

"I love you," he told her.

The numerals had been removed when Sinai had been painted, and he drove past the temple without knowing. But 47 was plainly marked on the house next door and he turned the car around and parked in the temple driveway. There was no sign. There would have to be a sign, small and dignified.

As he entered, he took a *yarmulka* from his back pocket and put it on.

Inside, it was cooler. Interior walls had been ripped out to make a large room for the sanctuary. The kitchen and the bathroom had been retained, and there were two small rooms off the central hallway which would be suitable for a general office and a rabbi's study. The floors were freshly varnished; he walked down a path of newspapers which led from room to room.

There was no *bema*, but an ark stood against one wall. He opened it and saw that it contained a Torah. On the velvet cover was a thin silver tag which informed him that the Torah had been donated by Mr. and Mrs. Ronald G. Levitt in memory of Samuel and Sarah Levitt. He stroked the scroll and then kissed his fingertips the way his grandfather had taught him so long ago.

"Thank you for this, my first temple," he said aloud. "I will try to make it truly a house of the Lord." The sound of his voice bounced back at him hollowly from the bare walls. Everything smelled of paint.

Number 18 Piedmont Road was not painted. Nor had it been washed for a long time. Dust covered everything. Small red spiders moved on the ceilings overhead, and a long white smear of dried bird-droppings defaced the front window.

Leslie had found a pail. She had filled it with water and placed it on the gas range, which she was trying in vain to ignite.

"There's no hot water," she said. "We need a mop and a scrub brush and soap. I'd better make a list."

Her voice was too calm, tipping him off about what to expect as he moved through the house. The furniture was summer-cottage borax and needed more than paint. A rung was missing from one of the rickety chairs, and another chair lacked a section of its back. In the bedroom, the stained brown mattress was folded back, exposing rusty and sagging springs. The wallpaper appeared to be ante-bellum.

When she returned to the kitchen he couldn't meet her eyes. She had wasted her last match trying to light the gas jet.

"Damn," she said. "What's the matter with this thing? The pilot light's working."

"Wait a minute," he said. "Got a pin?"

The only one she could find was on the fastener of a cameo brooch, but he used it to poke clear the little holes in the gas ring. Then he struck one of his matches and the burner caught with a puff, giving a steady blue-white flame.

"The water will be heated by the time you're back with the soap," she said.

But he shut off the gas. "Tonight both of us will work. But first comes dinner."

When they got into the car, each knew that the other was relieved to be free of the shabby, dirty house.

That night, while perspiration stung their eyes and dripped

from their faces, they scrubbed furniture and walls. When finally they finished, after midnight, they stood in the bathtub and washed each other clean. There was a serviceable shower but no curtain; Leslie turned on the cold water at full pressure, not caring when the spray glanced off their bodies and wet the entire bathroom.

"Let it dry," she said wearily. She walked naked into the bedroom and groaned. "There are no sheets." She pointed to the stained mattress and for the first time her mouth trembled. "I can't sleep on that."

Michael pulled on his trousers and walked barefooted and shirtless to the car, the trunk of which contained two blue Navy blankets purchased at a surplus-goods store in Manhattan. He carried the blankets into the house and spread them on the mattress and Leslie turned off the light. They lay in the dark together and, dumbly seeking to comfort her, he knew of nothing else to do but to put his arms around her and draw her nakedness to him. But she made a small sound in the back of her throat, half groan, half sigh.

"Hot," she said.

He kissed her head and flopped back. It was the first time she had denied herself to him. He forced himself to think of other things, the temple, his first sermon, plans for a Hebrew school. With the heat above them and the prickly wool blankets underneath, they somehow fell asleep.

In the morning Michael awoke first. He lay and looked at his sleeping wife; at her hair, straight and stringy from last night's shower and the humidity; at her nostrils, moving almost imperceptibly each time she exhaled, as if in afterthought; at the brown birthmark which surrounded a single golden hair beneath her right breast; at her flesh, pale and soft with the moist heat. Eventually she opened her eyes. For a long time they stared at one another. Then she tugged the hair on his chest and leaped from the bed.

"Come on, Rabbi, we've got a busy day ahead. I want to make this dump into a home."

They repeated the shower routine and then, wet, discovered that the other clean towels were still in the trunk of the car. They put underwear on their dripping bodies and let the air dry their skin tight as they breakfasted on milk and corn flakes they had bought the night before.

"The first thing you want to do is buy sheets," Leslie said.

"I'd like to get a decent bed. And a dinette set."

"Talk to the landlord first. After all, we're renting the furniture, too. Maybe he'll replace some of it." She frowned. "How much do we have left in the bank? We're going to have to pay ninety dollars a month for this palace, according to their letter."

"We've got enough," he said. "I'm going to telephone Ronald Levitt, the congregation president, and find out some of the businesses in town that are owned by temple members. I might as well buy whatever we need from the people who are paying my salary."

He shaved as well as he could with cold water, then dressed and kissed her good-by.

"Don't worry about me today," she said. "You buy what we need and keep it in the car while you get busy at the temple. I'll walk over to the General's square for lunch."

When he had gone she pulled her old jeans and a halter from the suitcase and put them on. She pulled her hair back with one hand and used an elastic band to make a ponytail. Then she heated water and, her feet bare, got down on her hands and knees and began to scrub the floors.

She did the bathroom and the bedroom first, then the living room. She was one third through with the kitchen floor, her back to the door, when she felt that she was being watched and she looked over her shoulder.

The man was standing on the back porch, smiling at her through the screen of the door. She dropped the scrub brush into the pail and clambered to her feet, wiping her palms on the front of the jeans.

"Yes?" she said faintly. He wore seersucker slacks and a short-sleeved white shirt and a tie and a Panama hat, but no jacket. I'll have to tell Michael, she thought, probably it's perfectly all right not to wear a suit coat around here.

"I'm David Schoenfeld," he said. "Your landlord."

Schoenfeld. He was on the temple board, she remembered.

"Come in," she said. "I'm sorry, I was scrubbing so hard I didn't hear you knock."

He smiled as he entered. "I didn't knock. You looked so pretty, workin' away like that, I thought I'd just look on for a while." She glanced at him warily, her feminine antennae catching emanations, but his smile was friendly and his eyes were impersonal.

They sat at the kitchen table. "I'm sorry I can't offer refreshments," she said. "We're not at all settled."

He made a small protesting motion with the hat in his hand. "I just wanted to welcome you and the Rabbi to Cypress. Temple Sinai is new at this sort of thing. I suppose we should have had a committee to get things ready for you. Is there anything you need?"

She laughed. "A vacation. This house certainly needed a going over."

"I guess it did," he said. "I haven't been in it since before the war. While I was in the Army an agent took care of it for me. I didn't expect you this soon, or it would have been ready." He looked at her perspiration-beaded neck. "Around here, we have colored girls to help people like you with this kind of work. I'll send one over this afternoon."

"That won't be necessary," she said.

"I insist. A free introductory service of the landlord."

"And I thank you. But I'm almost finished," she said firmly.

He looked away first, grinning. "Well," he said, jiggling the chair in which he sat, "at least I can replace these matchsticks. I'll see what else we can come up with in the way of furniture."

He rose and she saw him to the door. "There is one other thing, Mr. Schoenfeld," she said.

"Ma'am?"

"I would appreciate it if you would replace the mattress."

His lips did not smile. But she was glad when his eyes left her face.

"Happy to," he said, tipping his hat.

By the next day their future no longer seemed unbearable, even in their private thoughts.

Michael had mentioned the lack of a *bema* to Ronnie Levitt, and the following day a carpenter came to the temple to build a low platform at one end of the room according to the Rabbi's specifications. Folding chairs arrived for the sanctuary, and furniture for the office. He hung his framed diplomas on the wall and took a long time deciding how to arrange his study.

A van came to the house and two Negro men took out most of the old furniture, replacing it with attractive new pieces. Even while Leslie was directing the placing of the new things, Sally Levitt came to call. Five minutes later, while Mrs. Levitt was still there, two other ladies of the congregation rang the doorbell. The three bore gifts: a pineapple cake, a bottle of California sherry, a bouquet of flowers.

This time Leslie was ready for callers. She offered the sherry, she served iced tea, and she cut the cake.

Sally Levitt was small and brunette, with a pouting mouth and a tight youthful body that was betrayed by the crow's-feet wrinkles at her eyes. "I know a mill where you can get marvelous curtains," she told Leslie, casting an appraising eye around the room. "This place has tremendous possibilities."

"I'm really beginning to think so," Leslie said, smiling.

That evening, as she cooked dinner, her desk and their books arrived from New York.

"Michael, I hope we can stay here for the rest of our lives!" Leslie cried when they had unpacked the books and placed them on the shelves.

That night, on the new mattress, the Kinds made love for the first time in the new house.

Temple Sinai was dedicated on the following Sunday morning. Judge Boswell was the dedication speaker. He orated long and eloquently about the Judaic-Christian heritage, about the common ancestry of Moses and Jesus, and about the spirit of democracy in Cypress, "like fine wine in the peaceful Georgia air, allowin' men to live as brothers irregardless of choice of church," while a small knot of colored children gathered across the street to point and giggle or to gaze in wide-eyed silent curiosity at the white people on the opposite sidewalk.

"I am happy and honored," the Judge concluded, "to have been invited by my Hebra neighbors to participate in the christenin' of their new house of worship." He paused, realizing that all was not well, then beamed as the applause began.

Midway in the ceremonies Michael had begun to notice a stream of cars moving slowly and steadily past the temple. Courtesy had kept his eyes glued to the speakers' faces. However, at the conclusion of the dedication he was called upon to recite the blessing. Finishing it, blinking his eyes against the strong sun, he looked over the heads of the disintegrating crowd.

The line of cars still came.

There were vehicles of all models and makes. Some of them had Alabama and Tennessee registration plates. There were pickups and flivvers, farm trucks and an occasional Cadillac or Buick.

Ronnie Levitt bore down on him. "Rabbi," he said. "The ladies are serving coffee inside. The Judge is going to join us. You two will have a chance to talk."

"These cars," Michael said. "Where are they going?"

Ronnie smiled. "To church. In a tent. There's a minister who holds a prayer meetin' about three miles out of town. Pulls people in from all over the countryside."

Michael watched the cars continue to appear at one end of the street and disappear down the other. "That must be quite a minister," he said, trying unsuccessfully to keep the envy out of his voice.

Ronnie shrugged. "I think some of them just like to get their faces on the television," he said.

That Friday evening Temple Sinai was full, which pleased but did not surprise him. "They'll come tonight because it's a novelty," he had told Leslie. "It's the long haul that will count."

They welcomed the Bride of the Sabbath with fervor. He had chosen as his first text a portion from "A Song of Trust," Psalm 11 : 14.

> *The LORD is in his holy temple,*
> *The LORD, his throne is in heaven;*
> *His eyes behold, his eyelids try, the children of men.*

He had prepared the sermon with care. As he finished delivering it, he knew that he had held the interest of his congregation. When they sang *Ain Kailohainu* he could hear his wife's voice mingling sweetly with the others and as she sang she smiled up at him from the first row.

After the blessing they clustered around him babbling their praise and congratulations. In the kitchen the women prepared tea and coffee and thin sandwiches and small cakes; the *oneg shabbat* was as successful as the service.

Ronnie Levitt made a short speech, thanking the Rabbi and the various committees for making the opening of the temple possible. He gestured to the hallway, where a table was covered with bouquets of flowers. "Our Christian neighbors have demonstrated their friendship to us," he said. "I think it would be fitting for us to demonstrate our friendship to them. Therefore I am donating one hundred dollars annually for the purchase of two plaques to be given each year to the men chosen to receive the Temple Sinai Brotherhood Awards."

Applause.

Dave Schoenfeld stood. "I would like to commend Ron for a wonderful idea and a magnanimous gesture. And I would like to nominate the first recipients of our Brotherhood Awards. Judge Harold Boswell and the Reverend Billie Joe Raye."

Great applause.

"What have they done for brotherhood?" Michael asked Sally Levitt.

She closed her long-lashed eyes. "Oh, Rabbi," she said in a throaty whisper, "they're the most brilliant men in the world!"

CHAPTER TWENTY-SEVEN

The congregation wanted a Hebrew school limited to Sunday-morning sessions. When Michael insisted that classes also be held after public school sessions on Monday and Wednesday afternoons, they fought feebly and then gave in. It was the only friction, and the victory, although small, made him feel secure.

The Kinds' social life blossomed. Michael's evenings were busy and unpredictable, and they tried to limit themselves. They turned down membership in three bridge clubs, and Leslie began to play contract with Sally Levitt and six other women on Wednesday evenings, when Michael led a male seminar in Judaism at the temple.

One evening, at a cocktail party given by the Larry Wolfsons in honor of her sister and brother-in-law from Chicago, Leslie was asked what she had done before her marriage, and she mentioned her job on the magazine.

"We could use a good feature writer at the *News*," Dave Schoenfeld said, deftly snaring a gibson from a passing tray. "Can't pay New York prices of course, but I wish you'd give it a try."

"You've got yourself a girl," she said. "What are your sacred cows?"

"You can write about anything except early pregnancies and United Nations darkies," he said.

"That's too restrictive for me," she said.

"Come on down to the office in the morning," he said as he moved away. "We'll line up your first assignment."

That night as she and Michael got ready for bed she told him about the encounter.

"Sounds good," he said. "You going to do it?"

"I guess so," she said. "But I don't know if I can get away with it. They're so damn sick about skin color. Last Wednesday night at bridge the girls spent half an hour telling each other how impossible the *schwartzes* have become since the war. And they didn't bother to lower their voices because Lena Millman's maid was working in the next room. The poor girl kept right on working with her face a perfect blank, as if they were talking Hindustani."

"Or Yiddish." He sighed. "Actually, some of our members have very good attitudes about race."

"Privately. Very privately. They're so intimidated they're afraid to discuss it unless all the windows are locked. Darling?" she said. "Aren't you going to have to face this kind of thing from the pulpit sooner or later?"

"Make it later," he said, closing the bathroom door behind him.

He had already admitted defeat in the area of race relations.

The Temple Sinai *shamus,* or janitor, who in a Brooklyn *shul* would have been a pious old Jew using the job as an excuse for a life of prayer and study, was a plump Negro named Joe Williams.

Michael observed from the start that the trash bin was never emptied, the metalwork never shined, the floors unwashed and unwaxed unless he insisted repeatedly that they be done. Williams also did other things infrequently, as testified by the fact that he carried with him an acrid odor that matched the salt-rimmed stains which spread beneath both armpits of his shirt.

"We should fire him and get somebody else," Michael insisted to Saul Abelson, chairman of the Maintenance Committee.

Abelson smiled tolerantly. "They're all alike, Rabbi," he said. "The next one will be just as bad. You have to ride their tails."

"You mean to tell me I don't see clean, cheerful, and alert Negroes every day right here in town? Why don't we try to hire someone like that?"

"You don't understand yet," Abelson said patiently. "If Joe's been lazy I'll have to talk with him."

One day, irritated because the sacramental silver hadn't been polished, Michael invaded the *shamus'* domain.

The cellar was gloomy, smelling of dampness and molding newspapers.

He found Joe Williams in a drunken sleep on a grimy army cot. He shook him; the man mumbled and licked his lips but did not waken. There was a notebook and a stub of pencil on the floor next to the sleeping figure. Michael picked it up.

He read only the single line scrawled on the first page.

Nigger is six foot tall. World like a room with four foot ceiling.

He placed the notebook where he had found it and never bothered Joe Williams again.

Instead, he began to lock himself into his study for half an hour each Friday afternoon. Spreading newspapers on his desk, he used a rag and International Silver Polish to make the sterling Sabbath wine chalice gleam in time for the evening service. And sometimes, while he rubbed, getting the gray grit of the polish under his nails and setting his teeth on edge, he could hear thumping or an occasional curse from the *shamus'* domain in the cellar, proving that Joe Williams was still alive.

Leslie wrote a story for each edition of the *News*. They were light, humorous pieces or historical articles with a human-interest angle. For each she received seven dollars and fifty cents and a byline which her husband regarded with a certain amount of awe.

Their lives developed routine, and they found it good. The days fell predictably as tin ducks in a shooting gallery, and they both became certain that they had always been married to one another. She started to knit him a bulky sweater for a first-anniversary present, which he soon discovered hidden in the spare closet and thereafter studiously avoided.

As the seasons changed the leaves turned, not the bright colors splashed on the trees along the Hudson and the Charles, but shriveled browns and anaemic yellows. Then the rains came instead of the snows of their previous winters, the kind of rains to which they were unaccustomed.

One evening the rain came with a rush as Leslie walked past the General's statue toward the office of the *News*. She ran until she burst through the door and stood inside, dripping and gasping. The small editorial room was deserted except for Dave Schoenfeld, who was turning out lights and preparing to follow the example of the office staff and go home.

"Didn't you ever learn to swim?" he said, grinning.

She sat on a desk, tilting her head and squeezing water out of handfuls of hair. "The Atlantic Ocean just fell out of the sky in pieces no bigger than nickels," she said.

"That's news, but the edition's closed," he said. "We'll have to tell them about that on Thursday."

She took off her sodden coat and rescued her story from the pocket. Some of the pages had gotten wet, and she smoothed them flat on the top of a filing cabinet and started to edit the copy. The feature was about a man who had been a brakeman

on the Atlantic Coast Line for thirty years. After his retirement, he had confided to her, he had stayed drunk for three
months, living in a caboose in a siding outside Macon under the
care and protection of loyal former colleagues. "Don't print that,
if you please," he had said with great dignity, "just say I spent
the time traveling on my railroad pass," and Leslie had promised despite a vague feeling that she was breaking a journalistic
code. When the old man had sobered up, in sheer boredom one
day he had picked up a chunk of pine and a pocket knife and
had started to whittle. Now his American eagles sold as fast as
he could carve them, and at seventy-eight he was still making
bank deposits.

It was a good feature and she thought that she might try
to sell it to the Associated Press or the North American Newspaper Alliance and surprise Michael with the check. She edited
it carefully, making a low moaning sound when her pencil
point mushed through a wet spot in the copy paper.

Dave Schoenfeld came over to her and read for a few minutes over her shoulder. "Looks like a pretty fair piece," he said,
and she nodded.

"Rabbi's been pretty busy these nights?"

She nodded, still reading.

"Must get lonesome."

She shrugged. "It gives me time to work on these stories."

"You spelled chisel wrong, next-to-last graph," he said.
"*Ee-el*, not *el-ee*." She nodded and made the correction. She
was so engrossed in the editing of the story that it took her a
little while to realize that what she felt was his hand. By the
time she was ready to admit this somewhat astounding fact
to herself he had bent forward and covered her mouth with
his. She stood perfectly still, her lips closed, her hands by her
sides still holding a pencil and a piece of copy, until he took
his mouth away. "Don't be frightened," he said.

She carefully gathered up the pages of the story and walked
away from him to where her coat lay in a wet heap on the
advertising counter. She put it on and pushed the story into
her pocket.

"When can I see you?" he said.

She merely looked at him.

"You'll change your mind," he said. "I have things to teach you and you'll think about them."

She turned and walked toward the door.

"I wouldn't say anything to anybody," he said. "I can break your little *Yiddisheh* parson in ways you never dreamed of."

When she was outside, she walked very slowly in the rain. She didn't think she was crying, but her face was so wet almost at once that she couldn't be sure. She wished that she had left the story. The poor old man with the pocket knife and the pieces of wood, she thought, waiting for his name and his picture in the paper.

Their anniversary fell on a Sunday and they had to get up early because Michael taught a nine-o'clock class at the Temple. They exchanged gifts at the breakfast table, and he wore his sweater and she was very happy with the cameo earrings he had bought for her months before.

After lunch Michael took a rake and attacked the foundation beds, pulling out bucket after bucket of evil-looking leaves. He had finished one bed and was halfway through another when the parade of cars began.

This time he had a vantage point and plenty of time. He forgot the leaves and sat back to observe the cars.

The sick people usually sat in the back seat.

Many of them held crutches. Some of the cars had wheelchairs strapped to the roof or sticking out of the trunk.

Once in a while a rented ambulance rolled by.

Finally he could stand it no longer. He dropped his weeding tool and went into the house. "I wish we had a television set," he told Leslie. "I'd like to see what that fellow has that attracts so many people every Sunday."

"He's only a couple of miles away," she said. "Why don't you take a ride out to his tent?"

"On our first anniversary?"

"Oh, go ahead," she said. "It will only be for an hour or two."

"I think I will," he said.

He had no idea where the prayer meeting was held, but finding it was simple. He waited for the first break in the line of traffic and then pulled his car out of the driveway. The line

snaked over the curling road, through the General's square, out
the other side of town, past a Negro district of dilapidated houses
and unpainted shacks, and onto the state highway. Here it mated
with another motorized serpent which came from the opposite
direction. The new line, Michael saw, contained in addition to
Georgia cars a few vehicles bearing plates from South Carolina
and North Carolina.

Long before the big tent came into view, cars began turning
off the road and bumping over the fields to park under the
direction of Negro youths and straw-hatted white farm boys
who took money and made change, standing near homemade
signs whose prices rose as the cars drew closer to the tent:

PARKING 50¢.
PARK YOUR CAR 75¢.
PARK HERE $1.00.

Some of the cars, Michael's included, remained on the highway until they came to a huge red-dirt parking lot which had
been bulldozed to encircle the canvas church. The parking lot
was roped off from the highway. Entrance was gained through
a narrow ropeless opening, hardly more than the width of a
single car, which was manned by a bald man wearing shiny
black trousers, a white shirt and a black cotton tie.

"Bless you, brother," he said to Michael.

"Good afternoon."

"That will be two dollars fifty cents."

"Two-fifty. For parking?"

The man smiled. "We try to keep this lot reserved for the
lame an' the halt," he said. "Our method of doin' this kindness
is to charge two dollars fifty cents per car. Money goes to the
Holy Fundamentalist Preachers Fund to further the Lord's
work. If you rather not pay it, you can go back an' park in one
of the fields."

Michael looked over his shoulder. The road behind him was
solidly blocked. "I insist," he said. He reached for his money and
isolated two one-dollar bills and a fifty-cent piece.

"God bless you," the man said, still smiling.

Michael parked his car and walked toward the tent.
Ahead of him a thin, pasty-faced little boy leaned against a car
mudguard and made gargling sounds.

"Now you listen here, Ralphie Johnson, you cut that out," a middle-aged woman said as she stood over the boy. "Here we come all this way, with that healin' preacher only a few feet off from us, an' you start your monkey business. You just come on. Hear?"

The boy began to cry. "Can't," he whispered. His lips were light blue, as if he had stayed in the water too long.

Michael stopped. "Can I help you?"

"Perhaps if you can carry him in?" the woman asked hesitantly.

The boy closed his eyes when Michael lifted him. Inside, the tent was already crowded. Michael set his burden down on one of the wooden folding chairs.

"Say thank you to the nice man, Ralphie," the woman said brightly. The blue lips didn't move. The eyes remained closed.

Michael nodded and moved away. The chairs in the front of the tent were filled with people. He moved into an empty row about two thirds back and took a seat in the middle. In three minutes the entire row was filled. Ahead of him sat a fat woman whose head twitched spasmodically and with regular rhythm, left to right and then straight again, as if pulled by a string.

In the seat to his left sat a middle-aged blind man eating a sandwich held in long, narrow hands hooked into claws by rheumatoid arthritis.

In the seat to his right sat a well-dressed, attractive woman who looked fit and sound. She kept brushing her hand across her bosom. Presently she flicked her fingers over Michael's shoulder.

"Joy," the woman in the seat next to her said softly. "Leave the man alone."

"But the ants," she said. "Now they're all over him."

"Just leave him alone. He likes them."

The woman made a face. "*I* don't," she said, brushing her chest again and shuddering.

The tent was filling rapidly. A florid man in a white linen suit came down the aisle, leading two Negro men who carried between them an ambulance cot. On the cot lay the stiff form of a paralyzed blonde girl about twenty years old.

An usher came hurrying over to them. "Just set it in the

aisle close to the seats, an' you sit down right next to her. That's what the aisle seats are saved for," he said. The Negroes set down the cot and went away. The man reached into his pocket and pulled out a bill.

"Bless you," the usher said.

There was a curtain and a stage at the front of the tent, and a runway leading from the stage into the audience. Now two television cameras were driven out by cameramen who rode them like jockeys. Focusing, they turned the eyes of their cameras on the people in the seats, and faces swam across the screens of the monitors like schools of fish. The people stared up at themselves. Some of them whistled and waved their hands. The blind man smiled. "What's going on?" he asked. Michael told him.

Presently a handsome, dark-haired young man stepped through the curtain, carrying a trumpet. He wore no jacket. His white shirt was starched and he had on a blue silk tie in a stiff windsor knot. His hair was carefully slicked back and his teeth gleamed when he smiled. "I am Cal Justice," he said into the microphone. "Some of you might know me better as the Trumpeter of God." There was applause. "Billie Joe will be out in just a few minutes. In the meantime, I'd like to play you a little song you all know and love."

He played "The Ninety and Nine." He could play that trumpet. At first the notes were slow and mournful. But the second time around the tempo picked up and somebody started keeping time with his hands, and soon people all over the tent were clapping and singing, following the wild golden thread of the horn's music as it rose above their sound. In front of Michael the fat lady had become a human metronome, her tic keeping perfect time with the clapping.

The applause following the music was strong and sustained, but it heightened when another man in shirtsleeves stepped from behind the curtain. He was a large man, broad-shouldered, big-headed, and big-handed. He had a fleshy nose and a wide mouth. The lids of his eyes were heavy.

The trumpeter left the stage. The big man stood in its center, smiling, while the people below him clapped their hands and shouted words of praise.

Then he raised both hands to the sky, fingers outspread. The noise was erased. From overhead a microphone dropped on a boom until it was close enough to his face for the sound of hoarse, superhuman breathing to fill the tent.

"Hallelujah," said Billie Joe Raye. "God loves you."

"Hallelujah," said people all over the tent.

"A-man," muttered the blind man.

"God loves you," Billie Joe repeated. "Say it three times, with me: God loves me."

"GOD LOVES ME."

"GOD LOVES ME."

"GOD LOVES ME."

"That's good," Billie Joe said, nodding happily.

"Now, I know why you're here, brothers and sisters. You're here because you're sick in body and mind and soul, and you need the healing love of God."

Silence, and the amplified sound of breathing.

"But do you know why *I'm* here?" asked the preacher's mouth from the stage and from two dozen television monitors all over the tent.

"To cure us!" somebody near Michael shouted.

"To make me well again!"

"To help my boy to live!" a woman screamed, pushing back her chair and dropping to her knees.

"A-man," said the blind man.

"No," Billie Joe said. "I can't cure you."

A woman sobbed.

"Don't say that," another woman cried. "Don't you say that, hear?"

"No, sister, I *can't* cure you," Billie Joe repeated. More people began to weep.

"But *GOD* can cure you. Through these hands." He held them up, fingers widely spread, for everyone to see.

Hope was revived in a flurry of hosannas.

"God can do *anything*. Say it with me," Billie Joe said.

"GOD CAN DO *ANYTHING*."

"So God can cure *you*."

"SO GOD CAN CURE *ME*."

"Because God loves *you*."

"BECAUSE GOD LOVES *ME*."

"A-man," whispered the blind man, tears welling up in his sightless eyes.

Billie Joe sucked in a breath with an electronically amplified whoosh. "Once I was a dying boy," he declared.

The broadcast sound of breathing, slow and sorrowful.

"The Devil already had my soul and the worms were getting ready to play hide-and-go-seek in my flesh. My lungs were eaten with consumption. My blood was corrupted by anemia. My mammy and pappy knew I was dying. *I* knew I was dying and I was afraid."

Breathing like a chased-down stag struggling to suck one more portion of air into his lungs.

"I had wallowed in sin. I had drunk cheap whiskey. I had gambled like the soldiers who cast lots for the garments of the Son of God. I had fornicated with wild and diseased women as wanton as the whores of Babylon.

"But one day as I lay in my bed full of despair, I felt something strange happening inside of me. Something 'way down inside began to stir like the first soft stirring of a baby chick when it knows it has to start working away at the hard shell of the egg.

"And the tips of my fingers and the ends of my toes began to tingle, and the place where I felt that first stirring burst into a warm glow that no whiskey distilled by man could make, and I could feel the light of God streaming out of my eyes, and I leaped out of that bed and I shouted in my glory and *IN MY FULL HEALTH:*

"'*MAMMY! PAPPY!* The Lord has touched me! *AND I AM SAVED!*'"

Throughout the tent there passed a shudder of hope and happiness, and people lifted their eyes and thanked their God.

Next to the fat lady a young man sat, his cheek wet with tears. "Please, God," he was saying. "Please. Please. Please. Please. Please. Please."

Michael saw the young man's face for the first time, and with a feeling of numb unreality he realized that it was Dick Kramer, a member of the congregation of Temple Sinai.

From the stage, Billie Joe looked down benevolently at the

people in the seats. "From that day onward, although I was but a stripling, I preached the word of God, at first at meetings throughout these parts and then, as some of you good people know, as pastor of the Holy Fundamentalist Church over at Whalensville.

"And it wasn't until two years ago that I thought I was anything but a preacher of the Word.

"Some of our men were laying out a baseball field for the youngsters of the Sunday School, on land behind the church. And out of the goodness of his heart, Bert Simmons had brought over his light tractor, and was leveling some knolls. On a rock no bigger than a beehive, all at once his tractor bucked. It flipped over, pinning Brother Simmons' hand under its terrible weight.

"When I was summoned from the church, I could see blood coming out of the work glove. When we pried the machine off, from the way that glove was mashed and flattened, I knew Bert's hand would have to be cut off. And I dropped to my knees in the fresh earth and I lifted my eyes to the heavens, and I said, 'Lord, must this good servant be punished for having aided in Thy work?' And suddenly, my hands began to twitch and I felt power in them, surging and crackling like electricity was shooting out of the tips of my fingers, and I picked up Brother Simmons' crushed hand in mine, and I said, 'God, heal this man!'

"And when Brother Simmons took off his glove, his hand was whole and unhurt, and I could not deny that a miracle had taken place.

"And I seemed to hear the voice of God saying, 'Son, once I healed you. Now you will carry My healing power throughout the family of man.'

"And since then the Lord has healed thousands through my hands. Because of his goodness, the lame have walked, the blind have seen, and the afflicted have been relieved of the burden of pain."

Billie Joe bowed his head.

An organ began to play softly.

Presently he looked up.

"I want everybody here to touch the back of the chair in front of him and bow his head, please.

"Come on. Get those heads down. Everybody.

"Now I want every one here who wishes in his heart to seek Jesus Christ to raise his or her hand straight up in the air. Keep your head bowed, but raise your hand."

Michael looked around and observed perhaps twenty-five hands raised.

"Glory, glory what a sight, brothers and sisters," Billie Joe said. "All over this tent hundreds of hands are pointing toward God. Now, you people who are raising your hands, stand right up on your two feet. Stand right up, quickly now. Everybody who has his hand in the air.

"Now walk forward and we'll say a special little prayer." About twelve or fifteen people, men and women and three teen-age girls and one boy, came down to the front of the tent. They were taken behind a curtain by one of the preacher's assistants.

Then, while the organ played, Billie Joe went up and down the aisles, praying over the stretcher cases.

While he was doing this, one team of ushers passed the collection plates while another team passed out cards to those who wished to see the healer. All over the tent, people began to sign the cards.

"Will you show me where?" asked the blind man. As the man signed, Michael read the card. It was a release giving permission for the signer's picture to be used in periodicals and on television.

Cal Justice and the unseen organist played two more hymns, "The King of Love My Shepherd Is" and "Rock of Ages," and then Billie Joe was back on the stage. "If you will form a line in the aisle and be patient until it is your turn," he said, "we will pray to God about your afflictions, you and I."

All over the tent, people stood.

In front of Michael, Dick Kramer rose with them. He glanced around as he waited for others in his row to move out, and his eyes met those of his rabbi.

For a moment they stared at one another, something in the boy's face making Michael's breath catch in his throat. Then Kramer turned and plunged blindly toward the aisle, his elbow thumping into the fat lady's side. "Here!" she said, sitting down again.

"Dick," Michael called. "Wait for me!" He began to move down his own row of seats toward the aisle, repeating apologies as he pushed past people.

But ultimately the way was blocked by the stretcher of the paralyzed girl. The florid man was bending over it, his mouth slack. "God damn it, Evelyn," he was saying, "you move those limbs! You can move, if you want to." He turned to the usher, his head trembling. "You go fetch Mr. Raye, boy. You tell him to get the hell back here and pray some more."

CHAPTER TWENTY-EIGHT

Dick Kramer first learned that he had not gotten away free and clear one autumn morning in the middle of the pine woods outside Athens. He and his cousin Sheldon had been methodically working their dogs through some small hills. Since they were among the best shots at the University, the house committee of their fraternity had assigned them to supply the frat's kitchen with squab and quail, relieving them of less attractive duties so that they might hunt. The two boys were hunting competitors of long standing, and now Dick was feeling especially fine. He had counted only three shots from Sheldon's direction, and he knew that even if each shot meant a bird in his cousin's bag, he was far ahead. It was his virgin effort with a new 20-gauge Browning over-and-under. His old shotgun had been a 16-gauge, and he had been afraid that the smaller pellet area of the new piece would handicap him, but he had a brace of quail and two mourning doves in his bag, and even as the thought of this warmed him another dove rose with a sudden flutter, wings blurring black with motion against the blue sky, and he snapped the shotgun to his shoulder and at precisely the right instant pressed the trigger gently, feeling the jolt and watching the rising bird pause and then turn to stone and drop.

The Redhead recovered the dove and Dick took the bird and patted the dog and reached into his pocket. His hand closed over a dog candy—his right hand—but when he took it out of his pocket his fingers wouldn't uncurl to give Red his reward.

Sheldon came trudging over the hill, looking upset, with old Bessie panting and slobbering after him. "Son of a bitch," he said. "This keeps up, those guys are going to have to open a couple of cans of baked beans." He drew his shirtsleeve over his forehead. "I got only two. How'd you make out?"

Dick held up the dove he had just removed from the Redhead's muzzle. What he thought he said next was, "I got four beside this one." But his cousin looked at him, grinning.

"What?"

He repeated it, and the grin slowly faded from Sheldon's face. "Hey, Dick. You all right, Dickie boy?"

He said something else and Sheldon took him by the elbow and shook him a little bit. "What's the matter, Dickie?" he said. "You're white as a sheet. Sit down. Right here."

He sat on the ground and the Redhead came and nuzzled his face with a cold wet nose and in a few minutes his fingers opened and he was able to feed the dog the candy. His hand remained curiously numb but he said nothing of this to Sheldon. "I feel better now, I guess," he said instead.

At the sound of his voice Sheldon looked relieved. "Are you sure?" he said.

"Yes."

"All the same," Sheldon said, "we'd better go in."

"I feel fine," Dick protested. "Why quit this early?"

"Dickie, back there a few minutes when your face went so white. Do you remember saying something to me?"

"Yes. I guess so. Why?"

"Because it was . . . completely unintelligible. You were incoherent."

He felt a small fear, like an annoying insect that he chased away with a laugh. "Come on. You're giving me the business, right?"

"No. Honest to God."

"Well, I feel fine now," he said. "And you understand me, don't you?"

"You've been feeling all right lately, haven't you?" Sheldon asked.

"Jee-zuz, yes, it's been five years since I had that operation," Dick said. "I'm as healthy as a horse, and you ought to know it. When does a person stop being an invalid?"

"I want you to see a doctor," Sheldon said.

His cousin was a year older, as close to a big brother as he would ever have. "If it will make you feel better, dammit," Dick said. "Look at this." He held out his right arm. There was not the slightest sign of tremor. "Nerves of plutonium," he said, grinning. But the numbness was still there he noticed as he walked with Sheldon and the dogs through the pine woods toward the car.

He went to the doctor's on the following morning, and he told the old doc what had happened.

"Anythin' else been botherin' you?"

He hesitated and the doctor glanced at him appraisingly. "Lost some weight, haven't you? Hop on the scale." It was nine pounds. "Nothin' else been givin' you pains?"

"A couple of months ago I had a swollen ankle. It went away after a few days. And a pain down here." He indicated the right side of his groin.

"Been sportin' the girls a little too regular, I suspect," the doctor said, and they both grinned. Nevertheless, the old doc picked up the telephone and had him admitted to the Emory University Hospital in Atlanta for tests and observation.

"On the afternoon of the Alabama game?" Dick complained. But the old doc only nodded.

At the hospital, the medical resident who did the work-up observed for the record that the patient was a slightly pale, well-developed male of twenty, with right-sided facial weakness and some thickening of speech. He saw with a quickening of enthusiasm that there was an interesting history. The records showed that an exploratory laparotomy had been performed when the patient was fifteen years old, resulting in discovery of adenocarcinoma of the head of the pancreas. The duodenum, the distal portion of the common bile duct, the head of the pancreas, and a small section of the jejunum had been resected.

"They cut away some bellyaches for you when you were a kid, huh?" he said.

Dick nodded and smiled.

The patient's hand was no longer numb. There was a right-sided Babinski sign; neurologic examination otherwise revealed nothing.

"Can I get out of here in time to see the game?" Dick asked.

The doctor frowned. "I don't know about that," he said. His stethoscope revealed that a soft systolic murmur was audible over the precordium. He had the patient lie down and began to probe his abdomen with searching fingertips. "Do you think we can take 'Bama this year?" he asked.

"That kid Stebbins will pass them to death," Dick said.

The searching fingers located a firm, lobulated mass that was palpable midway between the umbilicus and the xiphoid and slightly to the left of the midline. It seemed to overlap the aorta. Every time the heart pulsated the mass pulsated with it, until it was as though two hearts beat in the boy's body beneath the doctor's hands. "I wouldn't mind seeing that game myself," the resident said.

Sheldon came to see him, and some of the boys from the House, and Betty Ann Schwartz, wearing a tight white sweater with long hairs of wool all over it. Nobody else came to see him the evening she was there, so there was nowhere else he could look, and the sight of her almost made him unglue. "No matter what anybody tells you," he said, "they don't put anything in the coffee here."

He had expected the remark to float up over her head, but she looked right into his eyes and smiled, as if what he said had pleased her. "Perhaps you can take up the problem with a nurse," she said, and he made a mental note to date her as soon as he was released.

His Uncle Myron came on his fifth night in the hospital.

"What did Sheldon have to tell you for?" Dick said in annoyance. "I'm feeling perfectly fine."

"This isn't a sick call," Myron said. "This is a business

meeting." For years Myron Kramer and his brother Aaron had run identical businesses in different towns, manufacturing hardwood dining room sets. With Myron in Emmetsburgh and Aaron in Cypress, they enjoyed the independence of nonpartnership, yet as brothers they felt free to enjoy such economies as sharing the same furniture designs and employing a single sales representative to push their twin line at the national furniture shows. When Aaron had died of a coronary two years before, Myron had taken over the management but not the ownership of his brother's business, with the understanding that Dick would assume this responsibility when he was graduated from the University.

"Something wrong with the business, Uncle Myron?" Dick asked.

"The business is fine," his uncle said. "What should be wrong with the business?" They talked of football, about which the elder Kramer knew almost nothing.

Myron Kramer sought out his nephew's doctor before he left Atlanta. "His mother died when he was a little boy. Cancer. My brother went a couple of years ago," he said. "Heart. So I'm the only one. I want you to tell me how my nephew is."

"There is a mediastinal mass, I'm afraid."

"Tell me what that means," Myron said patiently.

"There is a growth. In the back of the chest, behind the heart."

Myron grimaced and closed his eyes. "Can you help him?"

"I don't know how much, with a tumor of this type," the doctor said carefully. "And there may be others. Advanced cancer is a plant that seldom throws a single seed. We want to determine where else in your nephew's body there may be trouble."

"Will you tell him?"

"No, at least not yet. We'll wait awhile, and watch him."

"And if there are other . . . things?" Myron asked. "How will you know?"

"If metastasis has occurred," the doctor said, "it will be too easy to tell, Mr. Kramer."

On the ninth day Dick was released from the hospital. Before he put on his clothes, the doctor gave him a supply of multiple vitamins and pancreatic enzymes. "These will build you up," he said. Then he added another bottle of capsules. "These pink ones are Darvon. Take one anytime you feel pain. Every four hours."

"I don't have any pain," Dick said.

"I know," the old doc said. "But they're good to have in the house, just in case something comes up."

He had missed six days of classes and he had a lot of work to make up. For four days he crammed. Then he ran out of steam. That afternoon he telephoned Betty Ann Schwartz, but she had a date.

"How about tomorrow night?"

"I'm dated tomorrow, too, Dick. I'm sorry."

"Well, okay."

"Dick, it's not a brushoff. I want to go out with you, awfully. I'm not doing anything Friday night. What do you say? We can do anything you like."

"Anything?"

She laughed. "*Almost* anything."

"I heard you the first time. It's a date."

By the next afternoon he was too restless to study. Although he knew he couldn't afford it after missing school all the previous week, he cut two classes and drove out to the rod and gun club. There was a skeet shoot. Using the over-and-under for the first time in competition he hit forty-eight clay pigeons out of fifty, standing in the warm sun and knocking them off one after another, *bam, bam, bam, bam, bam,* to take first prize. Driving home, he felt that something was missing, and with puzzlement he searched for whatever it was. Then with a small laugh he realized that it was the sense of elation that usually accompanied winning. For some reason he felt down, not up. In his right groin there was a faint throbbing.

By two o'clock in the morning it had grown into a pain. He went to his bureau drawer and took out the bottle with the pink capsules. He shook a Darvon into his palm and looked at it.

"Screw you," he said.

He put it back into the bottle and put the bottle away in the drawer, under his jockey shorts. He took two aspirin tablets, and the pain went away.

Two days later it returned.

That afternoon he took the Redhead into the woods after birds but came home because his hand grew so numb he couldn't load the shotgun.

That night he took a Darvon.

Friday morning he went to the hospital. Betty Ann Schwartz visited him that evening. But she couldn't stay very long.

The old doc explained it to him, very gently.

"Will you operate," Dick said, "the way they did before?"

"It's a different kind of case," the doctor said. "There's something new that they've been having some success with. It's nitrogen mustard, the stuff they once used for war gas. Only this kills cancer, not soldiers."

"When do you want to start the treatments?"

"Right away."

"Can it wait until tomorrow?"

The old doc hesitated and then smiled. "Sure. Take the day off."

Dick left the hospital before lunch and drove the sixty miles into Athens. He stopped at a lunchroom but he wasn't hungry, and instead of ordering he stepped into the telephone booth and called Betty Ann Schwartz at the sorority house. He had to wait while they called her out of the dining room. She was free that evening, she said, and she would love it.

He didn't want to run into any of the boys from the House and he had all afternoon to kill. So he went to a movie. There were three motion-picture theaters in Athens, not counting the colored one, and two of them had horror pictures. The remaining one offered *The Lost Weekend*, which he had seen before. He sat through it again, eating cold buttered popcorn and scrounching down in the dark in the stale-smelling plush chair. The first time he had enjoyed the picture, but the second time around the dramatic parts seemed full of bathos, and he despised Ray Milland for wasting all that time searching for hidden bottles of booze when he could have been banging Jane Wyman and writing stories for *The New Yorker*.

After the movie, it was still too early and he bought a pint of bourbon, feeling like Milland, and drove out of town into the country. He looked carefully and found an ideal parking spot in the woods overlooking the Oconee River, and he simply sat there for a long time. The pain was very bad now, and he felt faint. That was because he hadn't had lunch, he told himself, only the lousy popcorn, and he felt disgusted that sometimes he was such a goddam fool.

When he picked up Betty Ann he took her to a good restaurant, a place called Max's, and they each had a brace of drinks and a beautiful sirloin for two. After dinner they had brandy. When they left the restaurant he drove straight to the parking lot overlooking the river. He took out the bourbon and she accepted the bottle when he opened it and she took a long swig and then gave it to him and he did, too. He turned the radio on softly and got some music and they had another drink and then he began to kiss her, and there was no resistance, only encouragement on her part, and soft nibblings all over his face and neck, and he felt a wild disbelieving realization that this was it, that it was finally going to happen, but when the time came he didn't react the way he should have, nothing happened, and finally they stopped trying.

"I think you'd better take me home," she said. She lit a cigarette.

He started the motor but he didn't drive off. "I want to explain," he said.

"You don't have to explain anything," she said.

"There's something wrong with me," he said.

"I can see that."

"No, something really wrong. I've got cancer."

She sat in silence, smoking. Then she said, "Are you kidding me? Is this some new kind of line?"

"This would have been important to me. If I die, you might have been the only one."

"Jesus Christ," she said softly.

His hand moved to the shift, but she touched him with her fingertips. "Do you want to try again?"

"I don't think it would do any good," he said. But he switched off the motor. "I'd like to really know how a girl is made," he said. "Can I look at you?"

"It's dark," she whispered, and he turned on the dashboard lights.

She lifted her heels to the edge of the seat and leaned back with her eyes shut tight. "Don't touch me," she said.

After a little while he started the motor again and when she felt the car begin to move she put her feet down. She kept her eyes closed until they were halfway home, and she turned her body away from him as she finished dressing.

"Would you like some coffee?" he asked as they neared a diner.

"No, thank you," she said.

When they got to the sorority house he started to say something to her but she wouldn't listen. "Good-by," she said. "Good luck, Dick." She opened the car door and slid out, and he sat and watched her run, up the front path and the stone steps and across the wide verandah, until the door slammed behind her.

He didn't want to go to the House and it seemed foolish to go to a hotel, so he drove back to the hospital.

He was in the hospital for the next ten days.

A pretty little nurse with wild-looking Italian-cut brown hair gave him the drug intravenously. The first day he joked with her and looked at her sweet body and hoped that the failing of the night before had been a mistake, a passing psychological thing, something that was not a by-product of his illness. By the third day he didn't even know that she was in the room. The nitrogen mustard gave him the runs and made him wretchedly nauseated. The old man came and corrected the dosage, but it still made him ill.

His Uncle Myron drove to Atlanta three evenings a week and came and sat and just looked at him, saying little.

Sheldon came once. He kept staring at Dick and finally he went away, muttering that he had exams. He didn't come again.

At the end of the tenth day he was released. "You'll have to come back to the hospital twice a week on an out-patient basis," the old man said.

"He'll stay at my house," his Uncle Myron said.

"No, I won't," he said. "I'm going to stay in school."

"School is out, I'm afraid," the doctor said.

"So is your house," he told Myron. "I'm going to Cypress. I'm not an invalid."

"What's the matter with you? Who do you think you are?" Myron demanded. "Why do you have to be so stubborn?"

But the doctor understood. "Let him alone. He'll be all right by himself for a little while yet," the old doc told Myron.

He packed his things late in the morning, when the House was almost deserted. He didn't even say good-by to Sheldon. He put his bags in the car and the Redhead on top of the bags, and he set the shotgun on a blanket on the floor behind the driver's seat, then he drove around the campus for a little while. The leaves were beginning to turn color. At one of the sororities an army of girls had turned out with brushes and pails to paint their house, and they had drawn a crowd of shouting, catcalling males.

He drove to the highway. Within minutes he had raised the speedometer needle to eighty miles per hour, screeching the little blue sports car around curves and rifling down the straightaways, while behind him the Redhead whined softly and he kept waiting for the car to miss a curve, to hit a tree or a wall or a telephone pole. But nothing interfered, not death or even a cop with a ticket for speeding, and like a man riding a rocket he flashed halfway across the state of Georgia.

He reopened his father's house and to clean and cook he hired a colored woman, the wife of one of the truck drivers who delivered dining-room sets for the business. He went to the plant on his second afternoon home and two of the men told him how terrible he looked and another man stared. After that, he stayed away from the furniture factory. Sometimes he walked in the woods with the Redhead and the dog whined and danced when he saw quail or mourning doves, but Dick made no attempt to hunt. There were days when he could have, when the numbness and the pain didn't show up on schedule. But he no longer felt like killing things. For the first time it occurred to him that he had been canceling life in the birds he had gunned from the sky, and he no longer shot, not even at clay pigeons.

Twice a week he made the long trip back to Atlanta and the hospital, but he drove slowly, almost listlessly, no longer seeking to hasten anything.

It grew colder. The mole crickets in the field behind the

house disappeared. Were they really gone, he wondered, or did
they burrow somewhere, to live again in the spring?

He began to think about God.

He began to read. He read all night long, when he couldn't
sleep, and most of the day, finally falling asleep over a book in the
late afternoon. In the Cypress *News* he read that a Jewish service
would be held, and he attended it. When they began to hold
services every Friday he became one of the regulars. He knew
most of the people and everybody there knew that he was home
from school because he was ill. They were tactful and the women
flirted with him bravely and mothered him, pressing him with
refreshments at the *oneg shabbat*.

But he got no answers from the services. Perhaps if they
had a religious leader, he thought, a rabbi who might be able
to help him work out some of the answers. At least a rabbi could
tell him what as a Jew he could expect from death.

But when the rabbi came to Cypress, Dick saw that Michael
Kind was young and a bit uncertain-looking himself. Although
he attended each temple service faithfully, he knew that he could
not expect from so ordinary a man the kind of miracle he needed.

One Sunday, sitting before his television screen and waiting
for the start of the sports spectacular, Dick saw the final ten
minutes of the videotaped Billy Joe Raye show. Following it he
saw fishermen at Lake Michigan, catching whitefish through the
ice, and then bronzed men and golden girls surfing at Catalina,
and he didn't allow his mind to dwell on the earlier religious
program. But the following Sunday without thinking about it
he shaved and dressed carefully and instead of watching television he drove his car into the line of vehicles wending their
way toward the healer's tent.

He sat still when Billy Joe asked for those who had come
to terms with Jesus, but he accepted and signed a card requesting
a personal interview with the healer, and as he stood in line and
inched toward the stage he noticed the people who left the
platform. A man and then a woman threw away their crutches
to a cacophony of triumphant cries, the woman actually dancing
up the aisle. Others went up the stairs maimed, wasted, or raving
and were apparently unchanged when they came down the seven
wooden steps at the far end of the platform. A woman took two

hesitant steps and then, eyes alight, hurled her crutches away.
Two minutes later, her face ruined by grief, she crawled toward
the crutches from the spot where she had fallen. But it was not
she, nor any of the other failures, who remained in Dick's mind.
He had seen the miracle of Billy Joe's hands, and now there
was further evidence.

Directly in front of Dick in the line was a girl about ten
years old. She was deaf, and after Billy Joe had prayed over her
he turned her around until she faced the crowd and could not
see the healer's lips.

"Say, 'I love You, God,'" he said to the back of her head.
"I love You, God," the girl said.

Billy Joe grabbed her head in both his hands. "See what God
hath brought about," he solemnly told the cheering crowd.

Now it was Dick's turn. "What's wrong with you, son?"
the healer asked, and Dick was aware of the lens like an accusing
eye pointed at his face and a little handle on one side of the
camera going round and round as it whirred.

"Cancer."

"Kneel, son."

He saw the man's shoes, brown, fine-grained pigskin, brown
silk socks stretched tight the way only garters will do, and beige
linen trouser cuffs that looked tailored. Then the man's huge hand
covered his face and eyes. The fingertips dug into his cheekbones
and scalp, and the palm, smelling of the sweat of other faces so
that Dick gagged slightly, pushed into his nose and mouth,
bending his head back.

"Lord," Billy Joe said, clenching shut his eyes, "this man is
being eaten by the demons of corruption. Cell by cell they are
devouring him.

"Lord, show this man that You love him. Save his life that
he may help me to do Thy work. Stem the advance of the foul
corrosion within his body. Erase the disease with a sweep of Thy
love, and prevent further damage by cancer, tumor, or other
devilish decay.

"Lord." The fingers, big as sausages and full of strength,
tightened painfully into a claw over Dick's face.

"*HEAL!*" Billy Joe commanded.

Strangely, there was no pain that evening or the next day. This sometimes happened, and he didn't dare hope until another day passed, and another night, and then two more days and nights, a vacation from suffering.

That week he drove to Atlanta twice and went to the hospital on schedule and allowed a resident to insert a canula into his veins and waited while the nitrogen mustard dripped-dripped-dripped into his bloodstream. The following Sunday he returned to the tent and he saw Billy Joe Raye again, and that Tuesday he didn't go to the hospital, nor did he go on Thursday. He got no nitrogen mustard but the pain stayed away, and he began to feel strong again. He prayed a lot. Lying in front of the fire, scratching the Redhead between the ears, he promised God that if he were spared he would become a disciple of Billy Joe Raye's, and he spent hours imagining himself conducting prayer meetings with the help of the Trumpeter of God and a girl. The face of the girl changed from dream to dream, and so did the color of her hair. But she was always well-built and beautiful, a girl whom Billy Joe had also saved and with whom Dick would experience the joy of living for God.

That Sunday after the meeting Dick went to an usher. "I want to do something to help," he said. "Contribute, perhaps."

The man led him to a little office behind a partition, where he was third in line, and when it was his turn a plump man with a kindly face showed him where to sign in order to become a Friend of Health Through Faith and pledge six hundred dollars over the next twelve months.

By the next Tuesday the doctor had telephoned several times and had notified his Uncle Myron that Dick had discontinued treatment, and Myron drove out to the house and there was an ugly scene. Dick came through it unmoved, telling himself that after all it was *he* who was being saved.

On Saturday afternoon he fainted. When he revived the pain was there, worse than before.

On Sunday it grew. Something within his chest seemed to press outward, perhaps against his lungs, making it difficult for him to draw a full breath, and he often felt faint.

He went to the tent meeting and he sat on the hard wooden folding chair and he prayed.

When he stood to await his turn to see Billy Joe he realized that seated in the row behind him was the Rabbi.

To hell with him, he thought, but even before he stopped thinking it he was running out of the tent and across the huge parking lot, his elbows pulled in clumsily by the pain under his ribs, his arms and his legs heavy and hard to lift. He was aware that there was really no place to run to.

When Michael got to the boy's house, nobody was home. It was a nice house, old-fashioned but built to last. It was not neglected, but it looked unfulfilled; it was the kind of house that should have been occupied by a large family.

He sat down on the front steps and in a little while a rangy Irish setter that walked like a sulky lion came around the corner of the house and moved to within a few feet of him.

"Hello," Michael said.

The dog looked at him without moving a hair. Then, apparently satisfied, he walked closer and lay across one of the stairs, resting his auburn muzzle on Michael's knee. They were like that, with the Rabbi scratching the dog's ears, when the blue sports car rolled into the driveway.

For a few minutes, Dick Kramer sat in the car and watched them. Then he got out and walked across the lawn to the porch.

"The old bastard loves that," he said. He took a ring of keys from his pocket and opened the front door, and without waiting for an invitation the Rabbi and the dog followed him inside.

The living room was large and comfortably furnished, but more like a lodge den than a living room, with antlers over a great stone fireplace, and a glass-covered gun rack.

"Drink?" Dick asked.

"If you have one," Michael said.

"Oh, I'll have one. They say an occasional drink is good for my nerves. I've got bourbon. A little water?"

"Fine."

They finished the liquor and sat there with the empty glasses in their hands, and then Dick poured another.

"Do you want to talk about it?" Michael asked.

"If I wanted to chat about it, damn you, I would have looked *you* up. Did that ever occur to you?"

"It crossed my mind." He stood up. "In that case, I'll be getting along. Thanks for the booze."

The boy's voice stopped him at the door. "Rabbi, I'm sorry. Don't leave me."

He came back and sat down. The dog settled himself at his master's feet and moaned softly. Michael reached for his glass and took a long swallow. In a little while Dick Kramer began to talk.

When he was through there was another small silence.

"Why didn't you come to me?" Michael asked humbly.

"You had nothing to offer me," Dick said. "Not what I was looking for. Billy Joe did. For a little while there, it looked as though he had come through. If he had, there isn't anything I wouldn't have done for him."

"I think you should go back to your doctor," Michael said. "That's the first thing."

"But you don't think I should go back to Billy Joe Raye?"

"That's something only you can decide," Michael said.

Dick Kramer smiled. "I think if I could have really believed him I might have made it. But my Jewish skepticism kept pushing me away from him."

"Don't blame your Jewishness. Religious medicine is an old Jewish concept. Christ was a member of the Essenes, a group of Jewish holy men who devoted themselves to healing. And only a few years ago sick Jews in Europe and Asia traveled great distances and suffered hardships in order to be touched by the hands of rabbis who were supposed to have healing powers."

Kramer took Michael's right hand, which was holding a drink. He held it up and looked at the fingers curled around the glass. "Touch me," he said.

But Michael shook his head. "I'm sorry," he said. "I can't help you that way. I have no direct line to God." The boy laughed and shoved the Rabbi's hand away. The liquor in the glass sloshed over the rim.

"In what way can you help me?" he asked.

"Try not to be afraid," Michael said.

"It's more than being afraid. I *am* afraid. I admit that. But it's knowing all the things I'll never do. I've never had a woman. I've never gone to far places. I've never done anything to leave my mark on the world, to make it a better place than it was before I got here."

Michael struggled, sorry that he had taken the liquor. "Have you ever felt love for someone?"

"Of course," he muttered.

"Then you've increased the worth of the world. Immeasurably. As for adventure—if what you fear is true, you will soon have the greatest adventure possible to man."

Dick closed his eyes.

Michael thought of his anniversary and of Leslie waiting for him, but something held him in his chair. He found that he was studying the rifles in the gun cabinet, and a shotgun leaning against a corner of the fireplace with a greasy rag poking out of one muzzle. He was remembering a night in Miami Beach, and a sad little man holding a German pistol. When he looked up, Dick's eyes were open and the boy was smiling at him.

"I won't," he said.

"I'm sure of it," Michael said.

"Let me tell you a story," Dick said. "Two years ago I was supposed to go into the swamp country with a bunch of fellas who have a hunting camp there, for the opening of deer season. When the time came, I had a miserable cold, and I told them to never mind about me. But on opening day I got the itch and I got up early and took my rifle and went into the woods not more than a quarter of a mile from where we're sitting. And I wasn't more than three steps from the road when I saw a big young buck and I snapped off a shot that dropped him.

"When I got to him he was still alive, so I took my hunting knife and I slit his throat. But still he wouldn't die. He kept looking at me out of those big brown eyes and his mouth kept opening and he made *baa*ing sounds just like a big old sheep. Finally I put my rifle to his head and fired it. But still he wouldn't die, and I didn't know what else to do. I had shot him near the heart and in the head and I had cut his throat.

I couldn't slit open his belly and dress him down while he was still alive. And while I was sitting there trying to make up my mind, he thrashed to his feet and took off through the woods. It started to rain, and it took me two hours to find him where he had finally dropped dead in the brush. I nearly got pneumonia.

"I thought a lot of that old deer," he said.

Michael waited until the Negro woman arrived to cook the boy's supper, then he left him sitting alone with the dog in front of the cold fireplace, drinking bourbon.

Outside, the air was sharper than he remembered, and sweeter-smelling. He drove home slowly, praying and at the same time noticing shadows and geometric shapes and variations of color and shade. In the house, Leslie was standing over the stove and he walked to her and put his arms around her, grasping a breast in each hand and burying his face in her hair. She let him hold her and then she turned to kiss him and he shut off the burner under the pot, pulling her in the direction of the bedroom.

"You damn fool," she laughed, half annoyed. "The supper." But he continued to press her toward the bed.

"At least let me—" she said, looking toward the bureau where the diaphragm was kept.

"Not tonight."

The thought excited her, and she stopped all struggling. "We're going to make a baby," she said, her eyes gleaming in the dim light from the kitchen.

"A king of the Jews," he said, touching her. "A Solomon. A Saul. A David."

She rose to meet him and as he kissed her she was speaking. "Not a David," it sounded as if she said.

CHAPTER TWENTY-NINE

The Temple Sinai Annual Brotherhood Awards, two handsome walnut plaques with silver face-plates, arrived in the mail from Atlanta, and at a board meeting Michael was urged to write a Brotherhood Day speech without delay.

"I'm a little troubled by the national epidemic of Jews giving brotherhood awards to *goyim*," Michael said pensively. "Why don't *goyim* ever give brotherhood awards to Jews? Or better still, why don't Jews give the brotherhood awards to Jews?"

The members of the board looked puzzled, and then they laughed.

"You just write that speech, Rabbi," Dave Schoenfeld said. "First we'll give 'em likker and a good dinner, then you talk 'em happy, then I'll hand out the awards." They set a date for a Sunday evening six weeks away.

Two days later, as Michael sat in his study and polished his sermon for the coming week, he had a visitor.

Billy Joe Raye sat on the edge of his chair with his feet flat on the ground and his hat in his lap. He beamed. "I figured it was time I was paying you a neighborly call, Rabbi," he said. "I brought you a little gift."

It was a copy of the New Testament in Hebrew. "I had it printed up especially for our Jewish friends," Billie Joe said.

"Well," Michael said. "Thank you."

"I ran into a young friend of yours on the street the other day. Young Richard what's-his-name?"

"Kramer?"

"That's the boy. He told me he wasn't going to be coming to see me anymore. Told me you and he had had a long talk."

"We did."

"A nice boy. A nice, clean-cut boy. Pity about him." He looked down and shook his head. "Of course, I wanted you to

understand I didn't try to get him to come to my meetings. I never
met him before he came into my tent."

"I know that," Michael said.

"Yes. Heaven knows folks like you and I have enough to
do without trying to steal from one another's flock like two
niggers raising chickens." He chortled and Michael smiled
thoughtfully as he stood to show him to the door.

Three full weeks went by before he forced himself to think
again of the brotherhood awards. Over the next ten days he
wrote three drafts of the brotherhood speech, working slowly
and laboriously. Each draft he ultimately tore up and threw
away.

Two days before the presentation dinner he sat down and
wrote the speech, quickly and with few revisions. It was short
and to the point, he thought, reading it over. And, he knew with
a sudden sinking of his heart, it was true.

When the dessert plates and coffee cups had been pushed
back he stood and greeted them—the members of his synagogue, the men being honored, the eminent gentiles at the head
table.

"When any clergyman comes to a strange town, he worries
about the religious atmosphere," he said.

"I must admit that I was worried when I came to Cypress.

"Here is what I found.

"I found a community in which the various churches be-
have toward one another in a remarkably civilized fashion," he
said, and Judge Boswell looked at Nance Grant and smiled,
nodding.

"I found a community in which the Baptists loan the Jews
the use of their church, and in which the Methodists buy tickets
to the Baptists' socials.

"I found a community where Episcopalians respect Congre-
gationalists, and where Lutherans work in harmony with Pres-
byterians.

"I found a community which recognizes the Sabbath and
which places a high value on it. A community where every man
is encouraged to worship God in his own way."

Judge Boswell lifted his eyebrows at Dave Schoenfeld and

nodded slowly and approvingly, projecting his lower lip slightly as he did in court when listening to a jury verdict.

"I found that in Cypress brotherhood flows from one denomination to another, like wells of sweet, God-given water which are interconnected by free-flowing, man-made tunnels," Michael said.

"But I also found a puzzling thing.

"Those tunnels go over and under and around almost sixty per cent of the population of this community."

Judge Boswell, smiling, had lifted a water glass to his lips. When he set it down his smile was still there, as if painted on. It faded slowly, like the closing of a flower.

"In Cypress, brotherhood is like a selective chemical that vanishes—*pouf!*—when it comes into contact with a colored skin," Michael said.

"Now, that is my impression of the macrocosm.

"As for the microcosm, I am familiar with my own congregation. So let us consider the fifty-three families which make up Temple Sinai of Cypress, Georgia.

"Three members of this congregation own businesses which refuse to sell food or drink to a man, woman, or child whose skin is not whiter than was the skin of Moses' wife.

"Two members of this congregation own businesses which refuse shelter and lodging to a person of color.

"Several of our members sell shoddy goods to Negro customers on credit, at premium prices which keep their customers in their debt.

"One of our members owns a newspaper which identifies each person by the title of Miss, Missus, or Mister—unless he or she is colored.

"The entire congregation patronizes a bus line which forces Negroes to sit in the rear or stand while there are empty seats in forward sections.

"This congregation lives in a town which contains a Negro district where much of the rented housing should be condemned and rebuilt for health reasons.

"This congregation helps to support an educational system in which Negro children are sent each morning to miserable schools which dare eager minds to survive." He paused.

"What the hell?" Sunshine Janes said to the Sheriff.

"Today we are gathered to give awards to two community leaders for brotherhood," Michael continued. "But are *we* entitled to confer such awards?

"The act of bestowing them says by implication that we are in a state of brotherhood ourselves.

"I say to you in all troubled earnestness that we are not. And until we achieve brotherhood ourselves, I do not believe that we are capable of recognizing it in others.

"I applaud the intent of what we have set out to do here today. Yet, because it points up the single greatest danger to our human souls in the days and years ahead, I am forced to issue solemn warning.

"Until we can look at the Negro and see Man, we are marked with the sign of Cain.

"Dostoevski said it: 'Until you have become really, in actual fact, a brother to everyone, brotherhood will not come to pass.'"

Two things he was aware of as he left the *bema*. One was the look in Judge Boswell's eyes. The other was his wife's loud, solitary applause, making a beacon of sound to guide him home.

Two nights later, Ronnie and Sally Levitt broke the wall of silence which the rest of the community had built around the Kinds.

"I must admit," Ronnie Levitt said, "that I agreed with the rest of them until a few hours ago. After all, it was my money that bought and paid for those damn awards. You've got to remember that Cypress isn't New York," he told Michael. "No, nor is it Atlanta or New Orleans, either. In those big places you might be able to alienate people and still stand a chance. If we alienate people here, we might as well close up our businesses. And we're not about to let you throw away our bread and butter."

"I don't expect you to, Ronnie," Michael said.

"Now. I think this may blow over if you just play it smart. I don't think you should apologize the way some are sayin'. Only make matters worse. We'll explain privately that you're young and a Northerner and that you'll watch what you say from now on, and perhaps eventually the whole thing will be written off."

"No, Ronnie," Michael said gently.

Sally Levitt burst into tears.

They left almost everything and packed small bags. "It's too hot to drive all the way," Michael said. They had saved some money, and Leslie agreed. They drove to Augusta and flew to New York from there.

Rabbi Sher sighed when he heard their story. "How difficult you make life for all of us," he said. "If only you were wrong." He forbade Michael to resume teaching. "If you're not careful you'll spend your entire life teaching Hebrew to little children," he said. "And then how horribly peaceful everyone outside your classroom would be."

It took three weeks of interviewing, and Michael finally flew all the way to California to preach a guest sermon, and then he was hired as rabbi of Temple Isaiah of San Francisco.

"They're all nonconformists out there, and it's three thousand miles away from this office," Rabbi Sher said. "You should only stay there until you die a happy old man."

They flew back to Augusta and drove the blue Plymouth into Cypress exactly eleven months and sixteen days after they had first driven into town.

The house on Piedmont Road was just as they had left it three weeks before.

Together they packed their books. Michael called Railway Express and arranged for the desk and books to be shipped to California. They had bought a rug and a lamp, and after much discussion they shipped the rug and left the lamp.

"I'll clean out my study at the temple," he told Leslie.

The first thing he noticed when he parked his car in the Temple Sinai driveway was the remains of the cross on the lawn. He stood and looked at it for a long time. Then he unlocked the door. There was no sign of Joe Williams, the *shamus*, and anyhow Michael assumed that Williams would not relish the job of cleaning up after the Klan or its equivalent. He found a rake and a spade in the utility shed and he raked the ashes and the charred chunks of wood carefully and then loaded the debris into a wheelbarrow and added it to the overflowing rubbish bin in the back yard. Then he came back to the front lawn and inspected what was left. The top of the cross evidently had been consumed before the entire flaming structure had toppled and burned itself out on the ground. The result was a T-shaped scar etched blackly into the turf, with each bar of the T about twelve feet long. Michael kicked the spade into the turf and began to turn the sod over along the burned lines. It was an old lawn, with a deep layer of interwoven roots that gave like a sponge before allowing the edge of the spade to cut through. Soon he was sweating.

A green Chevrolet, prewar but clean and shining, drifted slowly by. Three houses beyond the temple the driver stopped the car and then shoved it into reverse. A very black man got out and sat on the car's front mudguard, rolling up the sleeves of his blue workshirt. He was tall and thin and balding. What hair he had left was mixed with gray. He watched Michael in silence for a few minutes and then he cleared his throat.

"Trouble with that," he said, "is that the places you turned over are gonna have to be seeded. Then they're gonna come up a lighter green than the rest of the grass. That cross is still gonna be there."

Michael paused and leaned on his shovel. "You're right," he said, frowning. He looked down at the half-spaded T. "Why don't I just connect the corners?" he asked. "Then there'll be nothing but a green triangle."

The man nodded. He reached through his car window and took the keys from the ignition, then he walked around and unlocked the trunk and took out an edger. He came over to the place where the cross had been burned and began to stamp the half-moon blade into the turf. They worked together without speaking until the triangle was completed. The Negro's face had grown a crop of tiny water droplets, causing his pate to gleam darkly. He took a large handkerchief from his back pocket and carefully wiped his face and neck and bald spot and his circlet of hair and then his palms.

"My name is Lester McNeil," he said.

Michael held out his hand and they shook firmly.

"Mine is Michael Kind."

"I know who you are."

"Thanks for your help," Michael said. "You did a beautiful job."

The man waved a hand. "Ought to. I'm a gardener by trade." He looked down at the triangle. "Tell you what," he said. "All we need do is add three little corners and we can make this into one of them stars of yours."

"A Star of David, yes," Michael said. They fell back to work and soon it was done.

McNeil made another trip to his car trunk and came back with a cardboard box full of seed packets. "Get them at cost," he said. "It's not much of a bed. A lot of them won't come up. But some of them will. What kind of flowers shall we plant?"

They made the center of the star white verbena and the six points blue alyssum. "Kind of late to be startin' 'em from seed," McNeil said. "But I guess they'll be all right if you water 'em plenty."

"I won't be here," Michael said.

"We heard somethin' like that," McNeil said. "Well, maybe they'll be lots of rain." He returned the edger and the seed to his car trunk. "Tell you what," he said. "I'll stop by once in a while an' give 'em a little drink for you."

"That will be nice," Michael said. Suddenly he felt fine. "Maybe we can start a trend. Wherever a cross is burned, a flower bed will spring up."

"Be good for business," McNeil said. "Speakin' of drinks, could I have one? Work makes my throat like parched ground."

"Of course," Michael said.

In the kitchen he looked in the refrigerator, but found only half a bottle of orange soda left from a *bar mitzvah* six weeks before. It was flat.

"I'm afraid it will have to be water," he said, spilling the stale soda water into the sink.

"I never drink anything with bubbles except one bottle of beer every night after work, to clear the dust," McNeil said. They let the water run from the tap until it was cold and then Michael drank two glasses and McNeil drank four.

"Wait a minute," Michael said. He went to the *bema* and pushed aside the black velvet curtain behind the lectern and pulled out half a bottle of port.

He poured some into each of their glasses and they clinked them and grinned at one another. "*L'chayem*," Michael said.

"Whatever you said goes double for me," McNeil said. They knocked the glasses back and tossed off three fingers of warm Manischewitz, neat.

When it came time to go, Leslie called Sally Levitt and Sally drove over and she and Leslie clung to one another and cried and promised to write. Ronnie didn't come, nor did anyone else. Michael could think of nobody he really wanted to see except Dick Kramer, and they drove by his house on the way out of town. It was locked and the shades were drawn. A note tacked to the front door asked that mail be forwarded care of Myron Kramer, 29 Laurel Street, Emmetsburgh, Ga.

With Leslie at the wheel they drove past the pigeon-spotted statue of General Thomas Mott Lainbridge, past the Negro district, onto the state highway, past Billy Joe Raye's tent, and beyond the town limits.

Michael put his head back against the top of the seat and slept. When he awoke they were out of Georgia and he sat for a long while without saying anything, watching the Alabama scenery wheel slowly by.

"It was the wrong way to tackle the issue," he said finally.

"Forget it. It's over," she said.

"I should never have attacked it head-on like that. If I had been more tactful I could have stayed there and chipped away at it slowly over the years."

"There's no use iffing," she said. "It's over. You're a good rabbi and I'm proud of you."

They were silent for several miles and then she began to giggle. "I'm glad we left," she said, and she told him about how Dave Schoenfeld had acted toward her on the night it had rained so hard.

Michael slammed the heel of his palm into the dashboard. "That no-good *momser*," he said. "He wouldn't have tried that with the rabbi's wife if you had been a Jewish girl."

"I am a Jewish girl."

"You know what I mean," he said in a little while.

"Only too well," she said clearly.

It settled between them, like an uninvited and hated passenger, and for almost two hours they talked only in short and infrequent sentences. Then, after stopping at a gas station outside Anniston to allow her to go to the bathroom, he got behind the wheel, and when they were on the road again he put his arm around her and pulled her close to him.

In a little while she told him that she was going to have a baby, and for the next twenty miles they drove again without talk. But this time they were wrapped in a different kind of silence, his arm still around her even though it had fallen asleep long before, and her left hand, fingers spread, resting lightly on his right thigh, a gift of love.

BOOK III:

The Migration

CHAPTER THIRTY

The attendant they called Miss Beverly was a vivacious, wiry little girl who was working in the hospital to pay her way through the Sargent College of Physical Education at Boston University. She believed in the value of exercise. With the permission of Dr. Bernstein she had taken Leslie and a patient named Diane Miller for a long walk through the grounds. They had even held hands and jogged a little, so that when they came back into the ward they were cold and merry and ready for the hot chocolate Beverly had promised to make.

Leslie had been just about ready to take off her coat when the Serapin woman had thrown herself on Mrs. Birnbaum, screeching like a cat. They saw her arm rise and fall twice, the tiny blade in her fist glittering in the rather dim yellow light, and then they saw the unbelievable redness spreading on the floor and heard Mrs. Birnbaum's groaning, an ugly sound.

Miss Beverly had pulled Mrs. Serapin's hand behind her back and kept yanking the wrist upward, like some three-hundred-pound wrestler on television, but Mrs. Serapin was much taller and she wouldn't release the knife and finally Beverly began to shout and staff people began to come from every which way. Rogan, the night nurse, came running down from the nursing station with the other attendant and Peterson came charging in from the hall, her eyes bulging and her face the color of sour cream.

Mrs. Birnbaum kept crying and calling for someone named Morty and Mrs. Serapin continued to scream and in the struggle with her somebody had stepped in the blood on the floor, so that a large area was covered with red footprints, like a crazy Arthur Murray diagram.

Leslie felt faint. She turned and walked toward the door, which Peterson had left ajar. At the door she stopped. Only Diane Miller was staring at her. Leslie smiled at Diane reassuringly and then stepped out of the ward and closed the door behind her.

She walked through the hallway, past the vacant desk where Peterson should have been sitting and reading her television magazine, and into the little alcove between the hall door and the outside door. She stood there in the dark, smelling the cold fresh air coming through the bottom of the outside door, waiting for someone to come out and tell her she should not be there.

But nobody came.

In a few minutes she opened the outside door and stepped outside.

She would take another walk, this time in privacy, she told herself.

She walked down the long winding driveway, past the front gate and the two little stone statues of sitting lions with iron rings in their noses. She breathed deeply, in through the nose and out through the mouth, the way Miss Beverly insisted they should.

She no longer felt faint, but she was tired from the earlier exercise and the tension, and when she came to the bus stop she sat down to rest on the bench in the illuminated enclosure provided by the bus company.

In a little while a car came and stopped and a very pleasant woman rolled down the front window and asked if they could rescue her from the cold.

She got in and the woman told her they were from Palmer and bus service was not the best in the world in their neck of the woods, either. They would be glad to drop her off in town, the woman said.

It was quarter to eleven when she got out of their car. Main Street in Woodborough was not the great white way at that hour. Maney's Bar & Grille was open, so was the Soda Shop, a light burned over the window of the YWCA and the bus depot was illuminated; but the shop windows on both sides of the street were dark and blank.

She went into the Soda Shop and ordered coffee. The juke box was blasting and in the booth behind her three boys sat and slapped the table with their palms to the beat of the music.

"Call her, Peckerhead," one of the boys said.

"Not me."

"She's probably waitin' for you right now."

Go ahead, Peckerhead, call her, make some little girl's evening, she thought. They were just a little older than Max.

The coffee came in a cup just like those in the hospital; even the color was the same. She thought of taking a taxi back to the hospital but she was becoming frightened at the thought that she had walked away. She wondered what Dr. Bernstein would say.

"Call her, Peckerhead. You're chicken if you don't."

"I'm not chicken."

"Well, call her."

"You got a dime?"

Evidently the coin was passed, because behind her she heard the boy leave the booth. There was only one telephone in the Soda Shop, and he was still using it when she finished the coffee, but there was a sidewalk telephone booth outside the Y and she started toward it after making certain she had a dime in her change purse with which to call Michael.

However at the last moment instead of entering the telephone booth she walked past it and turned into the YWCA.

A girl with hair like a brown Beatle wig sat at the desk, scratching her scalp with the eraser end of a yellow pencil while she leaned over a very large book, the kind that could only be a college text.

"Good evening," Leslie said.

"Hi."

"I'd like a room. Just for the night."

The girl slid her a registration blank and Leslie filled it out. "That will be four dollars."

She opened her purse. Spending money at the hospital was paid directly into the commissary. The patients used chits. From time to time she took a couple of dollars in cash from Michael for the coffee machine and newspapers. The purse contained three dollars and sixty-two cents. "Can I pay you by check in the morning?"

"Sure. Or you can give it to me now."

"I can't. I don't have my checkbook with me."

"Oh." The girl looked away. "Wow . . . I don't know. This never happened to me before."

"I'm a Y member. Last year I was in Mrs. Bosworth's slim-nastics class," Leslie said. She smiled. "I'm really perfectly respectable." She dug into her purse and found her Y membership card.

"Oh, I'm *sure* you are." The girl studied the card. "It's just that if you forgot they would fire me, don't you see, or I'd have to pay for your room myself, which I really can't afford to do."

But she reached behind the desk and then held out a key with a numbered tag on it.

"Thank you," Leslie said.

The room was small but very clean. She hung her clothes in the closet and then got into bed in her slip. She felt very grateful to the girl at the desk. She would have to call Michael first thing in the morning, she thought drowsily.

But next morning the room was quiet; there were none of the early-morning hospital noises which now awoke her daily, and she slept until almost nine.

When she opened her eyes she lay without moving in the warm bed and thought how nice it was not to have had an electroshock treatment, which she knew was what would have happened that morning if she had been in the hospital.

A middle-aged woman with bland eyes and blue-white hair was at the registration desk when she turned in her key.

Outside the Y, she hailed a taxi. Instead of telling the driver to take her to the hospital, she gave him her home address.

I'm an escapee, she thought as she entered the cab. The idea should have terrified her, but it was so absurd it made her smile.

The house was quiet and deserted. She found the extra key where they always left it on the little ledge over the back door and she let herself in and brushed her teeth and drew a deep bubble bath and soaked in it and later, when she had changed into fresh clothing, she made herself a large breakfast of eggs and rolls and coffee and ate every bit of it.

She knew she had to go back to the hospital, that she was nearly finished there, but the thought was disgusting to her.

One-week vacations for long-term patients should be built into their schedules, she thought.

The more she considered the idea, the more it appealed to her. In the third drawer of her bureau, beneath her slips, she found the bankbook for the account that held Aunt Sally's money. She packed a small bag and then wrote *I Love You* on a slip of paper and placed it in Michael's bureau on top of his white shirts.

Then she called another cab and when it came she took it into town; when she paid for it she had eleven cents left, but at the bank she withdrew almost six hundred dollars.

At the Y she found out that the young night clerk's name was Martha Berg, and she left her an envelope with a ten-dollar bill in it.

It occurred to her that the note she had left for Michael was hardly reassuring, and she stopped at Western Union and sent him a telegram.

The first bus leaving the depot was going to Boston and she got into it and paid the fare. She had no real desire to go to Boston, but she hadn't thought this thing through, she really didn't know where she wanted to go. It was an old red bus, and she sat on the left side two seats behind the bus driver, trying to decide between Grossinger's and a plane to Miami.

But when the bus came to Wellesley she stood and pulled the cord. The driver looked surly as she gave him her ticket stub. "Paid to Boston," he said. "You want a refund, you'll have to write the company."

"That's all right." She got out and walked down Main Street slowly, enjoying the shop windows. When she reached the train station her arm was very tired and she turned in and checked her bag in a twenty-five cent locker, then she walked to the college campus unencumbered.

A lot of it was new and unfamiliar, but some of it was exactly the same. She walked until she came to Severance and then, feeling a little foolish, she went in. There were only a few girls around; it was the time of day when most girls would have a class somewhere. On the second floor she went to the right door without hesitation, as though she had left it only half an hour before to go to the library.

She had half-expected no answer to her knock and when the girl opened the door she stood tongue-tied for a moment.

"Hello," she said finally.

"Hello?"

"I'm sorry to disturb you. I had this room a long time ago. I thought it would be fun to see it again."

The girl was Chinese. She was dressed in a shortie night-gown and her thick, muscular legs were like ivory columns.

"Please come in," she said. When Leslie did she took a house-coat from the closet and put it on.

It was furnished differently, of course, and the colors were all different. It really didn't look like the same room. She walked to the window and looked out and the view really *did* take her back. Lake Waban was unchanged. It was frozen and snow-covered and near the shore some of the snow had been plowed away and the girls were skating on the ice.

"How long did you live here?" the girl asked politely.

"Two years." She smiled. "Do the toilets still stop up and overflow?"

The girl seemed puzzled. "No. The plumbing seems to be very efficient here."

All at once she felt like a perfect fool and she shook the girl's hand and started to edge toward the door.

"Won't you stay and have a cup of coffee?" the girl said, but Leslie could see that she was relieved to get rid of her and she thanked her and left the room and then the dorm.

The Old Grad, she thought. Ugh.

There was a new building, the Jewett Arts Center, and she went inside and into the gallery, which was good. They had a small Rodin and a small Renoir and a head of Baudelaire in light stone with large sightless eyes that she liked. She spent a long time in front of a St. Jerome by Hendrik Van Somer. The picture showed an old man with wrinkled dugs, a bald head, a hooked nose, a long beard and very fierce eyes, the fiercest eyes she had ever seen, and she thought immediately of the way Michael described his grandfather.

She went out the other side of the building and the moment she stepped through the door she knew exactly where she was.

There was old Galen Stone Tower and the courtyard and the trees and the stone benches, most of them snow-covered but one brushed clean. She sat facing Severance Hill, on which a solitary skier floundered and then fell. She remembered the hill in May, Tree-Planting Day with Debbie Marcus in a kind of bedsheet playing a vestal virgin.

A man in a black chesterfield and a woman in a gray cloth coat with a fox collar came out of the administration building. He had the kind of red face that made Leslie think he was a problem drinker without knowing a thing about him. "This seems to be the only bench without snow," the woman said to her husband.

"There's plenty of room," Leslie said, moving over.

The man sat on the other end of the bench and the woman sat in the middle.

"We're here to see our daughter," she said. "A surprise visit." She looked at Leslie. "Are you visiting one of the girls, too?"

"No," Leslie said. "I've just been visiting the museum."

"Which building is the museum?" the man asked.

She pointed it out to him.

"Is it all that modern business?" the man asked. "Junkyard scrap and framed paint rags?"

Before she could answer, a girl came running down the path, a high-colored brunette wearing blue jeans and a windbreaker. "How *are* you," she said, kissing the woman on the cheek. The man and the woman stood.

"We wanted to surprise you," the woman said.

"Well, I'm surprised." The three of them started to move down the path. "The thing is, I have a guest staying at the inn until tomorrow. Jack Voorsanger, the fellow I wrote you about?"

"I never heard about any Jack Voorsanger," the man said. "Well, why can't we all visit together?"

"Oh, we can. Of course," the girl said heartily. They walked away, the girl talking quickly and both her parents bending toward her as they listened.

Leslie looked up at the tower and remembered the carillon, how they played before chapel in the morning and before and after dinner. They always ended up with the same song; what was its name? She couldn't remember. She sat for a little while wishing that they would play now, and then she got to her feet, recalling what she had been told by the first boy who had ever kissed her: she had complained to him, a tall, bookish boy who was her father's prize Sunday-school pupil, telling him that she hadn't disliked it or liked it particularly, and he had said angrily, "What do you expect, chimes?"

She walked back to the railroad station and got her suitcase, then she bought a ticket and in about twenty minutes the New England States came in looking almost as it had when she had taken it home for the holidays, except a little shabbier, the way all trains were now. Right after the conductor took her ticket she fell asleep. She dozed intermittently and when she awoke the last time they were eight minutes outside of Hartford and she remembered with a small feeling of triumph what the song was; it was "The Queen's Change."

She and her father exchanged astonished glances when he opened the door in answer to her ring. He was amazed by her presence and she was astounded by his appearance. He wore a navy-blue sweatshirt and a pair of rumpled black pants marked with gray-white streaks and little lumps of something, maybe wax. His fine white hair was in disarray.

"Well," he said. "Well, come in. Are you alone?"

"Yes."

She walked past him and into the parlor. "New furniture," she said.

"Bought it myself." He took her coat and hung it in the closet. They stood and looked at one another for a difficult moment.

"What ever are you working on?" she asked, looking again at his clothing.

"Oh, my goodness." He turned and hurried away from her, into the kitchen. She heard him open the door to the cellar and then go down the stairs, and she followed him.

It was a warm, dry cellar, bright because he had turned on all the lights. In a big cast-iron cannibal pot a bed of coals glowed, and in the coals there was another pot filled with something thick that boiled and bubbled. "Must keep watching this," he said. "To leave it unattended is to invite fire." From a brown paper bag he took a handful of candle stubs and dropped them into the smaller pot. He watched anxiously while they melted, then he fished out the freed wicks with a long barbecue fork.

Senility?

She wondered, watching him closely. Certainly some kind of personality change, she told herself.

"What do you do with it?" she asked him.

"Make things. My own candles. Other things in molds. Want me to do your hands?"

"Yes."

Pleased, he utilized two pot-holders to take the molten wax off the fire. Then he took a jar of Vaseline from a cabinet drawer and watched critically as she followed his instructions, smearing the petroleum jelly thickly over each hand and forearm. He kept casting anxious glances into the pot. Finally he nodded. "Put them in. Once it gets too cool you might as well not do it."

She looked dubiously at the hot wax. "Won't it burn?"

He shook his head. "That's what the Vaseline is for. I won't let you keep them in long enough to burn."

She took a deep breath and plunged her hands into the wax and in a moment he pulled them out of the pot and she was holding them up in front of her face, hands covered with thick wax gloves. The wax was still quite hot but she could feel it cooling and hardening, and the heat and the slipperiness of the melting Vaseline, the oddest combination of conflicting sensations. She wondered how he was going to get the skin of wax off her hands without breaking it, and she started to giggle. "This is so unlike you," she said, and he smiled at her.

"I suppose it is. A man getting old needs something strange to do." He filled a pail with water, using hot and cold alternately as he tested the water in the pail with his fingertips.

"We should have done this together when I was about eight years old," she said, her eyes searching for his. "I would have loved it."

"Well—" He placed her hands in the pail of water and waited anxiously. "Temperature's the important thing. If the water is too cold the wax will break. If it's hot, the wax will melt." The water was warm. The wax became plastic enough for him to stretch it at her wrists, allowing her to pull her hands free. She jerked her left hand and the wax tore.

"Carefully," he said, annoyed. She withdrew her right hand slowly, and the wax glove that resulted was perfect. "Want to do the left one again?" he asked.

But she shook her head. "Tomorrow," she said, and he nodded.

They left the good cast hardening in a pail of cool water. "How long are you going to stay here?" he asked her as they climbed the stairs.

"I don't know," she said. She realized that she had not had dinner. "Can I have a cup of coffee, Father?"

"Of course," he said. "We'll have to make it ourselves. Woman down the street comes into make dinner, and to clean. I handle my own breakfast. Eat lunches out." He sat on a kitchen chair and watched her while she made coffee and toast. "Have you quarreled with your husband?"

"Nothing like that," she said.

"But you have some sort of trouble."

She found it tremendously moving that he understood her sufficiently to perceive this; she had not thought it possible. She was about to tell him this, then he spoke again—

"I see people in trouble every day."

—And she was glad she hadn't.

He spooned saccharine into the cup of coffee she served him and took a tentative sip. "Would you care to discuss it with me?"

"I don't think so," she said.

"Your privilege."

She felt the first stirrings of anger. "You might care to ask me how my husband and children are. Your grandchildren."

"How is your family?"

"Fine."

They said nothing for a few minutes, until they had finished the toast and coffee and there was nothing more to do with their hands and with their mouths.

She tried again. "I'll have to show Max and Rachel how to make wax hands," she said. "Better still, I'll have to bring them here and you can make some for them."

"All right," he said without enthusiasm. "How long has it been since I've seen them? Two years?"

"Eighteen months. Two summers ago. The last visit wasn't a pleasant experience for them, Father. They're very fond of their other grandfather. They could be of you, if you'll let them. It shook them to hear the two of you."

"That fellow," her father said. "I still don't understand how you might have felt I would be interested in entertaining him in my home. Nothing in common. Nothing."

She was silent, remembering an awful afternoon of shattered and bleeding personalities. "May I sleep in my old room?" she asked finally.

"No, no," he said. "It's full of cartons and things. Take the guest room. We make sure it always has clean sheets."

"The guest room?"

"Second on the left at the head of the stairs."

Her Aunt Sally's room.

"There are clean towels in the linen closet," her father said.

"Thank you."

"Are you . . . ah . . . in need of spiritual help?"

Towels and spiritual help dispensed cheerfully, she thought. "No thank you, Father."

"It is never too late. For anything. Through Jesus. No matter how far or how long we have strayed."

She said nothing, making a little motion of supplication with her hand, so small that perhaps he didn't see it.

"Even now, after all this time. I don't care how long you have been married to him. I cannot believe that the girl who grew up in this house could renounce Christ."

"Good night, Father," she said faintly. She got up and carried the bag upstairs and turned on the light and shut the door of the room behind her and leaned her back against it for a long moment, staring at the room she remembered from so many nights of burrowing into her Aunt's bed to sleep huddled against her dried-out virgin's body. She remembered exactly how her aunt had felt in her arms; even how she had smelled slightly, body odor and stale roses, probably the scent of a perfumed soap Aunt Sally had used in secret.

She changed into her nightgown, wondering if you still had

to light the gas ring in order to get enough hot water for the bath, too weary to find out. She heard him come upstairs and then the sound of his hesitant knock on her door.

"You run away when I try to talk to you," he said.

"I'm sorry, Father."

"What makes you so afraid?"

"I'm tired," she said through the closed door.

"Can you tell me that you feel as though you are one of them?" he asked.

She was silent.

"Are you a Jew, Leslie?"

But she would not answer.

"Can you tell *me* that you are a Jew?"

Go away, she thought, sitting on the bed in which her aunt had died.

In a little while she heard him go into his own room down the hall and she reached up and pulled the cord that shut the light. Instead of going to bed right away she went to the window and sat on the floor with her breasts crushed against the sill and her face pressing into the cold pane in the familiar old way, looking through a glass darkly at the street that had once been a part of her prison.

In the morning when they met for breakfast it was as though nothing had happened the previous evening. She made him bacon and eggs and he ate them with appetite, even a trifle greedily. When she served the coffee he cleared his throat. "Unfortunately," he said, "I have a full calendar of appointments this morning at the church."

"Then I had better say good-by now, Father," she said. "I've decided to take an early train."

"Oh? All right then," he said.

Before he left the house he stopped at her room and handed her two long yellow candlesticks. "A little gift," he said.

When he had gone she telephoned for a taxi and when it arrived rode in it to the depot. Inside the railroad station she bought a paperback Robert Frost collection and read it for twenty minutes. When the train was five minutes away she lifted her bag to the waiting-room bench and opened it, picking up the yellow candles to move them to make room for the book, and one of the candles came apart in her hand, the yellow wax crumbling away to show the flaw, a piece of undigested white wax at its heart. In disgust she picked the waxy crumbs out of her suitcase as best she could and threw them with the broken pieces into a trash barrel.

On the train she began to wonder what she could do with one candle and going through Stamford she removed it from the suitcase and dropped it down the crevice between the armrest and the wall beneath the window. Without knowing why, she felt better.

As they drew closer to New York she watched the scenery roll past like a long television plea for urban renewal. It was a warm day for winter. Off the tracks, mist rose from the snow in gray banks, and she thought of mornings in San Francisco where to look out the windows was to know that the earth was waste and void, and darkness was on the face of the deep, and the spirit of God moved upon the face of the earth and the face of the waters, disguised as lovely mother-of-pearl fog.

San Francisco, California
January 1948

CHAPTER THIRTY-ONE

The house, a narrow three-story gray shingle with a white picket fence, clung by the knuckles of its foundation to the side of a very steep hill overlooking San Francisco Bay. The man was middle-aged, short and broad. He stood with his foot on the running board of a discolored black panel truck laden with ropes and ladders and color-crusted buckets. He wore an air of somewhat raffish competence, clean but paint-spotted white coveralls, and a painter's cap with DUTCH BOY printed across the bill.

"So," he said, *basso profundo,* with satisfaction but no smile, "you made it. Lucky you caught me home. I was just leaving for my work."

"Can you tell us how to get to our new address, Mr. Golden?" Michael said.

"Never find it. Long way from here. I'll drive my truck, you'll follow."

"We don't want to cut into your workday," Michael said.

"Cut into my workday every day for the temple. Only way the temple gets anything done. Not an officer, like the *machers,* the big shots who talk-talk-talk all the time. Just a worker." He opened the door and climbed into the truck. He had a heavy foot on the gas pedal; the motor started with a roar. "You follow me," he said.

They followed, grateful for the truck ahead because Michael had trouble seeing the traffic lights; they were located in places an Easterner expected they had no right to be.

They drove for a long, long time. "Where is it, in Oregon?" Leslie said, whispering as though Mr. Golden were in the back seat instead of in the car ahead.

Finally they turned off into a street of small, neat ranch houses with closely clipped green lawns. "Michael," Leslie said, "they're all alike." Street after street of the same house, set in the same way on identical lots of land.

"The colors are different," Michael said.

The house Mr. Golden stopped in front of was green. It was set between a white one on the right and a blue one on the left.

Inside, there were three bedrooms, a good-sized living room, a dining area, a kitchen, and a bathroom. The rooms were half-furnished.

"It's very nice," Leslie said. "But all those other hundreds of houses just like it . . ."

"A big tract," Mr. Golden said. "Everything mass-produced. Get more for your money that way." He walked over and stroked a wall. "I painted these rooms myself. Good job. You won't find nicer walls even if you decide to look around."

He studied Leslie's face shrewdly. "You don't take it, we'll just rent it out to somebody else. Except this would be a good deal for you. The temple bought this house from our former Rabbi. Name of Kaplan, went to Temple B'nai Israel in Chicago. We don't have to pay taxes on it. Nonprofit religious institution. So it wouldn't cost you much." He disappeared through the doorway.

"Maybe we can live in a big old house with gingerbread. Or an apartment on one of the high hills," Leslie said in a low voice.

"I was told that good places are hard to find in San Francisco now," Michael said. "And very expensive. Besides, if we take this, it will mean one less headache for the congregation."

"But all the carbon copies."

He knew what she meant. "In spite of that, it's a nice little house. And if we find that we don't like living in a tract we can simply look around at our leisure and then move out."

"Okay," she said, and came to him and kissed him just as Phil Golden came back into the room. "We're going to live here," she said.

Golden nodded. "Want to see the temple?" he asked her.

They went for another drive which ended at a yellow-brick building. Michael had seen it only on the evening of his audition service. By daylight it looked older and wearier.

"Used to be a church. Catholic. Saint Jerry Myer. Jewish saint," Phil said.

The interior was roomy but dark and Michael thought it smelled faintly of age and the confessional. He had forgotten what an ugly temple it was. He tried to put down the disappointment that welled within him. A temple was people, not a building. But some day, he could not help thinking fiercely, he would have a temple full of light and air and a sense of beauty and wonder.

They spent the afternoon shopping for furniture, buying several pieces for more money than they had intended to spend and making an alarming dent in the bank balance.

"Let me use the thousand dollars Aunt Sally left me," she said.

He remembered her father's face. "No," he said.

She sat very still. "Why not?"

"Is the reason important?"

"I think the reason might be important. Yes," she said.

"Save it and someday use it for something our children really want," he said. It was the right answer.

The house was spotlessly clean and this time they had come prepared with clean sheets and towels. Nevertheless when night came they lay in the darkness of the unfamiliar room without sleeping. Leslie tossed.

"What's the matter?" he asked.

"I hate to meet those women," she said.

"What are you talking about?" he said, amused.

"I know what I'm talking about. Remember, I've been through it before. Those . . . *yentehs* . . . flock to the temple, not to pray, not even to hear the new rabbi, but to see the *shickseh*."

"Oh, God," he said heavily.

"They do. They look you up and down. 'How long are you married?' they ask. And then, 'Do you have any little ones?' and you can see their minds ready to go to work like little computers to see if their rabbi had to marry me."

"I didn't realize it was that bad for you," he said.

"Well, now you realize."

They lay next to each other in silence.

But a moment later she turned to him and covered his face with quick kisses. "Ah, Michael," she said. "I'm sorry. I don't know what gets into me." He reached to take her in his arms but she turned suddenly and slipped out of the bed and ran for the bathroom. He listened for a few moments and then followed after her.

"Are you all right?" he asked, tapping at the door.

"Go away," she said in a strangled voice. "Please."

He went back to bed and put the pillow over his ears, unsuccessfully trying to blot out the tortured noise of her nausea. How many nights had this happened while he slept undisturbed, he wondered.

All we needed, he thought.

Morning sickness.

Ech

Her beautiful belly will blow up into a balloon.

She's wrong about the women, he thought, this will take care of everything. She'll sit in the first row and during Friday night services the women will look from her swelling stomach to me and their lips will smile tenderly but their eyes will say, Beast, you did this to all of us.

Big. Very soon now.

Oy, I love her.

I wonder if we have to stop making love?

When she came back, limp with sweat and her mouth smelling of Listerine, he held her and touched her stomach carefully with his fingertips, finding it flat and hard and unchanged.

He looked at her in the growing light and the nausea was gone and unexpectedly she smiled a satisfied female smile, proud that she was in a position to have morning sickness. As he put his arms around her and his cheek on her cheek she belched into his ear and instead of excusing herself she burst into tears. The honeymoon was over, he told himself as he stroked her head and kissed her eyelids that were soft and wet like little flowers.

For two days he met and talked to people, the officers and the *machers* of the temple. The former rabbi's secretary had gotten married and was living in San Jose, and he spent a great deal of time simply trying to locate things. He found a membership list and started to work out a schedule of personal visits to help him get acquainted with the less-active members of the congregation.

On the second day Phil Golden came into the temple at noon. "Like Chinks? Place down the street does wonders with a moo goo gai pan. Owned by one of our members."

Golden wore a pin-striped blue suit that looked custom-tailored. "Aren't you working today?" Michael asked.

Golden grimaced. "I'll tell you," he said as they walked together toward the restaurant. "Years ago when I was a young man I worked like a horse. Paint, paint, paint. For a tough, bare living. Over the years my wife and I had four sons, thank God, all big, healthy boys. I taught them all how to paint houses. I

had a dream, some day I'll be a contractor, my boys will work
for me. Only now all the *boys* are contractors. I'm president of
the parent company, but that's what it is. A parent company.
The only time I get a paintbrush in my hands is when I do
something for the temple."

He chuckled softly. "That isn't quite true. Every six months
or so I can't stand it any more and I go out like a thief and take
a small job on the q.t. I hire a helper, a Mexican kid, and give
him all the profits. Don't tell the boys."

"I won't."

The restaurant was called Moy Sheh. "Morris in?" Golden
asked the Chinese waiter who brought the menu.

"He's at the market," the waiter said.

They were hungry and the pungent food was good. They
talked little, but finally Phil Golden sat back and lit up a cigar.
"So, how are you doing?" he asked.

"I think I'm going to like it here."

The older man nodded noncommitally.

"A peculiar thing," Michael said. "I've talked to a lot of
people. And from four different men I got the same warning."

Golden puffed. "What was the warning?"

" 'Watch out for Phil Golden,' they said. 'He's a rough one.' "

Golden inspected his cigar ash. "I could tell you the four
names. And what did you tell them?"

"I told them I'd watch out."

Golden's face remained expressionless, but the skin at the
corners of his eyes crinkled. "Make it easier for you to watch,
Rabbi, you and your wife come tomorrow for Friday-night dinner," he said.

There were eleven people around the dining-room table. In
addition to Phil and Rhoda Golden there were two of the sons,
Jack and Irving, their wives, Ruthie (Jack's) and Florence
(Irving's), and three of Phil's grandchildren, ages three to eleven.

"Henry, our other married son, lives over in Sausalito," Phil
explained. "Got two kids and a nice deck house. He married an
Armenian girl. They have two little William Saroyans, big brown
sensitive eyes and noses bigger than plain Jews could afford.

We don't see them much. They stay in Sausalito doing who knows what, maybe picking grapes."

"Phil," Rhoda Golden said.

Phil remembered about Leslie and felt impelled to explain to her. "He didn't convert, she didn't convert, and the kids are nothing. I leave it to you, is this good?"

"I guess it isn't," she said.

"What's the name of your fourth son?" Michael asked.

"Ai, Babe," Ruthie said, and the others smiled.

"I ask you to picture, Rabbi," said Florence, who was blond and well-built but skinny, "a handsome guy of thirty-seven. Still has all his hair. Makes money. Is a very tender person, a real booby-doll. Loves kids, they love him. Is all man, walks the streets of San Francisco on broken hearts instead of paving stones. Yet he won't get married."

"Babe, Babe, Babe," Rhoda said, shaking her head. "My Babe. If I could dance at his wedding. Even to Armenian music. Too much pepper in the fish?"

The fish was excellent, as was the soup and the roast chicken and the stuffed derma and the two kinds of kugel and the fruit compote. *Shabbos* lights burned in brass candlesticks on an upright piano in the next room. It was the kind of apartment Michael remembered but had not been in for a long time.

After dinner there was brandy while the women did the dishes and then the two sets of younger parents said good night and dragged their sleepy children home. Before leaving, Florence Golden made a date to take Leslie to lunch and to the De Young Memorial Museum the following day, which somehow turned the conversation to pictures and then photographs, and Rhoda hauled out a giant album which she and Leslie pored over in the kitchen, occasionally sending squalls of laughter into the living room where Michael and Phil sat over another brandy.

"So, now you're a Californian," Phil said.

"An old Californian."

Golden smiled. "*Zehr* old," he said. "*I'm* what you call an old Californian. I came out here when I was a little boy, with my mother and father from New London, Connecticut. My father was a drummer. Marine hardware. Always carried a trunk weighed a hundred and four pounds. When we first came here we tried a series of *shuls* in the old Jewish neighborhood around Fillmore Street. The *Yiddlech* huddled together in those days, like the Chinese. That didn't last long, of course," he said. "You can hardly tell the difference between Jews and Catholics and Protestants any more. Three good whiffs of California air and everyone becomes homogenized. Ah, Rabbi, its' a different story from the old days, being a Jew today."

"In what way?"

Golden snorted. "Take the *bar mitzvah*. It used to be a big thing for a little boy. He's called the *bema* for the first time, he sings a section of the Torah in Hebrew, like magic he becomes a man in the eyes of God and of his fellow Jews. Nobody sees anybody but him, you know?

"Today by comparison the boy takes a back seat. The show's the thing. There's more bar than *mitzvah*. Your temple congregation is mostly a cocktail crowd. Young American moderns. What do they know from Fillmore Street?" He shook his head.

Michael looked at him thoughtfully. "Why was I warned about you?" he asked.

"I'm the temple scold," Phil said. "I keep insisting that the reason we got a building is to have services in. That to be Jews you got to be Jewish. It doesn't make you popular in Temple Isaiah."

"So why are you a member?"

"I'll tell you the truth," he said. "My boys joined. My boys are as bad as the rest of them. But I feel a family should go to services as a family. I figured it won't hurt the rest of them to sit in the same temple as one old-fashioned *yiddel* when they come to their annual service."

Michael smiled. "Things can't be that bad. They can't."

"They can't, huh?" Golden chuckled. "They started Temple Isaiah eight years ago. You know why? The other Reform temples demanded too much time. Too much personal commitment. Your people want to be Jews, but not to the extent that it's going to take any of the free time they came to California to enjoy. Yom Kippur and Rosh Hashonah. That's all, brother.

"Now," he said, holding up one large hand like a traffic cop, "don't think they're unwilling to pay for this privilege. Our dues are fairly high, but this is a young, successful congregation.

Times are good. They make money and they pay their dues so *you* can be Jewish for *them*. You want to spend money for any temple project within reason, I can tell you here and now you can do it. Just don't expect to see many *people* at your services. Just . . . realize that you've got enemies, Rabbi. Rows of empty seats."

Michael thought about that. "The Ku Klux Klan doesn't bother you?"

Golden shrugged his shoulders and made a face. *Bist mishugah?* his expression asked.

"Then don't worry about the seats. We'll try to fill them."

Phil smiled. "That would take a miracle worker," he said gently, reaching for the bottle. He poured more brandy into Michael's glass. "I never have trouble with the Rabbi. With the board, yes. With individual members, yes. But not with the Rabbi. I'll be there if you need me, but I won't be a pest. It's your baby."

"Not for six months yet," Michael said, as Leslie and Rhoda came into the room.

And that changed the subject.

The following day some of the furniture came. Michael sat in a new chair in front of the television set formerly owned by Rabbi Kaplan. On CBS, newsreels were being shown of armies representing 40,000,000 Arabs of six countries directing their combined military hate toward 650,000 Jews. The film strips showed ruined *kibbutzim* and corpses and Israeli women huddled in olive groves, answering Jordanian fire with long bursts of tracer bullets. Michael watched the news programs closely. His parents heard from Ruthie infrequently now. She was evasive when they wrote to her with questions about what she was doing during the fighting. She would say only that Saul and the children were well and that she was well. Was that his sister Ruthie, Michael thought, lying behind a fallen olive tree and attempting to send a stream of bullets through an invader's flesh? He stayed in front of the television screen all day.

Leslie enjoyed the afternoon outing with Florence Golden. She came home with the name of an excellent obstetrician and with a framed print of Thomas Sully's *The Torn Hat*. They spent a long time hanging it, then they stood with their arms around one another and studied the sweet, serious face of the boy in the picture.

"Do you have your heart set on a son?" she asked.

"No," he lied.

"I really don't care. All I can think about is that our love is making a human being. That's all that matters. It doesn't make any difference whether he has a penis or not."

"If it's a he, I'd rather he had," Michael said.

That night he dreamed of Arabs and Jews killing one another and he saw Ruthie's dead body in his dream. Next morning he got out of bed early and walked in his bare feet into the back yard. The fog was thick and ropy, and he breathed it deep inside, tasting the fish-tang of the Pacific Ocean four miles away.

"What are you doing?" Leslie asked sleepily, coming up behind him.

"Living," he said. As they watched, the sun cut through the fog like a windshield defroster.

"I think I'll make a small garden and grow some tomatoes," he said. "And maybe an orange tree. Are we too far north for an orange tree?"

"I think we are," she said.

"I don't think so," he said crankily.

"Then plant it," she said. "Oh, Michael, this is going to be good. I just love it here. We were meant to stay here always."

"Whatever you want, Baby," he said, and they went inside, he to scramble the eggs and make the coffee, she to be sick with child.

CHAPTER THIRTY-TWO

On that first *shabbos* in his new temple he knew with a thrill of triumph that Phil Golden was wrong. His sermon had been short enough, bright enough and intelligent, stressing the importance of identification and participation by the members. The seats were four-fifths filled, the congregation was attentive, and after the service friendly hands grasped his and warm voices caressed him with words of support, even of incipient affection. He felt certain that his congregation would return.

Most of them did on the following week.

Fewer showed up on the third Friday evening.

When he had been rabbi of Temple Isaiah for six weeks, the empty seats were very noticeable from the *bema*. The backs of the seats were of polished wood veneer that reflected the lights like a great many mocking yellow eyes.

He ignored them, concentrating on the worshipers who filled the other seats. But the number of worshipers dwindled every week and the number of empty seats grew, so many unblinking eyes of yellow light on the backs of the chairs that he could no longer ignore them, and finally he knew that Phil Golden was right.

His enemies.

It was easy, he and Leslie found, to become Californians.

They learned not to drive behind cable cars going up steep hills.

They visited Golden Gate Park on Sunday afternoons when the air was the color of pollen and they sat and grass-stained their clothing and watched lovers walking and necking while all around them small children played and laughed and cried.

His wife's belly grew, but not into the ugly and swollen thing he had feared. It bloomed like a large, warm flesh bud, pushed outward by the growing life inside. At night now he sometimes turned back the covers and switched on the bed lamp and watched it while she slept, smiling to himself and breathing hard when he saw her belly shudder quickly as the baby within her kicked or tossed. He was haunted by thoughts of terrible things, of fatal miscarriages and hemorrhages and breech births and claw hands and no legs and vegetables with feeble minds, and he prayed through long sleepless nights that God would spare them from all of these.

The obstetrician was named Lubowitz. He was a fat grandfather and an old hand, and he knew when to be tender and when to be tough. He put Leslie on a regimen of walking and exercise that gave her a ravenous appetite and then placed her on a diet that kept her hungry all the time.

Michael spoke to her as little as possible about the temple as her pregnancy advanced, preferring not to disturb her. He was becoming increasingly disturbed himself.

His congregation puzzled him.

Phil Golden's family and a handful of others could be relied upon to attend services regularly. But his contact with the body of people who made up his temple remained almost nonexistent.

He went to the hospitals daily in search of sick Jews he might comfort and get to know. He found some, but rarely from his own congregation.

Calling at the homes of temple members, he found them polite and friendly but strangely remote. In a patio apartment on Russian Hill, for example, a couple named Sternbane regarded him uneasily after he had introduced himself. Oscar Sternbane was an importer of Oriental curios and owned a small interest in a coffee house on Geary Street. His wife, Celia, gave voice lessons. She had black hair and pink skin and was arrogantly aware of her looks, with a coloratura's chest tenderly displayed in a bulky scoop-neck sweater and flanks that deserved to be hugged by blue Pucci slacks, and nostrils that cost six hundred dollars apiece.

"I'm trying to reorganize the Brotherhood," Michael said to Oscar Sternbane. "I thought we might begin by having Sunday breakfasts at the temple."

"Rabbi, let me be frank," Sternbane said. "We're happy to belong to the temple. Our little boy can learn Hebrew every Saturday morning, and all about the Bible. That's nice, it's cultural. But bagels and lox! We were happy to leave bagels and lox behind when we came here from Teaneck, New Jersey."

"Forget the *food*," Michael said. "We have *people* in the temple. Do you know the Barrons?"

Oscar shrugged. Celia shook her head.

"I think you'd like them. And there are others. The Pollocks. The Abelsons."

"Freddy and Jan Abelson?"

"Hey," he said, delighted. "You know the Abelsons?"

"Yes," Celia said.

"We've been there once and they've been here once," Freddy said. "They're very nice, but . . . to tell you the truth, Rabbi, *square*. They don't"—he held up his hand and turned it slowly, like a man screwing in an invisible light bulb—"*swing* enough for us. You know? Look," he said kindly, "we've all got our own groups of friends, our own interests, and they just don't revolve around the temple. But what time will the breakfasts begin? I'll try to make the scene."

He didn't. In the end, eight men showed up on the first Sunday morning, four of them named Golden. Only Phil and his sons came back the second week.

"Perhaps a dance," Leslie suggested when he finally discussed his problems with her after he had consumed three martinis one evening before dinner.

They spent five weeks planning it; they prepared a flyer, sent two mailings, devoted the front page of the temple bulletin to the affair, hired a combo, ordered a catered buffet, and on the night of the dance watched with frozen smiles as eleven couples shuffled over the floor of the large temple hall.

Michael continued to visit the hospitals. He spent a great deal of time on his sermons, as if every seat in the temple were being fought over.

But this left a great deal of unfilled time. There was a public library two blocks away. He took out a card and began to draw books. At first he went back to the philosophers, but soon the jackets of the novels tempted him. He developed a nodding-smiling acquaintanceship with the ladies behind the circulation desk.

He returned to the Talmud and the Torah, studying a different portion each morning and reviewing it with Leslie each evening. In the stillness of the afternoons, when the temple building was quiet with the dead weight of undisturbed air, he began to experiment with the mystic theosophy of the Cabala, like a small boy dipping his toe into dangerously deep water.

St. Margaret's, the Catholic parish in which the Kinds lived, was building a new church. One morning, driving past the site, Michael double-parked for a few minutes to watch a steam shovel rip giant chunks of earth and rock from the foundation hole.

The next day he came back. And the next. He began making a habit of dropping by to watch the steel-helmeted workers when he had a few spare moments. It was relaxing to lean against the makeshift fence of random lumber and stare at the noisy mechanical monoliths and the leather-skinned construction crew. Inevitably he met the pastor of St. Margaret's, the Reverend Dominic Angelo Campanelli, a sleepy-eyed old priest with a huge strawberry mark like a sign of divinity on the right side of his face.

"Temple Isaiah," he said when Michael introduced himself. "That would be St. Jeremiah's. I grew up in that parish."

"Did you really?" Michael said, adding ten years to his original estimate of the age of the temple building.

"Served as choirboy for Father Gerald X. Minehan, who subsequently was associate bishop in San Diego," Father Campanelli said. He shook his head. "St. Jeremiah's. I carved my initials in the belfry of that church." He looked into the distance. "Right under an old gas lamp that used to hang from one of the walls." He colored and seemed to shake himself mentally. "Yes," he said. "Nice to meet you," and walked away, a black-cassocked figure whose fingers moved restlessly over the hundred and fifty beads on the cord around his waist.

That afternoon Michael overturned an old shoebox on his desk and one by one went through the tagged keys it had contained, until he came upon one whose tag was marked *belfry*.

The narrow door opened with a satisfying screeching. Inside there was gloom, and a short flight of wooden stairs, one of which cracked alarmingly as he set his weight upon it. How embarrassing it would be, he thought, to plunge through and break a leg—or worse. How would you explain it to the congregation?

The wooden stairs led to a landing. A diffuse gray light which fell from high, grime-colored windows revealed small round trays of rat bait set on the floor against all four walls.

A circular iron stairway spiraled to a trapdoor in the ceiling which opened noisily but with no difficulty. Birds exploded into the air as he climbed through. He held his breath against the stench. The walls were whitewashed with guano. Three drop-pings-encrusted stick nests contained incredibly ugly small birds. The baby pigeons were naked and fist-sized, with bulbous beaks.

The bell still hung. It was a large bell. He flicked it with his middle finger, getting only a bruised nail and a dull click. When he leaned over the side, careful to keep his clothing well off the befouled railing, San Francisco fell away below, looking older and wiser than it had ever looked to him before. Two of the adult pigeons came back, fluttering anxiously just above the belfry and making alarmed-mother noises as they cooed.

"Okay," he told them, picking a path through the guck. He pulled the trapdoor shut above him as he descended, grate-fully snorting in an attempt to clear the stench from his nostrils.

In the belfry landing he paused for a closer look. The old gas lamp was still on the wall. He turned the tiny spigot and was alarmed at the resulting hiss and gas smell. "Something will have to be done about *this*," he murmured, shutting it off.

The light was too dim for him to see whether the priest's initials were in fact there, but he took out some matches and after waving frantically to disperse any gas fumes, he struck one.

There was a heart, he saw as he held the flickering match. It was a large heart. Carved in its center were indeed the initials *D A C*.

"Dominic Angelo Campanelli," he said aloud, pleased.

Beneath the *D A C* there had been another set of initials. But they had been scrubbed out with a heavy black pencil which had remained heavy and black through the years. Instead of them, written in the heart with Dominic Campanelli's initials, was the scrawled word:

JESUS.

The match burned his fingers and he dropped it with a little grunt. He placed his fingertips in his mouth until the pain went away and then he ran them over the obliterated initials. The carved indentations still remained. The first letter was unmistakably *M*. There was another letter, either a *C* or an *O*, he couldn't tell which.

What had her name been?

Maria? Myra? Marguerite?

He stood there wondering whether young Dominic Campanelli had cried as he scrubbed out her initials.

And then he descended from the church tower and left his temple and went home to stare at his wife's comic-strip balloon belly.

In the slow peace of early morning Michael and the priest began to talk to one another as they leaned on the board fence letting the smoke from their pipes get lost in the fog and watching the giant steam shovel taking huge bites out of the hill. They steered their conversations away from religion. Sports was a good safe topic; they depended heavily on the status of the Seals and the team's running series with Los Angeles. While they talked of averages and clutch hitters, of the animal grace of Williams and the gallantry of DiMaggio, they watched the hole in the ground take shape and then the forms being built.

"Interesting," said Michael, seeing the outline of the forms emerge: an oblong leading to a much larger circle.

Father Campanelli would give no hints. "A departure from the stereotype," he said, and his head turned involuntarily to look up the street to where the old St. Margaret's, aged and too small but built of red brick along simple and beautiful lines, stood in ivy-covered dignity. His hand went up and his long thin fingers began to stroke the strawberry mark that stained his aquiline face. Michael had noticed the gesture before whenever they had discussed items that had cast ominous shadows: the Seals on a losing streak; Williams sullying his magnificence with a stiff finger for the fans; a slowing DiMaggio letting his light go dim with a hopeless love for Marilyn Monroe.

One Sunday, driving with Leslie through the golden afternoon deep into the Monterey peninsula, he saw a temple that had been built on a rocky cliff overlooking the Pacific.

The setting was magnificent. The building was all wrong. Redwood and glass, it looked like the offspring of a deck house that had been mated with an ice castle.

"Isn't that terrible?" he asked Leslie.

"Mmmm."

"I wonder what that church in town is going to be like."

She shrugged drowsily.

A little later she stretched and looked at him. "If you were asking an architect to design you a temple, what would you ask for?"

This time he shrugged. But he thought about the question for a long time.

Next morning, after he had studied the Talmud, he sat in his study and drank coffee and began to plan the ideal temple.

It was more fun than reading, he discovered, but full of frustrations, like a game of self-chess. He worked with pencil and paper, drawing rough plans which he promptly threw away, making out lists to ponder and rewrite. He went to the library and withdrew books on architecture. He found himself constantly confronted by stalemates which caused him to revise his image of what the temple should be, so many revisions that he emptied an entire filing-case drawer in his study for the storage of notes, volumes, and the crude drawings he made over and over again, filling the empty hours easily now, but with a kind of personal parlor game, a rabbinical version of solitaire.

There were occasional interruptions. A drunken merchant sailor, unshaven and with a cut under one eye, wandered through the doors one morning.

"Like say confession, Father," he said, slumping heavily into a chair, eyes closed.

"I'm sorry."

The sailor opened one eye.

"I'm not a priest."

"Where is he?"

"This isn't a church."

"Snow me, pal. Said confession here lots durin' the war. Distinc'ly remember."

"It used to be a church." He started to explain the facts concerning the building's conversion, but the sailor cut him off.

"Well Jesus," he said. "Jesus Christ." He got up unsteadily and walked away. "If this isn't church, what the hell you doin' here?"

Michael sat and stared at the door through which the man had lurched into the bright sunlight outside.

"I won't snow you, pal," he whispered finally. "I'm not sure I know."

CHAPTER THIRTY-THREE

He came home one evening to find Leslie's eyes red. "What's the matter?" he asked, his thoughts leaping to Ruthie's family, his parents, her father.

But she held out a small package. "I opened it for you."

He saw that it had been forwarded by the Union of American Hebrew Congregations. It contained a Hebrew prayer book bound in black buckram that was limp with age. There was a note in spidery Spencerian script.

My Dear Rabbi Kind:

I am sorry that I must tell you of the death of Rabbi Max Gross. My beloved husband died of a stroke in the synagogue on July 17 while reciting Mincha.

Rabbi Gross was not a talkative man, but he spoke to me of you. He told me once that if our son had lived he would have wanted him to be like you, only Orthodox.

I am taking the liberty of forwarding to you the enclosed siddur. It was the one which he used in his daily devotions. I know he would have liked you to have it, and it will give me comfort to know that Max's siddur will continue to be used.

I hope you and Mrs. Kind are very well and prospering in a lovely place like California, with such a climate.

Yours very truly,
Mrs. Leah M. Gross

She put her hand on his arm. "Michael," she said.

He shook his head, unwilling to talk about it. He was unable to weep like Leslie; he had never been able to cry at death. But he sat alone the entire evening going through the *siddur*, page by page, remembering Max.

Finally he crawled into bed to lie unsleeping next to his wife, praying for Max Gross and for everybody who remained alive.

After a long time, Leslie touched his shoulder apologetically. "Darling," she said.

It was 2:25 A.M. according to the alarm clock.

"Go to sleep," he said tenderly. "We can't help him."

"Darling," she said again, this time half-groan.

He sat up. "Oh my God," he said, a different sort of prayer.

"Take it easy," she said. "There's no need to get excited."

"You're having pains?"

"I think it's time to go."

"Are they bad?" he asked, by this time pulling on his pants.

"They're not even pains. Just . . . contractions."

"How often?"

"Every forty minutes in the beginning. Now, every twenty minutes."

He called Dr. Lubowitz and then carried her bag outside and came back and helped her into the car. The fog was very thick and he realized that he was very nervous; he couldn't take deep breaths and he drove extra-slowly, hunched up over the wheel with his head close to the glass of the windshield.

"What are they like?" he asked. "The contractions."

"I don't know," she said. "Like an elevator going up very slowly. They hang on up there at the top for just a little while and then they start sliding down."

"Like an orgasm?"

"No," she said. "Jesus."

"Don't say that," he said involuntarily.

"Oh, Moses?" she said. "Is that better?" She shook her head and closed her eyes. "For a bright guy you can be the biggest damn fool."

He said nothing, driving through the foggy streets, hoping he wasn't lost.

She reached out and touched his cheek lightly.

"My darling. I'm sorry. Ah," she said, "here's another one." She took his right hand from the wheel and placed it on her stomach. As she held it there the soft flesh grew hard and then rigid; then, gradually, soft again under his fingertips. "I can feel it inside like that, too," she whispered. "Making a hard ball."

He found suddenly that he was trembling. A taxicab was

parked on a corner curb under the light of a street lamp, and
he pulled in behind it.

"I'm lost, dammit," he said. "Can you move from the car into
the taxi?"

"Of course."

The cab driver was a bald man in chinos and a wrinkled
Hawaiian shirt. He had a red Irish face that was knotted in its
need for sleep.

"Lane Hospital," Michael said.

The man nodded, yawning gustily as he started the motor.

"It's on Webster between Clay and Sacramento," Michael
said.

"I know where it is, buddy."

He was watching Leslie's face and he saw her eyes widen.
"You can't tell me that was just a contraction," he said.

"No. Now they're pains."

The driver turned his head and took a good look at her for
the first time, suddenly fully awake. "Holy mackeral," he said.
"Why didn't you say so?" He stepped down on the gas pedal,
driving very carefully, but faster.

In a few minutes Leslie groaned. She was the kind of girl
who ordinarily refused to recognize pain; the sound that came
from her lips was animal-like and strange, and it frightened him.

"Are you timing the pains?" he asked. She made no sign that
she had heard his voice. Her eyes were slightly glazed.

"Ah. Jesus Christ," she said softly. He kissed her cheek.

She groaned again and he thought of barns and hay and
the sound of suffering cows. He looked at his watch and in a
little while another bovine groan sounded from his wife's lips
and he looked at his watch again.

"Oh, God, that can't be right," he said. *"Four minutes?"*

"Keep your legs together, lady," the cab driver called, as
though she were half a block away.

"What if she has it in the car?" Michael asked. He looked
down at the floor and repressed a shudder. A fat, wet cigar lay
mashed in a corner of the rubber floormat like an evil dropping.

"I hope not," said the driver, shocked. "Her waters break
in here, they tie up the cab for thirty-six hours while it's being

sterilized. Board o' Health." He slid the car around the corner. "Just a little while more, lady," he called.

Leslie had her feet against the front seat now. With each pain she slid lower and pushed, her shoulders against the back seat and her feet against the front seat, arching her pelvis toward the roof as she groaned. Each time she pushed she crowded the driver into the wheel as the seat jolted forward.

"Leslie," Michael said. "The man won't be able to drive."

"It's all right," the driver said. "We're here." He killed the motor and left them in the still-quivering car as he ran into the red brick building. In a moment he came out with a nurse and an attendant and they put Leslie in a wheel chair and took her bag and wheeled her away, leaving him standing with the cab driver on the sidewalk. He ran after her and kissed her cheek.

"Most women, they're built like ripe fruit," the driver said when he returned to the cab. "The doctor will give her a little squeeze and the baby will squirt right out, like a seed."

The meter said two dollars and ninety cents. The man had hurried, Michael thought, and he hadn't made any lousy jokes about expectant fathers. He gave him six dollars.

"Got sympathy pains?" the driver asked, stuffing the bills into his wallet.

"No," Michael said.

"Never lost a father yet," he said, grinning as he ran around to enter his cab.

Inside the hospital, the lobby was deserted. A middle-aged Mexican man took him up to the maternity floor in the elevator.

"That your wife they have just brought in?" he asked.

"Yes," Michael said.

"Won't be long. She is almost there," he said.

In the maternity ward a crewcut resident pushed through the swinging doors. "Mr. Kind?" Michael nodded. "She seems to be doing fine. We have her in the labor room." He rubbed a palm across his fuzzy head. "You can go home and get some sleep, if you like. We'll call you as soon as anything develops."

"I'd just as soon wait here," Michael said.

The resident frowned. "It could be a long time, but you're welcome, of course." He showed him the way to the waiting room.

The room was small, with highly waxed brown linoleum floors that reminded him of the home in which his grandfather had died. There were two magazines on the rattan sofa, a three-year-old copy of *Time* and a year-old copy of *Yachting*. The only light came from a lamp with an inadequate bulb.

Michael walked to the elevator and pushed the button. The Mexican operator was still smiling.

"Is there someplace where I can buy you a drink?" Michael asked.

"No, sir. I can't drink on the job no-how. But you want cigarettes and magazines and such, there's an all-night drugstore two blocks north."

On the ground floor he stopped Michael as he was about to leave the elevator. "Tell him I sent you, he'll give me a free smoke next time I go in."

Michael grinned. "What's your name?"

"Johnny."

He walked slowly through the misty darkness, praying, to the drugstore, and bought three packs of Philip Morris, an Oh Henry and a Clark Bar, a newspaper, *Life*, *The Reporter*, and a paperback whodunit.

"Johnny sent me," he told the clerk as he waited for change. "From the hospital." The man nodded.

"What's his cigarette?" Michael asked.

"Johnny? I don't think he smokes cigarettes. Cigarillos."

He bought three packs of cigarillos for Johnny. The fog was still thick but the first light was breaking as he walked back. Oh God, he said silently, let her be all right. The baby too but if only one of them then let her be all right, Please God Amen.

Johnny was delighted with the cigarillos. "Your doctor's here. Her water went and broke," he said. He looked dubiously at the load Michael carried. "You just ain't gonna be here that long," he said.

"The young doctor said it would be a long time," Michael said.

"Young doctor," Johnny said. "He has been here eight months. I have been here twenty-two years." The buzzer sounded and he slid the elevator door shut.

He opened the newspaper and tried to read Herb Caen's

column. In a couple of minutes the elevator was back. Johnny
came into the waiting room and took a seat near the door where
he could hear the buzzer. He lit up one of the cigarillos. "What
do you do?" he asked. "For a living?"

"I'm a rabbi."

"Is that a fact?" He puffed for a few moments. "Maybe you
can tell me something. Is it true that when a Jew boy is a certain age they hold a party and he becomes a man?"

"The *bar mitzvah*? Yes, at thirteen."

"Well, is it true that all the other Jews come to the party
and they bring money and they give it to the boy to open up
a business?"

Before he was through laughing a nurse stood in the doorway. "Mister Kind?" she said.

"He's a rabbi," Johnny said.

"Well, Rabbi Kind, then," she said tiredly, "congratulations,
your wife just had a little boy."

When he bent to kiss her the smell of ether almost took his
breath away. Her face was flushed and her eyes were closed and
she looked dead. But she opened her eyes and smiled at him and
when he took her hand she held it tightly.

"Did you see him?" she said.

"Not yet."

"Oh, he's lovely," she whispered. "He's got a penis. I asked
the doctor to check."

"How do you feel?" he asked, but she was asleep. In a few
minutes Doctor Lubowitz came in, still wearing delivery-room
greens. "How is she?" Michael asked him.

"Fine. They're both fine. Baby's eight pounds. Damn these
women," he said. "They won't learn it's easier to grow 'em big
once the baby is outside. Make the doctor work like a horse."
He shook Michael's hand and walked away.

"Do you want to see him?" the nurse asked. He waited
outside the nursery while she picked out the proper bassinet
and then as she held the baby close to the glass he saw with
a shock that it was a very ugly infant, with eyes that were red
swollen slits and a broad, flat nose. How will I ever love him,
he thought, and the baby yawned, stretching his lips and dis-

playing the pink ridges of tiny gums, and then started to cry, and he loved him.

When he let himself out of the hospital the sun was up. He stood on the curb and in a little while he hailed a taxi. The driver was a plump, gray-haired woman and the cab was very clean. There was a nosegay of spicy-smelling flowers in a vase attached to the back of the front seat. Zinnias, he thought.

"Where to, Mister?" the woman said.

He looked at her stupidly and then he threw back his head and laughed, stopping when she looked frightened.

"I don't know where I left my car," he explained.

CHAPTER THIRTY-FOUR

Leslie was awake when he returned to the hospital that afternoon. She wore fresh makeup and a lace-trimmed nightgown and had a blue ribbon in her brushed hair.

"What will we name him?" he asked as he kissed her.

"How about Max?"

"That's the homeliest, most unassimilated, *shtetl*-type name I can think of," he objected, tremendously pleased.

"I like it myself."

He kissed her again.

A nurse brought the baby into the room. Leslie held him gingerly. "He's so beautiful," she whispered, while Michael looked at her with pity.

But over the next few days the baby's appearance altered. The birth-swelling subsided from his eyelids, revealing eyes that were large and blue. The nose grew less flattened and more a nose. The red over-all color was replaced by a delicate pink-white.

"He's not ugly at all," Michael said in amazement one evening, giving his wife a headache.

The Plymouth eventually was found with the help of the San Francisco Police Department, parked where they had abandoned it. Only the hubcaps were missing. Their cost, and the fifteen-dollar fine which Michael had to pay three days later for parking in a forbidden area (taxi stand), he wrote off cheerfully as birthing expenses.

Abe and Dorothy Kind could not come to California in time to see their new grandson circumcised. But if they missed the *bris* they did not miss the *pidyon haben*. Dorothy refused to fly. They took a compartment on the City of San Francisco. For three nights and two days Dorothy knitted her way across the country. Three sets of booties and a little cap. Abe read magazines, he drank Scotch, he discussed life and politics with a freckled Pullman porter named Oscar Browning, and as a student of human behavior he watched with interest and admiration the progress of an Air Force corporal who two hours out of New York sat next to a haughty blonde in the dining car and was sharing her compartment when the train pulled into San Francisco.

Dorothy was ecstatic when she saw her grandson. "He looks like a little movie star," she said.

"He's got ears like Clark Gable," Abe agreed. The grandfather took over the job of bubbling Max after each feeding, carefully spreading a clean diaper over his shoulder and back to protect himself from spit-up, and invariably ending up with a wide wet splotch on his sleeve in the area of the elbow. *"Pisherkeh,"* he called the baby, a name spoken in equal parts of love and outrage.

He and Dorothy stayed in California ten days. They attended two Friday-evening services at the temple, sitting stiffly with their daughter-in-law between them, the three of them pretending that the empty seats around them did not exist. "He should have been a radio announcer," Abe whispered to Leslie after the first sermon.

On the evening before their return to New York, Michael and his father went for a walk. "Come, Dorothy?" Abe asked.

"No, you go. I'll stay with Leslie and Max," she said, her hand fluttering at her chest.

"What's the matter?" he said, frowning. "The same business? You want me to call a doctor?"

"I don't need a doctor," she said. "Go, go."

"What same business?" Michael asked when they were out on the street. "Has she been unwell?"

"Ah." Abe sighed. "She *kvetches*. I *kvetch*. Our friends *kvetch*. You know what it is? We're growing old."

"We're all growing older," Michael said uncomfortably. "But you and Momma aren't old. I'll bet you still lift weights in your bedroom. Don't you?"

"I lift," Abe admitted, smacking his flat belly with his hand.

"It's been nice having you here, Pop," Michael said. "I hate to see you go back. We don't see each other enough."

"We'll see you more from now on," Abe said. "I'm selling the business."

He was more surprised than he had a right to be. "Why, that's great," he said. "What will you do?"

"Travel. Enjoy life. Give your mother some pleasure." Abe was silent for a moment. "You know, our marriage was one of those late-starters. It took us a long time to really appreciate one another." He shrugged. "Now I want her to enjoy herself. Florida in the winter. In the summer, we'll visit a few weeks with you kids. Every couple of years a trip to Israel to see Ruthie, the damn Arabs should only let us."

"Who's buying Kind Foundations?"

"Two of the big outfits have made me offers in the last couple of years. I'll sell to the highest bidder."

"I'm glad for you," Michael said. "It sounds perfect."

"I figured it out so it would be," Abe said. "Just don't tell your mother. I want it to be a surprise."

In the morning there was an argument about whether Michael should take them to the train. "I don't like long good-bys in a railroad station," Dorothy said. "Kiss me here like a good son and let us take a cab like sensible people."

But Michael overruled her. He drove them to the station and bought magazines and cigars for his father and a box of candy for his mother. "Oy, I can't even eat it," she said. "I'm on a diet." She gave him a little push. "You go home now," she said. "Or to your temple. Get out of here." He looked at her and decided it would be better to do as she said.

"Good-by, Momma. Pop," he said, kissing them both on the cheek. He walked away quickly.

"Why did you do that?" Abe asked, annoyed. "He could have stayed with us another ten-fifteen minutes."

"Because I didn't want to start crying in a railroad station, that's why," she said, starting to cry.

She was better by the time they boarded the train. She knitted, saying little, until it was lunchtime. On the way to the diner Abe saw that Oscar Browning, the porter with freckles, was on board, too.

"Hello, Mr. Kind," the porter said. "Glad to have you returning with us."

"How much did you tip that man on the way out?" Dorothy asked when they reached the next car.

"No more than usual."

"So how come he remembers you?"

"We had a long conversation on the way out. He's a smart man."

"He sure is," she said.

In the diner he ordered a steak and a bottle of beer. Dorothy ordered only tea and toast.

"What's the matter?" he asked.

She closed her eyes. There was a white line around her mouth. "I feel *nisht gut*. Nauseous. It's this train. It keeps going from side to side."

"I told you we should fly," he said. He watched her tensely. In a little while the white line disappeared and the color came back. "Are you all right?"

"I'm all right." She smiled at him and patted his hand. The waiter came and left their food and she watched him eating. "Now I'm getting hungry," she said.

"Want a steak?" he asked, relieved. "Or some of this one?"

"No," she said. "Order me some strawberries, will you?" He did and they came as he was finishing his sirloin.

"I always think of that market basket and the ball of twine when I see you eating strawberries," he said.

"Remember, Abe?" she said. "You were courting me and we

used to go out all the time with that Helen Cohen, who lived next door and her boy friend, what was his name?"

"Pulda. Herman Pulda."

"That's right, Pulda. They used to call him Herky. They broke up later and he went into the meat business on Sixteenth Avenue and Fifty-Fourth Street. Non-kosher. But every night the two of you would bring us a bag of fruit, not only strawberries, but bing cherries, peaches, pears, pineapples, every night something different. And you'd whistle, and we'd lower the basket on the twine from the third-floor window. Oy, my heart would thump."

"Your bedroom window."

"Sometime's Helen's. She was a pretty girl. Stunning."

"Couldn't compare with you. Not even today."

"Yeh. Just look at me." She sighed. "It seems like yesterday, but look at me, hair all gray, four times a grandmother."

"Beautiful." Under the table he squeezed her *polkeh*. "You're a very beautiful woman."

"Stop it," she said, but he saw that she wasn't mad and he gave her leg another squeeze before he took his hand away.

After lunch they played gin rummy until she began to yawn. "You know what I'd like?" she said. "I'd like to take a nap."

"So, take a nap," he said.

She kicked off her shoes and lay down on the seat. "Wait a minute," he said. "I'll have Oscar make up the berth."

"I don't need it," she said. "You'll have to tip him."

"I'll tip him anyway," he said, annoyed.

She took two Bufferin tablets and after Oscar made the berth she took off her dress and her girdle and got under the covers in her slip and slept until last call for dinner, when he woke her as gently as he knew how. The nap had rested her and she was hungry. At dinner she ordered fried chicken and apple pie and coffee. That night, however, she tossed and turned, keeping him awake as well.

"What's the matter?" he asked her.

"I shouldn't eat fried foods. I have a heartburn," she said. He got up and gave her an Alka Seltzer. By morning she felt better. They went to the dining car very early and had juice and black coffee and then they went back to the compartment and Dorothy picked up her knitting again. It was attached to a tremendous ball of blue yarn.

"What are you making now?" he asked.

"Afghan, for Max."

He tried to read while she knitted but he wasn't a great reader to begin with and he was tired of reading. After a time he took a walk through the swaying train, ending in the men's lounge where Oscar Browning was stacking towels and counting small bars of soap.

"Won't be long before we reach Chicago, will it?" he asked as he sat down near the porter.

" 'Bout two hours now, Mr. Kind."

"I used to sell that town years ago," he said. "Marshal Field. Carson, Pirie and Scott. Goldblatt's. That's quite a town."

"Yes, sir," the porter said. "I live there."

"Do you?" Abe said. He thought for a while. "Any kids?"

"Four."

"Must be hard, traveling all the time."

"It ain't easy," the porter said. "But when I get home, Chicago is it."

"Why don't you get a job in Chicago?"

"Railroad pays me more loot than I could earn in Chicago. I'd rather come home to those four kids once in a while with money for new shoes than see 'em every day with no money for new shoes. Make sense?"

"It makes sense," Abe said. They both grinned. "You must see a lot of life on this job," Abe said. "Men and women stuff."

"To some people, travelin' makes 'em itchy down there. An' a train is worse than a ship. There's not much else to do." For a while they told each other stories, corset stories and railroad stories. Then Oscar ran out of towels and soap and Abe went back to the compartment.

The ball of blue yarn had rolled all the way to the door when it had dropped from her lap. "Dorothy?" he said. He picked it up and carried it to her. "Dorothy," he said again, shaking her, but he knew right away, and he leaned down hard on the button summoning the porter. She would have looked asleep except that her eyes were open. They looked sightlessly at the blank green wall straight ahead.

Oscar came through the open door.

"Yes, sir, Mr. Kind?" he said. He stared for a moment. "Our merciful Lord Jesus," he said softly.

Abe put the ball of yarn in her lap.

"Mr. Kind," Oscar said. "You better sit down, sir." He took Abe's elbow but Abe shook off his hand.

"I'll go find a doctor," the porter said uncertainly.

Abe listened to him move away and then he dropped to his knees. Through the carpet on the floor he could feel the vibration of the tracks and the straining and the swaying of the train. He picked up her hand and held it against his wet cheek.

"I'm going to retire, Dorothy," he said.

CHAPTER THIRTY-FIVE

Ruthie arrived ten hours too late for the funeral. They were sitting on stools in the Kind living room when the doorbell rang and she let herself in and walked over and put her arms around Abe, who began to shake with deep, gasping sobs.

"I don't know why I rang the bell," she said, and then she began to weep, quietly, her head twisting from side to side on her father's shoulder.

When things had quieted down she kissed her brother and Michael introduced Leslie. "How's your family?" he asked.

"Fine." She blew her nose and looked around. All the mirrors had been shrouded at Abe's request, despite Michael's insistence that this was not necessary. "It's over, isn't it?"

Michael nodded. "This morning. I'll take you out there tomorrow."

"All right." Her eyes were puffed and reddened from weeping. She was deeply tanned and there was gray in her black hair. The combination of dark tan and graying hair was very attractive, but she was overweight, with more than a suggestion of double chin. And her legs had thickened. She was no longer his sleek American sister, he saw with dismay.

People began to arrive.

By eight o'clock the apartment was filled. The women covered the table with things to eat. Michael started to go into his old bedroom to get cigarettes and two of his father's customers were sitting on the brass bed with their backs to the door, drinking Scotch.

"A rabbi and he married a *shickseh*. Can you tie that one?"

"My God, what a combination."

He closed the door softly and went back to sit next to Leslie and hold her hand.

At one o'clock in the morning, when everyone had gone, they sat alone at last in the kitchen and drank coffee.

"Why don't you go to bed, Ruthie?" Abe pleaded. "You had that long plane trip. You must be exhausted."

"What are you going to do, Poppa?" she asked him.

"Do?" he said. His fingers crumbled a toll-house cookie that had been baked by the wife of one of his cutters. "No problem. My daughter and her husband and their kids are going to move here from Israel and we'll be very happy. I'm selling Kind Foundations. There'll be enough money for Saul to go into any business he wants. Equal partners. Or if he wants to teach, let him go back to college for more degrees. We got kids here need teachers."

"Poppa," she said. She closed her eyes and shook her head.

"Why not?" he asked.

"To live in Israel you don't have to be a pioneer. You'd be like Rockefeller. If you come back with me there's a place near us with a little whitewashed courtyard shaded by olive trees," she said. "You can have a garden. You can exercise with your weights in the sun. Your grandchildren will come every day and teach you Hebrew."

Abe laughed without smiling. "Go let your kid marry a foreigner." He looked at her. "I would write lots of letters. Too many letters. It would take me ten days to know whether the Yankees beat the Red Sox or the Red Sox beat the Yankees. And sometimes they play two games in one day.

"You can't even buy a *Women's Wear Daily* there. I know, I tried the last time Momma and I—" He got to his feet and walked quickly into the bathroom. They heard the toilet flush as soon as he closed the door behind him.

There was a silence. "How's the plumbing over there now?" Michael asked.

Ruthie didn't smile, and he saw that she didn't remember, and then she did. "I don't mind it at all now," she said. "I don't know if that means it's gotten better or I've grown up." She looked in the direction her father had gone and she shook her head. "What do you people know?" she said softly. "What do you people *really* know? If you really knew, you'd be there instead of here."

"Pop said it," Michael said. "We're Americans."

"Well, my children are Jews the way you're Americans," she said. "They knew what to do when the planes came over. They ran like hell for shelter and sang Hebrew songs."

"Thank God none of you was hurt," Michael said.

"Did I say that?" she said. "No, I know I didn't. I said we were all *well*, and we are, now. Saul lost an arm. His right arm."

Leslie drew a quick involuntary breath and Michael felt tired and ill. "Where?" he said.

"At the elbow."

He had meant where had it happened, and when he didn't say anything she understood this. "A place called Petah Tikvah. He was with the Irgun Zvai Leumi."

Leslie cleared her throat. "The terrorists? I mean, weren't they a kind of underground?"

"They were in the beginning, with the British. Later, during the war, they became part of the regular army. That's when Saul was with them. For a very little while."

"Is he teaching again?" Leslie asked.

"Oh, yes. For the longest time. The arm makes it easy for him to control the children. He's a big hero in their eyes." She snubbed out her cigarette and smiled at them with something less than tenderness.

The morning after the period of *shiva* was over Abe and Michael drove Ruthie to Idlewild.

"You'll come at least to visit?" she said to Abe as she kissed him.

"We'll see. Remember the date. Don't forget to say *yahrzeit*." She clung to him. "I'll come," he said.

"It's a pity," she said when she hugged Michael just before boarding. "I don't know you or your family and you don't know me or my family. I have a feeling we'd all like one another." She kissed him on the mouth.

When she had left them they watched until the El Al plane dwindled into nothing in the sky and then they walked back to the car.

"What now?" Michael asked when they were on the road. "How about California? You're welcome in our house. You know that."

Abe smiled. "Remember your Zaydeh? No. But . . . thank you."

Michael kept his eye on the traffic. "Then . . . what? Florida?"

His father sighed. "Not without her. I wouldn't be able to do it. I'm going to Atlantic City."

Michael grunted. "What's there?"

"I know people who have retired there. I know other people who haven't retired yet, but who go there for the summer. Garment manufacturers. My kind of people.

"Come down there with me tomorrow," he said. "Help me pick out a place to live."

"All right," Michael told him.

"I like the waves. And all that goddam sand."

They found him a bedroom, kitchenette, sitting room and bath in a small but good residential hotel in Ventnor two blocks from the beach. It was furnished.

"It's expensive, but what the hell," Abe said. He smiled. "Your mother had grown sort of tight the last four-five years, you know that?"

"No."

"You want the stuff in the apartment?" Abe asked.

"Listen—" Michael said.

"I don't want it. Nothing. If you want it, take it. An agent will sell the apartment."

"Okay," Michael said after a while. "Maybe Zaydeh's brass bed." He felt angry, but he didn't know why.

"The rest, too. What you can't use, give away."

After lunch they walked a long way, stopping for a while at a fake auction where *shlahk* items were sold at three times their worth, and then they sat on deckchairs under a dazzling noonday sun and watched the Boardwalk pour its stream of people past them.

Fifty feet away two hawkers separated by a beer stand fought a battle of sex symbolism. A shirtsleeved man in a straw hat was spieling hot dogs. THE BIGGEST FRANKFURTER IN THE WORLD GET IT HERE GET IT HOT GET IT EIGHTEEN DELECTABLE INCHES LONG, the man screamed.

ALL COLORS BALLOONS BIG AND ROUND AND LOVELY AND BOUNCY AND JOUNCY AND BEAUTIFUL, he was answered by a short Italian-looking man who wore faded levis and a torn blue jersey.

A sweating Negro pushed a rolling chair containing a very fat lady holding a naked baby.

A covey of teen-age quail in bathing suits walked by, rolling their skinny hips in pathetic imitation of the voluptuous rotating behinds of their Hollywood favorites.

Carried on a salt breeze from a mile down the Boardwalk came the husky whisper of a distant crowd and faint far-off cries of terror.

"The broad jumped into the *yahm* on her horse," Abe said with satisfaction. He breathed deep. "A *michayeh*. A real pleasure," he said.

"Stay here," Michael said. "But when you get bored, remember we've got beaches in California, too."

"I'll come to visit," Abe said. He lit a cigar. "Don't forget, any time I feel like it here, I can jump in the car and visit her grave. That I can't do in California."

They were silent for a while.

"When are you going back?" he asked.

"Tomorrow, I guess," Michael said. "I've got a congregation. I can't stay away forever." He paused. "If you're all right."

"I'm all right."

"Pop, don't keep going to her grave."

His father didn't answer him.

"It won't do anybody any good. I know what I'm talking about."

Abe looked at him and smiled. "At what age does the father have to begin obeying the son?"

"At no age," Michael said. "But I see death, sometimes half a dozen times a week. I know it doesn't pay for the living to sacrifice themselves. You can't turn back the clock."

"Doesn't it depress you, your job?"

Michael watched a sweating Shriner, wearing a fez that looked too small for his fat bald head, put his arm around a tiny, cool-looking redhead who appeared to be sixteen years old. The girl looked up at the fat man as they walked. Maybe her father, he thought hopefully. "Sometimes," he said.

"People come to you with death. Sickness. A boy gets in trouble with the law. A girl gets pregnant behind the barn."

Michael smiled. "Not any more, Pop. Today that happens, but not behind the barn. In cars."

His father waved off the distinction. "So how do you help these people?"

"I do my best. Sometimes I manage to help. Lots of times I don't. Sometimes nobody can help, only time and God."

Abe nodded. "I'm glad you know that."

"But I always listen. That's something. I can be an ear."

"An ear." Abe looked out to sea where a trawler sat apparently motionless, a black fleck on the blue horizon. "Suppose a man came to you and said he was living up to his knees in ashes, what would you tell him?"

"I'd have to know more," Michael said.

"Suppose a man had lived like an animal most of his life," he said slowly. "Fight like a dog for a dollar. Screw like a cat at the whiff of a woman. Run like a race horse, round and round and round without even a jockey on his back.

"And suppose," he said in a low voice, "he woke up one morning and found that he was an old man, without anybody who really loved him?"

"Pop!"

"I mean *really* loved him, so that he was the most important thing in the other person's life."

Michael could think of nothing to say.

"You saw me once at a pretty ugly moment, for you," his father said.

"Don't start that again."

"No. No." he said, speaking quickly, "but I just want to tell you that it wasn't the first time I had other women while I was married to your mother. Nor the last. Nor the last."

Michael gripped the edges of his chair. "Now *why* do you feel you have to inflict this on me?" he said.

"I want to make you understand," Abe said. "Somewhere along the line all that stopped." He shrugged. "Maybe my glands, maybe change of life. I can think of half a dozen funny possibilities. But I stopped, and I fell in love with your mother.

"You never had a chance to know her, *really* know her. You didn't and Ruthie didn't. But now it's worse for me. Can you see that, Rabbi? Can you understand that, *m'lumad*, my wise man? I didn't have her for a long time, and then I had her for only a little while, and now she's gone."

"Pop!" he said.

"Hold my hand," his father said. He hesitated, and Abe reached over and took his son's hand in his own. "What's the matter," he said roughly. "You're afraid they'll think we're queer?"

"I love you, Pop," Michael said.

Abe squeezed his hand. "Shah," he said.

Gulls wheeled. The crowd poured past. There were lots of fezzes, an entire Shrine convention. Little by little the small black trawler crept across the rim of the sea.

THERE ARE MANY PRETENDERS TO THE TITLE BUT THIS IS THE ONE THE ONLY THE BIGGEST FRANKFURTER IN THE WORLD.

The girl on the horse must have jumped into the sea again. People screamed faintly. In front of them their shadows grew longer and less distinct.

When it was time to leave, Abe drew him toward the beer stand and held up two fingers. There was a young girl behind the counter, brown-haired and bored, an ordinary *zaftig* girl of about eighteen, slightly pretty but with crooked teeth and an imperfect complexion.

Abe watched her as she took the mugs off the tray and reached for the spigot. "My name is Abe."

"Yeah?"

"What's your name?"

"Sheila." In her cheek, a dimple.

He sampled it between his thumb and forefinger, then he went to the balloon man and bought a balloon, a passionate red one, and he came back and tied the string around her wrist so it floated above them like a big bloodshot wink. "This guy is my son. Stay away from him. He's a married man."

Coolly she took his money and made change. But she laughed as she walked away from the cash register, bouncier than she had walked before, the balloon bobbing above and just a little to the rear.

Abe slid him a schooner of beer.

"For the road," he said.

CHAPTER THIRTY-SIX

Life, he began to understand, was a series of compromises. The Temple Isaiah rabbinate had not worked out the way he had hoped, with hordes of people to sit at his feet and listen to his brilliant twentieth-century interpretations of Talmudic wisdoms. His wife was now a mother and he surreptitiously searched her eyes for the girl he had married, the one who had shuddered when he looked at her in a certain knowing way. Now sometimes at night in the middle of their lovemaking a thin wail from the other room caused her to push him away and run to the baby, and he lay there in the dark hating the infant he loved.

The high holidays came and the temple overflowed with people who remembered suddenly that they were Jews and that it was time to fill up with enough repentance to last another year. The sight of the crowded sanctuary excited him and filled him with new hope and firm resolve that he would not fail to win them over in the end.

He determined to make another try while the Yom Kippur sermon was still fresh in their minds. One of his former professors, Dr. Hugo Nachmann, was spending some time at the Los Angeles branch of the rabbinical institute. Dr. Nachmann was an expert on the period of the Dead Sea scrolls. Michael invited him to San Francisco to lecture at the temple.

Eighteen people attended the lecture. Michael recognized fewer than half of them as temple members. Two of them turned out to be science reporters there to interview Dr. Nachmann on archeological aspects of the discovery of the scrolls.

Dr. Nachmann made things easy for the Kinds. "This isn't at all unusual, as you know," he said. "People simply are not interested in lecturers on certain nights. Now, if you had offered them a dinner dance. . . !"

The next morning, leaning on the fence overlooking the half-completed church, Michael found himself telling Father Campanelli about it. "I keep failing," he said. "Nothing I do will get them inside the temple."

The priest fingered the mark on his face. "On many a morning I give thanks for the Days of Obligation," he said quietly.

One morning several weeks later Michael sprawled in bed feeling mildly dejected at the thought of another day. He knew enough about the psychology of personal loss to realize that the mood was a lingering remainder of his mother's funeral, but this awareness did nothing to bolster his spirits as he lay absentmindedly seeking comfort in his wife's warm thigh and staring at a crack in their bedroom ceiling.

There was little at Temple Isaiah to draw him out of bed; not even a clean floor, he told himself.

Just before the holidays the temple janitor, a gap-toothed Mormon who had kept the premises tabernacle-clean for three years, had announced his retirement to his married daughter's home in Utah to lull his sciatica and reawaken his spirit. The house committee, which met infrequently, had been lethargic about replacing him. While Phil Golden fumed and scolded, the silver and brasswork went unpolished and the wax yellowed on the floors. Michael could have hired a janitor, secure in the knowledge that his salary checks would have been issued at the rabbi's command. But it was the house committee's job to hire a new man. At least they would be held to that much commitment to the temple, he thought grimly.

"Get up," Leslie said, twitching her hip.

"Why?"

But seventy minutes later he was parking his car outside the temple. To his surprise the door was unlocked. Inside, he heard the rasp-rasp of scrub brush against linoleum, and following the sound downstairs he saw the man in paint-spattered white coveralls scrubbing the hallway floor on his hands and knees.

"Phil," Michael said.

Golden wiped a wet forehead with the back of his hand. "I forgot to bring newspapers," he said. "When you were a kid did your mother wash all the floors on Thursday afternoons and spread newspapers?"

"Fridays," Michael said. "Friday mornings."

"Nah, on Friday mornings she baked *chaleh*."

"What are you *doing*? A decrepit old *momser* like you, scrubbing floors? You want a heart attack?"

"I got a heart like a bull," Golden said. "A temple's got to be clean. You can't have a dirty temple."

"So let them hire a janitor. Hire one yourself."

"They'll *krahtz* around to it after a while. Start doing things for them, they'll never bother to think about the temple. In the meantime, the floors will be clean."

Michael shook his head. "Phil, Phil." He turned on his heel and went back upstairs. In his office he took off his coat and tie and rolled up his sleeves. Then he searched through several closets until he found another pail and brush.

"Not *you*," Golden protested. "Who needs help? You're the rabbi!"

But he was already on his hands and knees, rotating the

brush over the soapy water. Sighing, Golden returned to his own pail. Together, they scrubbed. The sound of the two brushes was friendly. Golden began to sing, in a breathless, grunting voice, snatches of opera.

"I'll race you to the end of the hall," Michael said. "Loser goes for coffee."

"No races," Phil said. "No kids games. Just work, a good job."

Golden reached the end of the corridor first and went out for the coffee anyhow. A few minutes later, sitting together in an empty Hebrew-school classroom, they drank it slowly and regarded one another.

"Those pants," Phil said. "Don't let the *rebbitzen* see them."

"She'll see I'm finally working for my money."

"You're working for your money every day."

"No. Come on, Phil." He sloshed his coffee round and round in its container. "I'm almost a full-time Talmudist. I spend every day with books, looking for God."

"So who knocks that?"

"If I find Him, my congregation won't come to hear about it until next Yom Kippur."

Golden chuckled and then sighed. "Ah, I tried to tell you," he said. "It's that kind of a congregation." He put his hand on Michael's arm. "They like you. You probably won't believe it, but they like you very much. They're going to offer you a long-term contract. With a good yearly increase."

"For what?"

"For being here. For being their rabbi. On their terms, sure, but still their rabbi. Is it a bad thing for a rabbi to be financially secure and still to be able to devote most of his time to study?"

He took the coffee container from Michael's hand and dropped it into the wastebasket along with his own. "Let me talk to you as if you were one of my sons," he said. "This is a good set-up. Relax. Be comfortable. Grow prosperous. Let your kid grow up with the rest of the lotus-eaters and go to Stanford and only hope that he ends up with this good a deal."

Michael said nothing.

"Another couple of years, we'll buy you your car. Later on, your house."

"My God."

"You want to work?" Golden said. "Come on, let's wash some more floors." His laughter was like blows on a drum. "I guarantee you, when I tell that lousy house committee who their acting janitor was, they'll have a permanent man hired by tomorrow!"

On the following day his muscles complained about the unaccustomed exercise. He stopped at St. Margaret's and leaned on the fence watching the steel-helmeted workers swarming over the new building, the knotted sinews in the backs of his thighs causing him to feel a new kinship with the workers of the world. Father Campanelli was not there. The priest now rarely came out to watch the work, remaining inside the red-brick walls of the old church, soon to feel the clout of the swinging iron ball.

Michael couldn't blame him. The new church had a roof like a poured cement derby. Its walls were of tinted glass block that sloped sharply inward, causing that portion of the building to resemble a huge ice-cream cone with the bottom tip broken off. A corridor of aluminum and glass led to a circular building that had all the spiritual appearance of an industrial powerhouse. On the roof of the round structure workmen were raising a gleaming aluminum cross.

"How's that?" one of the men on the roof shouted.

A man standing near Michael tipped back his tin hat and peered upward. "Fine," he yelled.

Fine, Michael thought.

Now anybody could tell it from a hot-dog stand.

He turned away, knowing he wouldn't be back for the same reason the priest no longer watched. It was a tastelessly conceived house of worship.

At any rate, there was nothing else to watch; it was finished.

So was his own research into temple architecture. He had worked out what seemed to him a reasonable verbal blueprint for a modern place of prayer. Since the former St. Jeremiah's Church could meet with ease the undemanding requirements of

Temple Isaiah, there seemed nothing to do with the accumulated data but publish it. He wrote a paper which he submitted to the journal of the Central Conference of American Rabbis, and subsequently it was published there. He mailed copies of the journal to his father in Atlantic City and to Ruthie and Saul in Israel, then he packed all his notes into a cardboard carton and took them home and stored them in the tiny attic, inside the lowboy from his parents' apartment which he and Leslie had not been able to bring themselves to sell.

The completed project left him with more time on his hands than ever. One afternoon he came home at two-thirty to find Leslie making out the marketing list.

"There's mail," she said.

The new contract had arrived as Phil Golden had promised. He examined it and saw that it was very generous, covering a five-year span with a substantial increase in income at the beginning of each year. At the end of the five years, Michael knew, there would be a contract with life tenure.

Leslie read it without comment when he dropped it on the table.

"It's as good as an annuity," he said. "I've been thinking about starting a book. I have plenty of time."

She nodded and busied herself with the marketing list.

He didn't sign the contract. Instead he placed it in the top drawer of his bedroom bureau, under his tray of cuff links.

He went back into the kitchen and sat with Leslie at the table, smoking and watching her.

"I'll do the shopping for you," he said.

"I can go. You must have things to do."

"I have nothing to do."

She glanced at him and opened her mouth as if to say something, then she changed her mind.

"All right," she said.

The letter came a few days later.

San Francisco, January 1948

23 Park Lane
Wyndham, Pennsylvania
October 3, 1953

Rabbi Michael Kind
Temple Isaiah
2103 Hathaway Street
San Francisco, California

Dear Rabbi Kind:

The Executive Board of Temple Emeth of Wyndham has read with no small interest your provocative article in the newly established and excellent CCAR Journal.

Temple Emeth is a sixty-one-year-old, medium-sized Reform congregation in the university community of Wyndham, twenty-three miles south of Philadelphia. Over the past several years we have hopelessly outgrown our twenty-five-year-old building. Faced with the necessity of determining what a new temple should be like, we found your article to be particularly fascinating. It has been the subject of many discussions here since its appearance.

On April 15, 1954, Rabbi Philip Kirschner, our religious leader for the past sixteen years, begins what we expect will be a happy and full retirement in his native St. Louis, Mo. We are seeking as his replacement somebody who will be both an inspiring religious leader and a man who has given thought to what kind of place a Jewish temple should be in modern America.

We would appreciate greatly an opportunity to discuss this with you. I will be in Los Angeles October 15–19, attending the 1953 meeting of the Modern Language Association at UCLA. If you could fly to Los Angeles at Temple Emeth's expense during this period, we would be grateful. If this is impossible, perhaps I can come to San Francisco.

I have notified the Placement Committee of the Union of

American Hebrew Congregations of our intention of discussing our rabbinical need with you. I shall eagerly await your reply.

> *Sincerely yours,*
> *(signed)* Felix Sommers, *Ph.D.*
> *President*
> *Temple Emeth*

"You're going?" Leslie asked when he showed it to her.

"I suppose it wouldn't hurt to fly down and meet him," Michael said.

On the night he returned from Los Angeles he came in quietly, expecting her to be asleep, and found her lying on the sofa watching the late late show. She made room for him and he lay down beside her and then kissed her.

"Well?" she said.

"It would be a thousand dollars less than I'm making now. And it would mean a one-year contract."

"But you can have it if you want it."

"There'd be the usual preliminary guest sermon. But I can have it if I want it."

"What are you going to do?"

"What do *you* want me to do?" he asked.

"You have to decide yourself," she said.

"You know what happens to rabbis who go through a string of short-term contracts? They become footballs. Only the problem congregations will consider them, at minimum wages. Like the one in Cypress, Georgia."

She said nothing.

"I've already told him we'd go."

She turned her face away suddenly, so that all he could see was the back of her head. He reached out his hand and touched her hair. "What is it?" he asked. "The thought of facing a new batch of women? The *yentehs?*"

"Damn the *yentehs,*" she said. "There'll always be people to whom you and I are freaks. They're not important." She turned swiftly and put her arms around him. "What's important is that you'll be doing more than collecting a fat annuity for serving as a rabbi in name only, because you're so much better than that, don't you understand?"

He could feel her wet cheek on his neck and he was filled with wonder. "You're the finest part of me," he said. "The very best of me." His arms were around her anyhow, to keep her from falling off the narrow couch, and now they tightened.

She placed her fingertips over his mouth. "What's important is that this is something you really want to do."

"It is," he said, touching her.

"I'm talking about Pennsylvania," she said in a little while, but she turned in his arms and lifted her face greedily.

Later in bed as he was falling asleep she touched his shoulder.

"Did you tell him about me?" she asked.

"What do you mean?"

"You know what I mean."

"Oh." He stared up at the soft darkness of the ceiling. "Yes, I did."

"That's good. Good night, Michael."

"Good night," he said.

CHAPTER THIRTY-SEVEN

He went alone to deliver the guest sermon and he liked what he saw as a hospitality committee drove him from the railroad station to Dr. Sommers' home for dinner before the Sabbath service. It was a small town, deceptively sedate-looking when seen from an automobile, as are most campus towns. There were four bookstores, a green bulletin board in the town square listing nearby concerts and art shows, and everywhere there were young people. The air crackled with autumn cold and the energy of the students. On the pond in the center of the campus there was a skim of ice. The bare limbs of stately trees were stark and beautiful.

At dinner the temple leaders plied him with questions about his ideas concerning their proposed new building. His long weeks of solitary research provided him with much more ammunition than he could use, and their frank admiration sent him from the dinner table glowing with confidence, so that when he mounted the *bema* later in the evening he was primed to deliver a dazzling sermon. He spoke to them of why it was that an ancient religion could survive all the things that worked in the world to snuff it out.

When he left Wyndham the following afternoon, he knew the pulpit was his, and when he received the call less than a week later it came as no surprise.

In February he and Leslie and the baby flew to Wyndham for five days. They spent most of the time with real estate agents. They found the house on the fourth day, a red-and-black brick colonial with a restored gray slate roof. It was in their price range, the agent said, because most people wanted more than two bedrooms. There were other disadvantages. The ceilings were high and the rooms would be hard to clean. There was no garbage disposal or dishwasher, both of which the house in San Francisco had. The plumbing was very old and the pipes banged and made gurgling-gasping noises. But the oak floorboards were wide-cut and had been lovingly preserved. There was an old brick fireplace in the master bedroom and a marble fireplace with a fine old raised hearth in the living room. The tall, eighteen-paned front windows overlooked the campus.

"Oh, Michael," she said. "What a set-up. This can be our home until our family grows too large. Max could go to college from here."

This time he knew better than to nod, but he smiled as he wrote a check for the real estate man.

From the very beginning his days in Wyndham were busy and full of people. Hillel and the Intercollegiate Zionist Federation of America had chapters at the university and he became chaplain to each. He made occasional trips with members of the Building Committee, inspecting new temples in other communities. Leslie registered at the graduate school as a special student of Semitic languages and they studied together twice a week with several of her fellow students. Temple Emeth was an intellectual congregation in an intellectual community, and Michael found that a considerable amount of his time was spent with similar study groups and in campus panel discussions. The cocktail parties resembled the fierce arguing sessions of old Talmudists, he found, except that most of the time these latter-day disciples argued about such prophets as Teller or Oppenheimer or Herman Kahn. The social functions of both the Brotherhood and the Sisterhood drew healthy numbers. The Kinds found themselves attending a variety of affairs; one winter night they served as chaperones on a youth-group sleighride, holding hands under the blanket as they glided over the snow and hoping that the gigglings and straw-thrashings in the blackness which surrounded them were sounds of innocent pleasure.

The weeks fell away so swiftly that he was surprised when the temple board came to him with a new contract and he realized that a year had passed. The new document was for two years, and he signed it without hesitation. Temple Emeth was his. Each Friday night the service was well attended and his sermon stimulated brisk discussion at the *oneg shabbat*. When Rosh Hashonah and Yom Kippur rolled around he was forced to hold services in double sessions. In the middle of the second service of the last day of Yom Kippur he suddenly remembered how lonely and useless he had been in San Francisco.

He did some marriage counseling, as little as possible. He found that he had a marriage problem of his own. The month after they moved to Pennsylvania he and Leslie decided that Max was old enough to have a brother or a sister and they stopped using birth control, confidently expecting that creation once achieved is easily duplicated. Leslie packed the diaphragm in talcum powder and hid the little box in the cedar chest with the extra blankets. Two or three times a week they made love with great expectations, and when a year had passed Michael found that he would lie awake when he had broken free of his wife, and she had curled her back against him, and, spurning afterplay, had gone to sleep. Instead of sleeping himself he would stare into the dark and see the faces of unborn children, and wonder why it was so difficult to call one of them into the world. He prayed to God for help and afterward he often walked on bare feet into his son's room, nervously adjusting the edge of the blanket so that it lay close to the small jaw, and looked down at the skinny figure that was so defenseless in sleep, stripped of six-guns and the belief that he could overcome all manner of evil by punching it in the stomach. And he would pray again, asking for the boy's safety and happiness.

And thus passed many of his nights.

People died, and he committed them to the waiting earth. He preached, he prayed; people fell in love and he legalized and sanctified their unions. The son of Professor Sidney Landau, who taught mathematics, eloped with the blonde daughter of Swede Jensen, the track coach. While Mrs. Landau took to her bed under sedation Michael went with her husband that night to meet with Mr. and Mrs. Jensen and their minister, a Lutheran named Ralph Jurgen. At the end of an uncomfortable evening Michael and Professor Landau walked together across the quiet campus.

"A troubled mother and father," Landau said, sighing. "Just as troubled as we are. Just as frightened."

"Yes."

"Will you talk to those young fools when they get back?"

"You know I will."

"Ahh. . . . It won't do any good. Her parents are religious people. You saw the minister."

"Don't anticipate, Sidney. Wait until they get back. Give them a chance to find their way." He paused. "I happen to be familiar with their problem."

"Yes, that's right, you are," Professor Landau said. He shook his head. "I shouldn't be talking to you. I should be talking to your father."

Michael said nothing.

Professor Landau looked at him. "Did you ever hear the old story about the grieving Jewish father who went to his rabbi and told him about his son's elopement with a *shickseh* and subsequent conversion?"

"No," Michael said.

" 'I had a son, Rabbi,' the man said, 'and he became a *goy*. What shall I do?'

"And the rabbi shook his head. 'I, too, had a son,' he told the man. 'And he married a *shickseh* and became a *goy*.'

" 'So what did *you* do?' the Jewish man asked the rabbi.

" 'I went into the temple and I prayed to God,' the rabbi said, 'and suddenly a great voice filled the temple.'

" 'What did the voice say, Rabbi?' the Jewish father asked.

" 'The voice said, I, TOO, HAD A SON. . . .' "

They laughed together, unhappily. When Professor Landau came to his street he seemed relieved to turn off. "Good night, Rabbi."

"Good night, Sidney. Call me if you need me." Michael could hear him weeping softly as he walked away.

And thus passed many of his days.

CHAPTER THIRTY-EIGHT

Michael stood on the gritty railroad-station platform and held Max's hand and the two of them watched the 4:02 from Philadelphia come in. Max's grip tightened as the engine thundered by.

"Scary?" Michael asked.

"Like big sneezes."

"Not scary when you're a big boy," Michael said, not believing it for a moment.

"No," the boy said, but he didn't let go of his father's hand.

Leslie looked tired when she got off and walked toward them. She kissed them both, then they got into the green Tudor Ford that had replaced the blue Plymouth almost two years before. "How did it go?" he asked.

She shrugged. "Dr. Reisman is a very nice guy. He examined me and he studied the results of your tests, and he said that when you and I get together there should be an explosion of life. Then he patted me on the back and said to keep trying and I gave his girl our address so they could send you a big bill."

"Great."

"Actually, he gave me some instructions. Things to do."

"What?"

"We'll have a rehearsal later," she said, sweeping Max against her and hugging him tightly. "At least we've got this palooka, thank God. Michael," she said, her face in her son's hair, "let's take a couple of days off."

Suddenly that was exactly what he wanted to do. "We could go to Atlantic City and see Pop."

"We just saw him. I've a better idea. We'll hire a sitter and take off, just the two of us. Drive up into the Poconos for two or three days."

"When?"

"What's wrong with tomorrow?"

But that evening as she bathed Max the telephone rang and Michael spoke for a few minutes with Felix Sommers, chairman of the Building Committee. The group had just come back from an inspection tour.

"Did you see that new temple in Pittsburgh?" Michael asked him.

"It's a beautiful temple," Professor Sommers said. "Not exactly what we're looking for, but very, very fine. The rabbi knew you and said to say hello. Rabbi Levy."

"Joe Levy. Good man." He paused. "Felix, how many temples does this make that we've inspected?"

"Twenty-eight. My goodness."

"Yes. When do we stop inspecting and start applying what we've seen?"

"Well, that's what I'm calling about, Michael," Sommers said. "We talked to the architect who did Pittsburgh. His name is Paolo Di Napoli. We think he's great. In the precise meaning of the word. We'd like you to meet him and see his stuff."

"Well, fine," Michael said. "You name the day."

"There's a difficulty. He can get together with us only on two dates. Tomorrow and next Sunday."

"Neither day is good for me," Michael said. "We'll have to make it some other time."

"That's the catch. He's leaving for Europe. He'll be gone three months."

"Next Sunday I have a wedding," Michael said. "And tomorrow—" He sighed. "Make it tomorrow," he said. They said good-by and he went in to tell Leslie that their trip was off.

In the morning he and Felix Sommers drove into Philadelphia. They left early and stopped for breakfast on the road.

"I'm bothered about the fact that Di Napoli isn't a Jew," Michael said in the restaurant.

Sommers paused in the act of breaking his roll. "What a strange thing for you to say."

Michael persisted. "I don't think a Christian can get the proper feeling into a temple design. The identification, the great emotion. The conception is bound to lack what my grandfather used to call the *Yiddisheh kvetch.*"

"What on earth is *Yiddisheh kvetch?*"

"Have you ever heard Perry Como sing *Eli, Eli?*"

Sommers nodded.

"Do you remember how Al Jolson used to sing it?"

"So?"

"The difference is *Yiddisheh kvetch.*"

"If Paolo Di Napoli agrees to take this commission," Professor Sommers said, "we'll end up with something better than a Jewish architect. We'll end up with a great architect."

"We'll see," Michael said.

But when they arrived at the architect's office Michael liked Di Napoli from the start. Without being arrogant he offered no apologies for his art. He sat quietly and smoked a short briar pipe and looked at them while they looked at his work. He had strong wrists and mournful brown eyes and thick gray hair and a big mustache like a small jaunty hairbrush on his upper lip; a mustache, Michael thought, that declared him in on whatever game the world was dealing. Among his accomplishments were four truly outstanding temples and half a dozen churches, as well as an unusual and striking children's library for a Midwestern city. They looked at his sketches and renderings, dwelling over the temple drawings.

On each of the temple plans a tiny sun had been drawn in the east, facing the building façade.

"Why the suns?" Michael asked.

"Personal idiosyncrasy. My private attempt to forge a weak link with the dead past."

"Explain?" Sommers asked.

"When Solomon's Temple was built some three thousand years ago on Mount Moriah, Yahweh was a solar god. The temple was positioned so its front gate threw a direct beam on the peak of the Mount of Olives, due east and some two hundred feet higher in elevation. Twice a year, on the days of the equinox, the first rays of the rising sun shining over the Mount of Olives entered the Temple through the open eastern gate. The rays shone down past the heart of the building into the recessed niche on the far western wall, which was the Temple's holiest place." His lips curved under the bush. "It just happened that an eastern exposure was fine for these four sites. If it's wrong for yours, I'm not restricted to temples that face the east."

"I like the idea," Michael said. "'Lift up your heads, O ye gates. . . . Yea, lift them up, ye everlasting doors; that the King of glory may come in.'" He exchanged a look with Sommers and they grinned at one another.

Yiddisheh kvetch.

"Do you have the list of rough specifications I asked you to bring?" Di Napoli asked Sommers.

Sommers took it from his brief case. The architect studied it for a long time. "Some of these things can be combined for economy without sacrificing design," he said.

"It should be a place for prayer. That above everything else," Michael said.

Di Napoli went to a file drawer and returned with a glossy reproduction of an architectural drawing. The base of the sketched building was a single-storied structure, low and rambling and as stark as the base of a pyramid. The second story covered a smaller area and rose in a group of soaring paraboloid arches to become a vaulted roof at once sensuous and ethereal as it pulsed beautifully upward, pointing to heaven as certainly as a New England church spire.

"What is it?" Sommers asked finally.

"A cathedral that will be built at New Norcia, Australia. Designed by Pier Luigi Nervi," Di Napoli said.

"Can you give us something that will invoke the same spirit of God?" Michael asked.

"I will try," Di Napoli said. "I would have to know the site. Do you have it yet?"

"No."

"The site will determine a lot of things. But . . . I lean toward the use of textured materials. Unfinished brick surfaces. Rough concrete, with warm colors to give the building life."

"When can you show us preliminary sketches of your ideas?" Michael asked.

"In three months. I will prepare them while I'm in Europe."

Felix Sommers cleared his throat. "Approximately how much will such a building cost?"

"We'll have to work within the limits of whatever sum is available, of course," the architect said, shrugging.

"Most of it will have to be raised," Michael said. "You've seen our specifications. Visualize the kind of temple *you* want to create. With economy. But nevertheless something that is art, a beautiful sanctuary for the worship of God, like Nervi's cathedral. How much is needed to make such a place?"

Paolo Di Napoli smiled. "Rabbi Kind, you are talking about half a million dollars," he said.

CHAPTER THIRTY-NINE

Several weeks later a large, handsome white sign with blue lettering was erected on the lawn of Temple Emeth: LET US RISE UP AND BUILD—*Nehemiah 2 : 20.*

Next to it was painted a twelve-foot-tall black thermometer, calibrated in thousands of dollars instead of degrees of temperature. At the top of the thermometer, next to the words OUR NEED, was the figure $450,000. The red line was only a little way up the thermometer, at forty-five or fifty thousand dollars.

Unfortunately, the sight of the device depressed Michael, reminding him of the basal thermometer Dr. Reisman had given to Leslie and which she now popped into her mouth each night upon retiring, lying propped against her pillow with the bed lamp on, an open book in her lap and the thermometer hung from her lips like a lollipop stick, while he lay on his side and waited for the verdict on how he would spend the next quarter of an hour.

Ninety-eight-point-two or above and he could go to sleep. Ninety-seven-point-two to ninety-seven-point-four meant that for twelve hours the goalposts were in sight and he would manfully rise to the occasion and become a plunging back.

No, he thought that night as he sat in the kitchen in his pajamas and waited for his wife to take a shower so he could do his duty: a bored intern inserting a canula, a milkman doggedly delivering the goods, a mailman dropping a letter, a worker bee struggling to unload his pollen in an inconvenient crouch Dr. Reisman called the Thighs Flexed Position, with his wife's soft tanned legs on his shoulders and her pelvis and vagina tilted skyward like the mouth of a lily, at an angle designed to reduce spillage and provide major receptivity. Guaranteed. By Dr. Reisman and *Good Housekeeping*.

Moodily he walked to the kitchen counter and sifted through the household mail. Bills. And Felix Sommers' first fund-raising effort. He poured himself a glass of milk and sat down at the table again to drink it.

Dear Congregation Member:

There are almost seven hundred reasons why Temple Emeth needs a new home. And you and your family are some of them.

These reasons are constantly growing in number, ken yirbu, *may then continue to increase.*

In little over three years, there has been a doubling in our membership. In twelve neighboring communities which do not have temples, builders are raising hundreds of new homes. With the reservoir of unaffiliated families only slightly tapped, there is no doubt that a corresponding increase will be experienced in the years immediately ahead. . . .

In the bathroom the shower stopped. He heard the hard whisper of the shower-curtain rings sliding along the metal rod and then the sound Leslie made as she stepped out of the tub.

> *. . . Yet it is a fact that we are presently not equipped to serve the needs even of our existing members.*
>
> *Our Hebrew School lacks the facilities which are so necessary to an educational institution. Our sanctuary is merely a large room without pews which is utilized as banquet hall, auditorium, carnival area and classroom. During the High Holidays double services have had to be held, splitting up relatives on the most sacred of occasions. Too many family simchas such as weddings and bar mitzvahs are held outside the temple. The reasons are simple. Our dining facilities are cramped and unattractive. The kitchen is small and inadequately equipped. Caterers find it difficult to work here.*
>
> *Clearly, we need a new home. An architect has been engaged to design it for us. But in order to make our dream a reality, each of us must sacrifice. Will you begin to consider what your fair share contribution will be? A member of the building fund committee will call on you in the near future.*
>
> *In giving, we must realize that we are not giving to strangers, but to ourselves and our children.*
>
> *Sincerely yours,*
>
> (signed) *Felix Sommers*
> *Chairman,*
> *Building Committee*

There was a cardboard scale attached to the letter, with a little sliding window labeled *Your Annual Income.* He moved the window to eleven thousand and saw that his suggested pledge was three thousand five hundred dollars. He grunted, dropping the letter on the table.

He heard Leslie run into the bedroom and the sound of the bed as she got into it.

"Michael," she called softly.

How could they ask a man for one third of his annual income? How many temple members would be able to meet such a pledge? It must be that the committee was asking far more than they expected to get, in the hope that this would make the "compromise" pledges higher than they would otherwise have been.

It troubled him; it was not the right note to begin on, he told himself.

"Michael?" she called again.

"Coming," he said.

"That's the way it works," Sommers told him the next day when he objected to the fund-raising letter. "Other congregations have found out that you have to do it that way."

"No," Michael said. "It's not honest, Felix. You know it and I know it."

"Anyhow," Sommers said, "we've hired a professional fund-raiser. It's his business to raise funds the right way. Let's just place ourselves in his hands."

Relieved, Michael nodded.

Two days later, the man came to Temple Emeth. The business card said he was Archibald S. Kahners of Hogan, Kahners and Cantwell. Fund-raising for Churches, Synagogues and Hospitals. 1611 Industrial Bankers Building, Philadelphia, Pennsylvania 10133.

He pressed the janitor into service and unloaded three large crates from the rear of a new black Buick station wagon. They made three trips. The cases were heavy, and by the end of the second trip they were sweating. When all the boxes were on the floor in Michael's office Kahners dropped into a chair and leaned back and closed his eyes. He looked like a dissipated Lewis Stone, Michael thought, gray-haired with a ruddy complexion and a little too much weight so that the flesh of his neck peeped just a tiny unpleasant bit over the collar of his carefully cut shirt. Both the shoes and the gray suit of heavy tweed looked very English.

"We don't want a high-pressure campaign, Mr. Kahners," Michael said. "We don't want to offend our membership."

"Rabbi . . . uh . . ." Kahners said, and Michael realized that the man had forgotten his name.

"Kind."

"Yes, Rabbi Kind. Hogan, Kahners and Cantwell have raised funds for two hundred and seventy-three Catholic and Protestant churches. For seventy-three hospitals. For one hundred and ninety-three synagogues and temples. Our business is to raise huge sums of money. We have developed proven techniques which accomplish this. Rabbi, you just sit back and let me handle it."

"What can I do to help you, Mr. Kahners?"

"Make out a list of half a dozen names. I want to meet with six people who can tell me about every member in the congregation. Approximately what each man makes annually, what he does for a living, how old he is, what kind of a home he has, how many cars he owns and what makes, whether his kid goes to private or public schools, and where he goes when he's on vacation. And get me a list of local donors to the United Jewish Appeal."

Michael peeked again at the business card. "Will Mister Hogan and Mister Cantwell be here to work with you on the campaign?"

"John Hogan's dead. Two years. Now we got an employee handles the Catholics." Looking down, Kahners noticed a smudge on his gray suit, and on his tie a tiny piece of brown paper from the flap of the cardboard carton. He flicked the paper off and rubbed the smudge with his handkerchief, spreading it. "My Protestant partner I don't need for just a four-hundred-thousand dollar Jewish drive," he said.

The mimeograph machine and two typewriters arrived early the next morning, and by mid-afternoon both secretaries were seated in front of folding tables typing lists. The clatter drove Michael out of the office to make pastoral calls, and when he returned to the temple at five o'clock it was deserted and ringing with silence. Papers littered the floor, the ashtrays were full, and he saw that two coffee rings like two thirds of a Ballentine's sign had appeared on the shining surface of his mahogany desk.

That evening he attended the first meeting of the Fund-Raising Committee with Kahners. It was more of an indoctrination than a meeting, with Kahners delivering the lecture. He used the United Jewish Appeal contributors lists for the past five years as his textbooks.

"Examine these," he said, flinging the small green UJA booklets onto the table. "See who your biggest contributor was each year."

Nobody seated around the long table had to look at the books. "Harold Elkins of Elkhide Knitting Mills," Michael said. "He gives fifteen thousand dollars every year."

"And below him?" Kahners asked.

Michael closed his eyes but didn't have to consult the books.

"Phil Cohen and Ralph Plotkin. They give seventy-five hundred each."

"Exactly half of what Elkins gives," Kahners said. "And who are the names under theirs?"

Michael wasn't sure.

"I'll tell you. A man named Joseph Schwartz. Five thousand dollars. One third of what Elkins gives. Now—" He paused and looked at them, Mr. Chips teaching his last class. "There's an important lesson to be learned here. Take a look at this." He threw another UJA booklet on the table. "This is the list for six years ago. It shows that for that year, Harold Elkins gave ten thousand dollars instead of fifteen thousand."

"Phil Cohen and Ralph Plotkin gave five thousand instead of seventy-five hundred.

"Joseph Schwartz gave thirty-five hundred instead of five thousand." He searched their eyes. "Do you get the message?"

"Do you mean to tell us there's always a proportionate pattern that stems from the highest contributor?" Michael asked.

"Not always, of course," Kahners said patiently. "There are always exceptions. And the pattern extends only so far down the line; it's very hard to predict about the nickel-and-dime contributors. But as a rule, this is how it works with the principal donors, the people who are really important to the success of a campaign. In every community we've handled, for a great many years, we've seen it work this way.

"Look," he said. "Sam X gives less than usual to charity.

So Fred Y says to himself, 'If Sam, who has twice as much money as I have, can give less this year, then who am I to deny that business has been *ahf tsorris*? I usually give two thirds of what Sam pledges, I'll give half this year, too.' "

"What if Sam increases his pledges?" Sommers asked, clearly fascinated.

Kahners beamed. "Ah. The same principle applies. But how much more happily. Fred says to himself, 'Who the hell does Sam think he is? I can't compete with him, he can buy or sell me; but I can stay in the same league as that phoney. I always give two thirds of what he gives, and that's what I'll give now.' "

"Then you believe that Harold Elkins' donation is the key to our entire campaign?" Michael said.

Kahners nodded.

"How much do you think he should be asked to contribute?"

"One hundred thousand dollars."

Somebody at the far end of the table whistled.

"He's not even much of a *shul*-goer," Sommers said.

"He's a member?" Kahners asked.

"Yes."

Kahners nodded, satisfied.

"How do you interest a man like that?" Michael asked. "I mean, sufficiently to cause him to donate such a large sum?"

"You make him your General Chairman," Kahners said.

CHAPTER FORTY

Michael and Kahners called on Harold Elkins together. The door of the refurbished farmhouse in which the manufacturer lived was opened by Mrs. Elkins, a white-blonde woman in a pink silk housecoat.

"The Rabbi," she said, shaking his hand. Her grasp was firm and cool.

He introduced Kahners.

"Hal is expecting you. He's out back, feeding the ducks. Why not go right out and see him there?"

She led the way around the house. She had a fine, free walk, entirely without self-consciousness, Michael thought. Beneath the swaying hem of the housecoat he saw now that her feet were bare. They were long and slender and white in the gathering darkness, with manicured toenails gleaming with dew, like little red shells.

She brought them to her husband and then left and returned to the house.

Elkins was an old man with gray hair and round shoulders over which he had draped a coat sweater despite the evening warmth. He was throwing corn to about fifty quacking ducks at the shore of a small pond.

He continued throwing the corn while they introduced themselves. The ducks were lovely birds, large with iridescent feathers and red beaks and feet.

"What are they?" Michael asked.

"Wood ducks," Elkins said, still casting corn.

"They're gorgeous," Kahners said.

"Mm-hmm."

One half rose in a flurry of wings, but got only a few feet off the water.

"Are they wild?" Michael asked.

"As wild as anything."

"Why don't they fly away?"

Elkins' eyes gleamed. "Pinioned 'em. Clipped their wings."

"Does it hurt them?" Michael asked, in spite of himself.

Elkins snorted. "How did you feel, first time you got your wings clipped?" He grinned at their silence. "They got over it, too."

He placed a kernel of corn between bloodless lips and bent over. A large duck with rainbow lights like jewels in her feathers paddled in and reached up regally and bit the corn from the old man's mouth.

"They're my darlings," he said. "I love 'em. I love 'em in orange sauce." He threw the last of the corn and then he crumpled the bag and dropped it. He rubbed his palms on his sweater. "You didn't come out here to admire my ducks."

They explained their mission.

"Why do you want me to become your chairman?" he asked, peering at them from under white eyebrows that stuck out wildly in every direction.

"We want your money," Kahners said clearly. "And your influence."

Elkins grinned. "Come into the house," he said.

Mrs. Elkins was lying on the couch reading a paperback with a naked corpse on the cover. She looked up and smiled at them and her eyes met Michael's and held them. He was aware of her husband and Kahners standing on either side of him but perversely he didn't look away. After what seemed like a long time but was actually a moment she smiled again and broke the contact as she resumed her reading. She had a good figure under the pink housecoat, but there were fine wrinkles in the corners of her eyes and her pale hair looked like straw in the yellow light of the living-room lamp.

Elkins sat down at a Louis XIV desk and opened a large checkbook. "How much do you want?" he asked.

"Hundred thousand," Kahners told him.

He smiled. He reached under the checkbook and pulled out a Temple Emeth membership list. "I looked this over before you came. Three hundred and sixty-three members. Among them some men I know. Men like Ralph Plotkin and Joe Schwartz and Phil Cohen and Hyman Pollock. Men who can afford to give a little money to support a good cause." He wrote out a check and tore it out of the book. "It's for fifty thousand dollars," he said, handing it to Michael. "If you were trying to raise a million, I'd have made it a hundred thousand. But for four hundred thousand, let everybody do his share."

They thanked him. Michael put the check in his wallet.

"I want a plaque in the main lobby," Elkins said. "'In beloved memory of Martha Elkins, born August 6, 1888, died July 2, 1943.' My first wife," he said. On the couch Mrs. Elkins turned a page of her book.

They shook hands and said good night.

Outside, as they got into the car, they heard a door slam. "Rabbi Kind! Rabbi Kind!" Mrs. Elkins called. They waited while she hurried to them, holding the hem of the pink housecoat high to keep from tripping as she half-ran.

"He said," she reported breathlessly, "that he wants to see the exact layout of the plaque before it's cast."

Michael promised that it would be done and she turned and went back into the house.

He started the car, and beside him Kahners gave a little low laugh, like a man who had just rolled a point in a crap game. "That's the way it's done, Rabbi."

"You got only half the amount you wanted," Michael said. "Won't this cut major contributions in half all the way down the line?"

"I told you we would *ask* for a hundred grand," Kahners said. "I was hoping we could get forty."

Michael sat silent and unaccountably depressed, feeling the presence of the fifty thousand dollars in his wallet.

"I've been rabbi here for two and one-half years," he said finally. "Tonight was the third time I set eyes on Harold Elkins. He has been inside the temple twice during that length of time. At *bar mitzvahs*, it seems to me. Or perhaps at weddings." He drove in silence for a little while. "The people who use the temple," he said. "The ones who come to services and send their children to Hebrew school. I'll feel a lot better about receiving money from them."

Kahners smiled at him but said nothing.

Next morning the telephone rang in his study at the temple and a woman's voice, hesitant and faint and slightly husky, asked for the rabbi.

"This is Jean. Jean Elkins," she added, revealing that she had recognized his voice.

"Oh, Mrs. Elkins," Michael said, aware that Kahners had looked up at the sound of her name and was smiling. "What can I do for you?"

"The question is what I can do for you," she said. "I'd like to help with the fund-raising drive."

"Oh," he said.

"I can type and I can file and I can use an adding machine. Harold thinks it's a good idea," she said after a tiny pause. "He's got to do some traveling and he thinks this will keep me out of mischief."

"Why don't you come down here whenever you feel like it," Michael said. As he replaced the receiver he observed that Kahners' face still wore the same smile, which disturbed him for reasons he had trouble defining.

CHAPTER FORTY-ONE

A Buick dealer named David Bloomberg donated four acres for consideration as the temple site, in memory of his parents, and when Michael visited the place with the committee they saw at once that it was ideal, a completely wooded tract on the crest of a high hill on the outskirts of town and less than half a mile from the campus. The view to the east was of broad meadow cut by a wandering stream, falling to young timber. "Di Napoli can build his temple on a height and facing the sun, like Solomon," Sommers said, while Michael simply nodded, his silence showing his pleasure more than words.

Acquisition of the site gave Kahners another talking point, and he scheduled a series of fund-raising parties. The first was a Sunday breakfast for men, which Michael was unable to attend because of a funeral.

The second was a champagne party at Felix Sommers' home. When the Kinds arrived, the living room was crowded with people standing and drinking champagne. Michael liberated two glasses from a passing tray as they plunged into the vocal hubbub. He and Leslie found themselves in conversation with a young Ph.D. biologist and an overweight doctor who specialized in allergy.

"They've got a fellow in Cambridge," the biologist was saying, "who is working in cryogenics, trying to find a way to quick-freeze human beings. You know, give them a blast of cold and keep them in a state of suspended animation."

"What on earth for?" Michael asked, testing the champagne. It was warm and rather flat.

"Think of the incurable diseases," the biologist said. "You can't cure something? Zappo, you freeze the poor shnook and keep him that way until there's been a breakthrough. Then you wake him up and cure him."

"That's all we need, that and the population explosion," the allergist said. "Where would they keep all the sleeping stiffs?"

The biologist shrugged. "Cold-storage. Warehouses. Refrigerated boarding houses, the natural answer to the nursing homes shortage."

Leslie made a face and swallowed warm champagne. "Think of a power failure. With all the boarders waking up right and left and hammering on the radiators for less heat."

Like a sound effect, someone started to hit a spoon against a glass pitcher for silence, startling her, and the three men laughed.

"Here comes the pitch," said the biologist.

"The commercial," the doctor said. "I already heard it, Rabbi. I made my pledge at the Sunday breakfast. I'm just here tonight as a shill."

Michael didn't understand, but the crowd was moving into the next room, where long tables had been set up. There were place cards to prevent random seating, and they found their places next to a couple they liked—Sandy Berman, an assistant professor of English at the university, and his wife June. Felix offered a short welcome and then introduced Kahners ("a financial expert who graciously is helping us with the campaign"), who spoke about the importance of their contributions and called for verbal pledges. The first man on his feet was the allergist. He pledged three thousand dollars. He was followed by three other men, none of whom pledged less than twelve hundred dollars.

Each of the four pledges was made quickly and cheerfully. Too fast and too pat, the work of amateur dramatists. An embarrassed silence hung in the room like a fat lady's bosom.

Michael saw that Leslie was looking at him and he knew that now she too understood what the doctor had meant when he had said he was a shill. Each of these bids had been made before. They were being made again in a mechanical effort to create a giving mood.

"Well?" Kahners said. "Don't be bashful, my good friends. Now is the opportunity. The need for sacrifice is now."

A man in the corner named Abramowitz rose and pledged one thousand dollars. Kahners' face lighted until he consulted a list in his hand and checked off his name. Obviously, he had expected more from Mr. Abramowitz. When Abramowitz sat down another man at his table leaned forward and engaged him in strenuous conversation. At each table now, a planted salesman began to sell. Nobody at Michael's table was urging anyone else to pledge. They sat and looked at one another in an uncomfortable muteness. Could it be, Michael wondered, that the committee had expected him to deliver a sales pitch? But Kahners was approaching them, smiling broadly.

"Ill fares the land, to hastening ills a prey, where wealth accumulates and men decay," he said.

"Goldsmith," Sandy Berman said gloomily.

"Ah, a student." Kahners placed a blank pledge card in front of him.

"Worse, a teacher." Berman made no move to pick up the card.

Kahners smiled. He placed a card in front of each of the men at the table. "What are you gentlemen afraid of?" he said. "They're only pledges. Take your pens and sign. Sign!"

"Better is it that thou shouldest not vow, than that thou shouldest vow and not pay," Berman said.

"Ecclesiastes," Kahners said, this time without a smile. He looked around the table. "Look," he said. "We've been working like dogs on this campaign. Like dogs. For you. For you and your kids. For your community.

"We've got advance gifts from principal donors that could knock your eyes out. From one man alone, from Harold Elkins alone, we got fifty thousand dollars. Fifty thousand. So come on now, be fair. Be fair to *yourselves*. This is a democratic temple we're trying to build. It's got to be supported by the little guy as well as the big guy."

"The trouble is, it isn't democratic at all," an owlish young man sitting at the front of the table told him. "The littler a guy you are financially, the more of a personal burden your contribution will be."

"It's all proportionate," Kahners said.

"No, it isn't. Look, I'm an accountant. On salary. Say my salary is ten thousand dollars a year. That places me in a twenty per cent tax bracket. If I give the temple five hundred dollars I can deduct one hundred dollars in taxes, so my donation actually cost me four hundred.

"But take another guy, a businessman who earns forty thousand dollars a year," he said, nervously adjusting his glasses. "In his bracket, he deducts forty-four and one-half per cent. If he gives two thousand dollars, which makes him four times the good guy I am, he saves almost half his donation."

The people seated near him began discussing this phenomenon.

"That's a lot of doubletalk. Mathematics can tell you whatever you want it to. Gentlemen," Kahners said. "Is anyone prepared to sign his pledge card now?"

Nobody moved.

"Then you will excuse me. It was a pleasure to meet you." He moved to another table. In a few minutes the party began to break up.

"Join us for coffee?" Leslie said to June Berman. "Howard Johnson's?"

June looked at her husband and then nodded.

As they passed Kahners, Michael saw that he was talking to Abramowitz, the man who had pledged one thousand dollars. "You'll come tomorrow night at eight-thirty in David Binder's house?" he was saying. "It's very important or we wouldn't ask. We appreciate it."

In the restaurant they ordered without enthusiasm.

"Rabbi," Sandy said, "I don't want to embarrass you, but that was pretty bad."

Michael nodded. "Bricks and cement cost money. It's a

miserable, thankless job, dunning for it. But they have to get it."

"Don't let them aggravate you," Leslie said. "Only *you* can tell how much you can give. Give whatever you can afford, and forget it."

"What we can afford?" June said. She waited until the waitress had served their coffee and sandwiches and left. "It's no secret how much assistant professors are paid at Wyndham. Sandy gets fifty-one hundred from the university—"

"Junie," Sandy said.

"Fifty-one hundred, plus another twelve hundred for teaching summer school. Because we need a car, this fall he'll teach two evening sections of business English; another eighteen hundred. That gives us an annual income of eighty-one hundred dollars, and those . . . *fools* . . . suggest we pledge seventeen hundred and fifty dollars to the temple."

"Those were preliminary suggestions," Michael said. "I know for a fact the committee will be happy to receive less. A lot less."

"Two hundred and fifty dollars," Sandy said.

"If that's it, then give them the check and when they say thank you, say you're welcome," Leslie said.

Michael shook his head. "They're going to set a minimum pledge at seven hundred and fifty dollars."

There was a small silence.

"I won't join, Rabbi," Sandy said.

"What will you do about Hebrew school for your kids?"

"I'll pay the tuition the way I always have. A hundred and forty bucks a year for the three of them, plus thirty dollars a month for transportation."

"You can't. The executive board has voted that only paid-up members can send their children to the Hebrew school."

"Wow," June Berman said.

"What happened to the grand old idea that the *shul* was a place where any man, no matter how poor, could seek God?" Sandy said.

"We're talking about membership, Sandy. You'll never be chased away from the temple."

"But there may not be a seat for me?"

"There may not."

"Suppose somebody just can't afford seven hundred and fifty dollars?" June asked.

"They've set up a hardship committee," Michael said wearily. "It won't be an ordeal. I'm on it. Your friend Murray Engel. Felix Sommers, your husband's boss. Joe Schwartz. All reasonable guys."

Leslie had been watching Berman's face. "That's horrible," she said quietly.

Sandy started to laugh. "Hardship committee. You know what the executive board can do? I'm not a hardship case. I'm a teacher. A university professor."

They finished their food. When the check came Michael struggled for it. Finally, knowing that tonight Sandy would insist interminably, he let him pay.

An hour later he and Leslie argued as they got ready for bed.

"Don't criticize the drive in front of congregation members," he said.

"Must it be this kind of a drive? Christians raise money for buildings without this . . . loss of dignity. Couldn't they tithe or something?"

"They aren't Christians. I'm a rabbi, not a minister."

"But it's wrong," she said. "I think the methods they're using are disgusting. They're an insult to the intelligence of the membership."

"Don't make things worse than they are."

"Why don't you tell them, Michael?"

"They know how I feel. Raising the money is their responsibility. They're convinced this is the one way to raise it. If I stay in the background, eventually the temple will be built and then perhaps I can make it something very fine."

She didn't answer. She put down the brush and he saw that she was actually taking out the thermometer, and something inside of him pulled back. "Don't wait up for me," he said. "I have some work."

"All right."

He read until 2 A.M. When he crawled into bed he was sure that she was asleep, and he drifted off almost immediately. But the luminescent hands of the bedside clock said 3:20 when he woke and realized that she was no longer lying at his side. She was sitting by the open window, smoking and staring out into the dark. The chirping of the crickets was piercing and he realized that it had been the shrill sound that had awakened him. "They're loud, aren't they?" he said. He got out of bed and sat on the window sill facing her. "What are you doing?"

"I couldn't sleep."

He took one of her cigarettes and she flicked her lighter for him, her eyes enormous and her face sad and wakeful, smooth light planes and dark hollows in the sudden yellow flare. "What's the matter, Leslie?" he asked gently.

"I don't know. Insomnia, I guess. I just can't seem to sleep lately." They were silent for a moment. "Ah, Michael," she said, "we've gone sour, haven't we? Too sour to make anything as sweet as a baby."

"What are you talking about," he said roughly, and immediately felt exposed as a liar and a hypocrite, knowing she knew him too well for pretending. "That's a great theory. Very scientific."

"Poor Michael."

"It will work out," he said. "There's always adoption."

"I don't think it would be fair to the baby." She looked up at him in the dark. "You know what our real trouble is?"

"Come to bed."

"You're no longer the young Jewish Lochinvar of the mountains. I'm no longer the girl you caught that big fish for."

"For God's sake," he said, enraged. He returned to bed alone but while she continued to sit in the dark and smoke he lay unable to sleep, and watched the red glow of her cigarette ember, recalling that vanished girl with a remembered love so intense it refused to be blotted out by the pillow he pulled over his face like a do-it-yourself slumber mask.

Kahners had reached the stage in the campaign where he was ready to sell the temple in sections. A mimeographed list entitled *Living Memorials and Tributes* was readied for the congregation members; it reminded them that a good name was rather to be chosen than great riches, and loving favor rather

than silver and gold. Certainly the highest virtue, it said, is a
name that attaches itself to the betterment of a community, the
education of youth, and the molding of good character. It offered
the unique opportunity of inscribing the member's name or the
name of a dear departed one in a building that would serve
through the years as an inspiration to future generations.

For twenty-five thousand dollars, the synagogue itself would
be named for the individual specified.

The chapel went for ten thousand dollars. So did the auditorium, while the religious school could be named for seventy-
five hundred, along with the recreation room and the air conditioning system.

The *bema* could be named for six thousand dollars. The
Torah (Complete—Cover, Yad, Breastplate, Crown), at twenty-
five hundred dollars was a bargain compared to the inscribed
brass nameplate that would be placed on the door of the cus-
todian's quarters for thirty-five hundred dollars.

The list was mimeographed on four pages, stapled. Kahners
used the same list for every Jewish campaign. He had brought
bundles of them with him in one of the crates, so that all that
was necessary was for Temple Emeth's name to be placed on
the top of the first page and then the bundles could be run
through the temple's addressograph.

Kahners came to Michael, groaning. "I've got both girls
to work late tonight, addressing. But the lists. Go depend on rich
volunteers. That Elkins woman took them home to cut stencils
yesterday and now she says she can't come in today. A summer
cold."

"I'll try to find somebody who can go out and get them
this afternoon," Michael said.

"By seven o'clock we need them. Seven-thirty the latest,"
Kahners said, leaving to answer a querulous secretarial summons.

The constant ringing of the telephones, the thunk-thunk-
thunk of the mimeograph and the steady clatter of the two typewriters blended into a claw of sound that raked him again and
again, until by midmorning there was dull pain in his forehead
and he began to search his mind for business that would take
him out of the office. He fled at eleven-thirty, stopping at a
sandwich shop for a light lunch and then making pastoral calls,

one of which yielded tea and strudel for dessert. At two-thirty he stopped at the hospital and sat with a woman who had just surrendered three gallstones to a surgeon, remaining until two-forty-eight, four minutes after she showed him the stones like gems on a black velvet cloth, future family heirlooms.

He was getting into his car in the hospital parking lot when he remembered the membership lists, and he took off his jacket and turned up his sleeves and rolled down the car windows and then drove through the town and into the country, squinting against the glare of the afternoon sun.

At the farmhouse he rang the front-door bell and waited, but nobody came to the door. Carrying his coat, he walked around the house to the barnyard. Mrs. Elkins was slumped on a chaise in the shade of a big oak, her long slender feet flat on the lounge and her knees spread so that through the brown V of her legs he could see the pan of corn on her bare belly. The ducks were all around her, quacking as she fed them corn with little flicks of her long fingers. Her short shorts revealed what clothing designers easily hid, the beginning of the age-dappling on the backs of her thighs. The shorts were white and her halter was blue and her shoulders were round but freckled. But it was her hair that surprised him; instead of straw blonde it was a soft shiny brown.

"Rabbi," she said. She took the pan off her stomach and stood, slipping her feet into loafers.

"Hi. Mr. Kahners would like the membership lists," he said.

"I'm all finished with them. Can you wait a few moments while I feed these monsters?"

"Go ahead. I have lots of time." While she threw feed they moved together through the puddle of greedy ducks, to a large wire cage in the shade of the house. The door opened with a rending of rusty hinges and she reached through the opening and set down the pan with the corn that remained, slamming the gate in time to prevent the escape of a large drake that rushed toward them on swift red web feet and with a convulsive trembling of wings.

"Why is this one penned?" Michael asked.

"We just got him and his wings aren't clipped. Harold will do it when he gets home. Please sit. I'll only be a moment."

She went toward the house. Carefully not looking at her walk, he went to the lounge. There were a few gathering clouds in the sky and, as he sat down, the first mutter of thunder, answered foolishly by the ducks. In a little while she returned carrying not the lists but a large tray containing ice, glasses, and things in bottles.

"Here. It's heavy," she called. "Put it on the lawn."

He took it and set it down. "This isn't necessary," he said. "I'm intruding, and you're not feeling well today."

"Not feeling well?"

"Your cold."

"Oh." She laughed. "Rabbi, I don't have a cold. I lied to Mr. Kahners so I could go to my hairdresser's." She looked at him. "Have you ever lied?"

"I guess I have."

"I lie a lot." She touched her brown hair. "Do you like it?"

"Very much," he said truthfully.

"I saw you looking at it. Before, I mean, that first night when you were here and then later when I came to the temple. I could tell you didn't like it the other color."

"Oh, it was pretty," he said.

"You're lying now, aren't you?"

"Yes," he said, smiling.

"But this is better? You like this?" She touched his hand again.

"Yes, it is. When is Mr. Elkins coming home?" he asked, realizing too late that as much as he wanted to change the subject, the question was not the best choice he could have made.

"Not for several days. He may go to Chicago from New York." She began to clink bottles. "What can I give you? Gin and tonic?"

"No, thanks," he said quickly. "Just something cool, if you will. Ginger ale, if you have it."

She had it and she gave it to him. There was no other chair on the lawn and she settled beside him on the lounge, bringing whiskey on the rocks for herself.

They sipped the drinks and then she set her glass on the lawn and smiled at him. "I've been meaning to ask you for an appointment," she said.

"What for?" he asked.

"I have . . . something I wanted to tell you. Discuss with you. A problem."

"Would you like to discuss it now?"

She finished her drink quickly and went to the tray to replenish it. This time she brought back the bottle and set it next to them. She slipped off the loafers and tucked her legs under her; a film of dust covered the red polish on her toes, inches from his knee. "Are you going to tell Mr. Kahners that I lied?" she asked. "Don't tell him."

"You owe nobody any explanations."

"I've enjoyed working near you." The tips of the toes touched his patella, contact but no pressure.

"Mr. Kahners says you're one of the best typists he's ever seen."

"Not that he's looked," she said, crunching ice between her teeth and extending her glass toward the bottle, and he saw with a small inner signal of alarm that once again it was empty.

He poured skimpily, adding the two largest ice cubes he could find to make it look like a generous shot. I must get out of here, he told himself, and he started to rise, but again she placed her hand on his arm. "This is the color it used to be," she said.

Her hair, he realized. He put his hand over hers to remove it from his arm and found that she had turned her wrist so that her palm snuggled into his and their fingers touched.

"My husband is much older than I am," she said. "A young girl when she marries an old man doesn't realize. The years ahead. What they're like."

"Mrs. Elkins," he said, but she let go of his hand suddenly and ran to the wire-mesh cage. The door squealed as she opened it and the drake dashed up to the opening and then stopped, confused when he saw that the barrier had not been slammed into place to block his way.

"Go ahead, you damn stupid thing," the woman said.

The drake sprang lightly, pushing with his big red feet, rainbow wings already whipping the air. He poised over their heads for a heartbeat in a gleam of white belly and long black tail and then the wing thrum sounded louder and he rose high in a projectile arc that carried him, triumphantly calling, into the woods beyond the farm.

"Why did you do that?" Michael asked.

"I want everything in the *world* to be free." She turned to him. "Him. You. Me." Her arms came up and tightened around his neck and he felt her against him and her mouth was warm and moving, but tasting of refrigerator ice and whiskey. He pulled away and she continued to hold him as if she were drowning.

"Mrs. Elkins," he said.

"Jean."

"Jean, that isn't freedom."

She rubbed her cheek against his chest. "What am I going to do about you?"

"As a starter, go easy on the booze."

For a moment she looked at him, and again sudden thunder rumbled over their heads.

"You're not interested, are you?"

"Not that interested," he said.

"You're not interested at *all*. Aren't you a man?"

"I'm a man," he said gently, two steps ahead of her so that the gibe didn't touch him.

She turned and walked back into the house and this time he stood and watched her fine free walk, virtuously feeling he had earned the privilege. Then he picked up his jacket and walked around the house to the car. As he opened the door something whistled by his head, so close he could feel it pass, and thumped against the top of the car, denting it. The box flew open when it hit the ground and some of the contents spilled, but luckily most of the file cards were sorted and held in bunches by elastic bands. For a moment he squinted into the sun, looking up at her standing at the open second-floor window.

"Are you all right? Do you want me to send somebody out here to stay with you?"

"I want you to go to hell," she said very clearly.

When she turned away he knelt and picked up the membership lists and placed them back in the wooden box, which was cracked on one side. Then he got into the car and started it and drove away.

He drove for a little while and then without knowing why he pulled the car off the road and lit a cigarette and sat there, trying not to think how easy it would be to turn the car around and go back. In a few minutes he killed the cigarette in the ashtray and got out of the car and walked into the woods. Smelling blueberry spice made him feel better. He walked hard until the perspiration started to flow and he was no longer thinking of Jean Elkins or of Leslie or of the temple. Presently he came to a stream, shallow and crystalline and about eight feet wide. The bottom was sand and drowned leaves and he took off his shoes and, carrying them, waded into the cold water. In the center it came to just above his knees. He saw no fish but on the far side he saw water-striders and under a rock he found a crawdad that he tracked downstream for twenty feet before it disappeared beneath another rock. In some rushes over a miniature rapids a large spider with yellow markings sat in a great web, and he thought suddenly of the spider in the bunkhouse the summer before college when he had worked on Cape Cod, the spider to whom he had talked. He considered briefly the possibility of talking to this spider, but the truth of the matter was that now he felt too old, or perhaps it was simply that he and this spider had nothing to say to each other.

"Hey," a voice said.

A man stood on the bluff looking at him. Michael didn't know how long he had been standing there watching. "Hello," he said.

The man wore the uniform of a farmer, faded blue overalls, milk-stained workshoes and a blue workshirt stained with sweat. The stubble on his face was the same gray as the battered and bandless hat he wore, a little too large so that the brim rested almost on his ears.

"This is posted land," he said.

"Oh? I'm sorry," Michael said. "I didn't see any signs."

"Too goddam bad. The signs are there. There's no huntin' or fishin' allowed on this land."

"I wasn't hunting or fishing," Michael said.

"Get your filthy feet the hell out of my brook before I get the dogs," the farmer said. "I know your kind. No respect for property. What the hell you doin' here anyhow with your damn pants rolled up like a four-year-old?"

"I went into the woods," Michael said, "because I wished to live deliberately, to front only the essential facts of life and see if I could not learn what it had to teach, and not, when I came to die, discover that I had not lived." He waded across the brook and stopped near the farmer to dry his feet very deliberately with his handkerchief, which fortunately was clean. Then he put his socks and shoes back on and rolled down his trousers, which were quite wrinkled. He walked through the woods thinking about Thoreau and what he would have told the farmer, and when he was about halfway to the road the rain began to fall. For a very little while he continued to walk, and then as the trees thinned and the rain fell more heavily he began to run. He hadn't run for a long time and although his wind was bad and it soon became hard to breathe he kept it up until he ran out of the woods and swerved to avoid hitting a large sign which told the world that the land was owned by Joseph A. Wentworth, and that trespassers would be prosecuted by law. He was breathless and soaked through when he got into the car, with a stitch in his side and a small trembling in the pit of his stomach and the feeling that somehow he had survived a narrow escape.

Three evenings later he and Leslie attended a seminar at the University of Pennsylvania. The colloquium was entitled "Religion in the Nuclear Age" and it brought together theologians, scientists, and philosophers in an atmosphere of guarded interdisciplinary good fellowship out of which were engendered few answers to the moral questions posed by nuclear fission. Max was being cared for by a Wyndham co-ed who had agreed to sleep over, and they felt no need to hurry home; following the meeting they accepted the invitation of a Philadelphia rabbi to stop at his home for coffee.

By the time they approached Wyndham in the car it was 2 A.M.

He had thought that Leslie was dozing, her head thrown back and her eyes closed, but suddenly she spoke. "It's as though everyone in the world has been turned Jewish," she said. "Only instead of ovens, now we all face the bomb."

He thought about it but didn't answer, driving slowly and

then not thinking about it, trying to forget the problem of whether God would be there if the world should suddenly dissolve into atomic mist. The night was soft and an August moon like a slice of carrot had dropped low in the sky. They shared the silence and in a little while she began to hum. He didn't feel like going home.

"Want to see the temple site?"

"Yes," she said, sitting up eagerly.

The tar road wound up the hill, narrowing and turning to rocky dirt halfway up and then petering out just before it reached the temple property. He drove the car as far as he could, past a house in which a bedroom light popped on and then was extinguished as their car bumped by.

She laughed, with bitterness around the edges. "They must think we're lovers," she said.

He parked at the end of the road and they walked past a fence and the looming shadow of a stacked woodpile, and then they were on temple land. The moon shed a lovely light but the ground was slick with the leaves of past seasons and uneven and she had to stop and take off her shoes. He stuck one in each of his jacket pockets and took her hand. They could see a path and they followed it slowly, and in a little while they were at the very top of the hill. He lifted her onto a rock and she stood there with her hand on his shoulder, looking down on a black landscape dappled in great patches by light from the sky, like the setting for a good dream. She said nothing, but her hand on his shoulder tightened until it hurt, and he wanted her as a woman for the first time in months.

He lifted her off the rock and he kissed her, feeling young, and she kissed him back until she saw what he was doing and then she pushed him back, half striking him.

"You fool," she said, "we're not juveniles who need to run off into the woods in the middle of the night. I'm your wife, we have a big brass bed at home and enough room to wrestle nude, if that's what you want. Take me home."

But that was not what he wanted. He fought her striking hands, laughing and then suddenly serious, until she stopped all struggling and took his face in her palms and kissed him like a bride, stopping only to whisper about the people in the house, with her husband past caring.

At first she started to do what Dr. Reisman had instructed, but he stopped her roughly. "This isn't for a baby. For a change for you and for me," he said, and they made love in the shadow of the rock on the rustling dry leaves, sweetly but like two wild things, like a duck and a drake, like lions, and afterward she was once more his darling, his *bubeleh*, his baby, his bride, the golden girl for whom he had caught the big fish.

They walked back to the car guiltily, Michael searching the dark windows of the house for sleepless peepers, and on the way home she sat very close to him. When they got to the house Michael insisted that they brush each other off thoroughly before going in, and he was pulling bits of leaf and twig off his darling's behind, with her shoes still sticking out of his pockets, when the front-door light flashed on and the babysitter told them shakily that she had thought it was burglars.

Ten days later Leslie came to him and held the back of his neck in her hand. "My period is lost," she said. "I can't find it anywhere."

"So you're a few days late. It happens."

"Mine comes with Yankee punctuality. And I feel like the Before girl in the vitamin ads."

"You're coming down with a cold," he said tenderly, praying.

Two days later nausea sent her into the bathroom to vomit away the early hours.

When hormone from her urine made a two-inch laboratory frog virile as a bull in the spring, Dr. Reisman jubilantly took full credit for the pregnancy. They didn't care.

CHAPTER FORTY-TWO

Seven weeks after Kahners came into town like a paladin borne by black Buick instead of white stallion, the fund-raiser packed up his crates, conned three strangers into carrying them out of the building, accepted a check for ninety-two hundred and thirty-eight dollars and disappeared from their lives.

The red line had risen to the top of the thermometer sign outside the temple.

Twelve families had resigned from temple membership.

Three hundred and fifty-one members had signed pledges to contribute sums ranging from five hundred dollars to Harold Elkins' fifty thousand.

Paolo Di Napoli returned from Rome with handsome pastel sketches that showed the influence of both Nervi and Frank Lloyd Wright. The committee approved them at once.

In October, ponderous machines lumbered up the hill on which the temple would be built. They bit open the red earth in great chunks, felled trees that were two centuries old, pulled up ancient stumps from their deep root sockets, and removed boulders that had not budged or trembled since the last great glacier had dropped them into place.

By Thanksgiving Day the ground had become hard down to the frost line and it had snowed for the first time. The machines were driven down the hill. The great gash of the foundation hole was softened by a thin white skim of new snow.

One day the Rabbi came up the hill carrying an attractive black-and-white sign that informed the reader that this was the site of the new Temple Emeth. Michael had nailed together and painted the sign himself. But the ground was frozen so hard he could not hammer the sign into the earth, and he decided to wait until spring and carried it down again.

He returned often, however.

He kept his trout waders in the trunk of the car and sometimes when he needed to be absolutely alone with God he would drive to the foot of the hill and pull on the rubber boots and climb until he reached the crest, to sit under the rock where he and his wife had made love. He watched the frozen excavation and swayed with the wind. There were many rabbit tracks in the snow, and others that he didn't recognize. He hoped that the construction of the temple wouldn't frighten the animals away. He always wanted to remember to bring food for them next time he came, but he never did. He envisioned a secret congregation of furred and feathered things that sat and looked at him with eyes that glowed in the dark as he preached the word, a sort of Jewish Francis of Assissi in Pennsylvania.

On the big rock there was a hump of snow that grew all through the winter. As spring approached it began to dwindle in inverse proportion to the growth of his wife's belly, until the snow of the rock was almost gone and her belly was full and humplike, their private miracle.

Seven days after the snow on the rock completely disappeared, the machines and the men returned to the hilltop to work on the temple. At first for Michael, watching the slow, laborious foundation-pouring was an agony of waiting, and remembering Father Campanelli's disappointment when the priest's new church had been completed in San Francisco. But from the beginning it was obvious that the temple would be a beautiful building and that he would not be disappointed.

Di Napoli had utilized the rough power of concrete to evoke the rugged splendor of the earliest temples. Inside, the sanctuary walls were of open-pored red brick, curved at the *bema* to aid the acoustics. "Encourage your people to rub their hands along these walls to see what they feel like," the architect told Michael. "This kind of brick needs to be touched to live."

He had designed gold-covered copper replicas of the Ten Commandments tablets to rise high above the ark, starkly illuminated against the dark brick by the eternal flame.

In the upper story, the classrooms of the Hebrew school were done in warm Israeli pastels, with splashes of soft color everywhere. The outside walls of each classroom were of sliding glass for light and air, with an exterior grid of thin concrete blocks to keep the children in and the sun glare out.

A nearby tall stand of old pines became a meditation grove, and Di Napoli had designed a permanent *sukkah* that was built behind the temple building not far from the large rock.

Harold Elkins, preparing to leave for a second honeymoon in the Mediterranean with his brown-haired wife, announced that he had acquired a Chagall which he would give to the temple.

The women of the Sisterhood began making plans for an independent fund-raising drive of their own. To raise money for a Lipchitz bronze for the new lawn.

After a minimum of polite bargaining on both sides, the old temple building was sold to the Knights of Columbus for seventy-five thousand dollars, with both purchaser and seller departing from the negotiations highly pleased. The sale should have brought a surplus to the Building Fund, but the Committee was forced to face the fact that although Archibald S. Kahners had gathered pledges, receiving payment in honor of those pledges was something else again. Repeated mailings drew little response from those who had not paid at once.

Finally Sommers turned to the Rabbi. He gave Michael a list of families who had not paid their pledges or who had not pledged at all.

"If you would visit them," he suggested delicately.

Michael stared at the list as if it puzzled him. It was quite long. "I'm a rabbi, not a bill collector," he said.

"Of course. Of course. But you could work these names into your schedule of pastoral calls, just to remind them that the temple knows they exist. A discreet hint . . ."

Sommers hinted on his own. It was, after all, because Michael had written a paper indicating that he was a "building rabbi" that he had been called to Emeth in the first place. Now they needed his help in making the building a reality.

He kept the list.

The first name on it was Samuel A. Abelson. When he called at the Abelson apartment he found four small children, two with bad colds, living in a furnitureless apartment with a dull-eyed twenty-two-year-old mother who had been deserted by her husband three weeks before. There was very little food in the house, which smelled badly.

He reported the name and address to the director of the Jewish Family Agency, who promised to send a caseworker that afternoon.

The next name was that of Melvin Burack, a wholesale clothing salesman who was on the road at the time of Michael's visit, in one of the family's three cars. Sipping tea with the Rabbi in her Spanish living room, Moira Burack promised not to forget again to send the check to the temple.

It was never quite so bad as he feared. Not even the seventh name on his list: Berman, Sanford. June served coffee and marble cake and Sandy Berman listened and then politely asked for an appointment with the hardship committee, in order to work out a settlement that would allow him to register his children in the Hebrew school.

What tipped the balance for Michael was that a few days later June and Sandy Berman crossed the street to avoid him when they saw him coming.

It wasn't an isolated phenomenon. If some of the others didn't cross the street when their rabbi came into sight, neither did they fill the air with joyous cries as they rushed to greet him.

He noticed that he was receiving fewer and fewer calls from his congregation for spiritual help in times of personal crisis.

In the late afternoons he began to sit in the still-unfinished sanctuary and ask God what he could do, praying while the smell of wet lime and new cement filled his nostrils and overhead the workmen dropped bricks, broke wine bottles, cursed one another out, and told dirty stories, thinking themselves alone in the temple.

Two days after the dedication of Temple Emeth on May eighteenth, Felix Sommers suggested that Michael prepare a speech for delivery at a champagne party to be held before the summer vacation period began. The goal would be to secure early pledges for the annual Kol Nidre donations which would be collected in the fall. The temple needed all the Kol Nidre money it could get in order to meet its mortgage payments to the bank, Felix explained.

While he was thinking about this the telephone rang.

"Michael?" Leslie said, "I've begun."

He threw a muttered good-by at Felix and drove home and picked her up. There was some traffic at the campus exits but the roads to the hospital were moderately traveled at midafternoon, and she was pale but smiling when they got there.

The little girl was born almost as fast as her brother had been, eight years before, arriving less than three hours after the first violent pain. The waiting room was too near the labor room, so that from time to time when a nurse pushed through the swinging doors at the end of the hall Michael could hear the moans and screams of the women, certain that he recognized Leslie's cries among them.

At twenty-eight minutes past five the obstetrician came into the waiting room and told him she had given birth to a little girl, six pounds, two ounces. The doctor asked him to come into the hospital cafeteria and they sat and had coffee and the physician explained to him that the baby's head had plunged through the wall of the cervix exactly when it was stretched thinnest by the dynamics of labor. The tear had included arterial ripping, and they had been forced to perform a hysterectomy as soon as the baby was out of her body and hemorrhaging had been controlled.

In a little while he went up and sat by the foot of Leslie's bed. Her eyes were closed, the lids blue and bruised-looking, but soon she opened them.

"Is she pretty?" she asked him faintly.

"Yes," he said, although in his worry he hadn't looked, taking the doctor's word that the child was all right.

"We won't have any others."

"We don't need any others. We have a son and daughter and each other." He kissed her fingers and then held her hand, and when she fell asleep comforted, he went and looked at his daughter for the first time. She was much prettier than Max had been at birth. She had a great deal of hair.

He went home with a box of bakery pastries for the baby-sitter and he kissed Max good night and drove through a spring rain to the temple and sat in the sanctuary until morning, in one of the comfortable new foam-rubber upholstered chairs in the third row. He thought of the things he had once wanted to do and the things he had done with his life, and he thought a great deal about Leslie and himself and Max and now the new little girl. In between conversations with God he discovered that although the temple was only a few weeks old a mouse played on the *bema* at night when the building was absolutely still.

At five-thirty-five he left the temple and went home and showered and shaved and changed his clothes. He got to Felix Sommers' house while Sommers was having breakfast, and he accepted a Mazel Tov and a cup of coffee, then he was aware that he was famished and he accepted an entire meal. Over the scrambled eggs he told Felix he was going to resign.

"Have you thought this out? You're absolutely sure?" Felix asked, pouring the coffee; and although he was, his ego bled a few drops when he saw that Sommers would not pretend to try to argue about his decision to leave.

He said he would stay until a replacement had been secured. "You should get two people," he advised. "A rabbi. And somebody else, probably a layman, perhaps a volunteer. With a business administration background. Let the rabbi be a rabbi."

He said it sincerely, and that was the way Sommers took it. Felix thanked him.

He waited several days before telling Leslie one afternoon as she sat feeding the baby. She didn't appear to be surprised. "Come here," she said. He sat gingerly on the bed and she kissed him and took his hand and touched it to the sucking baby's cheek, a softness so singular he had forgotten how it felt.

Next day he brought them home from the hospital. Leslie and the baby and half a dozen bottles of formula because her milk had dried up, and a large bottle of sea-green capsules the doctor thought would allow her to sleep. The capsules helped for a few nights and then lost the bout with insomnia, which returned to plague the mother although the child slept through the night.

On the day Rachel was three weeks old he took a morning train to New York.

Rabbi Sher had died two years before. He had been replaced by Milt Greenfield, Michael's classmate at the Institute.

"I know of an opening that's a real challenge," Rabbi Greenfield said.

Michael grinned. "Your predecessor, *alev hasholom*, once said the same thing to me, Milt," he said. "Only the way Sher put it was, 'I've got a lousy job for you.'" They both laughed.

"It's a congregation that has just voted itself Reform," Rabbi Greenfield said. "After a kind of civil war."

"Is there anything left of it?"

"Almost one third of its members are Orthodox. In addition to your regular duties you would probably have to officiate at

Shaharit, Mincha, and *Maariv* every day. You'd have to serve as rabbi to the pious as well as the liberal."

"I think I'd like that," Michael said.

On the following week end he flew to Massachusetts and two weeks after that he and Leslie drove to Woodborough with Rachel in a car bed and Max in the back seat. They found the big old Victorian house that looked as though it were haunted by the ghost of Hawthorne, with windows like wise eyes and an apple tree outside the back door. The tree had dead boughs that needed pruning, and there was a swing for Max made of a threadbare tire hung with heavy rope from a high branch.

Best of all, he liked the temple. Beth Sholom was old and small. There were no Chagalls or Lipschitzes, but it smelled of floor wax and tattered prayer books and dry woodwork and twenty-five years of people seeking God.

BOOK IV:

The Promised Land

Woodborough, Massachusetts
December 1964

CHAPTER FORTY-THREE

Columbia College Alumni Association
116th Street and Broadway
New York, New York 10027

Gentlemen:

The following is my autobiographical contribution to the Quarter-Century Book of the class of '41:

It is incredible to think that almost twenty-five years have vanished since we all left Morningside Heights.

I am a rabbi. I have filled Reform pulpits in Florida, Arkansas, Georgia, California, Pennsylvania and Massachusetts, where I now live in Woodborough with my wife, the former Leslie Rawlins (Wellesley, '46) of Hartford, Connecticut, and our son Max, 16, and our daughter Rachel, 8.

I find myself looking with surprising anticipation toward the twenty-fifth reunion. The present is so busy, we don't often enough have the opportunity to look back at the past. Yet it is the past which guides us into the future. As a clergyman in a religion almost six thousand years old, I am increasingly aware of this fact.

It has been my experience that faith, far from being an anachronism, is more important than ever in enabling modern man to grope his way into tomorrow.

As for me, I am thankful that God gives me the opportunity to grope. I have kept a fearful eye for the flash in the sky, even as you; I have given up smoking of late and have developed a paunch; recently I have noticed that a great many grown men have taken to using the expression Sir.

But deep down I am confident that the bomb will never

go off. I do not feel that I will be stricken by cancer, at least until I am very old; today, forty-five is a toddling age. And who wants a flat stomach? Are we a society of beach boys?

Enough of sermons; on to soda water; I promise not to open my mouth at Reunion, except of course to have another drink and to join in the singing of "Who Owns New York?"

> *Your classmate,*
>
> Rabbi Michael Kind
> Temple Beth Sholom
> Woodborough, Massachusetts

He had fallen asleep, finally, sitting fully clothed and slumped over on his desk, his head in his arms.

All night long, the telephone was silent.

At 6:36 A.M. it rang.

"We haven't seen her," Dr. Bernstein said.

"Neither have I." It was a cold morning, with the radiators gasping and clanking under a full head of steam, and it occurred to him to ask Dan how she had been dressed, whether she had been protected against the elements.

Her heavy blue coat and gloves and boots and kerchief were missing with her, Dan said. Somehow the information made him feel better: someone so sensibly bundled was hardly a Desdemona in the snow.

"I'll keep in touch," Dr. Bernstein said.

"Please."

Sleeping in the chair had made him stiff and uncomfortable and he spent a long time under the hot shower and then he dressed and woke the children and made certain they were ready for school.

"Will you come to PTA tonight?" Rachel asked him. "Each room gets two points for fathers. I take part. My name is on the program."

"What do you do?"

"If you want to know, you have to come and see."

"All right," he promised.

He drove to the temple in time to lead the *minyan* through

the *kaddish.* Then he shut himself in his study and worked on a sermon. He kept busy.

Just before eleven o'clock Dan called him again. "According to the State Police she spent the night at the YWCA. She signed the register with her own name."

"Where is she now?"

"I don't know. The detective said she left the Y early this morning."

She may have gone home, he thought; she may be there now. The children were at school and Anna was not due to come in until it was time for her to prepare the evening meal.

He thanked Dan and hung up, then he told his secretary that he would be working at home for the rest of the day.

But as he left the office the telephone rang and a moment later she ran out after him.

"It's Western Union, Rabbi," she said.

MICHAEL DARLING I'M GOING OFF BY MYSELF FOR A FEW DAYS. PLEASE DON'T WORRY. I LOVE YOU. LESLIE

He went home anyway and sat in the silent kitchen drinking hot coffee and thinking.

Where would she get the money to go away with, and to live on? He had their bank book in his pocket. So far as he knew, she had only a few dollars in her purse.

He was worrying the question like a dog with a bone when the telephone rang, and when he heard the Long Distance operator he started to pray. But then he recognized his father's voice on the line through a crackle and sputter of electronic noise.

"Michael?" Abe said.

"Hello, Pop? I can't hear you."

"I hear you," Abe said accusingly. "You want me to ask the operator?"

"No, now I can hear. How are things in Atlantic City?"

"I'll speak louder," Abe shouted. "I'm not in Atlantic City. I'm—" There was a burst of static.

"Hello?"

"*Miami.* I decided at the last minute. I'm calling to let you know, you shouldn't worry. I'm at 12 Lucerne Drive." He spelled Lucerne. "Care of Aisner," spelling that, too.

Michael wrote it down. "What is it, Pop, a boardinghouse? A motel?"

"A private home. I'm visiting a friend." Abe hesitated for a moment. "How are the kids? And Leslie?"

"Just fine."

"And you? How are you?"

"Fine, Pop. We're all fine. How are *you*?"

"Michael. I'm going to get married."

"What did you say?" he said, although there had been no static and he had heard his father. "Married, you said?"

"You're angry?" his father said. "You think it's a *mishugineh* thing to do, an old man like me?"

"I think it's wonderful, marvelous! Who is she?" He felt as much relief as delight and he realized guiltily that it might not be wonderful at all, that Abe might be mixed up with who knew what kind of woman. "What's her name?"

"Like I said, Aisner. Her first name is Lillian. She's a widow, same as me. Get this, she's the woman I rent the apartment from in Atlantic City. How's that for a move?"

"Shrewd. Very shrewd." He grinned into the phone. Ah, Pop.

"Her husband was Ted Aisner. Maybe the name is familiar? He had a dozen Jewish bakeries in Jersey. A baker's dozen."

"No," Michael said.

"It wasn't to me, either. He passed away in fifty-nine. She's a sweet person, Michael. I think you'll like her."

"If *you* do, that's enough for me. When will you be married?"

"We figured in March. There's no hurry, both of us are well past the age of impetuosity." From the way Abe said this, Michael guessed he was repeating something he had heard Lillian Aisner say, perhaps to her own children.

"Does she have a family?"

"Hey, you'll never guess," Abe said. "She's got a son who's a rabbi. Only Orthodox. He's got a *shul* in Albany, New York. Melvin, Rabbi Melvin Aisner."

"I don't know him."

"Well, he's Orthodox, you probably wouldn't cross paths. Lillian says he's very well thought of. A nice guy. She's got another son, Phil, I can't wait to avoid him. Even *she* says he's a *shnook.* He had me investigated. The damn fool, I hope it cost him a fortune."

Suddenly Michael was sad, remembering the double stone of hewn granite his father had had placed on his mother's grave, with Abe's name engraved next to hers and the last date left blank. "You can't blame him for protecting his mother," he said. "Say, is she there? I'd like to tell her about the gigolo she's getting."

"No, she's out shopping for dinner," Abe said. "I figure we'll take a little honeymoon in Israel. See Ruthie and her family."

"Would you like to have the wedding here?" Michael asked, forgetting for the moment his own complicating problems.

"She's strictly kosher. She wouldn't eat in your house."

"Hey. Tell her I'm going to have *her* investigated."

Abe chuckled; it occurred to Michael that he sounded younger, more buoyant than he had sounded in years. "You know what I wish for you," Michael said.

"I know." He cleared his throat. "I better hang up, Michael, that *shnook* Phil shouldn't think I'm running up his mother's phone bill on purpose."

"Take care of yourself, Pop."

"You, too. Leslie isn't there to wish me *mazel tov?*"

"No. She's out, too."

"Give her my love. And the kids, give them a kiss from the *zaydeh.* I sent them each a check, Chanukah money."

"You shouldn't do that," he said, but the line was dead.

He replaced the telephone in its cradle and simply sat. Abe Kind, survivor. That was the lesson of the day, the heritage passed from father to son: how to keep going, how to crash from today into tomorrow. It was a proud lesson. He knew men of Abe Kind's age and circumstance who chose to become permanent sleepwalkers, sinking into torpor as secure as death. His father had chosen life's pain, the double bed instead of the double grave. He poured another cup of coffee while he wondered what Lillian looked like; and as he drank it he pondered such matters as whether a double stone had been erected over Ted Aisner.

At seven-thirty he drove Rachel to the Woodrow Wilson

School and she abandoned him in the corridor. He accepted a mimeographed program from a serious boy in long trousers and walked into the auditorium. Sitting alone in the center of the middle row was Jean Mendelsohn.

"Hello," he said, joining her.

"Why, Rabbi! What are you doing here?"

"Same thing you are, I imagine. How's Jerry?"

"Not as bad as I was afraid he would be. He misses the leg. But it's not like stories I've heard about how they still feel the missing parts, how the toes cramp even though they're not there any more. You know what I mean?"

"Yes."

"It isn't like that. At least not with Jerry."

"That's good. How are his spirits?"

"Could be worse, could be better. I spend a lot of time with him. My kid sister Lois came in from New York. She's sixteen, wonderful with the kids."

"One of your children is on the program?"

"My Toby, the devil." She appeared to be flustered at the admission, and when he looked down at the program in his hand, he understood. The school was holding its annual Christmas pageant, an event he had expected to be able to skip when he had first seen the PTA schedule. The last line of the program listed Rachel as a property girl. "My Toby is going to be a Wise Man," Thelma said in a glum rush, getting it over with. "These children. They drive you crazy. She asked us if she could. We told her she *knew* how we felt, to make up her own mind."

"So she's a Wise Man," Michael said, smiling.

She nodded. "In Rome they tell us we don't have to feel guilty, and in Woodborough my daughter is a Wise Man."

The hall had filled. Miss McTiernan, the school principal, all bosom and steel-colored hair, stood at the front of the room. "On behalf of the pupils and teachers of the Woodrow Wilson School, I am happy to welcome you to our annual Christmas pageant. For weeks your children have been preparing costumes and rehearsing. The Christmas pageant is a tradition of long standing at this school, and all the pupils take great pride in it. I'm sure when you see the program, you will, too." She sat to loud applause, and the children marched down the aisles in costumes, nervous Shepherds with tall crooks, self-conscious Wise Men in wispy beards, giggling Angels bearing on their shoulders marvelous papier-mâché wings. After the costumed players trooped the pupils of the fifth and sixth grades, each boy wearing dark slacks and white shirt and tie and each girl in skirt and sweater. Rachel carried sheet music which she passed out to the rest of the children when they reached their seats, then she walked to the piano and stood there.

A small boy whose hair was still wet from the brush stood and began to speak in an incredibly sweet voice. "Now it came to pass in those days, there went out a decree from Caesar Augustus, that all the world should be taxed . . ."

The Nativity was acted out by the players, Jean Mendelsohn squirming when the Wise Men came bearing gifts. When the small drama was over, dissolving into "Silent Night, Holy Night," the children sang other carols, "O Little Town of Bethlehem," "The First Noel," "The Drummer Boy," "O Come, All Ye Faithful," "O Holy Night." Rachel, he noticed, did not sing. She stood by the piano gazing at the audience while all around her the voices of her classmates were raised in song.

When it was over he said good-by to Jean and went to meet his daughter.

"They were good, weren't they?" she said.

"Yes, they were," he said. They filed out of the overheated school building and got into the car and he drove home, but when they got there he didn't want to lose her company right away. "Do you have homework?" he asked.

"Miss Emmons didn't give us any, on account of the pageant."

"Tell you what, let's take a walk and get real tired. Then we'll go in and have some hot chocolate and go to sleep. That sound all right?"

"Mmmm."

They got out of the car and she put her mittened hand in his. No stars shone through the overcast. A raw wind blew, but without force. "Tell me if you grow cold," he said.

"We're going to have a New Year's program. Not for parents, just for the children," she said. "I can sing in that, can't I?"

"Sure you can, honey." He pulled her to him as they walked. "You minded about not singing tonight, didn't you?"

"Yup." She looked up at him hesitantly.

"Because you were the only one not singing, standing in front of so many people?"

"Not only that. The songs and the story. . . . They're so beautiful."

"They are," he agreed.

"Old Testament stories are beautiful, too," she said staunchly, and he hugged her close again. "If Max buys hockey skates can I buy figure skates with the Chanukah check from Grampa Abe?" she asked, sensing an advantage.

He laughed. "How do you know you're going to get a Chanukah check from Grampa Abe?"

"We always do."

"Well, if you do this year perhaps you should take the money and open a bank account of your own with it."

"Why?"

"It's good to have money of your own. For college. Or money that the bank can keep safely just for you, in case you want it some day—"

He stopped short and she laughed and tugged at his hand, thinking he was playing a game, but he was remembering the thousand dollars Leslie's Aunt Sally had left her before they were married. The money he had never allowed her to put into a joint account, so that some nebulous day she could use it in whatever way she saw fit.

"Daddy!" Rachel shouted in delight, tugging, and he became a tree that sank new roots every three steps all the way home.

In the morning after services he left the temple and walked over to the Woodborough Savings and Loan, where he and Leslie did their banking. The plate on the window said the teller's name was Peter Hamilton. He was a young man, tall and thin with a Saltonstall jaw and a little pinched furrow between his eyes. His black hair was sprinkled with gray and clipped close and high over his ears so that he looked like a Marine second lieutenant in a brown flannel Ivy League suit. Michael remembered Leslie asking him once if he had ever seen a fat bank teller.

Two people, a middle-aged woman and an elderly man, had gotten into line behind him, so when it was his turn in front of the cage he was a little self-conscious. He explained to Peter Hamilton that he wanted some information about a possible withdrawal made by his wife that morning, and as he talked he could feel the two people behind him lean forward.

Peter Hamilton looked at him and gave him a little smile with no teeth showing. "Is that a joint account, sir?"

"No," he said. "No, it isn't. It's *her* account."

"Then there is no question of . . . ah . . . dower rights, sir?"

"I beg your pardon?"

"The money in the account is all *hers* legally?"

"Oh, of course. Yes."

"Is it impossible for you simply to . . . ah . . . ask her? I'm afraid we're morally obligated not to . . ."

Vey.

"Where can I find the president?" he asked.

He was a man named Arthur J. Simpson in a large walnut-paneled office with high-pile rust-colored carpeting, a very daring shade for a banker. He listened to Michael with uncommitted courtesy, and when Michael had finished he pressed a button in the intercom and asked that Mrs. Kind's bank records be brought to his office.

"It was a one-thousand-dollar account to begin with," Michael said. "It would be more now with the interest."

"Oh, yes," the banker said. "Indeed it would." He picked out a card and held it up. "The account has fifteen hundred in it."

"Then she didn't get any money today?"

"Ah, she certainly did, Rabbi. This morning the account held two thousand and ninety-nine dollars and forty-four cents." Mr. Simpson smiled. "Interest mounts up. Figured every year, you know, with rates going higher all the time."

"The rich get richer," Michael said.

"That's exactly right, sir."

How far away could she get on six hundred dollars? But even as he asked himself the question, he told himself the answer.

Far enough.

When the telephone rang that night and he heard her name he felt his legs start to tremble, but it turned out to be another false alarm, a call *for* her instead of from her.

"She's not at home," he told the operator. "Who is calling, please?"

This is Long Distance, the operator repeated. When is Mrs. Leslie Kind expected?

"I don't know."

"Is that Mr. Kind," the caller, a strange voice, said.

"Yes. Rabbi Kind."

"I will talk to him, Operator?"

Yes, ma'am, thank you for waiting. Go ahead, please. She clicked off.

"Hello?" Michael said.

"My name is Potter, Mrs. Marilyn Potter?"

"Yes, Ma'am," Michael said.

"I live just three doors down from the Hastings Church? In Hartford?"

Good Lord, of course, he told himself, she's gone to her father's for a couple of days. Then he remembered again that the call was for her from there, and he knew that it couldn't be that. But what the hell was this woman saying, he asked himself numbly, suddenly aware.

"So I was the one who found him. It was a stroke."

Ah.

"Calling hours from one to three and seven to nine tomorrow and Thursday. With the funeral at the church Friday at two. Burial in Grace Cemetery, according to his written instructions?"

He thanked her. He listened to her sounds of condolence and he thanked her. He promised to extend her condolences to his wife and he thanked her and said good-by, and then without knowing why he reached up and switched off the lamp and sat in the dark until Max's harmonica pulled him upstairs, a lifeline of sound.

CHAPTER FORTY-FOUR

By Thursday she still had not come home. He had heard nothing more from her, and he was caught in indecision. The children should be taken to their grandfather's funeral, he told himself.

But they would ask why their mother was not there.

Perhaps she *would* be there, perhaps she had read the obituary, or had somehow heard that her father had died.

He decided not to tell Max and Rachel. Thursday after *Shaharit* he got into the car and drove to Hartford alone.

Two uniformed police officers directed the parking. Inside the church the organ vibrated soft hymns and almost all the white pews were filled.

He walked slowly up and down the aisles, but if Leslie was there he didn't see her. Finally he took a seat—one of the few remaining—in the rear of the church, on the aisle two rows from the back, where he would be able to see her if she came in late.

The flower-banked casket was closed, he saw with relief.

In the two seats next to him a middle-aged woman was discussing his late father-in-law with a younger woman who bore her a remarkable resemblance. Mother and daughter, he knew at once.

"Goodness knows, he wasn't perfect. Nevertheless, for more than forty years he served here. It would have been only proper for you to have gone to the funeral home. You can allow that Frank to do for himself for *one* evening, for goodness sake."

"I don't like to look at dead people," the daughter said.

"Dead, you wouldn't have known he was dead. He looked distinguished. *Handsome.* His face didn't look made up or anything. You'd never have known."

"I'd have known," the daughter said.

The clergymen appeared. One was young, one was old, one was somewhere in between.

"Three," the daughter whispered hoarsely as they rose for the invocation. "Mr. Wilson, the retired one. And Mr. Lovejoy, from First Church. But who's the young one?"

"They said from Pilgrim Church in New Haven. I forgot the name."

The middle-aged minister said the invocation. His voice was mellow and practiced, a voice accustomed to floating out over bowed heads.

A hymn: "Oh God, Our Help in Ages Past." The voices rose around him. The mother sang only a few lines in a tired croak. The daughter had a sweet, soaring soprano, just a little off key.

One thing have I asked the Lord that I will seek after; that I may dwell in the house of the Lord all the days of my life. . . .

Psalm Twenty-Seven. Ours, Michael thought, recognizing that his pride was senseless.

As for man, his days are like grass; he flourishes like a flower of the field; for the wind passes over it and it is gone, and its place knows it no more. . . .

I lift my eyes to the hills. From whence does my help come? My help comes from the Lord, who made heaven and earth. . . .

Psalm One Hundred Three and Psalm One Hundred Twenty-One. He had offered them himself at how many funerals?

But some will ask, "How are the dead raised? With what kind of body do they come?" You foolish man! What you sow does not come to life unless it dies. And what you sow is not the body which is to be, but a bare kernel, perhaps of wheat or of some other grain. But God gives it a body as he has chosen, and to each kind of seed its own body. . . .

New Testament, now. If he had to guess, he would say—First Corinthians. Next to him the middle-aged woman eased her weight from her right to her left buttock.

In my father's house are many rooms; if it were not so, would I have told you that I go and prepare a place for you? And when I go and prepare a place for you, I will come again and will take you to myself, that where I am you may be also. And you know the way where I am going. . . .

The middle-aged minister spoke in praise of the dead man and thanked God for the promise of eternal life and for the fact that the late Reverend Rawlins had labored in his behalf and in behalf of the entire community of souls.

Then they stood again and sang another hymn, "For All the Saints Who From Their Labors Rest," and the voices around Michael rose and fell, and he knew what Rachel had felt in school at Christmas-carol time.

The elderly minister gave the benediction, and the organ began to play and the crowd melted from the pews into the aisles and toward the exits. Michael stood there looking for her but not seeing her, until everyone had gone out and only the pallbearers remained, gathered around the box; then he went outside, blinking against the winter sunlight. He didn't know where Grace Cemetery was, but he got into his car and waited and then moved it into the line of vehicles well behind the hearse, which was a new black Packard, highly polished but speckled with a spattering of slush.

There were hillrows of soiled snow in the gutters on both sides of the street. The funeral cortege moved slowly across the city, snarling traffic all along its route.

Two cars behind Michael a driver gave up and moved out of line. It was a blue-and-white Chevrolet hardtop; as it passed him he caught a glimpse of her in the front seat, half-turned and talking to the young man at the wheel: the small hat was unfamiliar to him, but not the bronze-blonde hair or the blue coat or the way she held her head.

"Leslie," he shouted.

He rolled down the window and called again.

The car made a left turn at the next corner. By the time he had pulled his own car out of line and had negotiated the turn himself, it was nowhere to be seen. He left a huge moving-van behind, passing on the right with millimeters between his wheels and the curb, then shot by a bus and was held up by a red light at a broad avenue.

But the blue-and-white car had made a right turn here. He saw it two short blocks away, just beginning to move as a red light turned to green.

He didn't dare jump his own red light; the traffic was heavy.

When the light changed he slid the car around the corner with wheels spinning, like a teen-ager in a hotrod. There was a small hill and he didn't see the other car until he topped the rise, and then he saw it just making a left turn, and when he got to the corner he made the turn and then drove very fast, faster than he had ever driven in the city, weaving in and out of traffic.

Four or five blocks down he was lucky; they were stopped for another light and he pulled up short three cars behind them.

"Leslie!" he shouted as he got out. He ran to their car and hammered on her window.

But when she turned around, it was the wrong face. It was even the wrong coat, cut differently, a slightly different shade, with big gilt buttons where Leslie's were smaller and black. She rolled down the window. She and the man stared at him. They didn't say anything.

"I'm sorry," he said. "I thought you were somebody else."

He went back to his car and got in just as the light changed. The blue-and-white Chevrolet went straight ahead and Michael whipped his car into a U-turn. He slowly drove back the way he had come, trying to retrace the exact route, but when he had made all the turns there was no sign of the funeral procession.

But pretty soon he came to a cemetery and he swung the car through the gates.

It was a large cemetery, laid out in blocks formed by grids of road, and he drove in one direction on some of the roads and in the other direction on some of the others, trying to catch sight of the funeral. The roads were ploughed and well-sanded.

But all he could see were gravestones, no people.

Then he noticed a *Mogen Doved*. And another, and he slowed the car and read some of the inscriptions.

Israel Salitsky, Feb. 2, 1895–June 23, 1947.

Jacob Epstein, Sept. 3, 1901–Sept. 7, 1962.

Bessie Kahn, Aug. 17, 1897–Feb. 12, 1960, A Good Mother.

Oy, have you got the wrong cemetery!

He sat there, wanting to give up and go home. But if she were there, at the graveside?

He drove down one more block of graves and then there was an old man sitting there in a long brown coat and with a black stocking cap over his ears, on a metal folding chair next to one of the graves. Michael stopped the car near him.

"*Ah guten tag.*"

The man nodded, peering over horn-rimmed glasses that rode low on his nose.

"Grace Cemetery. How would I get there?"

"The one for *skotzim,* that's right next door. This is B'nai B'rith."

"Is there a gate connecting the two?"

He shrugged, pointing forward. "Maybe at the end." He blew on his hands, which were bare.

Michael hesitated. Why was the old man sitting here, next to the grave? He couldn't bring himself to ask. His gloves were next to him on the seat of the car. Not at all intending to, he picked them up and held them out the window.

The old man looked at them suspiciously. Finally he took them and put them on.

"It's going to be warmer tomorrow," Michael said, furious at himself.

"Gott tsedahnken."

He started the car and drove. There were graves on both sides of the road as far as the eye could see; it was a limitless world of graves, he felt like some kind of motor-age *molach ah mohviss,* the angel of death.

Then finally he was approaching the cemetery's end. There was a roadway and a cyclone fence and fifty feet on the other side of the fence he saw the funeral party standing with bowed heads, preparing to bury his father-in-law.

He stopped the car. There didn't appear to be a gate. Did they need an unclimbable fence to keep the dust and the souls from mingling? he asked himself furiously.

He was certain that if he turned the car around and sought to go all the way back out the front gate of B'nai B'rith Cemetery and then in through the front gate of Grace Cemetery, the funeral would be over before he found it again.

He drove the car along the road that ran alongside the fence. On the other side were graves and an occasional mausoleum. He stopped the car as close to the fence as possible next to a very impressive granite crypt and got out. The funeral was hidden by monuments and a small rise. He clambered uncertainly onto the hood of the car and then onto the roof, from which it was possible for him to pull himself onto and over the top of the fence, feeling the dull metal points of the heavy wire bruising his body through his clothing.

He had torn nothing, he noted with satisfaction. There was snow on the roof of the crypt. He walked through it to the far side and looked over the edge thoughtfully. The ground fell away and the drop was at least eight feet. But there seemed to be no other way to get down.

Geronimo!

He landed clumsily, like a dropped log, his heels sliding out from under him on the soft snow and sending him sprawling on his back. When he opened his eyes he saw behind him and overhead the stone-chiseled inscription on the large tomb.

Charles
Regina
BUFFINGTON FAMILY Lawrence REST IN PEACE
Curtis
Virginia

Nothing appeared to be broken. He stood and tried to dust the snow from his clothing. There were wet lumps of cold down his neck.

I beg your pardon, he told the Buffingtons.

There was no path through the deep snow to the ploughed lane within the cemetery; he collected more snow in his shoes and in his pants cuffs, then he was able to walk down the lane to where the funeral was being held.

He stood at the fringe of the crowd. There were a lot of people. She would be standing at the grave, he realized. He shoved his way forward.

"Sorry . . . Excuse me . . ."

A woman glared at him.

"Member of the family," he whispered.

But the people were standing too close together, he couldn't get through.

He could hear the minister reciting the benediction, *The peace of God, which passes all understanding, keep your hearts and minds in the knowledge and love of God, and of his son Jesus Christ our Lord. And the blessing of God Almighty, the Father, the Son, and the Holy Spirit, be among you, and remain with you always. Amen.* But he could not see which of the three ministers it was, or anyone else near the grave, and he realized that he might as well have stayed in the B'nai B'rith Cemetery.

He had a sudden mental picture of himself standing with his nose poking through the wire of the fence watching the funeral, a separate but equal mourner, and in spite of himself and to his horror he felt it as if it were a gathering gas bubble: a desire to laugh, an uncontrollable urge to laugh, a necessity to shake with mirth while only few feet away his father-in-law was about to be placed in the ground. He dug his fingernails into the skinned flesh of his palm, but then heads in front of him began to move and he could see that the minister was the young one. There was nobody standing near him whom Michael knew.

Oh God, he shouted silently.

Leslie, where are you?

CHAPTER FORTY-FIVE

When she got off the train at Grand Central Station she walked directly to the hotel and got a room that was smaller than the room she had had at the Woodborough YWCA and not nearly as clean, with half-filled set-ups and glasses all over the place and dirty towels on the bathroom floor. The bellboy said he would have somebody take care of it right away. But nearly an hour went by and nobody came and she grew tired of the mess, so she called the manager and told him that at fourteen dollars and seventy cents a day she felt entitled to a clean room. A maid came right up.

She had dinner alone at Hector's Cafeteria, across from Radio City. It was still a decent place to eat a lonely meal. A man tried to pick her up while she was eating her dessert. He was a polite man, not at all repulsive-looking although probably a bit younger than she, but she ignored him until she had finished the last of her chocolate pudding, and then she walked away. He began to follow her and she lost her patience. There was a policeman sitting at a table near the door dunking a cruller into his coffee and she stopped and quietly asked him for the correct time, looking over at the man. He turned around and walked quickly up the stairs to the second floor of the restaurant.

She went back to the hotel, still angry but consciously flattered, and went to bed early. The walls were very thin and in the room next door she heard a couple making love. They made love for a long time and the woman was very noisy. She kept making shrill little cries. The man made no sound at all, but there was the noise from the woman and the bed and she found it very hard to go to sleep. When she finally slept toward morning it was for a very little while; the noises woke her again at about five o'clock and there was nothing to do but listen.

But it grew light outside; the sun came up over the city and she felt better. She opened the window and leaned on the sill and watched the New Yorkers begin to crowd the sidewalks far below. She had forgotten how exciting Manhattan could be, and it made her want to get out and see it. She got dressed and went downstairs and had breakfast in a Child's and read *The New York Times*, pretending she had a job in an office to go to. After breakfast she walked down Forty-Second Street to the old building but the magazine wasn't there any more. She looked it up in the telephone book inside the Times Tower and she saw that it was on Madison Avenue, and then remembered reading some time back that it had moved. There was nobody still working there whom she knew well enough to look up, anyway.

She walked, breathing in through the nose and out through the mouth and seeing things. It was just as it had been on the campus; buildings that she remembered were missing and new buildings had been built in their places.

When she came to 6oth Street she turned west automatically. Long before she came to the roominghouse she was looking for it, wondering whether she would recognize it, and she did right away; the brick was freshly painted but it was the same shade of red. There was a *Rooms for Rent* sign on the door and she went up the stairs and knocked on the super's door and he sent her to Apartment 1-B, where the landlord lived. He turned out to be a

skinny middle-aged man with a freckled bald head and a scrag-
gly, dirty-looking gray mustache, the ends of which he chewed
in the corners of his mouth.

"May I see an efficiency?" she asked.

He led her up the stairs. When they reached the second
story she asked if 2-C might be vacant, but he said it was not.
"Why are you interested in 2-C?" he asked, looking straight at her
for the first time.

"I lived in it, a long time ago," she said.

"Oh." He continued to climb stairs and she followed him.
"I can give you a room on Three. Just the same as 2-C."

"Whatever happened to the woman who used to be my
landlady?" she asked.

"What might her name have been?"

But she couldn't remember.

"I don't know," he said indifferently. "I bought this property
four years back from a fellow named Prentiss. Owns a print shop
down in the Village somewhere." He led her down the hall; its
walls still were painted that incredibly ugly dark brown.

She had made up her mind that she would spend the rest of
the week living here and thinking about how it was when she
had lived here previously, but when he opened the door and she
saw the drabness and the discomfort, it overwhelmed her. She
made a show of looking the place over, wondering how she ever
had endured such ugliness.

"I'll think it over and let you know," she said finally. But
it was a mistake; she should have asked what the rent was before
telling him that.

"You're a fussy woman," he said, chewing his mustache. She
said good-by and, without waiting for him, went quickly down
the stairs and out of the building.

She went to a clam bar for lunch and had shrimp and dark
beer, then she spent the afternoon at the Museum of Modern
Art, thinking with happy scorn of the man on the Wellesley
campus. She had dinner in a small French restaurant and then
went to a bright and brassy musical. That night the couple she
had come to think of as The Honeymooners were at it again.
This time the man spoke quick, low words while the woman
sounded her cries, but Leslie couldn't hear what the words were.

The next day she spent at the Metropolitan Museum of Art and the Guggenheim. The day after that she wandered in and out of galleries. She paid sixty dollars for a painting by a man named Leonard Gorletz. She had never heard the name before but she wanted the painting for Michael. It was a portrait of a girl with a kitten. The girl had black hair and didn't look like Rachel, but you could feel Rachel's brand of vulnerable happiness when you looked at the way she was looking at the cat, and Leslie knew that Michael would like the picture.

The following morning she got to see the Honeymooners. She was giving her hair a final touch with the comb before going down to breakfast and she heard their door open and then close, and the sound of their voices, and she dropped her comb and grabbed her handbag and went out after them. She was very disappointed when she saw them. She had imagined them to be beautiful animals. The man was pudgy and soft-looking, with dandruff on the collar of his blue suit, and the woman was thin and nervous with a sharp little beak like a sparrow. Nevertheless, in the elevator all the way down to the lobby Leslie took admiring little peeks, remembering her remarkable range and versatility of soprano expression.

For the next two days she went shopping by herself and for herself. She bought several things she needed and she window-shopped for a great many things she didn't desire but were enjoyable to look at. She bought an English tweed skirt for Rachel at Lord & Taylor and a thick blue cashmere sweater for Max at Weber & Heilbroner.

But that night things took a subtle shift. She couldn't sleep and she had become sick of the four small walls of the hotel room. It was the sixth day and perhaps subconsciously she already had had her fill of New York. To top it off, there was no sound of passion from the honeymooners; they had checked out and abandoned her. In their place was someone who gargled and flushed the john a lot and used an electric razor and turned the television up very loud.

Early in the morning it began to rain and she stayed late in bed, half-dozing, until hunger drove her out. The entire wet afternoon was consumed in a place called Ronald's, a kind of matron's Playboy Club off Columbus Circle where customers

went from sauna to masseur to hairdresser in particolored muu-
muus with big fluffy bunny tails that wiggled with their behinds.
She baked at 190° F. while the Boston Pops played "Fiddle-
Faddle" and then a Marchessa de Sade with muscles in her
fingers kneaded and slapped and pinched her. A girl named
Theresa gave her a shampoo. While a pink cream soaked into
her facial pores a girl named Hélène gave her a manicure and a
girl named Doris gave her a pedicure, both at the same time.

When she left the salon the rain had tapered off but still fell
lightly, almost a mist. The Broadway lights threw shivering
streaks on passing cars and the surface of the street. She opened
her umbrella and walked downtown, feeling rested and very
attractive. Where to have dinner was the vital question. Her mood
called for a very fancy restaurant and then suddenly it didn't; it
seemed silly to go through the business of waiting to be seated at
a table and ordering and eating a large meal all by herself. She
stopped under a pulsing slab of neon and peered through the
wet window at a white-hatted psuedo-chef building a mountain
of yellow egg in a pan, trying to decide whether to go inside. Instead she walked another half a block and entered a Horn &
Hardart's. She swapped a dollar bill for a handful of change and
collected tomato juice, vegetarian vegetable plate, Parker House
rolls and jello. The cafeteria was crowded and she walked by
table after table until she came to a two-chair table occupied by
a fat man with a cheerful Stubby Kaye sort of a face, reading the
Daily News over his coffee while his bulging brief case rested
against his legs. She unloaded the tray and set it on the wagon
of a passing busboy and then discovered she had forgotten her
coffee. The coffee robot was only a few steps away and she
walked to it and drew a cup that was a bit too full and carried
it carefully back to the table.

Someone had propped a leaflet against her juice glass.

She picked it up and read the mimeographed lettering on the
title page, THE REAL ENEMY.

She started to read it as she sipped her tomato juice.

*The real enemy that faces America now is the Jew-Commu-
nist conspiracy to conquer us by diluting our white Christian
race with the blood of an inferior and cannibalistic black race.*

Jews have long controlled our banks and propaganda media

through the machinations of their international cartels. Now their sly sights have been set on education, in order to brainwash our children at a time when their minds are most malleable.

What do you want for your children?

Do you know the number of kike communists teaching in the Manhattan public schools?

She dropped it on the table. "Does this belong to you?" she asked the fat young man.

He looked at her for the first time.

She picked it up and held it out to him. "Did you see anybody leave this?"

"Lady, I was just reading my paper. Jesus." He picked up his brief case and walked away. One strap of the brief case was undone. Had it been that way before? She tried to remember, but couldn't. She looked at the people at the nearby tables, all of them ignoring her, eating, feeding blank faces. One of them? Anybody could have dropped the leaflet.

Why? she asked silently, speaking to the featureless face. What do you want? What do you gain? Disappear and leave us alone. Go into the forest and hold Black Masses at midnight. Poison dogs. Strangle small furry things. Walk into the sea. Or better, fall into a hole and let it close over you, clean earth.

What do you want for your children?

To begin with, I want them to have room to breathe, she thought. Just to breathe.

But you don't get it for them by hiding in a hotel room, she told herself. You begin by going home.

But there remained a thing important for her to do, she realized. There was no similarity between her father and the person who had written this poison. She had to look into her father's eyes and answer the question he had asked her, in a way that would make him understand.

On the train next morning she tried to remember when she had last given her father a gift and she wanted very much to give him something. When the train pulled into Hartford she got off and went to Fox's and bought a book by Reinhold Niebuhr. In the taxi on the way to Elm Street she saw from the copyright date that it was several years old and realized that her father probably had read it.

At the parsonage nobody answered her knock but the door wasn't locked.

"Hello?" she said.

An elderly man came out of her father's library, holding a clipboard and a pen. He had a lion's mane of white hair and wild grey brows.

"Is Mr. Rawlins here?" she asked.

"Here? No. Ah . . . You don't know?" He put his hand on her arm. "My child, Mr. Rawlins is dead.

"Here, here," he said in a worried voice. She heard the book strike the floor and she felt him leading her to a chair.

Rather surprisingly, in a few minutes he left her. She could hear him moving about in the back part of the house and she got up and walked to the mantel and saw a replica of her right hand in plaster of paris. He must have used the wax as a mould, she thought. The man came back with two cups of steaming tea and they drank it slowly together; it was very good.

His name was Wilson. He was a retired minister and he was assembling her father's church records. "The kind of job they give to an old man," he said. "I must say in this case it's no difficult chore."

"He was very orderly," she said.

She sat with her head back against the chair and her eyes closed. He left her alone again. But in a little while he asked whether he might drive her to the cemetery.

"Please," she said.

When they got there he pointed out the grave but he waited in the car, for which she felt very grateful.

The earth was still new-looking and she stood there looking at it and trying to think of something to say that would tell her father how, in spite of everything, she had loved him. She could almost hear the sound of his voice singing a hymn and she sang along with him silently.

Abide with me; fast falls the even-tide;
  The darkness deepens; Lord, with me abide
When other helpers fail and comforts flee,
  Help of the helpless, O abide with me.

On the fourth verse she almost faltered.

Hold Thou thy cross before my closing eyes;
    Shine through the gloom, and point me to the skies.
Heaven's morning breaks, and earth's vain shadows flee;
    In life, in death, O Lord, abide with me.

But she sang it through; that had been the gift. Now, although it was too late to make him understand, she answered the question with the prayers she had been saying for her mother for eighteen years. *"Yisgadal v'yiskadash shmay rabo, b'ol'mo deevro hir'usay, v'yamleeh mal'husay. . . ."*

CHAPTER FORTY-SIX

He had gone to bed the night before with the temperature at a chilly ten degrees, but when he awoke in the morning there had been a New England thaw. When he drove downtown the gutters were streams and the ground showed through the snow in shaggy brown patches, like holes in a blanket.

In the temple they gleaned nine men painfully, one by one the way it happened some mornings, and he finally had to call Benny Jacobs, the Brotherhood president, and ask him to come over and complete the *minyan* as a special favor to the rabbi. As always Jacobs came. He was the kind of person who made it easy for a man to be a rabbi, Michael thought. When he tried to thank him after the service, Jacobs brushed his thanks aside. "I'm going in to pick up the liquor for the temple New Year's party. Want anything special, Rabbi?"

He smiled. "I've had experience with your taste in alcohol. Whatever you get, Ben."

In his study he saw that there were absolutely no appointments on the calendar and he left the temple and went home to check the mail: bills and the Burpee seed catalogue. He escaped

for a fine hour looking at the new vegetables and reading the
mouth-watering promises before filling out his order blank the
same way he had the year before. He lay on the living room
couch for a little while listening to FM radio music and then the
station meteorologist predicted that the temperature would go a
few degrees higher before rapid cooling followed by a heavy
snowfall late that afternoon. He had neglected to fertilize the
garden the preceding fall and realized this might well be the only
time it would be possible all winter. He changed into worn slacks
and an old jacket and work gloves and put on his six-buckle
arctics, then he drove to the supermarket and picked up half a
dozen empty cardboard cartons. He had a long-standing arrangement with the owner of a turkey farm and he drove to the field
where each year after the Thanksgiving and Christmas rushes the
man built a mountain of bird droppings. The manure was weath-
ered and fine, the consistency of sawdust, full of long white ghost-
haunted feathers he knew would vanish beautifully into the
garden earth. It was odorless at that temperature and all the insects that made the job unpleasant during the spring and fall had
been winterkilled. He shoveled it into the cartons, careful to fill
them so there would be no spillage in the back of the station
wagon, which he had lined with newspapers. The sun was warm
and he enjoyed the work in the beginning, but he knew from experience that he needed five trips with the car to carry enough
fertilizer for the garden, and when he had hauled the third load
back to the house and carried it by hand to the garden and
dumped it the clouds were rolling in and it was cooler, so that he
no longer sweated. By the time he drove into the driveway with
the last load the snow had started, light flakes like small barley.

"Hey." Max was home from school, and he came to the car
and looked at his father's work clothes. "What are you doing?"

"Gardening," said Michael, while the snow gathered on his
lashes and brows. "Want to help?"

They carried the last of the cartons to the garden together
and dumped them and Max went into the cellar and brought out
the shovels and they began to spread the manure while the snowflakes grew larger, floating heavily through the gray air.

"Tomatoes like pumpkins," Michael called as he threw a

shovelful—swoosh!—and saw a yard-square skim of snow covered with a dark layer of fertilizer.

"Pumpkins big as tangerines," Max said. Swoosh!

"Corn sweet as kisses." Swoosh!

"Radishes full of worms. Squash covered with black sores." Swoosh!

"Punk kid," his father said. "You know I have a green thumb."

"This stuff stains through the gloves?" Max said. They worked steadily until all the fertilizer was spread and Michael leaned on his shovel like the character in the old WPA cartoons and watched his son finish the job. The boy needed a haircut badly and his hands were chapped and red. Where were his gloves? He looked more like a farmer's son than a rabbi's, and Michael thought how in the spring he and Max would turn this under together and plant the seeds and wait like *kibbutzniks* for the first pale green spikes to push up through the enriched earth.

"Speaking of kisses, want the car New Year's?" he asked.

"I don't think so. Thank you." Max threw a last shovelful and straightened up with a sigh.

"How come?"

"I don't have a date. Dess and I aren't going steady any more."

He looked for signs of scar tissue.

"She was asked out by this older guy. He's already going to Tufts." He shrugged. "That was that." He knocked manure from the shovel blades. "The funny thing is, I'm not even upset. I always figured I was ape over her. That if anything ever broke us I'd be real shook."

"You're not?"

"I don't think so. The thing is, I'm not even seventeen, this thing with Dess was like . . . well, a dry run. But later, when you're older, how do you tell?"

"What's your question, Max?"

"What's *love*, Dad? How do you know when you really love a girl?"

He saw it was a serious question, one that troubled the boy. "I don't have a workable definition," he said. "When the time comes, when you're older and you meet a woman you want to spend the rest of your life with, you won't have to ask."

They gathered up the cardboard cartons and placed them one inside the other for easy carrying. "Is it too late for you to get another New Year's date?" he asked.

"Yeah. I called a bunch of girls. Roz Coblentz. Betty Lipson. Alice Striar. They all had dates. Weeks ago." He looked at his father. "I called Lisa Patruno last night, but she was busy, too."

Oy. Steady, Zaydeh.

"I don't think I know her," Michael said.

"Her father is Pat Patruno, the druggist. Patruno's Pharmacy."

"Oh?"

"That make you sore?" Max asked.

"Not sore."

"But . . . *something?*"

"Max. You're a big guy, now, not quite a man. From here on in there are going to be decisions you're going to have to make on your own. Important decisions, more and more of them as you grow older. Whenever you want my advice, I'm right here to give it. You won't always make the right decisions—none of us does. But it's going to take an awful lot to make me sore at you."

"Anyhow, she had a date," Max said.

"There's a girl named Lois from New York. Sixteen. She's visiting Mr. and Mrs. Gerald Mendelsohn. If you want to take a chance you'll have to call information. They're not in the phone book yet."

"Is she bearable to look at?"

"I've never seen her. Her older sister is what at one time I would have called Good-Looking Head."

They started for the house and Max threw a punch that landed like a pole-ax, removing sensation from his shoulder probably forever. "You're not such a bad geezer to have for an old man—"

"Thank you."

"For a rabbi who stands around throwing bird crap into snowstorms."

Michael showered and changed and they had canned soup

for lunch and then Max asked if he could take the car and go to the library. When the boy was gone he stood by the window for a little while and watched it snow and then he got the idea for a sermon and he sat at the typewriter and developed it. When he had finished writing he went into the hall closet and found a can of Brasso and took it upstairs. Zaydeh's bedstead was becoming dingy. He worked on it slowly and carefully. After he had applied the polish he washed his hands and began to rub the bedstead with soft rags, enjoying it as the tarnish disappeared and the renewed metal shimmered through with layers of warm internal light.

He still had the entire headboard to do when he heard the front door open and the sound of footsteps on the stairs.

"Hello?" he yelled.

"Hello," she said, coming in behind him.

She kissed him in the corner of the mouth as he turned and then buried her face in his shoulder.

"Better call Dr. Bernstein," she said, the words muffled.

"We have time," he told her. "All the time in the world."

They simply stood, holding one another, for a long time. "I've been on the other side of the looking-glass," she said.

"Was it good?"

She looked into his eyes. "I shacked up in a room and experimented with whiskey and drugs. Each day I took a different lover."

"No. No, you didn't. Not you."

"No, I didn't," she said. "I went back to every place I had ever lived without you, trying to find out what I am. Who I am."

"What did you find out?" he asked.

"That for me nothing important exists outside of this house. Everything else goes up in smoke."

She saw in his face that he was tortured by the necessity to tell her. "I already know. I went to Hartford this morning," she said.

He nodded and reached out and touched her cheek. "Love," he said. This is what it is, he told the boy silently; it is what I feel for your mother, this woman.

"I know," she said, and he took her hand, seeing their compli-

cated images in the brass. Downstairs the front door opened and
they heard the sound of Rachel's voice.

"Daddy?"

"We're up here, darling," Leslie called.

He held her hand so tightly it was as if their flesh had grown
together, so that even God would have found it difficult to pull
them apart.

CHAPTER FORTY-SEVEN

On the last morning of the year he reached out and turned off
the alarm clock as Rachel crawled into his bed and burrowed
against him for warmth. Instead of getting up he held her head
against his shoulder, fingertips gently massaging the egg-shaped
little skull beneath the thick warm hair, and they both fell asleep
again.

When he awoke for the second time he saw with a pang that
it was after ten o'clock; he had missed the morning service for
the first time in months. But there had been no desperate telephone call from the temple, and he relaxed, realizing they had
gathered a *minyan* without him.

He got out of bed and showered and shaved and dressed in
chinos and lumberjacket shirt, taking only juice and then sitting
in his study with his feet bare, writing a long letter to his father
before lunch: *Leslie was overjoyed at the news. When are we
going to meet the bride? Can you come soon? Give us enough
notice so we can plan a suitable welcome.*

After lunch he went to the hospital. Bundled like Eskimoes
against the cold, he and Leslie tramped through the long bright
afternoon. They climbed the highest point on the hospital
grounds, a wooded hill with no paths so their booted feet had to
fight the crusted snow all the way, and when they reached the top
he was short of breath and he saw that there was actually a

round red Katzenjammer Kids spot on each of her cheeks. The sun was hard-bright on the snow and below and away was the lake, snow-covered but ploughed in places to permit skating, with the small clashing figures of hockey players. They sat in the snow and held hands and he wanted to hide the moment, make it last, stick it under his tongue like a piece of hard rock candy to be tasted at length and in stealth. But the wind blew snowdust demons into their faces and their behinds grew numb with cold and in a little while they deserted the hilltop and walked back to the ward.

Elizabeth Sullivan was brewing coffee in her cubicle and she invited them in for a libation. Before they could drink it, Dan Bernstein came striding in on morning rounds, and he pointed a blunt accusing finger at Leslie. "I've got a present for you. We just discussed you at staff meeting. We're going to kick you the hell out before long."

"Can you tell us when?" Michael asked.

"Oh, we'll have another week of treatment and take a couple of days to rest up. And then, good-by charlie." He patted Michael's shoulder and walked into the ward, Miss Sullivan following with the records wagon.

She opened her mouth to speak and couldn't, but she smiled at him and lifted her coffee mug and he touched his to it, trying to think of a very funny speech that would say it all and quickly realizing that speech was unnecessary; instead, looking into her eyes, he drank the coffee and burned his tongue.

That evening Max stopped the car in front of the temple and waited for him to leave.

"Good night, Dad. Happy New Year."

Without knowing he was going to, he leaned over and kissed the boy on the cheek, smelling his own after-shave lotion.

"Hey. What's that for?"

"Because you're too old for me to do that ever again. Be careful how you drive."

The downstairs function hall was crowded with people wearing silly little paper hats. Behind a makeshift bar, members of the Brotherhood dispensed drinks, making money for the Hebrew school. Five musicians thumped out a wild bossa nova and a double line of females moved their bodies to the beat like tribal communicants on the dance floor, eyes half closed.

"Ah, the Rabbi!" Ben Jacobs shouted.

Michael made his way slowly around the room.

Jake Lazarus grasped the Rabbi's hand. "*Nu,* twelve more months, another year. Fifty-two *shabbos* services," the cantor said, his eyes dreamy with vision and rye. "A few more years, it will be the turn of the century. Two thousand. Imagine it."

"Imagine harder and think of Fifty-Seven Hundred and Sixty," Michael said. "We began counting earlier."

"Two Thousand or Fifty-Seven-Sixty, what's the difference? I will still be one hundred and three. Tell me, Rabbi, what will the world be like?"

"Jake, am I Eric Sevareid?" He *potched* the cantor on the cheek, a love blow.

He reached the bar and came away with bourbon, poured generously. On one of the tables laden with food by the Sisterhood, amid platters of *tayglech* and cookies, he discovered a miracle, a dish of candied ginger, and he took two pieces and walked out of the hall and up the stairway.

When the door of the sanctuary closed behind him the sounds from below were coated in velvet. He stood in blackness but it was his temple and he needed no light; he walked down the center aisle to the third row, one hand curled around the rim of the glass to insure against spilling.

He sat and sipped the whiskey and nibbled at the ginger. A small sip to three or four nibbles, possibly the wrong ratio; the ginger was soon gone and much of the bourbon remained. He drank, letting his mind graze in the dark, nibbling at thoughts. Around him the darkness thinned as his eyes adjusted; he began to distinguish solid shapes. He could make out the lectern now, where in twenty-four hours he would be standing and leading the *shabbos* service.

How many sermons since that first sermon in Miami? So many services, so many words. He grinned in the dark. Not so many as still stretched in front of him; he felt it in his bones, he could almost reach out and touch it, a ladder of Sabbaths to be climbed into the future.

Thus shalt thou say unto the children of Israel, The Lord, the God of your fathers, the God of Abraham, the God of Isaac, and the God of Jacob, has sent me unto you: this is my name for ever, and this is my memorial unto all generations.

Thank you, God.

Downstairs the orchestra began to play something lilting. If Leslie were here he would dance—he felt like dancing; next year they would dance.

The taste of ginger was faint now. The last faint, bittersweet taste of ginger. Don't be afraid, Zaydeh, he said silently into the darkness. Six thousand years is not the wink of an eyelash or the beat of a bird's wing. There is nothing new on the face of the ancient earth, and what could not be erased by bloodbaths and ovens will not be erased by changed names or bobbed noses or the merging of our blood with mysterious bloodstreams.

He should tell Jake Lazarus he knew at least that much about the future, he thought. But instead he slumped comfortably and finished the last of the bourbon, relishing its warmth and filing the thought away.

He would turn it into a sermon in the morning.

ABOUT THE AUTHOR

Noah Gordon received a Bachelor of Science in Journalism degree from Boston University in 1950 and an M.A. in English from the same institution the following year. Mr. Gordon was a reporter on the Worcester, Massachusetts, *Telegram* for two years before he joined the Boston *Herald,* where he was the Science Editor for four years. Although *The Rabbi* is his first novel, Mr. Gordon has published articles and fiction in many leading national magazines, among them *The Reporter, The Saturday Evening Post, Redbook,* and *The Saturday Review.* Noah Gordon now lives in Framingham, Massachusetts, with his wife and three children.